GALAXY

High Table Hijinks Book One

CHRISTOPHER JOHNS

Copyright © 2021 by Christopher Johns

All rights reserved.

No part of this book may be reproduced in any form or by any electronic or mechanical means, including information storage and retrieval systems, without written permission from the publisher, except for the use of brief quotations in a book review.

This is a work of fiction. Names, characters, places, and incidents either are the products of the author's imagination or are used fictitiously. Any resemblance to actual persons, living or dead, businesses, companies, events, or locales is entirely coincidental.

This one is for my little sister. You were the first one to trod these pages even when they weren't finished, and now that you're gone and they're here, this milestone is all too bittersweet. You read everything I put out voraciously and told me exactly what you thought, even when it wasn't what I wanted to hear. You read even some things I couldn't share with anyone else. Here's hoping that the heroes in the worlds I make will be able to be the hero someone else needs to help them make it to the next day. Because sometimes, the next day is all we will have. I miss you, and I'm sorry.

ACKNOWLEDGMENTS

I would like to thank all of the awesome people who didn't know who I was and gave me a chance anyway. While this is something outside my usual fare, it'll be so much more familiar given time. Here's hoping that my awesome editors, alpha and beta readers were as amazing as I know them to be and that you like it as much as they did!

CHAPTER ONE

"Santa's Sleigh, this is Rudolf requesting elves immediately!" the radio stayed steadily broken with static as Cpl. Clay tried marking again with an ever-growing edge of panic rising in his voice. "Multiple injuries aboard convoy, requesting elves, fifteen mikes from North Pole. Over!"

"Take a breath, and keep trying, Corporal!" Lt. Mal ordered as he kept an eye on his side of the road. "What in the fuck happened back there? Bola! Did you see anything?"

I took a deep breath to try to explain the flashes of things I remembered, but Lance Cpl. Loretti's moaning became so high-pitched and insistent that I stopped, shaking my head as he shouted, "They're dead, sir! They're all dead! The whole fucking squad is gone—more than that."

"Secure that, Loretti!" Cpl. Clay barked as he reached for the radio dial to try again at another secured frequency. "I can't hear the damn radio to get the rest of the survivors help."

Visions of the scientists and researchers' cold, dead faces twisted in fear, and a ghastly pain flooded my mind as I tried to recall something—anything that could be useful. We should have never gone there, and whatever had chased us out probably wasn't far behind. That sent a chill down my spine and I wasn't one to respond to anything like that.

What the fuck did they send them there to investigate and why? They should have sent the whole damned battalion. I tried to regroup and gather my nerves, watching the side of the roadway for potential hiding holes and IEDs to get my mind off it, but the thoughts and questions kept coming. *What the hell kind of temple just appears after a goddamn sandstorm? And who the fuck sends Marines and eggheads in to check it out blind?*

I clenched my fist. *And what the hell was that amulet and why did it crumble like that when I touched it?*

Even in the dying light of dusk, the world was darker than it should have been. We had been on our way back to the FOB, forward operating base, after our mission when something hit our windshield and cracked it.

I grunted, "Fuck!"

Then all hell seemed to break out of its depths. Someone was taking potshots at us—not unheard of in the Middle East—but after that mission and three of the cars that we had been trailing being flung twenty feet up into the air? It felt like something big was up.

Our Lieutenant had the Lance Corporal slam on the brakes rather than drive through or around the car in front of us. Myself and the Corporal in our makeshift fire team braced as best we could. My helmeted head bounced off the back of the seat in front of me despite that.

"Contact!" The warning had been out of Cpl. Clay's mouth before the vehicle had finished skidding on the sandy road. "Unknown direction!"

I threw my door open and ducked behind it as I settled the buttstock of my rifle into my shoulder, safety off already. The pinging around me, from three round bursts, had my full attention. Fog of War threatened to engulf me, but our high stress training and experience helped mitigate it.

My eyes scanned the dunes around our position right to left, forcing me to find anything out of the ordinary. I found one of the people shooting at us, and sighted through the scope.

On a natural respiratory pause, my index finger squeezed lightly and the recoil bucked the muzzle upward slightly as I canted the weapon and scanned again.

Returning fire hit Loretti in his sappy plate three times, then he went down. I growled, scuttling back to check on him. His eyes were open and unseeing, a gaping hole in the side of his neck from a round hitting his artery. Deep red blood flooded from his neck guard hanging uselessly in front of him.

Rage roiled through me as I turned and fought my way to the other side of the Humvee, firing sporadically and stopping every so often to be sure I would make a more difficult target before I got to where the others hid.

"Lt. Mal—orders?" I called over the din.

He fired a three round burst and ducked back behind the open door. "Second and third Humvees are behind about a click, but they're on their way!" He leaned back a little further as a round slammed into the door. "Clay! Bola! Get your asses up to those cars and return fire before they flank us. Loretti and I will cover you."

"Loretti's down, sir!" My voice sounded so hollow suddenly.

"Shit!" he spat, then checked around us. "Fine. I'll cover you guys. Get up there and return fire, then I'll move to the other side. We can't let them flank us."

I nodded and looked over to Clay, the Lance looking around wildly. I grabbed his flak jacket and yanked him close so I could shout, "Get it together, Devil!"

He nodded wildly and mouthed a phrase all Marines dreaded, *I'm up, he sees me, I'm down*, repeatedly as he looked forward toward our destination.

"Firing!" Lt. Mal roared as his M-16 spat rounds at the enemy.

"Moving!" we responded as my feet churned beneath me. Clay was slower, but I lagged to let him get in front of me. I returned fire at someone who stood up randomly with an AK in hand, then got to the car. "Set! Firing!"

I shot at anything that moved, making sure to keep a steady rate as both Clay and I kept the enemy distracted and pinned down. "Moving!"

The Lieutenant made it to his position and prepared to yell again when a whining sound came toward us.

Boom!

A shockwave flattened me and Clay as the car the Lieutenant had chosen as cover blew up. Flaming car parts and material flew through the air, shrapnel decimating the already direly cracked windshield beside me. Some of it slapped against my flack, another piece shredded into my quad.

"Gah!" I snarled and held my leg. The pain was intense… so hard to focus as I blinked rapidly. I turned and saw that Clay's head hung at an odd angle as his body shifted and fell.

Ringing in my ears grew louder as another explosion rocked us. I looked about wildly before finding that the other vehicles had pulled up to us. My eyes closed slowly as my brothers and sisters fought.

I fell into a void, cold and vast. Welcoming. Something within watched me, but I couldn't see it. I just sort of knew it was there. *Waiting* for something.

———

"Marcus!" someone barked next to my ear.

I woke up on a cot, taking a quick inventory of my body. My leg was bandaged heavily, my ribs hurt like hell, and I was having trouble recalling things. Looking up at the full bird Colonel from my bed, I fought to stand, if not sit up, but he put a hand on my chest. "Relax, Marine."

I tried to sit up and his hand moved and tightened painfully on my shoulder, his eyes still holding some of the mirth that had been there. "That's an order, Sergeant."

"Yes, sir." I grinned and tried to relax.

"I'm Col. Brandt." He motioned behind him to where another Marine in service dress stood by the door. I recognized my Sergeant Major immediately. "As I'm sure you know, this is Sgt. Maj. Espinoza. We're here with… news. Unfortunately, some of the shrapnel from that car really did a number on you, Sergeant Bola. Nicked your femoral artery on its way out. If it hadn't been for the Corpsman with what was left of your unit, you'd have joined your irregular fire team in Valhalla. You've been in and out of consciousness for a few days."

Must've read my file. I rolled my eyes. Being reminded that my friends had passed was… hard, to say the least. You spend so much time with each other, you get attached. Those men and women who were there became family. Or more.

"With the extent of your injuries, broken ribs, your arm and leg torn to hell, we will be moving forward with sending you home and medically retiring you." Sgt. Maj. Espinoza stepped closer to us with a file in hand. "I know those Marines were family, son. But they need you to carry on."

"My place is out there then, Sergeant Major!" My voice raised without my meaning it to. "What about those assholes who attacked us?"

"They got theirs, Bola." Espinoza nodded with a grim look of finality on his face. "But not before they took a few others too. Rodriguez, Quint, Volan, and Daro. They got them too."

No. I yelled, my good arm lashing out at the small table that held uneaten food on it to my right. The food flew, table clattering to the ground. "Daro and Quint were kids! They just got to the unit."

"We know." Col. Brandt grimaced as he looked down at his legs, then he looked up into my eyes. "Did you see anything else out there? Anything strange?"

I scowled at him, trying to recall as my fuzzy memory refused to obey my will. Even then, I didn't know him, and from the look on my Sergeant Major's face, there was little trust there. I couldn't tell him everything, even what I could remember. "No. One minute, things were kosher, the next, people started dropping left and right and we got separated. Then less than ten minutes from the FOB, some group tried to ambush us. Other than that, nothing outside the norm."

Brandt looked almost... disappointed? As if he had expected some vastly different answer. To be perfectly frank, I didn't give a flying fuck. "Who were they? What did they want?"

"Just to create chaos before your unit could go home." Espinoza opened the folder and pulled out a few papers. Reading over it all, it was a debrief with a non-disclosure agreement. "You sign this, and say nothing of what happened other than what is in this debriefing packet, and we will ensure you're well taken care of, Bola. We want to do right by you."

"What about Clay's fiancée?" I challenged and the Sergeant Major didn't even flinch. "She's expecting. It was his first kid. What's she supposed to do? What about the others?"

"They will all receive compensation from the Marine Corps and VA, I can assure you." Brandt's hand was on my shoulder once more. "You survived. You feel guilty for it. What about *your* kid, Bola? You haven't taken leave to go back home in years, and he's how old now?"

My eyes narrowed at him dangerously. "You leave Connell out of this."

"All I'm saying is, think of your kid and *your* family." He leaned forward, his belt groaning a bit as he did. "You *do* have family, correct?"

"Yes, sir, I do." Something about the way he asked me made my skin crawl and my fight or flight reaction surge. Like he was trying to confirm if my disappearance would be easy enough for him to get away with.

I knew people like that all over.

"Good." He leaned back and looked satisfied, everywhere but the eyes. They seemed more dead than they had been our whole conversation. "Sgt. Maj. Espinoza, please explain the next few months to our friend the Sergeant here—I need to attend the General's daily briefing."

The Sergeant Major stood at attention and saluted the retreating man smartly before he cleared the doorway. Then, when he was gone, Espinoza turned to me with genuine concern, "Seriously, Bola, are you good?"

"Yeah, Sergeant Major, but who was that? Where's Col. Farnam?"

"Almost as soon as the head shed got wind of what was going on, Brandt was en route. He was relieved a few days ago while you guys were on mission in that… place. With the things and whatnot." He turned and watched the door, then began to speak louder, "You're on the first flight home tomorrow, son. We'll get you to medical, and get the ball rolling on your medical retirement—your physical therapy, VA consult—all of it will be taken care of. You got a place to go once you're out?"

I went to speak but Espinoza threw me that, *shut the fuck up, Devil* look before jokingly announcing, "Oh, yeah. I'd stay away from Cali too. Place is shit for a lot of reasons."

He stepped closer to the door and listened for a moment before he sighed, "We're in the clear. Bola, you really didn't see anything?"

I shook my head. "What the hell is going on?"

"There's been a real shift and it's been really weird. I have orders to go back with you because my replacement came too." I scowled at him and he nodded in understanding. "I know. That's unheard of in our beloved Corps. You only see that if the Inspector General finds some serious dirt. And we've been good on the IG's list forever. There's something going on, and everyone involved in that detail you were on a few days back has either disappeared or *been* disappeared."

I stared at him and he nodded. "Yes, we got your radio chatter on the way back. We had to scramble it so no one else could hear it. The others who survived are being treated for psych evaluations with the wizard. I had to fight for you because you had more pressing injuries."

"You think it's some kind of cover up?"

He frowned and shook his head. "Someone wants what was

in that place and they want everyone who knows anything gone in a real bad way."

My stomach churned. "You think we were set up?"

He nodded. "Brandt is taking orders from someone and it sure as shit isn't the General. Something is going on. I'll be investigating how I can, but I need you somewhere safe and where people would notice if you went AWOL. Got me?"

"Yes, Sergeant Major." He held a hand out to stop me going on.

"I don't want to know until I need to, just in case they get to me, or you. There's a nurse at the med bay that you can trust. She's an informant for me. Let her know where you'll be and she will tell me when the time comes." He eyed me with that same sort of senior enlisted contained rage and fury that a lot of them had. "You keep your head low. Stay safe and stay away from your family until we know what's going on. And for the love of Chesty, keep an ear out. Got it?"

I nodded and he smiled softly.

"Here's the plans we have for your med-sep, and Bola?" I stared at him as he closed the distance between us. "Don't let this eat at you. We will make them pay."

He looked down and grimaced at the ground. "We can see about getting you some good chow too. Rest up, I'll be back to ensure you're ready before we leave."

I nodded and laid back down to recover and rest while I could.

―――

Columbus Airport bustled like no other, which was different from the hospital atmosphere that I had been used to for the last six months. They had said that I healed faster than they had expected, and much better as well, but there was no hope for me to get back into the Marines.

It wasn't long before I arrived at the carousel for luggage when I saw my uncle. He wore a pair of loose jeans, a red

Hawaiian-style button up, and light cream hat. With his tanned skin, he looked like he should be in Florida or somewhere tropical.

Always the eclectically dressed man, he smiled at me and held his arms open. "Hey there, nephew. How you doin'?"

"Good, Uncle Yen, how are you?" I came over to him and pulled him into a big hug.

"Better now that I have you here, kid." He patted my back and grabbed me. "You bring much with you?"

I shook my head. "They're packing my house for me and shipping it to a storage place for me just down the road."

"Traveling light?" He eyed the backpack on my shoulder and the small one in my hand, and I laughed as he waggled his eyebrows.

He'd always known how to make me laugh, even if it had been almost twenty years. "Yeah. So, where to?"

"Well shoot, we're going to get lunch and then I gotta get you to the High Table to meet the boss!" He grinned at me and grabbed my shoulder. "Come on, son, we got to get to church!"

I eyed him, but he just laughed at me.

We got to his car, a nice, older-model Cadillac and he turned the radio off as it started playing some hip hop. "So, how was your time over there?"

"Rough, but I'm here." I was a little more closed off than I wanted to be, but it was for his protection.

Over the last six months, I'd been contacted incessantly to see if my memory had cleared, Brandt's goons bugging me to no end. I didn't want that for Uncle Yen.

"You don't want to talk about it, that's fine." He turned onto the roadway and we puttered on our way. "You kids have it so rough these days. Warfare is so much different from when I was your age. Yeesh."

I chuckled. He had been in 'Nam and that was a nightmare.

"All that house-to-house bullshit and IEDs—we had jungles and rice paddies! Persistent Viet Cong, mind you…but not like what you had to face!" My nodding just made him laugh. He turned into a parking lot and sighed happily. "Welcome to Church's, nephew."

I blinked up at the sign and saw that it was a fried chicken joint that I wasn't familiar with, then laughed so hard that I had trouble breathing.

"You thought I meant the other kind?" He snorted as I mouthed yes. "What problem is there that can't be solved or made slightly better by fried chicken? Let me tell you—not a damn one!"

We pulled into the drive-through line and ordered. The chicken was amazing and the biscuits were buttery and flaky. It was the best.

"Alright! Let's get you to the bar and the boss!" He wiped his hands on a napkin and started the car.

"You think I should change?" I motioned to the blue jeans and simple gray t-shirt I wore.

"Nah." He shook his head. "The name may *sound* fancy, but it's a pretty decent bar with no dress code other than shoes, shirt, and basic hygiene." He drove us toward the downtown area, High St., then onto another street I missed due to being enamored with the campus area.

Ohio State University had always been huge, and the massive statue of Brutus the Buckeye made me smile. A lot of the Marines I had known came from a few places, the most prevalent ones being from New York, Texas and Ohio. It was inevitable that one Ohioan would meet another in their unit.

My Lieutenant had been one. Remembering him hooting O-H to me on game days made me grin. Then the realization that his family was somewhere near here mourning his loss made the smile fade, slowly being replaced with a slight sense of guilt.

A few minutes after leaving the campus area, we pulled into a back alley and then into a small but well-kept parking lot.

A gentleman sat at the entrance in a guard uniform. He scowled and nodded to my uncle who eyed him equally as distrusting. Then Uncle Yen lifted his hand to him and held out a single finger.

The other man pulled it and my uncle acted like he was farting and both men devolved into laughter. The man smacked his knee. "You a funny man, Yenny. Don't ever change."

His perfectly straight white teeth contrasted with his dark brown skin, but his eyes sparkled and he looked really friendly with the smile on his face.

"Thanks Barley, I appreciate you." Uncle Yen smacked the man on the shoulder. "Barley, this is my nephew Marcus Bola, he's got an interview with the boss today. Wish him luck, yeah?"

The guard, Barley, whistled low. "Better be careful in there, boy, the boss is a mean ol' cuss."

I blinked at him and let my eyebrows raise. "Oh? Well, I've seen my share of mean in the Corps. But I appreciate the advice."

He winked and nodded at me as another car began to pull toward the parking lot. "Lot's closed to the public before hours!"

He got into an argument with the woman in the car but we were moving again. We walked around to the front and there was a blonde lady standing there. Her muscular build led me to believe that she might be some kind of security person. She wore black jeans, a black shirt, and sunglasses.

Her smile was nice though, and it looked as though she winked at my uncle quietly as we passed.

"Uncle Yen, why did it look like that young lady winked at you?" I raised an eyebrow at him jokingly and he just chuckled.

"Cause this ol' man still got it, boy." He shook his hips like the old man he was and I just laughed at him as he chuckled to himself.

The interior of the bar was what one might expect; a large floor for the patrons, some higher tables that required stools, lower ones with chairs. All of the wood in the room was stained dark, either from time or intentional, and it was all done with careful attention to craftsmanship. Everything was well-maintained, including a jukebox with everything from classic vinyl records to eight-track tapes to modern MP3s sitting in the corner of the room next to a wooden dance floor. I laughed, wondering if anyone used either.

The woman currently behind the bar gave us a nod, her willowy figure graceful as she moved from one task to the next. She raised a brow at me from where she watched us moving, her perfectly shaped eyebrow rising slowly as I moved.

Something banged into my shin painfully and I swore, "Damn it all!" She laughed and my uncle turned around and rolled his eyes. "Sorry, I'm coming."

I moved the stool out of the way, and focused on following Uncle Yen into the back and up a flight of stairs. The stairs were steep, and with his age, I wondered if he would be okay, but he was up them faster than I was. Luckily, physical therapy had kept me in shape—though my quadricep did burn like I had been working it too hard.

At the top of the stair was a hallway with a few rooms. All of them looked to be actual rooms for tenants with beds and desks. Uncle Yen pointed to the one on the left as soon as we came off the stairs. "Available, this one on the right is the boss's place, and the room at the end is the manager's office. That's where your interview will be."

He pointed me to a single chair outside. "Go ahead and have a seat while I get things rolling."

I shrugged and sat in the chair, finding it was actually very comfortable. He walked through the door and began to whistle a tune until he closed the door, then the sound stopped completely.

I worried that something was wrong, but even straining as hard as I could, I heard nothing. I tried to peek through the glass window, but it was one of those ones that was like it was shattered so you could make out lines of bodies, but not details. I saw someone moving around inside, but nothing reached my ears except my heartbeat.

Was Uncle Yen okay? What was going on in there?

I was about to get up to go in to be sure my uncle was okay when the door opened and my uncle smiled at me. "Come on in, Mr. Bola."

I frowned at him, giving him the side eye as I stood up fully and made my way into the office. It was sparsely decorated, the only real furniture in it being a table on the left-hand side with several chairs, the desk at the right-hand side, a coat rack and a chair behind the desk. My uncle sat down in the chair and eyed me knowingly. "So you wanna work at the High Table, huh?"

"I know you said you would get me a job, Uncle Yen, but you didn't have to go this far." I chuckled and rolled my eyes.

He didn't smile back. "I'm not giving you shit, kiddo. This is as much an interview as any other you might have been interested in taking. Please, pull up a chair and let's get to work."

I blinked at him, and when he steepled his fingers and continued to stare at me, I complied. As soon as my butt hit the seat, his smile returned. "Now, looking at your resume, I wanted to go over a few things with you. If you don't mind?"

I nodded mutely.

"Excellent. Served two tours overseas, saw combat and received an injury while serving your country in the Marine Corps?" I nodded quietly and he clicked something on his laptop. "Very good. And how do you feel that your service *here* would be done? I see that you were a Sergeant of Marines? I take it that this was a leadership role in the Marines, but how much responsibility did you have? I know things are a little different from my time in."

"Every Marine may be a rifleman, but true leaders are harder to find. I prided myself on being firm but fair, and my Marines knew that so long as they did what was expected and did their best in all things, I had their backs."

"We highly prize loyalty here at the High Table, so that same sort of ability to take command and lead in stressful situations is highly crucial." He hit a key and grimaced. "I see that the Marine Corps has you out as medically retired. I know some of what you have gone through based on our conversation before, but can you go into a bit more detail?"

"Other than the ones that made me unfit for continued service?" He nodded and I smiled as I took a deep breath and began to think. "I've been stabbed three times, bitten by a rattlesnake and a brown recluse spider, shot, had my arms broken in several places, injured my knee while training to become a Marine Corps Martial Arts Instructor. I've been bitten by military working dogs and almost drowned twice. I also had a few stints as the duty non-commissioned officer of the barracks and got into a few scuffles here and there."

"So you are in no way, shape or form, afraid of danger?" His question made me chuckle and I shook my head. "We like that here as well."

"I get that I could be working with heavily intoxicated people, but is this place really all that dangerous?"

He sighed and looked up at the ceiling before looking back down at me. "This is an odd place with a very… select clientele. Those clients who come here come to blow off steam and relax, but unfortunately tensions inevitably run high and someone speaks out of turn. Have things gotten as dangerous as you might be used to? Yes. Have they been fatal? No. However, I prefer that I and my staff remain as situationally aware and ready for no other reason than that I expect them to be. I want you safe. My staff safe. My clients happy. And my bar *whole*."

"I can understand that." I found myself smiling, remembering all the barracks parties on Miramar that I had been to with friends in the wing. Those had been wild. Destructive. Dangerous and so much fun. "What sort of clientele do you have coming here?"

"The kind that are very secretive and selective of whom they allow to know who they are." He eyed me carefully. "Once you begin your employment—if selected—you would eventually learn more about them all. I do have to ask a few more questions though, so let us continue."

He grilled me on some of my other qualifications.

Bartending was a lot of fun and I had liked it before I'd enlisted. I still knew a few tricks of the trade and I liked to watch videos of people making drinks even now. "I'd be willing to take some extra training for it though."

"Good, always learning is a sign of excellent character." Uncle Yen hit a key once more and the questions began anew. They ranged from anything about my parents—whom he had been ostracized from ever since he moved here thirty years ago—to my son.

"He lives with his mother here in Columbus, or in the surrounding area," I said uncertainly, as Connell had been a sore spot for me.

"Why wouldn't you know that?" he asked quietly. When he saw my face, he held up his hands. "I'm not trying to pass judgement, I'm just curious is all."

"She didn't like the way I reacted to the news that she was pregnant and then ran." I sighed, trying to get myself together. "I was excited, over the moon, I wanted to start a family, but she realized that she didn't want me. She was fine with Connell though, and his step dad. Stand-up guy from what I understand. She sends me photos in an email every now and then. I tried to hunt her down so I could see him, but any time I try, she threatens to stop sending me anything and leave."

He sighed, his hand gliding through his wavy hair. "That's rough, Marcus, I'm truly sorry."

"It's what I got." I shrugged. "He's about eight now, so in ten years, we can find each other and it will be different. I guess I just have to bide my time until then."

He nodded and smacked the table. "Good. I personally always value hope and seeing the silver lining. Sign this for me?"

He slid a paper over to me, then an older-looking red pen. The paper was a pretty standard non-disclosure agreement, which made me pause. I looked up and he motioned to the door. "For our clientele's comfort and safety."

I blinked, telling myself, *Uncle Yen hasn't lied to you before and he's been kind enough to take you in. Don't think about it too much, Marcus.*

I signed the sheet after initialing in the highlighted spots. As soon as I finished signing, a sharp pain jabbed my thumb and I pulled it away. The pen was perfectly smooth, but a droplet of blood fell onto the paper.

Uncle Yen looked at me oddly, as if something was wrong, but just handed me a small handkerchief from his desk and took the paper away.

"Excellent, Marcus—welcome to the High Table." He held his hand out and clapped me on the shoulder affectionately. "The room at the front of the hall is your room. You can go and get yourself ready for this evening. I take it you aren't too tired?"

"No, I should be okay." I frowned, as I really wasn't tired.

"Good, there's a shower and everything in your room, I have towels and whatnot for you to use as well. Go get yourself ready and come on down." He smiled at me and I went to do as he said. I made it to the door when he called after me, "Hey, Marcus?" I looked back at him and his smile widened. "I really am happy to have you here, nephew."

"Thanks, Uncle Yen. Happy to be here."

CHAPTER TWO

"Arden, this is my nephew and your new coworker, Marcus." Uncle Yen introduced me to the woman who was behind the bar. She wore silver bracelets and a hair tie the same color, the band tying back her mass of red hair so that she could see. "Marcus, Arden."

She stepped closer, toweling her hands dry. "Pleasure to meet you, Marcus." She winked at me, grinning as she held her hand out.

I shook it firmly, her grip equally as strong. "I'm not always so graceless, you know."

She just laughed and went about her duties getting ready for the shift.

Uncle Yen spent some time teaching me how to use the machinery, getting me good with the drink list and how to cash people out. It was tedious, but I took some notes on how to do everything and by the time people started to come in, I was able to keep up and not completely slow Arden down.

For the first night, it wasn't terrible and the crowd acted very interested in me. Some of the people, men and women of varying ages, watched me shyly for a while. I did my best to be friendly as some of the customers tried to make small talk with me.

A few hours into my shift, an older gentleman tottered in, by-passing the bouncer as she was busy. I rolled my eyes, knowing this guy's type from when I was in the Corps and put my best smiling face on. "Hey, pal. How can I help you?"

"I'll take a predator's tankard, thank you." His breath was rancid and rife with some kind of powerful alcohol and smelled almost like a wet dog. I eyed him, his unkempt hair had leaves and twigs in it, and looked almost like dreadlocks—nothing like some of the beautiful locs that I had seen all over the world that were well cared for. His eyes flashed to me and his teeth bared. "Why ain't you movin', son?"

I hit him with that smile again, "Well, seeing as though you made your way in here without the bouncer seeing you, I'm less inclined to give you anything. You know, since you had to sneak your way in here and all."

His mouth twitched and his fingers flexed just as I was setting my legs in case he pounced, but that didn't happen.

"Jolly, what are you doin' in here, you old goat?" The bouncer stepped inside as the other bouncer replaced her at the door. "You sneak past me again?"

He grinned. "Got a good one here, Cass, real good." He reached over and patted me on the shoulder. "He was ready for me to attack and didn't balk at all. You sure he ain't part of our security?"

The bouncer, Cass, shook her head and just closed her eyes. "You think that just because you used to head security that you get to come in and test every new 'tender?"

"I called him in, Cassia, don't be too rough on the old man." Uncle Yen clomped down the stairs and grinned widely. "He pass inspection, Jolly?"

"Flying colors, Yen." He winked and suddenly had a large tankard of liquid in his hand. He took a deep drink before spitting it out and scowling at Arden, "This is water, you dunderhead!"

She eyed him steadily. "I'm not letting you poison yourself, old man." She crossed her arms as he growled angrily.

"All alcohol is poison, Arden, and a customer has a right to their drink." Yen eyed her severely.

I watched the unspoken battle between the two of them for longer than was comfortable and turned to Jolly whispering, "How do I make the drink?"

"Full tankard of the darkest beer on tap with that there plant in it." He pointed to a large jar with a swath of purple bulbs in it. I eyed my uncle and Arden, stepping around the latter to get to the tap, and grabbed the jar without a second thought.

The tap reset, beer almost to the top, I crushed the plant up before putting it into a tea infuser. I wasn't too familiar with this, but I figured that stirring the beer with this would be good enough.

Once I finished, I put the mug on the table in front of Jolly and stepped between the two now-bristling people and smiled. "So, who's Jolly again?"

Uncle Yen eyed me, then tilted his head toward the man who was whistling a happy tune as if I had given him an elixir from the gods. "He's the former head of security here, and a close personal friend. I hire him freelance whenever I get a new body for the bar to see how they'll do. He comes in, finds the right buttons to push for that person and sees how they'll respond. If they do well, good. If not, they need more training."

"So my giving him the thing he wanted right now?" I lifted my eyebrow with uncertainty.

Arden flinched and turned to find the old man grinning ear to ear. "You did *not* drink all that in a fuckin' heartbeat, did you?"

"Oh yeah, I dish." He blinked and looked down at his mouth. "Oh dears. I'm already drunk."

Arden rounded on me, grabbing the front of my shirt to pull me close. "That's fucking *poison* to his kind!"

"Arden!" Uncle Yen snarled and she turned her head to look at him. "He doesn't know."

Her fists unclenched and she looked stricken. "What do you mean he doesn't know?"

"What don't I know?" My pulse sped and I was beginning to get a little angry at having things withheld from me.

"Ya work at a bar for monsters, boy." Jolly giggled, the white skin of his face darkening as the veins under his eyes began to blacken and bulge. His eyes rolled back in his head and his head lolled to the side before he slumped forward onto the bar.

"Is he okay?" I started to reach for him.

"Don't touch him!" Cassia bellowed, the others around us surprised and shocked as the old man suddenly reared up.

His teeth were larger—sharper—and snapped at my hand almost faster than I could blink, but they just missed my hand. I reached out to grapple him, but was flung away as Arden and Cassia surged around me.

Jolly fought back, hard, but Cassia and Arden held him back as the other bouncer came in behind him. Uncle Yen stepped forward, calling, "Take him up to my office and lock the door!"

They grunted and struggled as his body bulged and bucked, his growling laughter shifting into a barking, baying cackle as they hauled him upstairs.

"Uncle Yenasi—what the hell is going on?" I grabbed him by the shoulder.

Frowning at me, he replied, "Been a long time since someone called me by my given name; almost forgot what it sounded like." His wry smile almost made me shake him. He turned and waved a hand, indicating the people in the bar that had begun to go back to their conversations and drinking. "All of these fine folks are what most people would call monsters."

"I could see some alcoholics, sure, but monsters?" I rolled my eyes and he thumped me in the chest.

"Easy, son." He pulled me out from behind the bar and toward the stairs. I worried that someone would go behind the bar, but no one seemed interested in the alcohol and those who had been near us stared at me with open interest. "These men and women, and things in between, are called monsters by Normies out in the streets because they are myths and legends."

He pulled me toward the stairwell and waited for me to see something, but before I could offer any kind of rebuttal or observation, he tapped the wall inside the stairwell. The formerly off-white plaster and drywall were shredded down to the brick in lines that looked like claw marks.

A guttural cry of rage rang down from above and I could see that Jolly was still struggling and howling up the stairs, his hands on the walls in much the same manner as what caused the rents. As soon as the latest low and mournful note left his mouth, chairs fell behind us and three very large men stomped closer.

"Ah, Id, Jeff, and Logan, thank you." The three men nodded to my uncle before bounding up the stairs. One of them even looked to be *crawling up the wall* like he was some kind of web-slinging superhero. "Their next round is on me."

"What the *fuck* is going on?" I snarled at Uncle Yen as he sighed.

He grabbed my shoulders and pulled me down to look at him in the eyes. It wasn't far, but it was enough out of the norm that it brought me out of the shock I was going into.

"This is a bar for the preternatural and supernatural—a *neutral* ground where they can come to relax and put their differences aside." My mouth opened and closed as he stared at me in amused silence before he just shook his head. "I know that you're confused and this is a lot. I'll send Arden down in a minute, but I need to see to my friend. Can you handle the bar?"

I felt my left eye twitch a bit, but—like all challenges—I'd face this one head on. "Yeah, but I *will* have answers."

He nodded once and fled up the stairs as I turned toward the bar, wondering, *Could it have been some kind of preternatural creature like Jolly who murdered my Marines and those eggheads?*

One of the patrons at the bar hailed me with a raised hand,

breaking me out of my thoughts. I walked over to him and tried to put on my best smile, but he just gave me a placating look and said, "Don't put the show on for me, darling, I heard it all. It's okay to feel out of your league—I won't judge you for it."

He was what a lot of women might call handsome, a little more wiry than most of the guys I knew, myself included, but he had long hair and his angular face wasn't all that bad.

I sighed. "I am a little out of my depth here, sorry. What can I get you?"

"How about a Bloody Mary?" That I could do. Then he added, "Could you make it *extra* bloody?"

I paused as I reached for the vodka and tomato juice, looking back up at him where he stared at me sweetly. "Is that code for *actual* blood?"

He laughed, a throaty, barking sound. "Heavens no, dear boy. I just like extra hot sauce is all. Is this your first time making one that way?"

I opened my mouth, then laughed. It was probably the hardest that I had laughed in a while, and the guy just watched me as if I had done the most adorable thing. "Thanks, sir. I needed that. How spicy you want it?"

"Oh? A treat? Por moi?" He put his chin on his fist and smiled dreamily. "Surprise me."

I just chuckled and went about making the drink. First, I poured coarse salt and some Tajin I kept in my bag from a friend of mine onto a napkin, lightly rubbed a lime on the rim of the glass, then put the rum into the mixture. From there, I turned it right-side up and added the hot sauce first, just a few bumps, then the vodka and tomato juice. More juice than liquor, but still a good amount of the latter. After that, I added a small dollop of Worcestershire sauce and a little pickle juice.

He eyed me, but I wasn't done yet. I took some cold bacon out and looked to my patron. "You aren't against meat, are you?"

"I certainly am not, mister man." His response made me

roll my eyes before using the slice of bacon to carefully stir the mixture.

Once I was finished, I wiped the glass below the salt line and handed it to him. "Voila! An extra Bloody Mary, Devil Dog style."

He just raised a brow and tipped the glass into his mouth. His eyes closed as the liquid permeated him. I had seen this look on someone's face before.

He swallowed the drink before opening his eyes to stare at me. "I absolutely despise pickles, but this?" He tapped the glass twice as he ran his other hand through his shoulder-length hair. "Is to die for. Tell me, for just having started working here and all, you seem at ease with the phrase 'Devil Dog,' why is that?"

"Oh, that's easy—my brothers scared the hell out of the German soldiers at Belleau Wood in France." The man seemed fascinated, so I grabbed a glass to clean and continued. "They were said to have been so afraid of the bloodshot eyes of the Marines who fought them, and the way they fought, that they were like Teufel Hunden, which translates to devil dogs."

He laughed then. "And so these Marines have worn that like a badge of honor since then?" I nodded and he just laughed some more. "Have you ever wanted to see a *real* devil dog?"

I raised a brow at him and he leaned forward. "I'll make a little deal with you. Make me a few more of these like this, and I'll *give* you a hellhound. What do you say? Do we have a deal?"

I started to answer when Arden wrapped her arm around my shoulder and fixed the man with a disapproving look. "You know the rules, Luci. No deals with the staff at the High Table without Yen's say so."

Luci rolled his eyes. "You're such a buzzkill, Ardent Flame. You know I was only teasing him." She just stared at him and he held his hands up. "Fine! I won't make any deals, but I will tip heftily if he keeps these coming! Mind me now, boy, and keep them coming. Daddy's feeling *dancy*!"

I snorted and Arden just clicked her tongue as he wriggled away from us. "He seems interesting."

"He likes to come in occasionally and have his fun." She laughed as she looked to be remembering something. "You should really see him on karaoke night. He kills it."

I washed a glass and noted that he was getting empty so I made another drink and set it on the bar. Arden looked at me oddly, so I caved. "What?"

"You really have no issue giving *the* Morningstar booze?" I stared at her blankly. "Lucifer?"

Wait... "You mean he's *the* devil?"

Arden laughed along with some of the other patrons in earshot. "Sure is, kid."

"He seems so nice." I frowned, wondering if I was doing the right thing by serving him. I wasn't a devoutly religious man, but I'd always heard the devil was a dick.

"He's got a reputation, but he has *always* played by the rules." Arden smiled at me, almost like she had read my mind. "He likes to push the envelope at times, and press buttons, but he wouldn't break the rules like this. He likes us too much."

I snorted and shook my head. "Fine, I'll go take him his drink, you good?"

"I was fine before you, but I think I can manage." She just shook her head and turned back to the other customers.

I grabbed the Bloody Mary and headed over to where the king of darkness swayed to the beat of the song playing through the speakers. The dance floor lit where I stepped and I watched him look up at me, a thrill of adrenaline coming over me as something dark and radiating red slithered behind his eyes.

What in the fuck was that? I muttered to myself, frozen to the spot.

He blinked and it was gone, and I could move again, as he smiled kindly. "Oh! Thank you so much, I was just about finished with this one!"

I smiled as best as I could and nodded once before heading back to the bar. Arden watched me knowingly, then tossed me a shot glass that I caught deftly.

"What's this for?" I stared at her in confusion as she pointed a thumb to the clock where it struck ten.

"Tensies!" She poured a shot of something silver that I knocked back. It burned fiercely but after, I felt like I was calmer and more collected than before. She leaned closer to me and stage whispered, "The real creepy fuckers come in about now. That will help you keep cool without any magic or power to protect yourself."

Magic was real? I sighed. *Of fucking course it would be, Marine. You've literally just met the devil. How can it not be?*

CHAPTER THREE

The rest of the night progressed well as I came to the realization that this was really happening and no, I wasn't in some kind of dream. Though that last bit did little for the paranoia that edged in my mind that I might be serving the murderer who had done the majority of my platoon.

I kept Luci supplied with plenty of booze, experimenting a little more with various flavors that I thought he would enjoy. The other customers were curious about me, but kept a respectful distance. Arden made it clear I was still a baby when it came to the supernatural world.

After that, *all* of them wanted to get to know me. I spent the majority of my night talking about myself until last call at two a.m., though Arden was adamant that I not give anyone my full name.

"It's too much of a liability with the fair folk." I had to pick my jaw up off the floor after she moved away and one of the people at the bar just laughed uproariously.

"Oh, sweet summer child, I like you." She had the absolute greenest eyes I had ever seen. "You seeing anybody?"

I found myself preening a bit as I straightened up. "Not currently, no."

"I'll keep that in mind." She finished her drink and winked at me lasciviously as her tongue flicked across her lips.

After all was said and done, I had racked up quite the load of tips. And true to his word, Lucifer had left the majority of it.

Though how he had left it was a little more interesting than the others leaving it in the jar with my name.

I felt a hand in my pocket as I bent to grab another can of juice out of the back of the fridge, my hand automatically grabbing it and twisting, the pocket ripping at the violent motion.

"Feisty!" he muttered blearily as he stared at me with a lopsided grin on his face. "I promised you a tip if you kept the booze comin' an' you did jus' that. Sho here it is."

He held up a slim black card that looked like a credit card between his index and middle finger, like a magician making a card appear as a trick.

"Luci, I can't take your credit card, that's not right." I pressed it back toward him when the devil just glanced askance at Arden who stood behind me.

"He gives us all one." She explained as she held one up to me from her pocket. "Lucifer is a firm believer that everyone gets what they are owed, and if he means to tip you, the exact amount will be on the card. Take it and keep it."

"Lishen to the flame, boy." He gripped my shoulder and patted it. "Buy new pants too, on me. Make that booty look *goooo...*"

Someone appeared behind the slurring demon king and grabbed him from where he had begun to lean too heavily on my shoulder. "Thank you for your time, mister 'tender. Don't worry, I'll see him home."

"Thanks Azazel!" Arden waved and the man winked at her before they both just disappeared in a cloud of putrid smoke that stank of rotting eggs and pickle fart.

"Ugh, I hate it when he's too drunk to teleport on his own."

Uncle Yen waved a hand in front of his face and coughed loudly.

I watched him sit at the bar and motion me to him, so I joined him. "Arden, come sit with us for a time. You may be able to help me explain things a bit better than I can think to at the moment. And pour us all a pint of the good stuff?"

She nodded once and did just that. Soon, two large mugs of frothy alcohol sat in front of each of us. Two would hit the spot if I had a decent eye, and I could really use them right now.

Uncle Yen eyed her darkly and she just rolled her eyes. "It was a long, good shift. And I want to celebrate Marcus making it without melting down too much."

Yen snorted and laughed before taking a swig of his drink, sighing contentedly before glancing at me, then my mug.

I took a drink and sighed myself. It was damned good alcohol.

"The High Table was, and always has been, a place where the creatures of the shadows and magic can come and relax," he began, his hand waving in the air. As his fingers moved, shapes began to form at the ends of his fingertips.

Motes of dust, light, and shadow wove together to form images of creatures sitting at a single table.

"Wars, fights, arguments and grievances were always put aside at the High Table." The images threw their weapons down and lifted mugs high, cheering. "Bitter enemies could come and speak without fear and resentment. It hasn't always been easy, not by any measure, but it's always *been*—and that's what matters most."

Images flickered at the peripheral around those at the table, their weapons raised. "We here at the High Table pride ourselves in our ability to maintain this truce, this forced peace in our establishment, as was dictated in the Accords of Farnellan, the Maker of the Table."

"The reason it was so important that you be tested was to see that you could assist in keeping the peace," Arden added softly, then belched before her hand could cover her mouth. "Excuse me."

"Sign of good booze, Arden, don't apologize." Yen thumped the table and winked at her.

"So wait, this bar has always been here?" My mind wasn't fuzzy yet, but I was confused for certain.

"No." He tapped the top of the bar itself, the deep mahogany color of the wood shimmering. "This is but a piece of the table, and where it resides, so does peace. There are bars and clubs like this scattered all over the world in various nooks and crannies. Just gotta know where to look."

"Okay, and how are a few mortals going to compete with literal demons, and demi-god level creatures?" I scratched my head, wondering where I could hide a rifle in here.

Arden snickered. "We aren't mortals, Marcus." Uncle Yen threw her a warning glance and she just rolled her eyes. "You just did magic in front of him and your closest friend is a suicidal werewolf—I think he knows you aren't vanilla, Yenny."

"She has a point, Uncle Yen." I frowned at him, then at her. "And just who, or *what* are you?"

"That's a pretty rude question, Normie." Arden crossed her arms in front of her chest and glared at me.

"He doesn't know the do's and don'ts yet, Arden, and you kind of started it." He glared at her and crossed his own arms.

"Sorry if I offended either of you." I sighed heavily and shook my head. "You were kind to me and helped a lot today, thank you."

She stared at me sourly before rolling her eyes and saying, "Jinn. I'm a jinn. And before you ask, I will *not* grant you any wishes. I've been free for four thousand years and I do *not* plan to go back into service for anyone."

"Oh, that's so cool!" I leaned forward and looked at her closely.

"What are you doing?" She raised a single brow at me questioningly.

Uncle Yen laughed. "I think he's looking for jinn-like traits."

"We aren't close enough for you to see me in my natural form, Marcus." Arden snorted and drank from her mug. "Some day, but not this day. And Yen? What do *you* have to say concerning yourself?"

Uncle Yen rolled his eyes and looked at me. "I'm what would be called Touched."

"Stupid?" I raised an eyebrow at him and Arden began to wail with delight, beating the table hard enough that our drinks jostled.

"No, Marcus, a different sort of Touched." He shook his hand and the images shifted and became that of normal-looking humans standing in a line on the bar top. One of them lit up with an aura of light and the others began to shift all around them. "One in every hundred thousand humans in a given area may be Touched. Always to varying degrees and strengths."

Arden pointed to the image. "Some might find they can sense the weather a little better, or have more affinity to animals than others—like they always seem to like you no matter what you do?" She saw that I had begun to understand. "Then there are those like your uncle, who have the ability to manipulate magic in different ways. Almost as good as the creatures he serves and protects here."

I glanced over at Uncle Yen. "Is that true?" He nodded silently. "So then what is it that I can do here? I'm just normal."

"You're a little more brave than your average human—or foolish," Arden observed wryly.

"You aren't normal, Marcus." Yen spoke softly, but in the empty bar with no music playing he may as well have shouted it. I stared at him and he patted my shoulder. "You've touched something recently that left something inside you. You went somewhere, likely somewhere ancient and in a desert that could house so many secrets, no less. Where was it? *Which* was it?"

I blinked at him, carefully considering what I could say, but finally answered, "I can't say it."

"But he didn't deny that he went somewhere. NDA? Some

kind of gag order?" Arden looked excited, like a detective as I just nodded. "You deployed to the…" She leaned forward and sniffed me twice. "Middle East. Akkadian maybe? Or was it the Medes? No? Don't know? Feh, humans."

She rolled her eyes at my confusion. "And while you were there, you were a part of some kind of expedition to go and explore something ancient. Right? Don't speak! Just nod or shake your head."

I frowned and nodded. "Escorting someone?" Another nod. She clapped and spoke again. "While there, something happened. You touched something, something touched you. You walked into a room or something that no one else saw?"

I blinked, uncomfortable with how good she was at this.

"Can you do magic now?" Her hushed voice was curious and held notes of the drink in her fist.

"No, he can't," Uncle Yen interrupted gently. "Magic like that needs to be awakened, and by someone who won't try to take it."

"How does that happen?" The question left my lips before my brain caught up. "And what will that mean for me?"

"It means that you will be able to cast spells, though how powerful they might be will be up to you and the magic within you, I suppose." Uncle Yen scratched his head. "And it will happen by me calling in a favor, I think. We shall first see if they come in tomorrow and speak to them about it. If not, I'll call them to me."

"Thank you, Uncle Yen." I took a deep drought of my drink and sighed as the alcohol eased my mind a bit. Thoughts and images beginning to swirl at just what had happened back in the desert.

"Go and get yourself some clothes and things tomorrow that you will need, I don't care what it is, just get it for you." He noticed me thinking for a minute and sighed. "You get paid weekly here as well, so don't worry about money for now."

"Don't forget, you have that card from Luci too, and if you don't use it, he gets upset and throws more money at you."

Pulling back from the beginnings of my inner turmoil, I frowned and rolled my eyes at her. She pulled my tip jar over and I saw just how full it had become. There were wads of bills and coins that were so massive they couldn't be quarters or even silver dollars. "This is for you too. Yen will take the old money and give you Normie money."

"Seems like my nephew is pretty popular!" Yen grabbed the jar and began pulling things out of it. "Quite a bit here. Stop by my office in the morning and I'll have all this converted for you."

He scooped things back in, then popped off his stool and went to walk away, but I stopped him with a "Hey!" He paused and turned to look at me with my jar in his arm. "How's Jolly?"

A look passed over his face, unreadable but dark, then answered, "He will live, but his choice of poisoning himself strains our ties."

"I'm sorry." My heart fell into my stomach and he shook his head. "Don't tell me not to be. What I did was wrong, and even if I didn't know, I was wrong. I'm going to feel bad about it."

He snorted. "No one is going to tell you not to be sorry, kiddo. I've been in this biz for quite some time, and I've done things I regret and resent others for. You unknowingly allowed my friend to poison himself, and I wasn't against it. Granted—you were heavier-handed with his chosen poison than anyone should have been, but I wasn't against it."

"Why?" Arden interjected sourly.

Yen rubbed his head irritatedly. "It's complicated and it's not my place to judge him for it because I don't know his pain." He stared at me for a long moment. "So that you know, a lot of werewolves can't consume enough alcohol to actually feel the effects before their metabolisms flush it from their bodies. We have to use special tools that slow down their bodies enough to feel the effects. Tomorrow, you'll learn how to use those tools properly."

Something in the set of his shoulders and footing almost

dared me or Arden to defy him. He nodded once and turned to go back upstairs without another word.

I finished my first drink, then hefted the second mug and downed it in a steady set of gulps. Arden eyed me appreciatively as I did and smiled.

She had finished hers and winked at me. "Good work today, rookie. Want to go shopping in the morning? I know some places."

"You have a car?" I raised an eyebrow at her and she rolled her eyes.

She dug into her pocket and lifted a set of keys. "Boy, I'm four thousand eight hundred and twenty-six years old. Of course I have a car."

The sound of my jaw hitting the top of the bar was enough to make her laugh. "I'll pick you up around ten?"

I nodded dumbly and went up to my spartan room. It consisted of a bed, simple dresser, and a desk.

I stripped my clothes off and set an alarm on my phone for eight am. Five hours of sleep? Perfect.

CHAPTER FOUR

I woke up to the sound of birds chirping loudly from my phone, pulled it from the charger and stretched on the bed. It was softer than I was used to, but it worked.

I stood up, dressed in some workout clothes and laced up my tennis shoes for my morning run.

The doctors and therapists had encouraged me to remain active to avoid muscle atrophy and personally, I didn't know how else to start my day. PT had been an everyday thing for me for more than eight years, even on weekends. Some of the younger Marines liked to have me along on hikes and runs just to challenge them and because I knew the area we were stationed at well.

It was nice.

Having just gotten out not too long ago, there was still the culture shock to adjust to as there were no other Marines around. I felt isolated and alone here, despite being so close to family.

I growled to myself, *Get over it, Marcus. There are Marines out there dying in a shit storm and you're whining because you miss the camaraderie? What would Chesty say?*

I snorted at my little joke and threw my ratty old headphones into my ears and turned on some music as I locked the door to my room with the key I'd been given, then walked outside through the front door.

One of the bouncers stood there. "Hey, you must be Marcus! Yenny's little nephew. How're you doing, man?"

I blinked at him and smiled. He looked like he could have just turned eighteen, but maybe he was different. "Hey, I'm good, just going for a run. You going to be here when I get back in an hour or so?"

"Yeah, I'll be here." He grinned happily, his fresh and freckled face pleasant and friendly. "I'm Keith, by the way. It's nice to finally meet you."

"I take it my uncle talked about me a lot?"

Keith snorted. "Wouldn't shut up, and that's weird for the guy. But I digress—enjoy your run."

I grinned at him and took off down the sidewalk. It felt good to get my legs pumping again as the music flowed through my ears.

Granted, these headphones were on their last legs, but they worked and I appreciated that about them.

I ran as far as I could for half an hour, stopping to do some basic body weight exercises and other calisthenics before heading back.

This time, I incorporated wind sprints between street signs, fighting to stay out of other peoples' way at times.

My breathing came and went in bursts, as I hated sprinting, but it was good for me so I dealt with it. Embracing the self-inflicted suck. Besides, this helped me better come to terms with my world having been turned upside down from what I had always thought it was.

Keith smiled at me as I rounded the corner and cheered me on loudly as I sprinted to the doorway. He whooped for me as I crossed the shadow of the door. "Yeah!"

I heaved a sigh and caught my breath, before eyeing him dangerously. "You always cheer people on like that?"

Keith just chuckled and crinkled his nose, "Oh, come on! That was pretty fast for a human."

I stilled and watched him carefully, making him pause. "Shit. Did I mess up?"

"No. You looked like a kid and now I have no idea who or what I'm talking to."

He rolled his eyes and his shoulders fell. "Normies and their racist constraints… Look, I'm staff, specifically security." He pointed emphatically to his shirt that said as much. "So you can tell that I'm either an oni, or a werewolf. We have some other kinds of security, but the majority of us are either of those. So it's safe to assume that humans like you impress us, being strong or fast for your kind."

Now it was my turn to stare at him. "Now who's racist?"

He grinned. "That's fair." He glanced around before leaning closer. "Don't ask someone *what* you're talking to; kind of a dick move. Just roll with it, and assume anyone working here is more than they seem and if they want you to know, they'll tell you what they are. Like me—I'm a werewolf."

I nodded, my hand running through my short fade. "Sorry, Keith. I'm still getting used to this."

He crinkled his nose again. "I know. I can smell it on you." I stared at him and he tapped his nose. "Super strong sense of smell, bud. I know you haven't been near many of our kind before last night because all the scents are new."

"Oh, that's really cool, actually." I had to admit I was impressed. "So, do you like, have all the same kinds of abilities and stuff as the movies and books say you do?"

He laughed, nodding. "And then some. My kind age super slow too, so I may look like a kid to you, but I'm old enough to be your dad." My eyes widened and he laughed harder before shaking his head at me, grabbing my shoulder. "Ha, I'm just shitting you, man. I'm only a few years older than you. I'm still a pup to my pack. But you should've seen your face!"

I tried to feel indignant about it, but he had me dead to

rights and honestly, he had been pretty cool to me so far. I laughed with him and we bumped fists. "We cool, Keith?"

"We're definitely cool, Marcus." He unlocked the door and swung it open for me. "You let me know if you need anyone to howl at the moon with, and I'll be there, 'kay?"

I grinned at him and patted his shoulder as I walked by. He closed and locked the door before retaking his position while I crossed the bar to the stairs, shaking my head to all of this. Was this really my life now?

I showered quickly, resolving to buy my own towels and everything with the tips I had earned.

I changed into a set of clean clothes, then went about putting the few sets I had into the dresser, barely taking up any space.

A note on my desk made me frown.

Nephew,

Leave any dirty clothes or towels at the foot of your bed in a pile, or basket, before you leave your room or go to sleep for the night. There's a brownie on staff who takes care of that for us.

Uncle Yen

P.S. If you want to leave him a tip, he loves chocolate and cookies. I'm sure you can figure that out.

I laughed and complied, then grabbed my wallet, keys, and phone before heading out the door.

I turned and spoke to the air, "I'm not sure how this works, but thank you. And I'll bring you back some chocolate chip cookies, okay?"

I waited for there to be some kind of response, but when nothing came, I closed the door and went down the hall into the office where I found an envelope with my name on it.

I grabbed it and opened it up, pulling out crisp, fresh hundred-dollar bills. *You have got to be shitting me.*

I counted more than six grand in tips; it was almost enough to make me feel hollow. Had it been too much? I called Uncle Yen and when he picked up, he grunted, "Yeah?"

"There's way too much money here." I set the wads of cash

on the desk and I heard his door open up, his feet shuffling down the hall and into the room.

"That's what, six thousand, four hundred, and a couple ones?" I nodded to him and tapped the desk. "Yeah, that's all there was in your jar."

"Uncle Yen, there's no way." I insisted, remembering that the jar was full, but it wasn't like, *stuffed* full.

"There are conversions, Marcus." He walked around the side of his desk and pulled a small coin out of the top drawer. "This? This coin is worth more than three hundred dollars on its own, and there are creatures out there with *loads* of cash like this. This is the one place they can spend what they want and don't need to worry. Best part? That was a *slow* night, boy."

"What do I do with it?" I frowned and he just laughed at me. "Seriously, how do I get anything accomplished? If I open a bank account, there will be an investigation. If I want to do anything with credit, I'll be outed for some kind of crime!"

Yen just snickered and shook his head. "Listen, kid, you get paid here weekly, and our clients are *very* generous. But that just means you have to be smarter than the government—ain't hard." He grabbed the money off the table and took out four hundred-dollar bills. "This? Weekly earnings and three nights' tips. You put that into your Normie bank account with the base three hundred and five or so, then a tip of a minimum of a hundred every week."

"What about the rest?" I blinked at him and he just rolled his eyes.

"The rest you get a safe for, you hire someone to manage for you in hedge funds, or something else. I can personally suggest a dragon who owns an accounting firm." I stared at him and he paused. "You think I'm kidding, but I'm not."

I shook my head, a soft, disbelieving chuckle escaping my mouth. "Okay. If that's what you think I should do, then yeah, let's get them on it."

"Good man." He smacked my shoulder affectionately. "Have you eaten anything yet?"

"I was about to go find a place to eat." I took the wad of cash and pocketed it.

"I know a place we can go; give me ten to get dressed." He started to walk out of the door, then stopped and turned back to me. "You may want to check that card that you got from Luci."

I rolled my eyes, taking the card out and only expecting possibly a hundred or so, then remembered that everyone was generous. And he had called himself a hefty tipper.

I looked at the card and saw that it was a Visa and it had the image of a halo with horns on it on the numeric side, then on the back, it had a whopping ten thousand dollars.

"What the hell?" I bellowed and my uncle's laughter ringing from the doorway only made my distress seem that much less of an issue.

"Lucifer likes to give back." Uncle Yen's eyes twinkled as he watched me where I stood in disbelief. "He loves us and takes care of us, because we give him a place to just be himself away from the stigma of what he is—who he is forced to be."

I opened my mouth, and found that I had nothing to say. He had been a perfect gentleman to me and he had tipped me well just for putting forth the effort to make his night easier.

"Okay." Uncle Yen eyed me with a smirk and nodded to the door. "But breakfast is on me."

"You bet your butt it is, boy." Uncle Yen howled with laughter as he went to his room and I headed down to the barroom to wait. Once he was ready, we made our way out the door.

We went to a small mom and pop diner down the street he frequented and had the *best* scrambled eggs I'd had in more than a decade. While we were there, we spoke about what my duties would be while I worked at the High Table.

"Look, all I want is for you to keep your head on a swivel, be a sweetheart and the guy to talk to, but don't take any crap either." He held up his fist to motion like he would whack me and the woman who served us eyed him dangerously. "You know me, Jeanine, always the teaser!"

"He's not teasing." I teased him back and he kicked me beneath the table.

"Things will be even more manageable when we find out how strong your… cardio is." I caught on to what he meant and nodded. "So keep your chin up, your eyes open, and you'll be okay."

"Do we have anyone I need to watch for?" I kept my voice low so as not to attract too much attention as more people began to come into the diner.

"Not particularly, but there are VIP guests and customers that come in occasionally." He shrugged, clearly trying to think of someone. "The courts could be an issue, their people tend to be a little more vindictive and volatile, but they know our rules."

"The courts?" I tilted my head and he nodded. "What are those?"

"The denizens of the Fae, the fair folk." He watched me as I motioned for him to go on. "Fairies, boy. The courts of the Summer and Winter? The Seelie and Unseelie?"

I sighed, my head in my hands. "I thought they were just myths."

"Think again, nephew." He sipped his coffee and sighed deeply. "They're as real as you and me, and every bit as dangerous as the legends say. They're older than the mob and three times as brutal. They have men everywhere—outfits everywhere. Where there's a High Table affiliation, they follow."

"If they're like mobsters, then why do we allow them in?"

He eyed me severely. "It's not our place to judge, but to remain neutral and serve our people for the good of the land."

"How is serving these people for the good of the land?" I couldn't help the incredulous snort leaving me as I thought about the absurdity of that statement.

"What happens when your Marines are pent up all the time with nothing to do, and then suddenly you put them with a bunch of people weaker than them?" he asked me with a raised brow as our server refilled our coffees.

The very thought of that scenario made the hair on the back of my neck stand on end. "It would be absolute madness. The command would have to write so many non-judicials that the commander's hand would likely fall off and run away."

"Imagine that with creatures who used to actively hunt humans." His voice was soft compared to the din of the room around us. "Imagine that very situation with creatures whose magic could level a city block, and all because they felt slighted and a little aggressive without release?"

"So that's another reason we do the things that we do?" He nodded as I made the connection. "Okay. I'll do my absolute best."

"Good." Uncle Yen relaxed and tapped the table where the check was with a wink. I didn't even look at it and left a hundred-dollar bill. He grinned and nodded his head. "Good boy."

I snorted at him and we left the diner to go back to the bar with plenty of time for me to spare before Arden showed up.

Cass sat the door this time, eying me steadily. "Not gonna say something stupid to me like you did Keith this morning, are ya?"

I chuckled to myself and shook my head. "I learn my lessons quick, Cass. I appreciate him teaching me."

She scowled at me for a few seconds before her mean mugging halted and she fixed me with an easy smile. "Good man. By the way, I don't care if you know that I'm an oni."

I held my hand out and she took it. "Glad to finally meet a yokai."

Her eyebrows rose slowly as her face slackened, but it was Uncle Yen hitting me that made me flinch and her look to him. "You mean to tell me you know Japanese folklore but not about the Fae? What the hell is that about?"

"Yokai are mentioned in a lot of anime, manga, and video games, Uncle Yen." I tried to explain but he just harrumphed and threw his hands up as he escaped the source of his annoyance.

Cass watched him leave then turned back to me. "You a weeb?" Her face was stoic as she asked the question.

I couldn't help the bark of laughter that escaped me. "I guess? I'd settle for slight otaku, though." She frowned, so I continued. "One of the Marines I served with overseas brought a huge collection of anime and had a lot of manga stored so that he had something to keep him out of trouble. He'd share his passion with me, and I thought it was interesting, so I guess I could be called that?"

She shook her head, then thumped my shoulder. "We'll make one of you yet, Marcus."

She wore the biggest grin and I just laughed as she beamed at me. She was a beautiful woman, short blonde hair that hung to her ears, sunglasses that just let you see the outline of her eyes. A muscular physique but not at all unsightly or anything. And a real life oni to boot. "Well, if you have anything you want me to read or watch, just let me know?"

"I'd be delighted, and I know where you sleep, so I can always leave things for you." My face heated a little at the hint of a huskier tone in her voice but her phone being thrust into my sternum knocked me out of it. "Here, why don't you give me your number? I'll text you some things."

I added myself in her phone and she immediately sent me a smiley face emoji. "And that's me. Any plans today?"

"Yeah, Arden is going to take me shopping for some necessities and whatnot today."

She grinned wider. "You'll be in good hands then; Arden is a super nerd." She laughed at something and I turned to find Arden glaring at the bouncer. "Hey, babe."

"Don't you 'babe' me after referring to me in such a base way, you heathen." Arden stomped forward and flicked Cassia on the nose, making the oni just giggle in delight. She rolled her eyes, then faced me. "Are you ready? I find my desire to be here suddenly tainted."

"Ouch!" Cass muttered sullenly, but perked up when Arden glared at her. "At least take him to all the good places!"

"What kind of jinn do you take me for?" Arden threw her hands up. "Come on, Marcus, the yokai here are cramping my style."

She tossed her hair toward Cassia while turning to walk away and I just snorted and followed along.

We got to the parking lot, the same man sitting there this morning as had been there yesterday. "Back already?"

Arden smiled at him. "I've always preferred speed, Barley, you know that."

He just shook his head and let us in with a mischievous glint in his eyes. Arden screeched and he began to laugh hysterically.

I caught up to her and found her staring with her fists clenched at her sides while she stared at a massive pile of bird crap on what looked like a brand new, cherry-red Lamborghini Huracan EVO. "You did this on purpose, Barley!"

He nodded at me, then when she looked at him, he started to shake his head earnestly. "Not a clue what you're talking about, Miss Arden." He waved his hand dismissively and the pile evaporated into nothing. "See? What are you so upset for?"

She glared at him and he just played the fool, before she growled and turned to the car and me. "Get in."

I touched the handle on the outside of the passenger-side door and it popped out at an angle so I could pull it open. The interior was beautiful and the seats a little stiff, but I could be okay with that, especially since I was about to drive with a jinn. "I thought we needed to keep a low profile."

Arden snorted and stared at me for a moment. "Low profile? We're not the boogeyman, Marcus. I am a jinn, a creature of air, flame and speed. I desire to go fast and I will do so. Besides, no one ever said that we had to lay low. You'll get used to us."

She whipped the vehicle out of the parking space and out of the lot onto the street. "I was planning to go to Polaris or Easton today, those places alright?"

I nodded as the machine beneath us began to really let out.

"So you're almost five thousand years old. How do you keep the humans and authorities off your back?"

"We've had to adapt, us immortal and nearly immortal creatures." She switched lanes and the car sped on. "For the longest time, we could just grift and hoard money, blending in with the times, but now it's much more… bothersome. Now we typically start bank accounts and find suitable employment or excuses to be wealthy, fake growing old and having children, then when we're too old to be alive anymore, our *children* take over family affairs."

"So the reason you look like you're only twenty-five is because you can make yourself look that old?" She nodded at me and I relaxed a little. "That's pretty cool."

"Magic is absolutely amazing." She smiled and we sped on in silence for a few minutes, her hand flicking over the metrics on the display in her dash like it was second nature. "Are you nervous about trying to develop your magic?"

"A little bit. It makes me wonder what I'll be able to do, and not do." I scratched my head and paused, really wondering about something. "If I tell you something about what happened, you have to swear not to tell anyone else."

The car slowed down immensely, almost to the point that it felt like we were barely driving. "I will tell you this—jinn are terrible with oaths. And by that, I mean if you make a promise to me and break it, I would be well within my rights to kill you for it, and I might. It is much worse for us the other way round. So if I make you a promise, or an oath, you could place me into servitude if I break it. That is how we operate. So no, I will not bind myself that way."

"I'm sorry, Arden." I almost added that I didn't know, but she knew that.

We drove in silence for a minute before she put a hand onto my knee. "I will not swear to anything, but I will listen to you as your friend if you feel you need to speak about it."

She squeezed lightly before taking her hand back and I felt a little better about it. The NDA I had signed said that I could speak of nothing I saw to any human being alive or dead in any manner. Arden was a jinn, so she didn't count. *Right?*

"The ruins that we went to were like some sort of temple that had been uncovered in the middle of a sandstorm, and found by one of our helicopters while searching for insurgent supply routes." She turned onto a side street and nodded for me to continue. "We were scrambled to go with some scientists and archeological teams to see what was there. Me and my platoon went, all forty-three of us, with these egghead researchers. They flew us in by Ospreys, along with heavier aircraft bringing us Humvees too.

"You flew birds?" She seemed highly concerned but I chuckled and she seemed to get it. "That is a nickname for an aircraft, isn't it?"

I nodded. "When we landed, a squad stayed outside to secure the perimeter and another squad set up the tents and everything. We'd be there for a few days at a minimum, so we needed a perimeter and base for things to be easier to deal with." I stared out the window before continuing. "My squad went in with the researchers."

I closed my eyes, remembering everything as if I were still there, some of my memory having returned over the months I'd been recovering. "The inside was massive, the stone on the outside was tan, but the inside was white as bone, with markings in red that still dripped as if fresh. We walked in and stood on a catwalk of sorts that surrounded the lower level. We split up by fire teams to try to find a way to the lower level that we could see below us, but no easily discernible way down to it."

I gripped my knee as the sounds of weapons fire and shouting echoed in my mind, my heartbeat racing as I tried to find the team that I had been separated from. Their cries of fear and rage making me frown. It was so hard to remember everything from then on.

"Marcus?" Arden's voice swept through me and I mentally shook myself.

"I got lost and ended up in some room by myself. There was

a stone coffin inside, with bodies and skeletons surrounding it." A chill ran up my spine as I remembered their eyes having been clawed out, some of the skeletal remains having their eye sockets smashed wholly. "I turned around and there was a door there that hadn't been before. I started to look for a way out but found nothing and started to fire at the door, my rounds doing little more than chipping the stone."

"What did you do?" She blinked at me, then whipped her head to the road in front of us and corrected the car's path.

"I checked the walls again and while I did, I realized the cover of the coffin was slightly open, so I shoved it aside and looked in." I shook my head and frowned. "There was a human skeleton inside with a necklace around the spine that rested on the rib cage. It was like it *called* to me, maybe it was some kind of key that could be inserted into the wall like a video game. Anything to get out and back to my platoon. I grabbed it, and as soon as I did, it crumbled and I noticed that the door had been opened. I booked it and tried to find my fire team. They were gone. Couldn't even find their bodies. But the researchers were still there… their corpses and what remained anyway."

"Everyone else?" She pulled into a parking space and stared at me. I shook my head. "They didn't make it?"

"A few of the others survived something hunting them while we were inside. All in all, we had about three or four fire teams left. We saddled up in our Humvees and got out of there, not trusting anything or anyone to wait long enough for air transport." I scratched my head. "It took us days to get back after that, having to backtrack and take scenic routes to make sure we weren't followed or intercepted. We had almost made it back to the FOB when we were ambushed."

"Holy shit, Marcus, I'm so sorry." She put her hand on mine and I flinched at the contact. Remembering what I went through did this to me at times, but it had been the first time I had been able to fully see it all at once. "Do you think that whatever was in that room with you did this?"

"It has crossed my mind, and now all of this?" I shook my

head and sighed. "We can talk about it more later if you're open to it."

"I think I could be convinced to listen if you want to talk about it more." She smiled and pushed me toward the door. "Let's go get you some clothes and other necessities first though."

Turned out that 'other necessities' for Arden was more than I had planned for. We got clothes and shoes for a few occasions outside work, then shoes and clothes for work.

We made a stop at an Apple store and she pressured me into the latest phone, which I wasn't terribly upset about, and a set of rechargeable headphones to replace my old, dying ones.

I got a case for my phone to protect it and made sure I ported over all my contacts, then eyed her. "Where to next?"

"Cassia said to take you to the good places, so I'm going to." She grabbed my shoulders and turned me toward the wall behind me. "We're going to need to stop and get you a TV."

I rolled my eyes and then we were off. To Barnes and Noble, which made me pause. "Since when do you need a TV to read books?"

"That's for later, these are for other things." She grabbed an e-reader and put it in a little shopping basket, then pulled me toward the fiction section. "There are some authors out here who are actually some of us that sprinkle truth into their works, making things seem a little more *fantastical*. We'll grab those, and then the rest you can get for the e-reader online."

She grabbed a few books and placed them gently into the basket, reading the names and putting some more in there. The last one she held up to me. "This guy is a Normie, but he is surprisingly insightful, so I recommend it."

I shrugged and we were off to the myth and legend section, where Arden grabbed a few more books before taking me to check out. I spent more money on books than I think I ever had in my life.

The clerk asked if I wanted to opt into the store card and I shook my head, but Arden swiped hers for me and grinned, which made the clerk smile as he scanned. "Let's see here, we have… Chapman, Dean, Price, and Wong—I think I sense a theme here! You have really good taste."

I laughed. "Thanks. You can blame the lady, though. She turned me on to them, and I'm ever the voracious reader."

I spent the money, more than two hundred bucks, and hauled my possessions out to the trunk with the other bags of stuff. It took a little rearranging, but it all fit into the trunk, then when

Arden tapped it, there was even more room. I looked up at her; she winked and walked around to the driver's side door where she climbed in easily.

I shut the trunk and climbed in as people crowded around the car with cameras and phones clicking for photos.

We stopped by Best Buy and bought a large TV, around seventy inches, because I had always wanted one and she assured me it would fit with ease.

After getting the TV, she took me down the road to a place on Morse and my jaw dropped. "Really? A video game store?"

"The good places, Marcus." She grinned and pulled me inside with a giggle. "This is also for research."

"You don't have to convince me—I like video games." I shook my head at her. "What, you aren't PC master race?"

"I have it all, but we're here for you—oh, they have that in?" She skipped over to a rack and picked up one of the games before scowling at the clerk who had just walked out from behind the desk. "Masonai! Why didn't you tell me that this was in?"

"Check your damn phone!" The man snorted, pointing to her pocket. She pulled it out and glared at the screen, then narrowed her eyes at him. "See? I do care."

"You're off the hook for now."

Masonai turned to me, his hair reminding me of some of the Marines I knew and I was instantly more at ease with him. His nose wrinkled as he smiled at me and offered his hand. "How's it going? As you can likely tell from Arden's obvious over-familiarity, my name is Masonai. How can I help you today?"

"I'm Marcus, and I guess I need the works?"

He put his hand on my shoulder like he was consoling a dying man. "Don't worry, my friend, I'll be gentle with your wallet." I laughed with him as he pulled me to the consoles he had on display. "What's your poison?"

"I'll go PlayStation, I suppose, as it was what I had before I served." He stiffened a bit, then leaned close to me. "Yes?"

"You a jarhead?" I leaned back and his eyebrows raised suspiciously as I nodded. He just shook his head. "Army. Glad to meet you, brother."

I wrapped an arm around his shoulder and patted him like I was consoling him. "I'm sorry for your loss."

We both laughed and Arden stepped closer. "What was that about? Why be rude to my friend?"

Masonai shook his head. "Nah, it's not like that." He motioned from him to me. "What the crayon muncher was trying to do was a little playful ribbing. See, if anyone came in here and disrespected the service in front of either of us, or disparaged the other, I have a strong feeling he and I would be neck and neck to lay them out."

I bumped the fist that he offered, and stated, "Damn right. Hoo-ah."

Arden rolled her eyes, muttering something beneath her breath before turning away from us.

He snorted and let me go. "You're good people, man. Just don't break anything, alright?"

I lifted my eyebrows and acted hurt. "A Marine not breaking something in a new place? You wound me, sir."

We traded more half-hearted jabs at each other's branch of service as he helped me get everything I needed and more that Arden added to the pile. Around a thousand bucks later, I was ready to tap and Masonai was ecstatic. "You'll have to game with me, Arden, and Cassia. Do you know her?"

"He works with me, Masonai; yes, he knows her." Arden

thumped the game she held and eyed him dangerously. "I need this."

"She's always on if she's not at work or out and about, man—do you even sleep?" Masonai just snatched the game out of her hands and scanned it. "Don't bother, I know your credit card number by heart with how often you come in."

Arden smiled and batted her eyes at him. "Who needs to sleep when it feels like you spent hundreds of years asleep in a bottle?"

I stilled, eyeing her for her reference but she glanced from me to him and Masonai just chuckled and handed the game back with a retort of, "Well, you may be that good, but everyone needs rest."

"I'll rest in another thousand years or so, buddy." She winked at him and we left with me promising to give my gamer tag to Arden for her to share so he could add me.

"I know that he thinks you're joking, but what if he didn't?" We were in the car by now and on our way back to the bar.

"I've been joking like that with him for years, he's used to it by now." She thought a little more, then blushed. "Besides, he's cute. Did you see the way his brown eyes lit up when he saw me? His dark skin is beautiful too. He is a handsome man, and I do not think I would mind him knowing I am a jinn."

"It doesn't break any rules to tell him?" She shook her head, then something occurred to me. "It doesn't because it would just implicate you. And you would outlive him. Knowing that, he would keep your secret because he would love you for you, right?"

"As would I him. Yes." Something akin to remorse flitted across her gaze before she sped us toward downtown. "I have done this only once before, in Macedonia. He was a good man. We never had any children because the jinn can only reproduce with another of their kind, but we adopted many. Watching them all go before me was… heartbreaking. I watch over their lineages from time to time. Bring them good fortune in his name. It brings me comfort."

I had nothing to say to that because I couldn't imagine it, so I stayed quiet until we got back to the bar.

Cass let us in, calling for someone to come and take the door so that she could help us get everything in. She took bags and bags of clothes like she was hiking groceries into the place. Then proceeded to walk up the stairs like it was the simplest thing in the world. Which, to an oni, it likely was.

She stared around the room and grunted. "Nice digs, Marcus. But a little disheartening, don't ya think?" I scowled at her as she waved to my sparse furniture. "I know a guy, and we can hook you up with some stuff to help out."

I rolled my eyes and smiled. I noticed that the laundry and towels were gone from the floor and neatly folded on the bed, but it was what I had forgotten that made me grunt, "Shit!"

Arden looked over at me from where she was hooking up my TV and system. "What?"

"I promised the brownie some chocolate chip cookies and I totally spaced."

She rolled her eyes and took a step toward me before she was gone, a gust of wind blowing by my head. A moment later, she stepped through my door with a package of twelve chocolate chip cookies. "Seamus loves his cookies, so I couldn't very well just allow him to go without."

She put them on the floor and slid them under my bed, then went back to what she had been doing.

Cass piled the bags of new clothes on the floor before the bed, then looked through the games I had gotten. Her eyes lit up as she held up the same game that Arden had just bought. "This is out? Why didn't Masonai tell us?"

Arden just grunted at her without looking up. "Check your phone."

Cassia pulled out her phone and her shoulders fell. "Damn, he's such a good dude."

I laughed. "He sure seems like it. What's the big deal about this game?"

I looked at it, but it looked like a standard four-man party role playing game, not to say that I didn't want to play it.

"It's a co-op game with a party system that encourages group play." She turned to Arden who just nodded. "So since we all have it for the same system, we can play together!"

"If you want to play with us?" Arden asked politely. "I know we work together, but I also know this is a lot for you to take in. You don't have to feel like you need to."

I shrugged. "I played with the guys I worked with all the time when I was in. This is my life now, and I'm just glad to have some people who won't judge me."

Arden and Cass glanced at each other, then at me before Cass snorted. "Who said anything about not judging you? You'd better be a good player and not a newb."

Arden and I both laughed, then I checked my watch as it read about 16:00. "What time does your shift start?"

She checked her watch and grinned. "Now." She flitted out of the room humming a tune.

Cassia just shook her head and winked at me. "I get off early tonight, but I'll stick around and help you get some things in. I already called my brother."

"You what?" I turned to follow her and she just winked at me before she followed Arden down the stairs.

I set everything up, taking a photo of my new gamer tag before heading down stairs in time to be early for my shift. I found a burger and french fries on the table waiting for me. Arden pointed to it and, with a note of command in her voice, ordered, "Sit and eat that. I know humans get hungry if they don't eat enough."

"I don't usually get too hangry, but thanks." She eyed me and I finally asked, "What?"

"How humans survive anything is beyond me." She grinned and turned away.

I rolled my eyes and dug in, adding ketchup and mustard to the burger as well as some ketchup for the fries. Both were probably the best I had ever had. "I didn't know we had a kitchen."

"We do, we just don't sell a lot of food on a normal day like yesterday. We will today." Uncle Yen's voice surprised me as he joined me at the bar. "How was your day? I see that you got some good stuff."

I told him about where I had gone with Arden and he just scowled. "Video games? You'll be learning how to wield magic if I can help it, you won't have time for that."

"So what is that process like?"

"For us, it's simple—someone who is familiar with awakening latent power, or with immense power of their own—will come and take a look at you." He winked at Arden and she headed into the back wordlessly. "As to everything else? It varies from person to person."

"That is absolutely awesome!" I stared at him for a second as he looked around, his attention finally falling back on me. "How did your magic come about?"

He chuckled and scratched his head. "I always had a little, but when I was in my youth, I made some pretty powerful friends. When they found out I had a knack for it, they awakened the rest of it." He tapped the bar. "Shortly after I mastered it, I was asked to start running this branch of the High Table."

"So is that kind of the end all beat all?" I raised a brow at him and he just shrugged. "You don't know?"

"Not that I don't know, nephew." Arden appeared on the other side of the bar and set a steak and fries in front of him. "It's mainly that there are so many options out there that I couldn't justify calling it that. What is best for me could be terrible for you, or Arden here."

"I'd hate to be in your position, Yenny." She smirked and walked away to get someone else a drink.

"See?"

I shook my head at his wry comment and finished my meal sitting amicably next to him.

My curiosity got the best of me and I finally whispered, "When will we do it?"

"We will see if he comes here tonight." He checked his watch. "If he's not here by eight, I'll call in a favor."

"Thank you." I stood up and rubbed my stomach. "My compliments to the chef."

"I will let them know." Uncle Yen belched happily and I left him to go change for work.

Entering the room again, I noticed that my clothes were gone and that the blue jeans and plain black shirt that I had bought with work in mind were neatly folded on the bed.

"Thank you, Seamus!" I called and I could have *sworn* I heard a soft reply under my bed.

I didn't look, but I did shiver a bit. I dressed in the bathroom and left my clothes in there so that he didn't have even more to do right now.

I walked out of my bathroom and heard a small thump near my bed. I turned and saw a small, furry brown hand with three fingers placing a sticky note.

I picked it up as the hand disappeared.

Marcus,

Don't leave clothes about, and let me do my job, lad.

Seamus.

Also, thank ya for the cookies, boy-o.

I laughed loudly. "You can thank Arden for that, Seamus. She saved my bacon because I forgot. But you got it, buddy."

A soft huffing noise came from under the bed that made me think of laughter.

My clothes in a neat pile on the floor at the foot of my bed, I left the room and got to work.

CHAPTER FIVE

Customers really liked the new blood apparently, as they kept calling for me to come chat with them.

At one point Uncle Yen had to save me from a table. "Now, now. You ladies and gentlemen need to let the boy work. He's a permanent fixture here now, just like yours truly. You'll be able to learn all about him soon, I promise."

They laughed and threatened that they would do just that before I got away and back to the bar. Arden snickered at my exasperation. Her smirk made me laugh as she shook a cocktail.

I took my time to make sure that all the drinks I made were as good as possible, even getting a few compliments for slight additions and changes I made.

One of the people at the bar who looked to be much younger than I would let in made a request. "Can you put on a show with my drink? I've seen other human bartenders toss their cups and juggle bottles while they make things. I hoped that you might be able to do that too?"

I looked over at Arden and she crossed her arms as she stepped back to give me room. I laughed bashfully. "I suppose I could try."

"I'd like something fun, I just turned six hundred!"

I nearly spat in surprise, remembering that there were exceptionally long-lived creatures here.

I thought about a drink and smiled, since Arden had shown me we had the ingredients for it earlier. I grabbed a clear glass and placed it on the bar before filling it with crushed tonic water ice, then flipped my shaker over my shoulder where I caught it in front of my chest then placed a small amount of ice in it. I filled it with normal-looking vodka and shook it three times swiftly, chopping the shaker to release it and poured the alcohol into the cup as I added more tonic water over that.

As it started to settle, it took on a blackness, then small motes of light appeared as if they were stars. A miniature galaxy in essence.

"Wow!" the customer whispered in awe.

I tapped the cup and put it under a black light that we had on the bar and it *really* lit up. "Here you go, the galaxy is yours for your birthday."

They took the drink and stared into it with wonder before drinking it.

"Color-changing alcohol?" Arden asked me as they walked away, so I nodded and she smiled. "Cool trick."

"I had meant to save that one for Luci, but I can't just let someone not have something cool for their six hundredth."

She shook her head and walked off to pour some beer and left me to my own devices. I took some food from the serving table just outside the kitchen to the appropriate tables. The entire time I worked, I checked my watch on the inside of my left wrist. Old habits die hard and all that.

It was fifteen after twenty-hundred and I still hadn't been summoned to Uncle Yen. I just sighed and went back to work, smiling and joking as best as I could.

I washed some dishes quickly in the sink behind the bar and turned around to find a man staring down at me from the other side of the bar top. He was at least seven feet tall and had a large walking stick that came to the top of his head.

His skin was pale white, almost sallow and sickly, that clung tightly to the bones of his body. His eyes were pitch black and his hair was plastered to the side of his face on one side. If there was anyone who could have been the grim reaper, it was this guy for sure.

I blinked at him and tried to smile, but there was something off about him, "Hello, sir, how can I serve you?"

"It be not how ye can serve me, but how I might be of service to thee." His voice was the deepest and most gravely that I had ever heard in my life.

"Cut the crap, Anubis." Uncle Yen stepped closer and thumped the man on the shoulder.

The massive man looked down at my uncle and deflated sadly. "You never let me have any fun, Yenasi."

I watched as his face and body filled out, and his skin became more and more tan and healthy until he cut an even more intimidating figure. "I had him thinking I was the grim reaper! Do you know how pissed that guy would be if he heard that I could pass in his stead?"

"Pretty pissed, which is why I don't want to have you doing it here—you know how vindictive he can be." Uncle Yen wagged his finger at Anubis threateningly before pulling him into a great big hug. "Good to see you again, my friend. I'm sorry it took this long to get a hold of you."

"Yenasi, I'm a death god, I know it's hard to get a hold of each other." He held out a small black object. "I did get a mortal device though, a cellular phone?"

Uncle Yen took it and flipped open the object only to laugh. "This thing is almost as old as me!"

Anubis looked defeated, almost sullen. "I thought it was neat."

"It is." I smiled at him and reached into the backpack I left under the table. "Have my old one."

I handed him the Android phone and he took it as if it were going to break in his hands. He looked down at me and asked, "You're sure I can have this?"

"You and Uncle Yen are friends, right?" He nodded and Uncle Yen just watched me as I continued. "Friends should be able to chat, right? Plus, I'm assuming that the reason you're here is because of me, so it's the least I can do."

Yen smiled at me and mouthed, *thank you,* as Anubis stared at the phone. His head dipped, then bounced back up as he stuck the item in the satchel on his hip. "I will need to turn it on, correct? Can I count on you to assist me, Yenasi?"

"Of course, old friend." Uncle Yen patted his arm and motioned to me. "The reason you are here is, as Marcus said, to help awaken his magic."

Anubis glanced around. "Then let us go to the VIP room and get started."

Yen nodded and went to turn when we heard Cassia shout, "You know damn well you aren't going to come in here armed!"

"Get out of the way, you stupid bitch!" A man snarled and a scuffle ensued.

I started around the bar with a blade in hand which I kept hidden in my belt, carefully watching as four figures entered. Three of them spread along the wall and the fourth adjusted his black suit jacket, then ran a hand through his greased hair as he glared around the room.

"What, is no one going to offer to take my damn coat?" He spread his hands and laughed as if he were the funniest guy on the block. He took his jacket off as one of the other suits stepped forward to take it. By the time he turned around, I stood in front of him and Cass stepped into the room. "See? This guy knows how to greet the new boss. Go get me a drink, dumbass, I'm thirsty."

His cronies laughed and he turned to throw a dirty look at Cass. My fist moved, clocking him in the stomach, then my blade was at his throat as he bent slightly in the middle. "I don't appreciate you being so gruff with my friends and then coming into our establishment to act like an asshole. I'm going to have to ask you to leave."

He snickered and stood up, the blade moving on his throat

did nothing but make him laugh. "You're going to use a Normie weapon on a preternatural creature? On *me*?"

He stood fully and the three men behind him were on top of me in a heartbeat; someone's fist plummeted into my stomach painfully, then the hands grabbing me were gone.

I collected myself as best I could, having been through all kinds of shit, but that punch to the gut felt like it had rearranged my innards.

"Let them go, old man." The cocky piece of shit growled at Anubis. The Egyptian god had one of the men gripped by the throat with his legs dangling in the air as the other two tried to get to him around Cassia and Arden.

Three more bouncers were ready to hop in before Uncle Yen bellowed, "High Table order: All Calm!"

A vacuum-like sound rumbled around us and the wood on the table glowed amber. I had been angry before, and more than a little concerned as I was out of my depth, but now?

Now, I was calmer than I had ever been in my life.

Uncle Yen stepped forward and spoke in a firm and authoritative tone, "I don't know why you think it okay for the Summer Court to come here armed to the teeth and expect to be served, let alone allowed to come in. You know the Laws of the High Table, boy, no weapons outside of staff, and only then for your protection and with permission."

"What about the Normie who pulled a knife and attacked me?" He pointed to me and smiled. "Are you going to give him to me to appease my wrath?"

"He's staff, and you broke the rules," Cassia snarled, her skin beginning to turn a mottled shade of red. "Get the fuck out."

"Who are you to order me around, oni?" the younger man spat as he stepped forward in challenge.

"She's the current head of security and staff—which means you go." Yen sighed tiredly. "It also means that I'm more than within my rights to tell you that you're banned for a hundred years."

He snorted and rolled his eyes. "Whatever, old man. Let's go, boys."

Anubis pulled the man in his hand close. "You may want to find better company to keep, Fae. I can smell death on you—it's yours."

One of the others leaned forward toward me and grunted. "Smells the same."

"Let's go!" the leader barked and snapped his fingers so that they had to follow him outside. As he walked, he put his hands in his pockets and thrust his hips forward. "I'll own all this anyway, soon." The bouncers mean mugged them the entire way and as soon as they were out, the door shut behind them.

Uncle Yen pointed to the three other bouncers. "Front and side doors. Vince, guard the back door. You even see any Summer Fae, you get backup just in case. Am I clear?"

They nodded and split up and Yen turned to Cassia, "Cassia, calm down. There's no need to blow up and attack them now, you're off shift. Come have a drink on me?"

She nodded and stepped toward the bar and then Anubis stopped her. "I will buy you a couple drinks as well, as a vote of solidarity."

Cassia grinned at him with her best attempt and plodded toward the bar then growled, "I wanted to punch one of them! Fuck." She was obviously still very worked up.

Arden walked around the bar and started to serve her and some of the others.

My uncle grabbed me and tugged me toward the back of the bar and made a vague gesture with his hand. The wall shimmered and a door appeared there. He touched it and it flew open just before he pulled me inside.

The room was a deep green color with a sort of garden-like feeling to it. Plants and trees grew within the space and though I could tell there was a roof to the room, the stars above us looked as real as if I was in the desert again. There were couches, a low table made of roots woven together, and a small bar in the corner.

Once Anubis and I were in, he shut the door and rounded on me. "You have no powers and you attack the heir to one of the most powerful houses in the Summer Court?"

Anubis chuckled to himself, both Yen and I turning to stare at him as he tried to give a small cough to cover the sound. "I thought it was rather brave. Brash actions are typically entertaining."

"Dangerous is what they are!" Uncle Yen seethed, his normally serene face having turned older and enraged.

I mumbled in response, "Not that I knew who he was."

Meanwhile Uncle Yen continued seething, "I had wondered what was going on in this city of late, but now I know what it is."

"What?" I stepped forward and put a hand on his shoulder.

"The Summer Court is making a move for the criminal underbelly of this city." Yen swatted my hand away and walked over to the plush couch in the room and flopped onto it. "Every now and then, we would get wind of a rumor about some of the seedier, lesser preternatural creatures being found dead in spectacular ways. Human dealers drained of blood, or lying dead in craters with no real meaning to it. We've been doing what we can to keep people off the trail and the Wardens in the city have been hunting the culprits. Now, I'm pretty sure they just walked in and handed us the news with trumpets blaring."

"But why would he do that and walk in here claiming to be the new boss?" I frowned and looked at both of the men.

"He's young, likely only a few centuries, and probably looking to make a name for himself. If he were to take over the High Table here, he would be untouchable." Anubis ran his hands through his hair. "Remember when my pantheon tried to do this in Egypt? Tried to take back everything and make the country theirs again?"

"The Nile nearly flowed with more blood than it did in their prime." Uncle Yen shook his head and stroked his chin.

"What can we do about it?" I crossed my arms and stood ready to hear the plan.

"We?" Yen scoffed and waved me away. "*You* need to have your magic awakened and then with that, train and get as strong as you possibly can."

"Speaking of, you might want to have a seat, Marcus." Anubis rested his massive hand on my shoulder and gently guided me toward the sofa across from Uncle Yen.

I sat down and he stood behind me. "This will not be comfortable, and for that I apologize."

I was about to ask him what he meant when his fingers rested on my shoulders, and his forefingers tapped my temples.

Discomfort built where he touched, then a savage rolling agony lanced through me to the pit of my stomach, then back.

I could vaguely hear Anubis hiss, "Oh… this isn't good."

He was right. It wasn't.

CHAPTER SIX

I blinked and found myself floating in the ocean under a sea of dark stars, the outlines of them being the only thing visible in the darkness. The voice that had spoken to me had been a breathy, feminine voice that echoed out of the darkness.

"Who's there?" I called, my voice sounding muffled until I realized that, since I was floating, my head was under water. I lifted my head and my hearing returned to normal. "Where are we?"

This is your mana pool, what magic you will be able to use will come from here. We've had several months to fill it slowly so as not to draw any attention to ourselves, and I have to say, you have much untapped potential.

"You never told me who you are," I called back. "Show yourself."

You aren't strong enough to gaze upon me, Marcus. Not yet.

"What happens now?"

You grow, as all of my blessed have before and, with a little luck, even more than they ever could have.

"How will you know?" I stared out into the nothingness and waited.

Because I will be there with you, you will see.

I closed my eyes and when I opened them once more, I was sitting in the room with my uncle and Anubis still touching my shoulders and head. He was breathing quicker and quicker as I rolled the stiffness from my neck.

"This is not good, not good at all." Anubis' hands left my body and as I turned to look at him, his staff appeared and dark energy wrapped around the top of it.

"What the hell is going on?" Uncle Yen asked him quickly, bolting over to stand in front of him. "What's wrong?"

Oh, he does not like me. Her voice rustled through my mind again, then a weight formed on my shoulders and I felt claws dig into my clothes.

I looked up and found a black cat with irises of the purest green I had ever seen. Her tail flicked back and forth as she watched Anubis blanching at the sight of her.

"This is old power. It predates even myself, and I am *old*." Anubis took his staff in both hands and pointed the swirling end toward me and the cat hissed violently.

Tell him this name. The voice paused, then purred. *Garellia.*

"Garellia." I blurted out the name and Anubis' staff dropped onto the floor with a dull thud. "What does that mean?"

Anubis was quiet for a moment as he stared at the cat before shuddering. "I don't know, but for some reason it makes me feel… small."

Because he is, but no matter. I will be teaching you how to use your magic in the old way.

"What is the old way?" I whispered to her as she crawled down my arm.

Adaptive.

She faded from view and a fierce itching overtook my right forearm. I lifted it so that I could see and found a tattoo of a starry cat against my skin.

Touch it.

I did as she said and as soon as my fingertips touched the object, a small screen hovered over it. "Woah!"

I looked up and both Anubis and Uncle Yen looked at me as if I were either daft or losing my mind.

I moved my forearm and the screen moved with it, so I moved it back up and looked it over more in depth.

Level 1
Stats
Brawn: 2
Dexterity: 3
Physique: 2
Mana: 4
Charisma: 5
Points to spend: 20
Spells Known
None

"I thought you said that she was old?" I scoffed at Anubis and motioned to the screen on my wrist. "She's basically treating this like a video game!"

"A what?" He frowned and turned to Yen, leaning toward the man who motioned to him and whispered in his ear. "Oh! Like those games that you like to play? What is it, Obliviate?"

"Let's leave my down time out of this," Uncle Yen whistled and stared pointedly at me. "What do you mean she? Is your magic talking to you? Is the cat her?"

I stared at the new ink on my forearm and nodded; that felt right. "It's like an RPG system." I saw that there were arrows next to the stats that could increase them. "I can level up and spend stat points right now."

Some of what you have is either human level, or slightly above human level. You are strong but not too strong, and your scores reflect that. I am surprised that Anubis did not think to correlate his power this way as well. How far they all have fallen.

"It looks like my two highest scores are Mana and Charisma." They seemed shocked by that, but just stayed quiet. "I think I might need some time to think over what kind of selections I'll make."

"Okay, nephew." Uncle Yen stretched, but even then, he

looked a little worn down and concerned. He grabbed me by the shoulder and stared into my face. "I'm going to go see what I can dig up on ancient beings with Anubis. We may not find anything but it would be better to know than not. You okay to go back to work?"

"Sure am!" I grinned at him before smiling over at Anubis. "Thanks for the help, Anubis. I really appreciate it."

"Keep that thing away from me, and we'll be even." The god of death scowled at me.

"Why the sudden distaste, Anubis?" I watched the emotions playing over the old god's face and could swear I saw his fist clench.

"The old ones ate the younger ones, and this thing in you feels *old*." He shuddered visibly. "I am serious, keep her away from me, Marcus. I like you, boy. I love your uncle like a brother and will help him in this. But I will kill you to stay alive if I must. Please, do not force my hand."

The look of horror on my uncle's face was telling and I just nodded to him once as I turned and walked out of the room.

"Who's the cat?" Arden watched her for a moment between orders.

"She's mine, magical and whatnot." I grinned only just realizing that she was no longer just a marking on my arm, but a decoration for my shoulders and she went back to work, but stared at her occasionally before more people piled in.

The bar was busier and it was a good thing too, as I thought better when my hands were busy. There were some drinks out there that I had to follow cards for, but otherwise it wasn't bad. While I went over the drinks and checked things, I decided to have a chat with Garellia.

"So how does all this work?" I filled an order and ran for some food, then started making another order. "And why video game stats?"

They are something that you understand and something that my people used to quantify their abilities. I do not know where your game makers found the old texts, but they created some masterful systems from them.

"You got that information from my memories?"

She nodded her head.

I stilled, then decided that it couldn't be what I thought and just let it go for now. I snorted and rolled my eyes as I left a table of people who were nice, but ignored me for their conversation. Arden had said they were like this though, so I paid it no mind.

"Okay, so what's with the cat?"

The voice was quiet for a time, then the tattoo on my arm faded and the cat once again stood on my shoulder. *I am still in a vastly weakened form due to having slumbered in an almost-larval state for millennia, and this manifestation takes little energy for me to make and manipulate.*

"Is Garellia your real name?"

The cat's head shook side to side.

"What is it?"

Her tail flicked for a time, several customers walking closer to her to observe and pet her. She looked like she enjoyed it.

Finally she turned back to me and stated, *I don't know.*

I stared at her. "Do you wanna be called that?" She blinked then shook her head, and I was still long enough that Arden had to touch my shoulder to get my attention.

"Can you bring a pitcher to table seven? Group of ladies in the back corner? They asked for you."

I obliged, filling the pitcher they wanted, and another for the wait on me. "Hi ladies, how are we doing?"

One of them, a tall and leggy woman with a sweater dress on, glanced behind me and said, "I like your kitty. I didn't know we were allowed pets in the bar."

I set the pitchers on the table. "This one is from me for the wait, and as far as she's concerned? I think we're a package deal."

Indeed. The cat purred at me.

"What's her name?" another of the women asked. This one looked like she could have come straight from the runway. Her dark skin had highlights and makeup that would have made any of the models I had ever seen want to crawl under a bridge.

"We were actually just discussing that—I don't know." I was a little uncomfortable with the third degree I was getting from them, but it seemed cordial.

"She's beautiful, as all cats are," the final woman announced with her nose held high. She looked like a tell-tale Karen, down to the haircut and snobbish looks. "Is she not, Bastet?"

The model-looking woman nodded appreciatively as she watched the cat.

"Well, I think we could take suggestions?" The cat suddenly appeared on my shoulders and purred loudly.

"Isis." Karen suggested.

"What?" The first woman raised her eyebrows and looked around.

Karen sighed. "Beautiful name, but hardly for the intelligent."

I shook my head. "And what's your name, miss?"

She lifted her chin. "Inanna, but you might know me as Ishtar."

I tried to act like I was considering it but the cat batted my head. *No.*

"Sorry, seems she doesn't like it." I offered a placating smile as the woman just stared open mouthed at me and the cat. "But please, enjoy your drinks."

Isis touched my arm as I went to move away from them and pulled me close. "I'd call her Galaxy because of how stellar her fur looks." She then slipped something into my hand with a smile. "For you, and maybe the little kitty too."

Isis reached up and stroked the cat's chin so fast that she hadn't gotten the chance to react before the touch was over.

"What do you think of Galaxy?" I whispered softly as we traversed the crowd back to the bar area.

It's basic, but I suppose it will do. She lifted her front right paw and licked it clean, then washed her chin with it. *I will be staying off you for a short time to adjust to myself and my surroundings.*

I worked for another few hours with Arden as the night

progressed, Galaxy asleep on the bar, or watching the crowd passively.

"So what do you think I should do with those points?" My question lifted her head and she turned it in my direction.

It would depend on how you would like to grow. She walked over to Arden and purred softly. *This jinn is magically powerful, fast, and at least six times stronger than a human, but she cannot change these aspects of herself. The drunken one over there?*

She padded down to the end of the bar where Cassia's head lay on the wood with her drooling happily. Galaxy set a paw on her head and stared at me. *This one is at least a dozen times stronger than a human in this form alone and more than twice that in her true form. Her magic is okay, and she is much faster than a human too. Physically, there would be nothing that you or anyone could do to her without a special weapon, due to the toughness of her skin and her amazing physique.*

She once more appeared on my shoulder and butted her head against me. *As with all of the people in the past, you will have the ability to make whatever you wish of yourself. So it depends more on your whims and how you desire to grow from here on out. I will tell you that the reason all of these beings appear as normal humans to you is because your Mana is so low. If you were to raise it to at least a ten, you would be able to glimpse their true natures. The higher your Mana, the more you can see of them.*

"Will I be able to cast spells?" The cat nodded and I began to hoot and holler, drawing attention to myself. I laughed. "Sorry, guys, just talking to my cat."

One of the guys at the end of the bar, big biker-looking fella, called, "I do the same thing, buddy. Don't you feel ashamed at all!"

He laughed and Arden snickered. "You're a literal feline, Balthazaa; your cats can talk back to you."

"His is magic though." The man pointed to Galaxy. "You can tell from her aura how powerful she is."

I looked at her and whispered, "Is that okay?"

Galaxy hopped off my shoulder and faded from sight only to step out of his shadow on the wall beside him onto the bar.

She tilted her head at him and sniffed the hand he offered before rubbing her teeth, then head against his knuckles. *He means no harm, and he smells good.*

I chuckled and he looked extremely pleased with himself as he scratched her shoulder blades gently.

Well, I guess that means he's friendly. I snorted again and poured another drink.

No one said that. Her voice echoed through my mind. *You could think of your questions to me to seem less crazed, if you like.*

Oh. My cheeks heated wildly. *I'm so sorry.*

I am a part of you now, Marcus. I can sense everything about you.

I thought about it some more and she eyed me. *Yes. Every single thought that you have had since you picked up my husk in my temple.*

Oh no… My palm hit my forehead hard enough to give me a headache. *That's so embarrassing.*

A throaty laugh vibrated down the back of my skull. *You're a healthy young man. It's expected that you feel and think those things.* She paused as she stared pointedly at Cassia and then Arden. *I cannot say that I disagree with your desires either.*

Then you know what question I was going to ask you next.

She looked at me and her tail flicked twice before she answered. *You'll be able to make choices as you like and whenever you want. Let me know if you would like to make selections and I will open your status for you.*

I nodded and she opened it for me in the same spot that it had been the first time. I made my selection, adding six points into my Mana stat to make it an even ten.

Thinking about it, I added five to Charisma too, because I worked in the service industry and being charismatic could help me make more money. Seeing as though being able to buy things and not really worry about it was a very nice feeling. That, and Uncle Yen's advice seemed wise as well. That left me with nine points and there were only three other stats.

You are decently strong for a human, Galaxy purred for a moment to let me think on that before continuing, *No points you use now will be a waste, but being smart about it may help you.*

How so? I blinked and realized that there were shapes and outlines that started to glow around all of the people surrounding us.

If you have strong magic, you might be able to strengthen your body. To reinforce yourself. Or, if you have enough of another stat, you could do other things.

"How the hell am I supposed to pick?" I grumbled to myself out loud.

"Pick what?" Arden bounced over toward me, but paused as she looked at me. "Did you do something with yourself? Exfoliate or something?"

I blinked at her and narrowed my eyes suspiciously. "No?"

She stared at me for a minute more and shrugged. "Must be the clothes then, they look good on you."

My jaw dropped a little and I muttered, "Thanks?"

"So what are you picking?" She stared at me for another second then smiled. "Are you trying to decide on the class you want to play in the game we got?"

I forced a smile on my face. "Yeah, that's right."

Galaxy looked back at me from where she sat with her tail slowly moving through the air, her eyes sparkling with mirth.

Arden grabbed my hand and pulled me to the back of the server's side of the bar excitedly. "Right? I've been wondering if I should go the stealthy route or if I want to be a caster."

"I don't know what I was thinking of doing either." I grunted and scratched my head. "I've got a character I'm thinking of with good Mana and Charisma, but I don't think his other stats are all that good. Constitution, Strength, and Dex are pretty low. What do you think I should do?"

She crossed her arms. "Is that how it is? Are the stats randomized?" I shrugged and she rubbed her chin. "Well, it's a co-op game, right? So if you wanted to min-max, you could, and the other party members could round things out or cover for your character's shortcomings."

She snorted to herself and offered with her hand motioning to me. "Or you could just remake your character."

The nervous laughter that bubbled out of my throat made her snicker before I cleared my throat and said, "I don't know if that's possible right now."

She shook her head. "Well duh, you're at work. Cass would be livid if she found out you started without the rest of us. I'd be pissed too if you weren't looking so yummy in those jeans." I blinked and my jaw dropped as she laughed. "Relax. I'm teasing you, Marcus. It's what friends do, right?"

Friends... Galaxy chortled loudly and turned to sit and watch the two of us. *Indeed.*

"Sure is." I decided to just wait and do a little more research into my options before spending that many points. Plus, I would be grilling the hell out of Galaxy for information too.

I had a feeling there was a lot she wasn't telling me.

CHAPTER SEVEN

Uncle Yen took my tips for the night to exchange and count them for me, and I was about to head up to my room when a hand wrapped around my wrist.

I glanced down and saw it was Cassia's and she was smiling at me, her eyes bleary from sleep. "Hey, you want to play?"

I gently extricated my wrist from her grasp and touched her shoulder kindly, explaining, "You've been drinking, Cass. We should wait for that?"

She stared at me, hurt. "What are you talking about, Marcus?" She grunted and belched, waking up a bit more. "You don't want to play at all tonight?"

I almost screamed aloud, but kept it together before saying, "Sure! If you're feeling up to it, that's fine."

She waved me off dismissively. "I'm no lightweight, Marcus. That little beer nap was a catnap! I'd been up for a week straight. Now I'm good for another few days."

What in the hell? She blinked at me, her eyes clearing more and more, so I asked. "Is that something you do often, or is it an oni thing?"

"It's an oni thing, but I can make it a little longer than some others. I'm tough." She flexed her arms and for the first time, I could see a little of the auric outline around her shift into a more massive female form with a single horn-like protrusion sticking out of her head.

"Alright, how long will it take you to get home so we can play together?" I frowned. "Don't you have to go get the game as well?"

"I live in the basement, and had bubba Kenshi go get it for me, so not long at all!" She pulled out her phone and tapped a few keys before she was on the phone with someone. "I knew you'd be up. Me and Marcus are going to play tonight, so you and Arden need to get it in gear and get ready!"

She gasped and looked at me. "Masonai has already started making his character!" She shouted into the phone, "Traitor!"

My eyes widened as she turned and sprinted outside, turning to lock the door and whoop wildly.

Better go up and get ready, Marcus. Galaxy yawned and stretched. *Though I am eager to see what all the fuss is about.*

"So am I, let's go!" I sprinted up the stairs with her popping out of the shadows across from my door and waiting patiently for me to unlock it. I opened the door and she was in and on top of my bed in a heartbeat.

I closed the door and turned on the TV and system just before a knock on my door drew my attention. I stalked over to it and opened it to find three massive men with horned auras standing outside my door.

"Sissy Cass said bring furniture." The speaker turned and patted a large sturdy box that the other two held as if it weighed absolutely nothing.

"Oh, sure!" I opened my door wider and they came in with a stand and large bookshelf. They set the bookshelf up, then put the stand on the back side of my desk and turned to the door and plodded out of it.

A moment later, they brought up another shelf and a rack that clothes could hang on. One of them even brought in a couple of bottles of booze and left them on the desk. Once they were done, the one who had spoken first turned and grunted, "Enjoy game with sissy Cass, new friend."

"Thank you!" He smiled back at me and waved then took off out the door.

Galaxy had already managed to maneuver some things to the point where I could actually set up my new account, another way that I'd be able to be tracked and made to disappear if I was found. "How did you do that?"

I have access to many memories of yours that I find odd, but useful. Galaxy turned and batted the joysticks until she had spelled a gamer tag name that made me laugh—Galaxy_Marine75.

I texted it to Arden and Cassia so they could use it and I found that a moment later I had three friend requests. I added them and got a party invite as the game was downloading and updating on the new system.

"I like that name!" Arden's voice bubbled over the new headset I wore.

I snorted and shook my head. "I had a little help with it." I looked down at Galaxy as she watched things moving around on the screen.

"Enjoying the new system, Marcus?" Masonai's voice echoed slightly and I could hear some moving and static on his end before his voice returned. "Sorry, I was streaming earlier and forgot that it was still on. I sound okay?"

"Yeah, man, it's all awesome. Thanks again for the help with everything." I smiled wide. It almost felt like I was in my element again. Now all we needed was that one drunk Marine and we would be set.

"First one to take damage takes a shot!" Cassia roared at us through the headphones and I started to laugh uncontrollably.

I opened my mouth, smacking my lips as I realized that the inside of my maw felt like I'd decided to eat the Sahara and wash it down with salt.

My eyes tried to open against the bright light streaming into the room. Slowly they adjusted as I peered about.

The first thing that caught my attention were the glasses of water that sat on the new bedside table on my right. I reached over and downed the first one, grateful that I could feel my mouth and throat without needing to cough now.

I groaned inwardly and outwardly, sighing and putting the water down before glancing about again. The TV was still on, but the game on screen wasn't the one that we had been playing. It was another RPG, one that I was excited to play. But why was it on?

He awakens. Galaxy came out of the bathroom, her paws still a little wet for some reason, then I looked over to the cups of water. She sat next to the controller on the floor and actually rolled her eyes. *No, Marcus, I simply wished some privacy to relieve myself and this body is tiresomely annoying when it comes to washing.*

I grunted, "Can't cats reach like, everything?"

Yes, as can I, but I simply do not wish to. I had research to do. She turned toward the controller and pressed pause so that the game began playing again. Her paws danced oddly over the controls and she played exceptionally well. *I like this game, and the stronger you become, the more of this sort of control I will have once more. The stronger I will become again.*

"So, where did the water come from?" I sat up and downed another glass of water before she deemed it okay to answer me.

Or she started to, but my door opened and I turned to see Cassia poke her head in. "Oh! You're up, awesome." She opened the door further and stepped inside before closing it and smiling at me. "Boss said that you and Arden had the day off since you'll be her protégé for a little bit."

"How do the days off here work?"

"Two on, two off." She motioned to my bed and I nodded that she could join me. She stared at me for a moment quietly before a slow smile worked over on her face. "You really suck at video games."

I snorted and threw a half-hearted left jab at her and she

just took it on the shoulder like it wouldn't bother her. "It's been a while since I've played anything other than the systems that they had at the junior enlisted club. I'll get back into it."

She nodded and eyed me a little more. "I know you will. You'll have all of us teaching you and training you. But that's not what I'm here about."

"What's up?" I frowned at her; that last bit had seemed almost bashful. Like she was worried about something.

She scratched her head and stood up, careful to avoid bothering Galaxy—who had paused her game and slyly moved the controller over close to me. She paced for a second before I finally spoke, "Listen, Cass, I know we don't know each other too well, but you can talk to me."

She stopped and her fists balled up next to her hips as she stared me dead in the eyes. "I want to fight you!"

I blinked at her and frowned as Galaxy hopped onto the bed next to me. *Well, this is an interesting development. Unexpected too. How long have I been asleep, Marcus?*

"Believe me, I wish I fucking knew," I muttered back and saw that Cassia had heard my reply. "Sorry, had a stray thought and I'm still sobering up a little. I think a little tussle might help me get my shit together though, so yeah—let's go have a spar."

"Great!" She grinned at me and I could see that her teeth looked slightly less human than they had before. Her eyes sparkled and she leaned forward, the tank top she wore dipping dangerously before she grabbed my chin and stared me in the eyes, hard. "Follow me."

She lifted me out of bed so that I could follow her through the bar and out into the daylight. Keith, sitting at the door, barked with laughter. "You smell like a brewery, brother. Tell Kenshi to get you a bite of the wolf. He'll know what you mean. You gonna need it, boy."

He laughed some more as we walked away, Cassia taking me toward one of the buildings beside the bar. She walked straight toward the wall and passed through it. I paused and touched the wall a heartbeat before a hand reached out of the stony brick and mortar to pull me inside.

Cass watched me for a moment, then sighed as she poked her head out and then back in. "The glamour only works on the rest of the world if you come in fast. So you can't hesitate like that, Marcus."

"Yes ma'am."

The inside of the 'glamour' that she was speaking about was a high tech-looking gymnasium.

"Welcome to the top floor of the barracks, Marcus." She motioned toward all the equipment, benches, weights, and machines in here, including treadmills so advanced-looking I could imagine only professional football teams being able to afford them. "State of the Normie-art facilities for all of our members and team, magically enhanced for our needs. You technically fit into that section as undesignated within the High Table, so you can come and work out with us any time you like."

"What else is in here?" I stared around us in wonder as the other men and women who worked with the High Table began to trickle into the room in workout gear. People who looked like normal folks loaded hundred-pound weights onto the bars and machines and started cranking out reps that made me green with envy.

To be honest with myself? They looked groggy and still half asleep, so it was likely only a warm up for them and that was galling.

"We have the mats and dojo across the hall this way, then down on the bottom floors we have the barracks and everything for the security staff and visiting delegates." She waved over at one of her massive brothers and smiled as he stared pointedly from me to her. "On the floors above us are the mess and more living quarters."

"Wouldn't it be easier for you to be directly attached to the bar?" She glanced back at me as we moved toward the dojo area.

"We are, we just keep them secret until there's an emergency." She opened a door on our left, revealing several large red and blue figures that looked like the oni I had seen in fiction all over the world but in high definition. Their massive muscled bodies and their horns were almost obscene but at the same time—I wasn't scared.

This was now my normal and I needed to accept it because my friends were here and different. Just like how the Marine Corps had all types, green and dark green were the same damned thing.

One of the blue ones turned and glanced down at me and when I didn't cower at the sight of them, offered me a fist to bump with a toothy grin. I bumped it and it felt like I had hit stone.

"Kenshi!" The blue oni stood straight and turned back to stare at Cassia. "Bite of the wolf for Marcus, please?"

"Okay, sissy." I recognized the voice as the same man who had spoken for her brothers last night.

Once he had cleared the room, Cassia stepped closer to me and whispered, "Sorry, my brothers aren't much for talking if they don't have to. Thousands of years being mindless muscle before coming to work for the High Table have made them shy and self-conscious."

"I get that, it's something leadership looks for all over." I knew more than a few Marines who were content not to talk and just listen to those around them.

It was a few minutes before he came back and handed me a Solo cup that looked hilariously tiny in his massive hand. I took it gratefully with, "Thanks, Kenshi. Nice to see you again."

He grinned down at me, his large, tusk-like teeth clacking as he offered me his fist again. "Fight hard."

I nodded and hit his fist gently and his deep voice echoed creepily as he walked out chuckling darkly.

"You going to take your normal form for this too?" I watched as Cassia turned to a wall in the corner and tapped it.

Something clicked softly and a panel opened. She reached in and pulled out a gi of sorts that she tossed to me.

"I will, but I want you to wear this." I frowned at her and glanced down at my clothes. Sure they were a little less than clean thanks to the shift and my drinking while gaming, but they were fine. I could move perfectly in them as well. She added, "I would hate to ruin them when you just got them."

I nodded, respecting the lady's wishes and turned around to change. She snickered at me and I looked over my shoulder where she stood watching me. "You don't have to turn around on me. I'm a big girl."

I shook my head and laughed before I pulled my shirt over my head and replaced it with the gi shirt. I dropped my pants, having taken my shoes off first. I slipped into the pants and then folded my clothes before placing them on top of my shoes.

She nodded to the Solo cup I'd placed on the floor. "Drink up."

I shook my head; she looked more and more eager as I stood here, so I took a drink and found that I couldn't stop. Even though I tried to. I finally noticed that Cassia was standing behind me and her finger was under the cup, tipping it into my mouth. "Swallow it all down, there you go."

I coughed, almost choking at how sensual she had made that one phrase sound.

My stomach churned momentarily as the taste of energy drink ladened with pennies and something else raged through my mouth.

I grimaced. "What was in that?"

"Something you likely will be upset about, but since you have magic of your own now, it won't be bad." She was about to say something more but my left forearm itched fiercely. I sent a thought to my partner and she opened my screen for me.

Bite of the Wolf – A crass mixture of an energizing drink with the saliva and blood of a lycanthrope.

"You dosed me with lycanthrope spit and blood?" I snarled

and she looked taken aback as I stepped forward. "What if I didn't want to become a werewolf, Cassia?"

"You're a mage—you can't." Her smile made me frown; there was another emotion on her face that I couldn't quite place. Hurt? "Magic kills the curse. I don't know why, but the Touched can't turn into a lycan unless they were born one, and those are ten times more rare than the Touched themselves."

Do not be overly hasty here, Marcus. This is a good thing for us, Galaxy purred through my mind. I shot her an inward glare and she opened the screen once more.

Bite of the Wolf promotes increased healing and wellness as well as heightened senses for a short time.

Oh, that is cool, I suppose. I could no longer feel the effects of the hangover I'd had and I honestly felt better than I ever had.

It gets better. Galaxy opened another screen and my jaw almost dropped.

It looked like a sort of tree that had various clouded things within it, but one of them stood in stark contrast to the others, colored blue and crimson.

I tapped it and it expanded.

Lycanthropic Curse – Devoured – Your body will heal at an accelerated rate permanently as a new standard.

"Woah." I whistled to myself as I looked over my body. I felt normal, but better? It was an odd feeling. Sucked that I couldn't keep the other things like the improved hearing and sight though. Sense of smell could be okay, but in certain places? Maybe not.

I looked up at Cassia as she watched me uncertainly. "I'm sorry I reacted that way."

"This is all new to you, I understand." She motioned to herself and sighed. "I was born into this knowledge. Learned it the way humans learn arithmetic and to read—it's as ingrained in me as your knowledge of your nation is to you."

"I'm certain it is." I stepped closer and punched her lightly on the shoulder, a soft smile spreading on my face. "I appreciate you just wanting to help me however you can."

Her eyes half lidded for a moment then she stepped back. "Time for you to see more of me."

I raised my eyebrows a couple times at her just to be funny and she laughed.

Mission successful.

Her loose basketball shorts appeared to shrink slowly as her muscles bulged, her alabaster skin mottled, then darkened until it was completely red. Her body grew until she met and matched the aura around her completely. The loose tank top she had worn before now looked like a tight crop top that fit her well. Her hair was no longer blonde, but black and shining, flowing down past her shoulders.

The horn that erupted from her head stood out almost six inches above the top of her head. She reached back and put her hair into a loose ponytail before turning her deep black eyes at me. "Well. Scared?"

I rolled my eyes. "Kenshi looked like he could slam dunk me into a pro basketball hoop and steal my lunch money for a year and not bat an eye at anyone who stood up to him. You?" She seemed taken aback as I pointed at her. "Are fucking terrifying. But you look awesome as hell. So this is what you normally look like?"

She nodded, a smile making her look slightly less intimidating. "I can pick and choose what I look like in my human form as well. I won't be blonde anymore though. I change my hairstyle and color every time I change into my natural state. Keeps it fun."

"That's really something, Cass." I took a step closer to look her over and she watched me carefully. "Why did you want to fight me?"

She blushed, hard for her crimson face, but her skin turned purple at her cheeks and along her neck so it had to be something. *Woah wait, that must be the enhanced senses at work.*

Her scent was different as well. Not bad, but not necessarily the prettiest scent I had ever gotten a whiff of. Kind of acidic smelling and alkaline?

"It's an oni thing, but I'll explain it afterwards." She took a step back and stretched her massive arms. "You ready?"

I laughed. "Not at all—let's go."

She laughed and lunged toward me with her arms set to go around my waist. I dropped to my back, my arms slapping the mat to disperse my weight as I caught her midsection with my feet and rolled, sending her flying ass over tea kettle.

She hit the wall and stood up as if she had just stumbled. "Nice work."

"Thanks, I love it when all the pretty ladies attack me." I waggled my eyebrows and she was suddenly in front of me, her fist flying at my stomach.

Grimacing, I turned to let the attack glance across my hip. It felt like something broke but I roared and grabbed her massive neck and dropped my weight to throw her again, sweeping my foot under hers and just hanging there as she stood perfectly in place.

"Fool me once, shame on you." She reached down and grabbed me around the waist before lifting. "Fool me twice, shame on me!"

She whipped her body into an arc. The German Suplex should have shattered me, but for some reason I was still hanging on. Barely.

The enhanced healing in your body is working as it should, but you will not hold out for much longer, Galaxy warned me mentally. *What would you like me to do?*

Can you throw all my points into Brawn? There's no way that I'm going to be able to beat her like this. She let me drop and stood up, clapping her hands like she was dusting them off. *Better yet, make that six Brawn and three Physique. If I get hit before I can heal it all, I'll fucking die.*

It's done, good luck. Galaxy's mind left mine as I stood.

My muscles bulged painfully as my body bucked and spasmed before settling.

"You okay?" Cassia asked me as she stepped closer. "You look like you're really hurting."

"Nah, I'm good." I stood up and really did feel like I was better than before. I felt heavier than I had been, but that wasn't in a terrible way.

She scowled at me and moved in, still faster than me. I timed my attack and sent my right fist in a punch to her jaw. She didn't try to dodge it and let me catch her on the chin.

A solid smack and her head actually turned with the strike before she whipped her face back toward me as if she wasn't sure what she was seeing.

I kept on the offensive, striking her twice more on her chin, each landing blow making her eyes narrow at me in disbelief. I lifted my foot and jumped up, snapping my heel into her chest. She didn't move, making her a springboard for me and I rolled away from her before she could react.

She stood up, frowning. "Are you sure you're a mage?"

I grinned as I stood up and dusted off my gi, nodding.

She grinned and bolted toward me, her right fist cocked back as she howled, "Hold still!"

"Not happening!" I laughed and stepped aside, but she grabbed my gi with her lead hand. I slipped out of it but she still managed a glancing blow on my shoulder, the bone popping out of the socket painfully. *Fuck, you asshole*, I grumbled mentally as I tried to get the offending limb back into place.

I couldn't get it to move without agonizing pain and focused on just evading her strikes. It was increasingly harder and finally it was too much to bear. I ducked under her swing as my back hit the wall and she punched where I had been.

The wall crumbled and before she could react, I jumped onto her broad shoulders and wrapped my legs around her neck, squeezing as hard as I could.

She coughed slightly but her left hand lurched up and wrapped around my leg, fingers nearly cracking as she gripped.

I grunted and tightened my grip to the point that my hips

adjusted loudly as she yanked. My hip popped out of place and I bellowed, "Shit!"

I kept as much tension as I could on her neck, grabbing my legs with my good arm to keep the lock. The sheer pain of it all grating at my ability to keep upright, but I felt like if I just gave up and tapped out, she would just ignore it.

Did I want to do that if I really wanted to get stronger? I grit my teeth, growling and snarling at the agony moving along my limbs as I squeezed with all I had.

It felt like I was making some kind of headway in time for her to just reach up and pull me off, tossing me aside like a rag doll.

She growled savagely as the door opened, several things happening in rapid succession. She launched herself at me, only to be caught by Kenshi and several other people. They dropped her, then dropped *onto* her to keep her down while someone I didn't recognize knelt next to me.

The person kneeling beside me frowned, muttering, "He smells like a shifter, is he one?"

"No, he mage with bite in his system." Kenshi grunted and snarled as something snapped. "She not coming out. Get sissy out room!"

Strong arms gripped me and pulled me into the hall after the mob had managed to wrestle Cassia outside. I could hear her screaming and guttural calls to let her go, she needed to get to me, but then someone closed the door behind us.

The room they brought me to was sterile, almost like a clinic and it smelled lemony. The pain started to truly register without the adrenaline to suppress it a bit and was climbing higher until someone poured something else down my throat.

More of the Bite drink they gave you earlier, Galaxy informed me carefully, my arm itching again. *It is making the healing process stronger—much stronger—and has boosted the ability you gained.*

"So I grow by consuming things?" The room around me grew intensely cold, then hot and I started to convulse as whoever was in here with me spoke in a language I couldn't comprehend. My leg lifted painfully, then a tug and pull that resulted in a popping noise that churned my stomach and offered some minute relief.

I grow, and with me you reap the benefits. So when you are attacked or affected by magic, like from a hostile spell, I take a small portion of it for myself, and give you incentives for having been put in danger. I have done something similar here.

"So I get boons when you get to eat?" I grunted as the good doctor jerked my arm back into place, and howled as it separated once more, only to pop right back in. "Fucking hell, Doc!"

"Shh… it'll be okay soon, don't worry." His voice reassured me softly before I felt something pierce my arm and looked down to see a needle sticking out of my elbow.

Stop him! Galaxy yowled and my body moved of its own accord, my left wrist smacking the needle out of my skin as soon as it showed the first signs of drawing blood. The needle bent and the plastic tube flew across the room.

"What are you doing?" the man growled at me. "I need to do blood work to make sure that you haven't contracted lycanthropy. Hold still and let me—"

"I can't get it, I'm a mage." I started to sit up, my stomach grumbling noisily. My head was a little fuzzy and I was ravenous but otherwise my body was whole again. I could move and stand without wincing and that was great.

His hand wrapped around my wrist again and he started to speak, but my right hand moved the same time as I twisted my left hand. I grabbed his wrist and twisted it savagely as I pressed his elbow away from me, his head dipping toward the bed. "Touch me again without my permission, or with intent to take from me, and I'll break your arm."

The rage surging through me fled my system as someone opened the door. It was Cassia in her human form, with blue hair that fell past her shoulders and stopped mid chest. Her clothes looked worse for wear, torn here and there and baggy against her frame, but she didn't look like she was trying to kill me anymore.

So there was that. Which was a nice change.

"Marcus, are you okay?" She stared at me, pinning the doctor against the examination table. "Why are you twisting the doctor up? How are you twisting him up like that? And how were you suddenly so much stronger than you were before?"

"What do you mean, how am I twisting him up?" I turned and looked down at the doctor, the man indignantly watching me as I kept the pressure on his joints. His aura flared to life around him and I saw that he had a large, cat-like form that radiated around his body. "Lycanthrope?"

He grunted, "Yes." And I let him up as he appeared to be fighting something. "It's my saliva and blood running through you right now. But it's also not. You smell like me, but not like me. It's concerning and I should run some tests to make sure that you're okay."

Galaxy and I both growled, "**No**," and he leaned so far away from us that he almost fell over the table.

I blinked, *us?* Galaxy and I were still separate beings, were we not? And why had my body moved on its own like that? What was going on?

Yes and no. I will explain later; we need to be vigilant now.

If I could have glared at her, I would have, but for some reason, she didn't want my blood taken and I would give her that respect. For now.

"I feel fine, Doc, but let's compromise—if I feel any adverse effects or like I'm going to start howling at the moon, I'll come get you. Okay?" He just stared at me in disgust. "That was a really insensitive comment, wasn't it?"

"I'm not a werewolf, so it would really be more along the lines of hacking up a fur ball without having fur." He offered me a sort of half smile, and looked to Cassia. "You okay, kiddo?"

"Yes, Doctor, thank you." She blushed and looked at him bashfully. "Can I have a minute with Marcus?"

The doctor raised an eyebrow and glanced over at me. "Leave the mess, I'll get it after you kids are done."

I frowned at him and watched as he left the room while shaking his head. The door clicked and Cass watched me. "You aren't a normal mage, are you?"

I chuckled nervously, my heartbeat rising as I countered, "Are any of the Touched normal?"

"No, but you aren't like any of the others I've met." She crossed the room to stand closer to me. I was still a little wary of her and stepped back, but the damned table was in my way so I couldn't move further without going over it.

As she closed the distance, her nose crinkled and she frowned. "You really do smell like a lycan, but that should be fading."

"They gave me more of that drink when I got in here." I watched her accept that and felt a little more at ease. "What happened back there? Why did things get so bad, so fast?"

"Oni are a combative race to begin with, even among the yokai." Her head hung a little bit. "It's why we get compared to demons so often. Part of why some of the other yokai keep us around as muscle."

"Okay, so you guys really get into a fight—I can respect that." It was true. Hell, I knew some Marines who thrived on fighting. The more violent the encounter they had, the better they felt.

"Thank you, but that's not all." Her face turned another shade of red and I thought she was about to transform again, but she looked away. After a moment, she took a heaving breath and shrugged before turning back and blurting, "It's also how we figure out if we're compatible lovers with someone."

"Woah!" I barked, the sudden realization making me blush and bump the table behind me in shock. "Wait, so you…?"

"I was trying to see if you would make a good lover." She hid her face with her hands, her voice leaking through. "I thought you were cute when I met you, but when you attacked that Fae when you thought he'd hurt me, I thought you were so cool. I had to know."

"Oh." My cheeks hurt with all the blood rushing to them, but now I was curious. "Well, how did I do?"

She peeked out from behind her hands, then eventually put her hands down to her sides. "Well, you didn't win—but you aren't an oni, so that was never going to happen. But the fact that you hit me so hard and kept coming at me even when I was confused about how strong you were suddenly..." She closed her eyes and smiled. "When you tried to choke me out after I dislocated your arm? Oh, that was so smart."

My eyebrows knit together, suddenly I was as confused as she seemed to be smitten. "It was a good thing that I tried to choke you?"

She nodded emphatically. "I'm bigger and stronger than you, Marcus. You have to be able to defend yourself somehow, and fighting smarter and dirtier was just good thinking."

"Then why did you insist on attacking me more after you popped my leg out of socket?"

She got bashful again and muttered something that if there hadn't been lycanthropic senses raging through my body, I wouldn't have been able to hear it at all. "It was hot, and I wanted to see what you would do."

"Wow." I could hear Galaxy laughing in my head and it only made things worse.

You cannot hide your shame from me, child—nor your infatuation with her. I believe you think her 'hot' as well?

I nodded and knew she could feel it.

"I'm sorry," Cassia whispered and straightened. "I shouldn't have just thrown you into my cultural shit storm without warning you. Or explaining anything."

I grinned like an idiot, rubbing the back of my head. "I mean, yeah, it's a lot to take in, but that just means that you like me. So, that's really nice."

"You think so?" She frowned at me, some of the blood in her cheeks fading.

"Yeah, of course." I rubbed my face to try to get some of the soreness from smiling so much to go away. "I mean, who doesn't like having a beautiful woman confessing their feelings to them?"

She smiled, genuinely and looked hopeful. "Do you want to fight me again?"

A coughing, barking surprise bout of laughter escaped me before I could yelp, "No!" She pouted and I held up a hand as I finally calmed myself enough to speak through the laughing. "My kind don't need to try to kill each other to tell someone we like them. And I know damn well how strong you are."

She smiled again, then frowned. "Wait…" She watched me suspiciously and pointed at me. "Is that your way of saying that you like me too?"

I decided. "Yeah. Yeah, it is." I grew a little bolder when she straightened up. "I thought you were weird and quirky, and I thought that was cute. But now I know that you're an awesome gamer and a complete badass who can hold her own. So yes—I like you."

Her eyes widened and she grinned happily before rushing into me. She lifted me into a massive hug that cracked my back.

"Oof!" I grunted and wheezed. "Too much hug. Can't breathe!"

"Oops." She dropped me and I landed in a heap, coughing and regaining my sight. "Sorry, I'm just so excited."

She knelt down and rubbed her forehead against mine with a soft smile on her face, the contentment and excitement she looked to be feeling making the pit of my stomach explode into butterflies. "What are you doing?"

She stopped and stared at me blankly, "Oh, this is a way that oni show affection in a non-violent way."

"I appreciate the non-violence." I snorted and she cocked her head. "Yes?"

"Do you want me to not do that?"

"You can show affection however you choose to, just don't break me." She laughed and offered me a hand. I clasped it and she effortlessly pulled me up until I was standing. My stomach gurgled violently, a cramp beginning to form in the pit of my stomach. "Uh, Cass?"

"I can tell how hungry you are from the rumbling gut. Let's go up to the chow hall." She pointed her thumb up and when she mentioned the chow hall, I think I could have fallen in love.

"Now that is a capital idea, Cass." I grinned and she walked toward the door with me.

CHAPTER EIGHT

When we walked into the hallway, the doctor and Cassia's oni brothers stood vigil, their gazes questing and uncertain in the sterile white of the area. But once they saw the smile on her lips they all grinned and turned their attention to me.

Kenshi pushed his chest out and pounded it twice. "Good job, bubba Marcus."

I blinked at him. *Bubba?*

It is a term of endearment saved for those who the oni consider family, Galaxy explained with an edge of delight in her tone. *Forgive me, but I decided to do a little digging on the creatures around us in the books that you have and found them horridly lacking. I used your cellular device and e-book thingy to get some books and access to the interweb. Fascinating place.*

"Oh, I see," I muttered aloud, Cassia looking down at me curiously. I smiled at her, then her brothers and mimicked their greeting. "Thank you, bubba Kenshi."

Cassia took my hand and the contact made me think of a grade-school crush, but I just laughed it off and followed where she tugged me.

We raced up a set of stairs into a large cafeteria that largely reminded me of the chow halls I had eaten in while in the Marines. Those had been some happy, gross memories and the nostalgia of it made me smile.

"So, just to warn you, there is normal food here, and then there is other food here." She motioned to the side where the majority of the people in oni form milled about in line. "Unless you like bugs and worms and the like, you wouldn't care for it."

"Got it, I will stay away from that side of the chow hall." I laughed and she laughed with me. We walked over and grabbed trays, the cooks behind the counter eyeing me because I was new, but I was used to that.

I ordered eggs, bacon, sausage, fries, and yogurt, all of which looked amazing. Cassia loaded her plate with food, and I smiled—had to like a lady who could eat!

As we moved, the sensation of eyes drilling themselves into my back made my skin crawl, but every time I looked over my shoulder, no one was watching me.

"Are people staring at us?" I asked quietly.

Cass glanced at me and sighed softly. "Yes, but I like to think it's because they haven't seen you here before and not because you're with me." She had a large muffin that wouldn't fit onto her already overloaded plate, so put it onto her tray. We turned and walked toward one of the walls of windows and sat together, her across from me and close to the window.

I sat at a point where I could keep the entrance to the room in sight, something I did unconsciously at times, but purposely now.

As we ate, I realized just how hungry I was, and how delicious the food here tasted. It was amazing.

"So, Cassia—what does this mean for you and me?" I took another massive bite of eggs and she watched me for a moment longer before I added, "If you had any thoughts on it?"

"Well, to be completely honest, oni don't have the normal relationships humans do." She frowned and thought for a bit before shrugging. "I don't really know. What is it that humans do when they find each other attractive and think the other has desirable traits?"

"Date," I offered around a mouthful of bacon. She laughed at me and I remembered that I should represent myself a little better here. "Humans who like each other and want to be with each other, date, so that they can learn more about one another. If they're serious, it can lead to marriage, or if it's not exactly what either of them wants, they can just stop dating."

"What happens then?" She frowned at me, clearly concerned. "Do they kill each other? I've seen some TV shows that had that in it and even as an oni, I think that's a little on the extreme side."

I laughed out loud at that, the noise making some of the other patrons turn toward us. "No, they don't have to kill each other. It sounds like you were watching some kind of soap opera or something. It depends on the relationship and the people involved. If you like each other but not enough to marry, or continue to date, then you stop dating and see other people. You can remain friends if you're comfortable with each other, or you can just distance yourselves and move on."

"What other factors can play into this decision?" She put her fork down and took out her phone and a stylus to write notes, making me laugh some more. "Come on, Marcus, I'm trying to learn!"

"Oh God, okay—okay!" I heaved, my sides hurting from laughing so hard and trying to keep food down. "Well, if they have pets together, they may want to stay cordial, or they will have to decide who will keep the pet. If they have mutual friends, they will need to ensure that everyone is comfortable and that there's no bad blood between them—even if it isn't anyone else's business but theirs. And this is if there are... children involved."

"I assume that if there are children involved that the mother takes them and the fathers are free to go and do as they see fit." She was writing that when I stopped her. "Yes?"

"No, not always." I went quiet for a little while, my thoughts with Connell and how big he was getting. How I hadn't even gotten a choice in how he would be raised. Who he would become would be left entirely up to someone else. "Usually both parents would decide if they could, but sometimes that choice isn't given."

"Why would it not be given?" She looked genuinely confused and upset by that thought.

"I don't know," I stated simply. I never learned about why his mother had kept Connell from me, only that she hadn't wanted me.

While I spiraled into the unknown, thinking of all the things I had done that could have been construed or misconstrued as wrong that would make her run from me like that, I lost track of my surroundings and someone touching me brought me out of it. I glanced up and saw Cassia sitting across from me angrily watching someone behind me. I looked up above me to see what I could only think of as a body builder type guy grinning down at me condescendingly with two of his buddies as backup.

"Did you not hear me, Normie?" He stuck his head forward a little as if talking down to a child. "I said, 'Get fucking lost, Normie.'"

"So far as I was aware of, this place belonged to all staff and security at the High Table, so I think not." I smiled up at him as best I could as I took another bite of bacon. "But you and your girlfriends are lookin' real cute today, big guy."

"Are you seriously going to let this loser Normie talk to a fellow security guard like that, Cass?" One of the other men grunted first at her, then turned to me. "You can piss off, human. Your kind aren't welcome here."

"I'm getting real tired of having to repeat that I'm a mage, but I take it you all don't give a shit about that." I glanced over at Cassia to see that she agreed that they likely wouldn't.

"Only mage we respect is old man Yenasi," the third body advised coldly. "Anyone else is just in our way. You need to leave —now."

"And what if I don't want to?" I scooped up a big bite of

eggs, shoving them into my mouth and moaning in exaggerated delight. "See, it's been a minute since I had chow this good, and I just got my ass kicked by the lovely lady across from me. Look at this as a date."

"That's the fucking problem!" big and butch bellowed, smacking my tray away from me and all my food on it. Eggs and bacon dotted the floor, biscuits and sausage wasted. Something massive stood behind him, some flavor of lycan, but bigger than a wolf and the cat that the doc had exhibited.

"Alright, game on." I caught Cassia's eye as she smiled and I snarled, the fork in my hand slamming into the man's throat with all my fury at the wasted food and interrupted conversation. His being a dick. I could go on, but when it didn't cut him, I grimaced. The small point of pressure helped me put exact pressure on a specific spot in the trachea to make him wheeze and grab his throat, though, so there was that.

The other two were highly trained and didn't hesitate to converge on me, their hands reaching and grasping as I squirmed and rammed my foot into the big guy's inner knee. A sickening popping snap made him cry out as he dropped and the others managed to pull me away from him.

Cassia reached over and grabbed the one on his right, breaking his grip on me long enough that I only had to deal with the stooge on his left.

I shoved my palm against his nose so hard the bones cracked and he grunted in pain before loosening his grip long enough for me to hop onto the bench I had been sitting on and elbow him in the throat.

He stumbled back, righted himself, and lunged at me.

"Enough!" a resounding bass voice roared as the three men began to disrobe as if they would shift. A large bear of a man stepped out from behind the counter with a large spatula in his left hand, his chef's hat tilted to the side. He had a paunch of a stomach but the rest of him was muscle.

He glared at all of us, the three men next to me huffing as

they looked to be gathering their mental faculties to stop what they were going through.

"Who's fighting in my chow hall?" His growl sent a familiar sort of thrill down my spine, the way a drill instructor's screaming can make a recruit shit themselves.

I sighed and stepped forward. "I threw the first punch."

He stepped closer to me, his bulk dwarfing me as he fixed me with a scowl. "I don't like fights in my chow hall. This is a sanctuary for food and camaraderie." He lifted his gaze to look behind me. "Sabbath, Argil, Fred—get your asses in the back and apron up."

I turned to see the three of them looking confused. The leader stepped forward to speak, but the chef fixed him with a glare and growled, "No one disrespects my cooking, Sabbath. No one. Get your asses in back and start cleaning dishes. You have mess duty for the next week."

They looked like what they wanted to say more, but his deep growl sent them scurrying into the back before he turned and regarded me with what was beginning to look like his trademark scowl.

His meaty hand reached out and grabbed my shoulder and pulled me close so he could mutter, "Next time you come to my chow hall, you keep your crayon-eating ass in line, son. You hear me?" I stared at him, wondering how he could tell when I saw that he had a horseshoe cut. "And call me Gunny. I saw what they were doing to you and Cassia; that shit ain't sat. You go on up and get yourself some more chow, Devil, and don't you skimp."

I snorted and shook my head. "Thanks, Gunny."

He smacked my shoulder and turned to stalk back into the kitchen where he raised his voice and began to bark orders.

I walked over to the line, grabbed some food to go and Cassia and I left the area as the asshat crew came out to begin cleaning up the mess they made.

"You fought them very well." Cass observed as we made our way out into the hall.

"Thank you for the assist there. I think I would have been in a little bit of trouble if it hadn't been for you stepping in."

She crossed her arms over her chest. "They interrupted our conversation and I couldn't abide that. Not to mention Sabbath is just angry that I won't pay any attention to him."

"Why not?" I glanced over at her as we walked, her face serene, almost happy. "The guy's built like a god."

"I know many gods, and there are many of them more humble than he," she replied with a grin that made me laugh. "Besides, I found someone I have more in common with."

She reached out and held my hand. "I think the term I would like to use is a 'boyfriend'?" She squeezed my hand and let it go. "If you want to be that, that is. I have a lot to learn about human culture where this 'dating' is concerned, so I will ask for patience, but if you are willing to help me, I will help you."

I grabbed her hand and held it firmly. "That's what it means to be in a relationship. Learning about each other and helping each other."

As we walked back outside, Keith smiled wildly as he opened the bar for us and let us in. Cass opted to wait downstairs for me while I showered and I told her I wouldn't be too long. I bounded up the steps.

As soon as I was in the room, Galaxy paused her game and turned on me. *About time. That fight leveled you up.*

"Wait, seriously?" She opened my status screen and sure enough, I was level two with five points to spend. "How is that possible?"

You 'defeated' them by doing more damage to them than they did to you before the fight stopped. It is not an exact science, this gaining of experience.

"Okay, so I get that I can spend my points but as everyone keeps pointing out, I'm a mage." She stared at me for a long moment before I continued. "So does this mean that I get to start casting spells? Flinging fire, or zapping the hell out of people?"

I have been deciding on how best to give you spells and I think that I've come up with something similar enough to how it used to be done. I've also been researching new methods and I like those even more, so please bear with me.

She yowled. My eyes squeezed tightly, and my head rang so much from the assault on my ears that I quickly clapped my hands over them to help dull the pain.

The ringing echoed and pulsed down my body until it touched my feet and came back up into the pit of my stomach.

I tentatively opened my eyes and saw that I had a HUD in my vision.

If you mean to use spells, you will need to use mana. Most mages feel how much magic they have left with constant monitoring and meditation training so that they learn their limits. You are special and we don't have that sort of time.

I scowled at the blue bar in the top left corner of my vision and it solidified, giving me the exact digits of how much mana I had.

100/100.

"Oh, that's too cool." I glanced around and saw nothing for health. "How will I know when I'm close to dying without a health bar?"

Do you not know your own body? The dry retort from the cat almost hurt the one feeling I had, and she just batted her tail side to side as she watched me. *Physique is more a representative number to your overall defense and endurance. You can endure much already that most humans would find excruciating. But you will know when you're about to die.*

"Fair enough, and what about spells?"

I have opted to give you a sort of list of spells that, as you grow stronger, will be able to evolve and grow as you do. She turned and watched the screen as she spoke. *I rather enjoy this aspect of these new-fangled video games. I almost wish we had these in my time. How much stronger my servants would have been!*

"How much stronger indeed." I chuckled nervously as I tried to contemplate how much more wildly powerful they were than me. An itch on my arm drew my attention to the status screen that opened and went to a new tab called Spell Matrix, where I saw that I had six points to spend.

It was a large, tree-like system of lines and bubbles with the upper echelons after the first line grayed out and hidden from view. Very RPG-like.

"In all this time you've been researching, this is what you came up with?" She turned and narrowed her cat eyes at me. "I like it!" I held my hands up as if to show I was being honest and she just continued to stare. "Why do I have six points, though? Is that every time I level up?"

She lifted her paw and began to lick it clean as she explained, *Three points are for your first level that you should have gotten but I did not know how to proceed. You will gain three points until I see fit to give you otherwise, so spend them wisely.*

A thought occurred to me, and I sat on the bed with her in front of me on the floor. "Does doing all this weaken you?"

She watched me carefully before stating, simply, *Yes.*

"Then why do any of it?"

Because I already grow stronger by the hour thanks to this new, mana-rich world. You fighting and gaining power also gives me a little something as well. As you grow, I grow. And as I grow, I will be able to dote on you more.

At that last statement, she hopped onto the bed and head-butted my arm. *I find myself fascinated by this world and particularly you. That you were strong enough to be my host is telling. You are something special, Marcus, and I intend to find out what that is. Even as I try to recall who I was and am.*

"Thank you." I scratched her head and she purred violently as I looked at the five options available.

Physical Buff – Make yourself physically stronger, faster, or more resilient for sixty seconds. 25 Mana.

Shield – Summon a malleable shield to repel attacks. 5 mana to summon with an equivalent cost spent in mana to damage defended against.

Wisp – Create a small bit of flame in your hand to attack with. 10 mana.

Bolt – Create a small bolt of electricity in your hand to attack with. 10 mana.

Blade – Create a weapon of pure mana to attack with. 15 mana.

"All of these are pretty awesome, but why isn't there anything for ice? You would think there would be."

Who knows what may come the stronger you grow, Marcus? Galaxy watched me as I tried to decide.

"Each one only costs a point to buy." I frowned and chose Blade, the spell lighting up for me and glowing. As soon as it lit completely, there was a small space on the upper right-hand corner that had a 1/6 to it. "So each one can be upgraded?"

She nodded. *They will grow stronger, become cheaper, and possibly last longer or have other effects once you put more points into them.*

"How do I unlock the stronger spells?" I stared at the gray bubbles hungrily and tried touching them.

Use the spells you have and you may yet figure it out.

I went ahead and bought Bolt, Wisp, and Physical Buff, then spent the remaining two points on Blade and Bolt, giving each a boost.

Even though it looked like this point just made each of them more potent, I was okay with that.

Level 2
Stats
Brawn: 8
Dexterity: 3
Physique: 5
Mana: 10
Charisma: 10
Points to spend: 5
Spells Known
Blade 2/6
Bolt 2/6
Wisp 1/6
Physical Buff 1/6

Do not forget that you can still spend points as needed, Marcus, Galaxy reminded me just before there was a knock on my door.

"Come in!" I called and Cassia came in. "Oh! Hey, sorry. I had something take my attention and haven't had time to shower yet."

"That's okay, I can still wait downstairs if you like?" She pointed her thumb to the door and went to open it.

"No, no, that's okay." I set my food on the table next to the bed, then thought better of that and put it on the desk. "You can help yourself to my room. I mean, we're dating now, so mi casa and all that."

"You speak human Spanish?" She quirked her head and I paused.

"There's a difference?" She nodded and I just laughed at my ignorance. "Great. More to learn."

She laughed with me and paused as she stared at my screen. "Were you playing this?"

I turned and looked at her as I was beginning to take my shoes off. I saw that Galaxy's game was still paused on the screen and she sat next to the controller.

How much can I tell people about you? She looked at me and I just knew she found this entertaining.

Your friends, I do not mind if they know—I do not fear that they will tell on you for my being with you. She hopped into Cassia's lap and purred like a boat engine. *But be selective who you tell outside of them. The jinn, your uncle, Anubis, Cassia and the drunkard are fine.*

"Thank you, Galaxy," I said aloud as the oni stroked her head, a confused look on her face. "Cass, Galaxy was playing it."

"I know she's magical, but gaming takes skill, Marcus." She waggled her fingers as she pointed to them with her hand. "And thumbs."

Galaxy hopped off her lap and began to play, as if showing off. The cat's head lolled back as if daring her to speak again, *Feel free to take that back. At least the skill bit.*

"Wha—How is she playing like that?" Cassia blinked at her

in fascinated horror. "She's good." She pointed to me with her eyes on Galaxy. "You're better than he is!"

"Ouch!" I grumbled half-heartedly. "She's an old being, I don't know what exactly, but she really seems to like video games. She's playing constantly."

"Does she have a gamer tag?" Cassia watched as the cat paused the game and popped out to base menu screen to show that she was StarLionGal and the oni took a photo of it. "Arden would never believe me."

"Can you talk to her, Galaxy?" I eyed her and the cat scowled in thought.

It may work... have her hold her hand out. I did as she asked and Cass held her hand out.

Galaxy reared up and bit her hand hard enough to draw blood. Then lapped up the blood that was there, leaving behind a silvery star-shaped scar.

Can you hear me, Cassia? I heard the cat speak as she stared intently at the other woman.

"Oh my God, this is what you hear? Why you look like you're carrying a conversation with her all the time?" I nodded and she reached down to grab Galaxy. "You are the coolest cat of all time!"

I'm delighted you think so. She faded from the oni's grasp and appeared on my shoulder. *I have marked you as mine.*

"What does that mean?" Cass pointed to the mark on her hand. "I like this, by the way."

It means that when I grow stronger, I may be able to make you grow as Marcus can.

"Wait, so you can do the same for her as you do for me?" I was almost hurt that I could become obsolete so quickly. The thought of it made me plop onto the bed forlornly.

You misunderstand, Marcus. Galaxy batted my ear painfully before hissing at me. *She may grow, but she will never grow the way you do. You're pure and untapped potential. She has the trappings of her race and racial abilities. But she will be stronger than some of her kind soon —if you grow stronger.*

103

"What do you mean 'do the same'? About what?" Cass seemed confused and I had Galaxy summon my stat sheet. "Oh my God, what is that?"

I spent some time explaining things and she screamed aloud, making my ears ring, "Don't ever keep these things from me! I could have helped you!"

She stopped talking and turned to me. "That's how you got so strong so fast! You added points to your Brawn." I nodded at her and she just grinned. "And you say that I can have something like this?"

I think so, yes. Galaxy watched us both. *I used to have multiple blessed, I believe.*

"So she draws power from you, and in return she gives some back?" I nodded and she clapped. "I have an idea!"

What is that?

"What if we had multiple people who were your blessed for you to draw power from?" I stared at her as she motioned to me, Galaxy watching her hands move to me. "Marcus is the first, then me, then someone already powerful who understands game mechanics and whatnot!"

"Arden?" She nodded and I had to admit, "Based on the talk we had the other night? I can agree she would make sense."

"And Masonai."

I was surprised about it being another human. Would that divert some of her attention from me and give me back a semblance of normalcy, or control?

I will think on this a time. Galaxy walked toward the window and into the sunlight that warmed the floor to lay down as Cassia started to open her mouth to speak. *He is a human, Cassia—Marcus was the first in thousands of years to survive my blessing. I cannot say with certainty that he would survive.*

"Thank you for considering it, Galaxy." I leaned back and stood once more to take my shirt off.

"I noticed them before, but you have so many scars." Cassia's fingers traced over my back and lower back along some of the rough skin. The sweet caress of her warm breath made my heart pound as it hit my shoulder and neck.

"Yeah, I've been in a lot of fights." She wrapped her arms around the front of my body along my stomach and pulled me closer to her while she took a deep breath. My stomach flip flopped and I glanced back at her, her eyes having bled red like her oni form.

She nibbled my shoulder lightly, her canines lengthening a little as she did. "You want to fight?"

I laughed. "The reason I'm about to shower is because fighting you made me sweaty and bloody."

She bit a little harder and growled low as she grasped my hips. "Not that kind of fight, Marcus."

I blushed fiercely as she pulled me toward my bathroom for a nice, long—hot—shower.

I stepped out of the bathroom a little more bruised than when I had gone in, but otherwise content, to spy Galaxy sitting on the desk where she watched me intently. "Yes?"

You need to learn magic to nullify sound. Her sourpuss reply almost made me snort. *It's bad enough I could feel everything, but hearing it as well?* She sighed heavily and stared at the controller. *I had to stop my research because I couldn't give it the focus it required.*

"I'm sorry?" I offered her a small frown, still puzzled. "You know, when you get your own body, will we still be tied together like this?"

I have my own body now, it is just not the one that I would prefer because I need you to grow stronger.

"That means we go out and hunt tonight!"

Cassia's chipper statement made me turn to her in confusion, "I'm sorry—what?"

She kept drying her hair as she explained, "We hunt. Every now and then the other oni and I will go out to protect the city in little ways here and there. Stop a mugging, prevent an assault. It gives us a chance to unwind from all the protecting we do here. Less posturing and more… pummeling."

"Is that not against the rules or something?" I pulled on a loose pair of jeans and a faded green t-shirt. "I thought Uncle Yen said there were people out there that were killing humans or lesser supernatural creatures in spectacular ways."

"And there are Wardens out searching the city and investigating the murders too." She nodded excitedly.

"One: what the hell is a Warden?" She was about to answer me when I held up a second finger. "Two: what makes you think it's so fine to go out with them nosing about, and three—why the hell are you so excited about it?"

"Wardens are an elite force of mages and demi-gods who patrol the world to make sure that us supernatural and preternatural creatures don't go on killing sprees and stay secret." She thought for a moment and shrugged. "What we are doing is technically a way to keep our populace a secret by lessening the amount of work and investigations that Normie law-keepers have to do, and I'm excited because it means I'll get to punch someone I don't care about!"

My mouth opened and worked for a moment before closing again so that I didn't shove my foot into it on accident. *This has to be an oni thing, right? Fighting and proving herself to herself and her people so that she can hold her head high. That's commendable to me, in an odd way.*

How many times had I had to bust my ass on days I was feeling out of it, or in a funk, because my junior Marines deserved to see what they could aspire to become? I truly knew where this was coming from.

Not to mention she is the head of High Table Security here, this is also a way of making sure that the bar is safe, and with it—the patrons too.

"Okay, we can go hunt, but let's just be careful, okay?" A crushing force gripped me and lifted me up, my legs shaking back and forth. "Fuuuuuuuuu…"

The air had cleared from my lungs fully for a good five

seconds before Galaxy's yowling and hissing got through to the excited oni. "Do you have any weapons?"

The question startled me a bit. "No. Medical staff confiscated them from me so that I wouldn't be one of the twenty-two."

She blinked at me with a frown on her face. "Twenty-two?"

An emptiness filled me at the thought of having to explain it to someone, but letting them know was part of informing. "Twenty-two veterans are estimated to die every day from suicide due to everything from losing friends, to injury, and more. And that was only in 2012. Now it's probably higher."

"They took your weapons because they thought you were going to kill yourself?" She scratched her head, then shook it. "I don't understand, Marcus. Why would warriors kill themselves when there are so many enemies they could fight and prove themselves against?"

"There are some battles that even if you win—you lose." I rubbed my head, thinking about the Marines who had watched their brothers and sisters die in combat. The ones who thought that they had lost everything when they got out because no one seemed to understand them, or their mentality. How many times that it had crossed my mind too. That feeling of being all alone in a place where you were revered as a hero one minute, then brushed aside as soon as the day was over. "And there are times where the battle is internal and eternal. No matter how much you think you won, that one stray thought can build into a torrential downpour of negativity that just eats you alive until you feel there's nothing left."

She stared at me, mouth agape, but it was Galaxy who asked, *What does one do when faced with that yawning maw of despair, Marcus?*

"It can be anything from calling a friend, to calling a hotline for someone to just listen and talk to you." I pulled out my phone and showed them some of the people I had gotten messages from over the years through social media asking for help, or just someone to talk to because they were alone and afraid of what might happen. "All it takes is reaching out. Hell, I've even heard of people reaching out to authors they like because their worlds bring them so much solace and joy that there's almost no way they wouldn't understand."

I can imagine that not everyone knows the right thing to say in those times, Galaxy mused more to herself than anyone else.

"Sometimes all it takes is listening and telling someone that you care enough to be there." I clapped my hands after a moment, the attention in the room back on me. "But yeah, I'll need to get something. I really do need to get a gun too."

"Those won't work on supernatural beings, but they work on humans!" She smiled and cupped my back, pulling me into her chest. "I'm sorry about the twenty-two of your fellow warriors that fall because of these things, Marcus." She pushed me away so that she could stare me in the eyes. "If you ever feel that way, you can fight me, and then you'll feel better."

She patted me on the arm and walked out of the room with a wink and left me to watch her with Galaxy.

The cat batted my hip to make me look down at her. *I am sorry as well, but I don't think I want to fight you the way she does.*

I shook my head. "Really going to have to get her to specify, huh?"

She nodded her head once and I walked out the door to follow Cassia. "You know where I can get a weapon?"

She grinned at me from near the door. "Of course I do—what kind of warrior would I be if I didn't know that?"

I rolled my eyes and followed her out of the bar to the parking lot where she pulled a set of car keys out of thin air and pressed a button. A large blacked-out SUV clicked and the lights flashed at me. "Is that a Kia Mohave?"

She smiled back at me. "You bet it is." She climbed in before saying anything else. The interior was cherry red and smelled earthy. "Red to hide the blood."

"Blood?" I raised an eyebrow at her and she just laughed as she put the vehicle in gear and gunned it. The door to the gate was already open, the person sitting there just reading a book waved to us like they could care less.

About twenty minutes later we arrived at a large, apartment-like building with a sign hanging above the door that I was certain wasn't visible to the naked eye. I couldn't read it, but it was there. The building could have passed for a defunct, derelict, or foreclosed section of this city by itself. It looked to be falling apart, but I knew from the last couple days that perception wasn't always reality.

We ground to a halt on the somewhat unkempt cement outside the front door and got out. Cassia stopped me at the front of the car and looked me squarely in the eyes. "You don't have any weapons on you, do you?"

I blinked, thinking about the one I kept in my belt. "My belt knife?"

"Throw it in the car." She ordered and crossed her arms as I stared at her in disbelief. "They will take it and roast you alive for it. They will pick it apart for hours and we just don't have that kind of time today."

I tossed the knife onto the floorboard and closed the door so she could lock it before we headed inside.

Once we were inside the building, I gasped in hushed awe. The first floor had been knocked out and made into a factory-like floor on the left-hand side where bulky men and women worked together at presses and lathes. Metal grinders and hammers added to the din of machinery hissing and pumping almost deafeningly.

"Welcome to the Forge!" Cassia grinned at me and took me to an elevator on the right side of the opening and pressed the only button there.

Some of the figures not actively doing anything waved toward the oni, and she waved back as the double doors in front of us yawned open with a single platform inside. "Come on."

Cassia pulled me in as the doors closed, then out again as they opened once more.

"What?" I blinked, then rubbed my eyes in disbelief as the scenery in the room we stood in was just too unreal.

There were weapons of all sorts lining the walls on shelves. Axes next to spears and swords with spears standing in an umbrella holder in the corner. Knives that made my fingers itch and my wallet ache. On the wall opposite were racks on racks of guns. Everything from shotguns and rifles to pistols, and even a couple sniper rifles. My mouth began to water and Cassia just crossed her arms and grinned as I walked into the room with sheer pained joy.

I could never afford all this. I grumbled to myself, resolving to probably make myself even more charismatic to get better tips if for nothing more than to spend it all here.

"That you, Cassia, you one-horned fighting freak of nature?" A gruff voice called from behind the counter on our right. I turned to spy a stout-looking man, almost too short to see over the counter, eyes as black as coal staring at her almost gleefully.

"You know me, Jayvali, I'm constantly in the market for new toys." She grasped my hand and pulled me forward. "Jay, this is my lo—boyfriend—Marcus. We're going hunting tonight and despite having magic, he wants something that he can protect himself with." She looked at me and motioned to him. "Marcus, this is Jay. He's the dwarf I go to for all the fun toys."

"Cassia, did you go and land yourself a mage?" He rolled his eyes. "Look at him, he's skin and bone! Probably never held a weapon in his life, and look at the way he eyes the swords!"

I blinked at him, turning my gaze from the massive zweihander which was hard because that thing was absolutely gorgeous. "I'm sorry?"

"See?" The man pounded the counter in front of him. "Downright lustful! Probably fancies himself the spellsword type. Some kind of chosen one or some ripe shite like that. Don't you, boy? Fess up!"

I frowned, looking pained because I damned well was and said, "You're right, I am lusting after that sword—it's magnificent. But I have no clue how to use anything more than the NCO sword I bought for the Marine Corps Ball two years ago, and even that was just for sword manual, using the sword for drill with platoons and stuff for the ball. I'd have no clue how to do anything more than salute with it. What I would love to see are some of the knives you have, a couple pistols in nine-millimeter if you have them, and maybe an M-16 or an M-4?"

He opened his mouth and closed it like a flounder in the ocean until he finally got out the words, "Cassia! You found a proper man!"

I laughed and she crossed her arms but he just waggled a finger at her. "Don't you be looking at me like that, lass—you wallop things and leave. This one knows the good stuff!"

"We're hunting humans; guns work on them and not on us. Don't get so excited, or shitty." Jay rolled his eyes and she laughed at him, clearly used to his antics by now.

He grabbed the pistols first. The ones he placed in front me looked like your run of the mill pistols. "These the Walther Q4 Steel Frame and Beretta APX semi?"

"They look like them, don't they?" Jay grinned and tapped the Walther. "This is the MB S6 Fae Frame, but we modeled it after the Walther model due to—well, due to Normies not being able to tell the difference between dwarven forged weapons and other kinds."

"Why is that?"

"You really think some drunken, scared humans were the ones to come up with the idea to make weapons that spewed fire and death?" He chuckled darkly. "Nah, that was us dwarves seeing how they would do it. We leaked our ideas to see how they could do it and we improved upon them."

Cassia rolled her eyes at him and corrected, "You mean they won the plans and details from your sorry drunk asses in games of chance, and you had to make changes to be better than them so as not to get in trouble."

Jay stared at her, hard. "I'd watch your tone, missy."

She leaned forward and stared him right in the eyes as she

smiled slowly and remarked, "I seem to recall someone coming to me to help him recover the plans for a factory that a certain horse guy used to industrialize the gun industry in this country." She tapped her face as if trying to remember something or someone, never once taking her eyes off him. "I wonder who that could have been…"

"Shut up!" He hissed and smacked the table. "They still don't know about that, okay?" She continued to eye him and finally he blanched. "Okay, okay—I'll give you a good deal today."

He touched the Fae Frame, "This one has no iron in it and requires special ammunition and magazines, so that the Fae can't sense its closeness. The pistol to the right of it is the Silvaero APX Semi-Auto. This one can switch between two kinds of munitions, simple Normie rounds and silver rounds that will slow down lycans."

"I thought weapons like this couldn't hurt your kind?" I frowned at Cassia and she looked to Jay.

"They can't," he said simply. "But still, you shoot someone in the eye with a BB gun and what happens? They can go blind. You shoot a Fae or lycan with these things and it will sting at best, and distract them long enough to get the real weapons out. Or magic, as a mage."

He went to the other side of the counter, flipped up the partition, and walked over to the rack holding several kinds of rifles in a variety of calibers. "Hey, jarhead. I heard you wanted something like your M-16?"

I nodded and he just shook his head as he grabbed a few different weapons to bring back to the counter for me. "Alright, we got the Ogre Basher, this one here that looks like your typical M-16. The Sour Krout Kid—that's the one that looks and handles like an MP-5, not my favorite mind you, just to show."

I touched the one that resembled the M-4 I'd carried while deployed. "What's this one called?"

"Thumper." Jay rolled his eyes at me. "No, seriously, that's what we call it. Each of these weapons is specifically designed to throw lead like its Normie counterpart, but with the caveat that the ammunitions can be changed out for anti-super ammo. You take your pick, I can scratch your itch."

He disappeared while I appreciated the fine craftsmanship of each weapon. A submachine gun in an area where a lot of people were tightly packed together didn't seem practical to me, so I rolled the MP-5 look alike out. The Ogre Basher looked amazing and brought quite a few boot camp memories back to the surface of my mind, but this wasn't about being able to sling weapons and do drill.

This was about hunting down bad guys and defending my uncle's bar.

I looked to my left and my breath caught—several blades of differing sizes and complexity now lay on display for me to peruse. "All dwarven made, and all of them deadly in the proper hands."

Jay crossed his hands over his chest and smiled, Cassia grinning. "I think I know which ones we're going to be buying." She pushed both pistols forward. "I'll be buying the Fae Frame for him as a gift, he can buy the others."

I smiled at her gratefully as I lifted the nearest knife. The blades all looked amazing, but I wanted to try something new as well. "Do you have any that would fit into a belt-style sheath?"

"What?" Jay looked at me as if I were suddenly making terrible faces at him. "All of the sheathes we have for the fixed blades will go on a belt or a harness, are you daft?"

"No—I mean *in* a belt." I reached down and grabbed my belt buckle. "I saw a punch knife that I really liked once and if I'm unarmed elsewhere, having one would be nice."

He eyed me and turned his head toward Cassia as if she were going to say something, but she was off looking at some of the more grotesquely large swords. He turned back to me and muttered, "One minute."

He stepped aside and picked up what looked like a land-line phone and spoke into it fervently before turning back to me and motioning for me to wait patiently. About thirty seconds passed before a younger-looking dwarf sprang out of the elevator with a tablet in his hands.

"Sorry it took s'long, got stuck behind a boomer." His Irish accent made me smile, since this was how I had thought dwarves sounded all along. "Can ye describe the weapon to me? In detail?"

I spent a few minutes describing the style of punch blade that I liked, thicker and almost-leaf shaped with a decent two to two-and-a-half inch 'hilt' that was really just a piece of plastic to grasp and punch with. It could be put into a leather belt and made to look like a latch, or a portion of the belt itself. Hell, there were Marines I knew who had these same sorts of blades tied into their boot strings or on ankle sheaths. There was some really top notch work out there.

"We will take the time to research this and come up with a suitable, workable piece that you can test out in about three to four days." The younger dwarf shook my hand, then looked over at Jay. "I'll be takin' this up to management to have it looked over right away, sir." The dwarf bowed his way out of the room as if I were royalty.

"Was all that really necessary?" I frowned at Jay and he nodded. "Why? This isn't a very new concept. It's highly likely that your people started this too."

"Nah." He surprised me and tapped the counter before him. "My kind believe in open carrying weapons, never really had it in us to stow away beautiful things and sneak 'em in places. Not us. But people out there like Cassia and her brother Kenshi? Ol' Jolly? Those guys deserve the utmost respect and to have the ability to conceal their weapons if needed."

"Okay, I can understand where you come from with that." He pulled out a tall bottle of amber liquid and three small glasses that reminded me of shot glasses at work. "What's that for?"

"This..." He tapped the bottle and whistled softly to get Cassia's attention before he continued to explain. "Is an eons-old tradition of dwarves predating the dawn of Normie kind. You just sold us a blueprint, Marcus; my kind will be making those weapons for generations and any and all variations on it will be your doing."

"I doubt there's much that's really worth drinking over." I chuckled and he just stared at me as if I were putting my foot in my mouth.

Cassia proved I was when she whispered, "Refusing to drink with a dwarf for any reason other than a life-or-death fight or alcohol allergy is the most offensive thing you can do to a dwarf." She waved a hand in front of the stone-faced dwarf's eyes and he just glared at me. "You could probably mount his mother and kill his father in front of him, and he would hate you less for it."

"I'll drink!" I raised my hands as Jay smiled and nodded as if I had made the best decision of my life. I glanced at Cassia and muttered, "Did you have to be quite so vibrantly gruff about that?"

"She's right, Marcus—I'd have probably hated you less. Drink." The last was growled, his teeth bared at me. I lifted the glass to my mouth and shot the drink in one go as he and Cassia's eyes widened in shock. "Oh gods!"

Cassia panicked, grabbing my shoulders to turn me toward the elevator. I didn't think much of it until I took a surprised breath in through my nose, the most virulent and horrible burning sensation I had ever felt in my life roiled through my body.

It felt like I was going to vomit, Jay shouting, "Don't fight it, lad—spew!"

The heat and burning wasn't going anywhere but up, so I leaned forward and opened my mouth wide. A guttural roar emanated from my mouth as the elevator doors opened and the young dwarf sprinted in. He caught sight of me just as flames jettisoned from my gullet onto him, his squeak of surprise lost in the roar of the flames. He managed to jump to the side as the last of it cleared my throat and I could breathe again.

Cassia pulled me upright and poured something into my mouth that numbed the burning sensation as Jay cleared the counter and threw himself on top of the younger dwarf. His hands patted the poor man's beard, almost like he was pummeling him, both of them grunting as Jay growled, "Be still, boy, or it'll all burn!"

Finally, they looked to be done and they both stood. The younger dwarf's reddish-brown beard was singed and blackened in places, but hadn't all been burnt.

"I am so, so sorry. If there's anything I can do, please just let me know."

Dragon's Brand Whiskey – A particularly strong brand of alcohol favored by dwarves. If consumed too fast, can cause the drinker to spew forty feet of flame.

Dragon's Brand Whisky – Devoured – Spells with the fire element will now be stronger thanks to the distilled dragon flame.

"That's distilled dragon flame?" I eyed the dwarves who stared openly in horror at me. "I have a special ability that allows me to know what is in stuff that I consume. How the hell do you guys drink that and survive?"

"Slowly?" Jay shrugged, then motioned to me and Cassia menacingly. "I like the two of you, but no one can ever know what we drink, hear me?"

"Why?" I frowned at him and he grimaced, tugging on his beard.

"We worry the dragons will try to avenge their fallen if they find out that we harvested their fire glands to make booze." My eyebrows shot up and Cassia stood up straighter. "This was thousands of years ago when the world was still wild and even then—before the Cull."

I'm going to have to do some serious research, I resolved for myself and sighed. "Fine, I'll forget that it's here, or anywhere else for that matter. How much do I owe you for the pistol and the Thumper?"

"Not the Thumper, just Thumper," he corrected me. "She's

a one of a kind, and for the kindness of not revealing our brand of whiskey, I'll give you a good price on her. Did you want to take a blade as well?"

I turned and walked back over to the counter, choosing one with a boxy sort of look to it like a tanto. The thick blade had a good weight to it, not too heavy or light, and the balance was exceptional. The only thing that I could think of that bothered me was that the metal had a light blue shimmer to it, the veins that ran through it white and almost spectral. "This is going to be weird if people see it, will it not?"

"It'll look to most like Damascus steel." He took the blade from me and flipped it in the air. "Good for throwing, good for fighting. Metal is tough, but not brittle; pliable, but not able to be bent. Oni steel is good like that. Good choice."

"This steel is made by oni?" I turned to see the look of pride on Cassia's face deepen.

"Yeah, our kind can take normal steel and enhance it with our blood." She crossed her arms and grinned. "We don't do it too often because it takes some of our strength from us. But there are quite a few of my cousins out there who make the stuff exclusively for this forge, and you can always trust it."

Jay looked over at the younger dwarf. "Seem doable?"

He nodded sheepishly, eyeing me hurt, but understanding. "They said that the normal price is good. And if he has other requirements, they are to be notified immediately."

"Good, good." Jay clapped him on the shoulder. "Take the day and go see the barbers, huh? See if they can't make that look more presentable for you. On me."

The younger dwarf bowed his head and left the room at a sprint. I tried to say something, but Jay shook his head. "Beards aren't as important as they once were. Machinery and forging being what they are now, they become a liability. This will teach him not to style it differently—I hope."

He chuckled at that last bit to himself, then looked to me and explained, "The normal price for a blueprint that is so open to interpretation and differences is about twelve grand."

I whistled low—it was a good amount of money—but he continued. "You also get exclusive rights to royalties, usually about one percent per purchase of the items made, and you get a yearly selection of the new models made. Also, any time a blade needs to be treated or repaired, we will do it free of cost to you."

"That's so much." I scratched my head and he just waved it away. "Seriously, Jay. It's a lot for my so-called design. Is that normal?"

"Of course it is!" He actually hit me in the stomach, the sudden attack making me flinch and almost break his nose in retaliation. "Hehe, good reflexes, lad. Listen, this could well be the thing that makes our craftsmen gain the expertise they need to make master-crafted items! We dwarves prize the ability to make and though we have imagination, we always like to have things to fall to in times of mental drought. This could be what inspires a novice to new heights. We take that very seriously."

"Fine, I suppose that has to be okay." I shook my head and took the knife and sheath from his hand.

I paid about six grand for everything including the normal ammo and a sheath for the blade. The two guns having been about two thousand each thanks to the deals that they gave me, but the blade had been the most expensive. I almost thought of putting it back, but that wouldn't have been good. I needed a blade just in case my magic failed me. And they had almost literally given me everything for free thanks to my blueprint, hell I even managed to make money off it.

"Can I see your identification please?" I frowned at him, but Jay just made the gimme motion and I handed it to him. He ran a few things, grumbling about a lack of a record, then handed me my ID back. "Okay, you are now the 'registered' owner of those two weapons. Any run-ins with Normie law enforcement will come back that you have licensure to carry both, and that they are both perfectly legal."

"Thanks, Jay." He grinned at me and we shook hands. "I'm sure I'll be back for all kinds of fun stuff."

Once we were back into the car, I sighed and Cassia glanced at me. "Are you okay?"

"No, I forgot to get extra magazines, some holsters and other stuff." I finished speaking just after I heard her grunting and found her speaking into her cell phone. "What was that?"

She tapped a button and turned to smile at me. "Making a request."

"Well, let's go in real quick and get those so we can go ge—" I stopped speaking as a tall human man walked out of the building to the side of the car that Cassia was on with a small backpack and nodded to her once before she opened her door and grabbed it. He smiled and turned to walk away from the building completely and jogged across the street. "What was that? What's in that?"

She tossed the bag onto my lap and the rattling made me roll my eyes. "How much do I owe you?"

"Nothing, that's from the High Table's security stash. We keep our extra armory here—just a precaution." She touched my face, pinching my cheek. "Whatever we take, they replenish."

"If I could have gotten whatever I needed for free, why did I have to buy—never mind." She laughed at me as I ran my hand through my hair. "What should I wear for our date tonight?"

"Something hot." She growled happily as she threw the SUV into reverse. "And a mask too!"

CHAPTER NINE

The cool night air washed over me; we had been in a darkened portion of the largest parking garage on campus. I had my mask, this one was magic, according to Cassia, and had been Kenshi's before he had opted to use a new one. The simple black ceramic item fit snugly over my features and left my face blank. I could see out of the mask perfectly with no hindrance to my vision. I let my hands fall to my sides and my fingertips grazed my weapons as I still worked on getting used to their presence.

The holsters I had for my pistols were amazing. An inner pants holster on my left hip for the Fae Frame and the open carry on my right hip that was a thigh holster. I wore a long, dark green flannel over it so that both my weapons were hidden. The oni blade attached to my belt so that the hilt could be accessed from the small of my back on the right-hand side. I made it a habit to reach for them while we were getting ready earlier. There was a surprising amount of briefings to go through for a hunt like this.

Reports of local crimes that they had missed in the last week, photos of the local missing posters, and other things that made me truly appreciate the force I was with. They weren't just out here killing for fun like I had originally thought. They had a purpose, and I could respect that.

We waited in the shadows for about an hour or so waiting for any kind of news from the other teams of hunting guards.

I do not understand why they hunt so fruitlessly, Galaxy grumbled inside my head, Cass frowning at her.

"What do you mean by that?" she challenged with her arms crossed. "Do you have a better way?"

Let me see your phone, Marcus. I complied, opening my map. She pressed a couple things, really making me do it for her until she had a decent overview of the area. *Now, see if you can find local crime reports.*

I spent a few minutes piddling with my phone, but it was Cassia who pulled a website up first. Galaxy scanned it for a few minutes, then my head ached fiercely.

I blinked and a mini-map populated in the upper right-hand corner of my vision and Cass gasped. "Is that what I think it is?"

Yes. That is a mini-map. I find it quite useful when I am researching things. I couldn't see her, but I could just tell that she was preening herself over it. *You will be able to use that and find enemies. As a matter of fact, there is a report of a drug den nearby that could be of use?*

"You want to check it out?" I shrugged at her and she nodded. "Where to, Galaxy?"

A red dot populated in the north-eastern section of the map, which we followed.

We walked for twenty minutes, a few of the groups having moved with us from other directions at a text from Cassia.

"Okay, so when we go in here, we have no idea what to expect," Cassia started to explain to me, but I just smiled as she lifted her mask to look like a beanie. I took off my mask while we moved so that people wouldn't see us and automatically call the police. To most people, we would likely look like a couple on a date or walking home from a class. She lifted an eyebrow. "What?"

"At least wait until we get there before you start making a plan." She chuckled. "We had to do blind sweeps, entry, and clearances of houses in Fallujah. We went house to house, street to street. We had no idea what would be waiting behind every door and that kept us sharp. We can do some recon and see if there are multiple entrances, but making a plan now is just a waste of time."

"Normie battles must be hard, huh?" She shook her head and explained as I gave her a withering glance. "Not having anything other than what little armor can protect you from such fierce technology. Your skin is weak, your bones fragile, and your teeth would shatter on a blade. It must be truly terrifying to fight each other."

"It can be," I agreed, trying to understand that she came from a wholly different experience than I did. "Humans have to be cunning and wily because we are so fragile and short-lived. Our mortality is what makes us dangerous."

"Indeed it is," she agreed solemnly. It took us half an hour to make it to the area and already I could sense something was off.

There were no cars in the area, the street lamps and outdoor building lights in the area had been busted out, and the buildings with lights in them had windows that were dark with little to no coverings.

"They have lookouts all along this street." I growled softly as I pulled Cassia up against a building like I was going to make out with her. I kissed her fiercely, one because I wanted to, and two because it gave us a little credibility. "There are at least three that I could make out in some windows, did you spot any?"

"Yes." She kissed me back, her hips grinding against mine. "Pretending to fight is a good idea. We need to get somewhere a little more secluded so I can let the hunters know what to do."

I nodded, wishing I had gotten a suppressor for my rifle, and that I had brought it in the first place. Picking these bastards off would have been so much easier with it.

She kissed me again, my breath ragged as she motioned toward an alley that was just outside what I hoped their visual range might be.

Once we were there, she started texting her people, then looked up at me. "What would you suggest in this kind of situation?"

"I would like to have guardian angels as we move forward into the territory, that way they can watch our backs and the area surrounding for people closing on us." I pointed to the rooftop as I spoke softly. "After that, I'd want to get people into those buildings to take out the lookouts as we moved."

I poked my head around the corner, wishing I had some kind of night vision on me, but settled for just seeing vague shapes in the windows.

"There's no way I could take one out without a suppressor for my rifle and I don't have it—so moot point." I scratched my head as I watched one of the lookouts disappear. "Wait, what was that?"

"Lycans." Cass grinned at me, pointing behind me as a shape skittered along the wall above one of the watchers on a second-story balcony. "They may be furry and have weird allergies, but they can scale a wall like it's a floor and kill in an instant. We can do this."

Three other lookouts died quickly, all of them failing miserably at putting up some kind of fight.

Part of me wondered if this was really okay, but Galaxy didn't let me dwell.

From what I read online, this is an area that the authorities will only come to with SWAT and heavy numbers, Marcus. These people are bad people. You are doing a good thing.

"Are you saying that because you want to grow?" I growled more to myself than her.

Yes. But also because your morality has begun to affect me slightly and I want to see these fuckers pay for the atrocious things they've done.

Cassia handed her phone and the site over to me and my blood began to boil, even as I had been smiling because she cursed like that for the first time. This place had been a known hub for narcotics, prostitution, and human trafficking. The people here had warrants and criminal histories longer than my body and then some. Some were even known cop killers, murderers, and rapists.

"These people need to pay, Marcus," Cassia grumbled to me with her hand on my shoulder. "We are the justice this city needs right now, and this is how we can continue to keep the Normies and humans from investigating the High Table."

I nodded once, my jaw set and ticking slightly. "Let's go. I don't need any more reason than all that." With that said, I slid my mask on as did Cassia.

We closed in on a larger building that looked like a broken-down factory or something to that effect when someone walked around the corner with a lit cigarette. He had a gun in his right hand and a cell phone in his left.

"Come on, Julian, pick up the phone, you were supposed to come and replace me, man." While he was distracted, I lowered myself into a crouching position and ghost walked up to him, my oni blade clearing its sheath and resting against his throat. "Why the fuc—"

"Shut the phone off and throw it down now." I tightened my grip on his forehead as he pulled the device away from his ear. The screen should have blinded me but I closed my right eye to conserve what little night vision I had.

Cassia snatched the pistol in his hand and snickered. "Safety's still on."

I growled in the man's ear, "Then we must be dealing with the low man on the staff. Better just kill him." I upped the pressure on his throat and he started to plead, so I eased up. "Tell me what you know. Why all the watchers in this area?"

"We got product, man." He started to sweat profusely, his body shaking like a leaf against me. "Something new that hasn't hit the streets big yet, got the supplier here tonight. Big wig.

Ain't heard of 'em before. Please don't kill me. My cousin just told me this was a place to watch for a while and get some quick dough and roll, man. Please!"

Is there any way to know if he's telling the truth? My internal question to Galaxy made the cat appear on my shoulder. *He looks like he's just a kid.*

And he did, his clothes and mannerisms just made him appear a little older.

I don't know, I'm not strong enough to tell.

"His heart beat is going crazy. He could be lying." Cassia sidled over in front of him as I tugged him out of sight of the building. She removed her mask, then leaned down in front of him, letting her eyes turn with a grunt, the glow around them an eerie blood red, horn growing from the top of her head as her voice deepened. "Do you believe in monsters, human? I will know if you lie to me."

"What the fuck are you?" he cried, his voice a hoarse, fear-filled whisper as tears began to stream down his face.

"I am a demon, and I eat the souls of the wicked." She leaned forward to take a large sniff of him. "Were you being honest? You lie to me and I will eat you."

"I was being honest, I swear it on my moms!" His pleading made him seem even younger.

I leaned forward and whispered, "You turn away from this life, kid. And if we find out that you have done anything wrong or told anyone about us being here?" I lifted his wallet from where I had picked it out of his pocket. "We'll know who we're looking for. Walk away from here—don't run. Walk."

I pushed him away and nodded him off as Cassia took a deep breath to pull her partial shift back and retain her human form. Letting him go would likely be foolish, he would say something to someone about me and Cassia just to end up called out for being crazy or hallucinating. Either way, I hoped he got his shit together.

"Good improvising." I nodded to Cass and she returned it

with a nod of her own. "Let's get closer and see what we can figure out."

We moved closer, my hands free as I put the oni blade away. I pulled the Silvaero on my right hip and peered around the corner slowly, keeping an eye out for any other lookouts or goons. No one was immediately visible and from my peripheral vision I could see multiple lycans wandering the walls and taking out lookouts in high positions.

"We go in slow and quiet," I whispered to Cassia and she opted to let me take the helm, but texting commands to the guards in the area. "Have them post up and get inside if they can. Be our eyes from above."

"Already done," Cassia replied with a smug smile. "What next?"

"We penetrate." I grinned at her and she giggled knowingly as she replaced her mask. I shook my head and rolled my eyes before we started forward. I kept both hands on my gun, the high firm grip with it canted to the side and held at my chest as if it were the most natural position in the world.

We moved surely, eyes forward and roving the area to be certain no one watched, and made it to the entrance. Cassia whispered, "Eyes on some kind of large group on the factory floor. Through here, to the right, and then a left. Guards all over."

She put her phone away as I tensed and sprang up the stairs, checking for lines and wires along the doorframe. I found nothing and checked the door—locked.

Cassia reached down and grasped the door before shaking it once violently. The door creaked and the sound of metal crunching made me eye her nervously before I looked around again. The door moved inward without another peep, which I was grateful for.

"All it needed was some coercing." She winked at me, the door handle mangled beyond all recognition.

We followed the simple instructions to get into the factory floor and what we saw honestly wasn't all that impressive. The sides of the walls were littered with refuse and junk. Scrap metal and garbage with a number of tables and other things strewn about haphazardly made the place look more and more like a dump than a factory.

Sofas and televisions like this place was a flop house of sorts, lived in, almost. In the center of what could have been the production floor was a massive, singular vat, looking to be about twenty to twenty-five feet tall and half as wide. It was filled with a whitened substance that men and women stood over on cat walks with long poles, stirring like chefs tending soup. No vapor came from it, and nothing emanated from it or from within, it was just *there*.

How had it gotten there? What was so special about it that it just needed to be stirred like it was? From where I stood, I couldn't even see if there was a source of heat beneath it to boil or refine it. It was just big and full of the stuff.

A large group of people stood in the center of the floor next to the vat, surrounded by armed guards who watched their fields of fire like that was all they ever did.

I couldn't hear what was being said, and Cassia didn't look to be able to either. *Galaxy, can you go spy on them?*

She sighed heavily and appeared in front of us, then dropped down lower to one of the cat walks and stilled. *Oh, this is interesting.*

What? I responded, looking over at Cass to see if she knew what was up.

The liquid in that vat is condensed mana.

What did that mean? I blinked and watched as she slunk around the feet of one man and dropped into the vat with a soft plop.

"What the hell did she just do?" Cassia's panicked whisper drew my attention back to her and away from the goings on below.

I shook my head and shrugged before someone shouted something below. A man jogged forward, the guards turning to watch him as he moved toward what I assumed was their

127

charge. Their weapons raised until a single figure stepped forward and I thought I recognized them. But I couldn't place them.

They spoke and the figure raised their hand and the weapons stilled, they didn't fall—just stilled. The panting man spoke in gasps and the guards surged forward toward them. A mousy-looking man in a suit stepped away as the guards ushered the middleman out under their protection and the rest of the figures on the floor galvanized each other.

"Find them!" one of the men roared.

Cassia looked askance of me and I just shook my head. "Leave the one they left behind. He may know something."

She grinned and leaped over the railing in front of us with a joyful whooping cry. Gunfire rang out below as I sighed and sighted in on the one calling the shots down there. I squeezed the trigger and his head rocked back, his body falling to the ground, dead.

I moved and ducked shots, halting and dipping sporadically to make myself a harder target.

Some of the people on the vat abandoned their posts and sprinted toward me. *No time like the present to try out some magic, Marcus!* I growled and cast Bolt.

Something in the pit of my stomach roiled and floated up into my chest and down into my shoulder and arm before electricity rippled around my hand and shot into the first man who was running at me like a linebacker ready to smear me on the metal walkway. His body stiffened like he had been tased, a round from one of his buddies hitting him in the stomach, then one of mine took him in the neck. My sights aligned on someone's forehead; bang, they fell.

Someone almost reached me and I push kicked them before they could get too close. They stumbled over the rail and down to the floor. It was too much to be able to do any kind of pistol work up here with so many people close enough to overwhelm me.

I cast Physical Buff and suddenly I just *knew* I was faster than I had been. I blinked and saw that I did, indeed, have a speed buff floating in the upper left-hand corner under my mana bar.

My hands slapped and moved people's fists and feet out of the way as I shuffled forward into the fray. My knee cracked against the inside of a woman's leg, her failed attempt to drive a knife into my neck leaving her wide open. Her knee popped and she cried out as I relieved her of her weapon and slid it into a man next to her. He fell into her and sent them both falling over the side of the cat walk and into the vat. The impact made a huge splash and when the liquid hit one man in the side, he screamed wildly and tore at his clothes as if it was acid.

When his shirt came off, I could see a huge purple stain where the mana had seeped through, his eyes glowing bright blue as he tottered drunkenly toward me. At first, I wasn't going to hurt him and just try to incapacitate him, but his fist hit me so hard that all the air was driven from my lungs and I rocketed off the catwalk and into the wall behind me twenty feet away.

He cackled madly as he walked slowly forward, his wide-open mouth making him look manic and almost goofy, but I knew I was sporting broken ribs from that, at least for now. I pulled the Silvaero and unloaded on him, but his skin just welted a little where the rounds collided with him.

I wheezed, "Shit," as he towered over me, his foot just missing my head as he lost his balance and gained a look of panicked confusion as the glow leached from his eyes. The weapon's slide had locked in place, indicating that I was out of ammunition, but that didn't mean I was unarmed. I reached up as I summoned a Wisp and slapped his leg with it.

He howled and tried to slap the flames away from his clothes and leg, giving me the chance to shove his foot and send him into the rail. He didn't fall, but it gave me enough time to cast Blade. A shimmering sword of blue erupted in my hand as I climbed to my feet and rushed forward.

My clenched fist slammed into his chest as he tried to back away, stopping the blade that was embedded between his ribs. I stared him in the eyes as blood flowed from his mouth and down his bare chest before I let the spell go and threw him over the side. The sickening thud of his body smacking against the floor would have made most people balk, but I felt nothing, surprisingly.

By the time I made it down the catwalk ladder to the factory floor, my ribs felt normal-ish, and I could walk without needing to hold them now. Bodies littered the floor and several of the other High Table security force milled about in the shadows. Watching. Waiting for some kind of signal.

"He refuses to talk." Cassia sighed, the mousy man already bloodied and shivering in fear of her.

"Well, you beat him—I'd hardly want to talk to you either." I lifted my mask and glared at her reproachfully as she blinked in my direction in surprise. I reached toward the man only to have him flinch away. I stilled my reaching and offered a gentle, "It's okay, I'm not going to hurt you."

He still raised his arms as if to defend himself, but I just grabbed his shoulder and pulled him away carefully, winking at her over his head so she might realize what I was doing.

I patted some of the dirt off his suit and spoke softly, "Sorry, bud, she gets a little bit overly excited and forgets that manners can be useful from time to time." He glared at me as if I were a snake ready to strike at him. "Listen, I know that you got the raw deal and had to stay behind to oversee the product, and personally, I don't want to see you get into any trouble that could get you killed."

He stiffened, looked at the body I motioned to about three feet from us, the head laying at an odd angle compared to the body with the weirdly contorted limbs akimbo.

"See, I can be a nice guy—all I need to know is who it is running this show, and I can go take care of them." I offered him a genuine smile, trying to be as real as possible. He watched me quietly and didn't answer at all. So I sighed heavily and turned back to Cassia. "Seems he doesn't want to chat, Cass.

You mind throwing him into the vat? I'm sure whatever is in there is plenty of fun."

"No!" he shrieked as she stomped forward, the men and women around us chanting loudly for her to throw him high. "No, please no—not that!"

"What's in there that has you so spooked, Mr. Mouse?" I grabbed him by the back of the neck and pulled him closer to the man that still twitched on the ground, the purple spot on his body spreading over his skin even in death. "Does it have something to do with this?"

He fought and squirmed against me, and even as he fought, he grew steadily stronger and stronger. Something was wrong.

I glanced down and caught a syringe in his arm, his eyes glowing a blue so vivid they could have held the sky in them. His mouth twisted up into a snarling grin, his voice sounding deeper and almost whispered at the same time as he explained, "It's an incomplete blend is all."

His fist rocketed out and I threw myself backward in time to avoid the majority of the damage he could have caused. He still hit my left shoulder hard enough to send me skittering instead of rolling back onto my feet, my entire left arm numb from the contact.

Cassia roared into action, her human form forgotten, and clotheslined the bastard as he grew. His suit shredded and several of the other guards joined the fight in their various supernatural states of being. Three of them were werewolves and the other two were oni, one blue and the other green-skinned.

They dog piled onto the not-so-mousy man and still got tossed aside as he stood up and growled, "Now who's the mouse?"

I rolled my eyes and frowned; Galaxy wasn't saying anything, and I wanted to be sure she was okay, but this guy was a problem.

I pulled the oni blade from my belt with my right hand and rushed forward as he swung his bulk in my direction. I slashed at his heel, the tendon in his left leg snapping from the immense weight on the leg.

"Raaaaargh!" His spittle splashed against my back as I tumbled to avoid his other leg attempting to stomp on me. The pain in his injured leg didn't look to be enough to stop him from trying to kill me, but it was enough to slow him.

One of the wolves snarled and hopped onto his back, teeth tearing at his shoulder as the red oni grabbed his damaged leg and heaved with a loud bellow, like a powerlifter grunting and shouting for added strength.

The burly man tried to correct, but I cast Bolt again and his body stiffened just long enough for him to fall and land on his back. The other wolves leapt onto his chest and arms as Cassia and the other oni piled onto his legs. I still had the oni blade in my hand as I clambered around them all so I could go for his throat.

His massive mitt wrapped around my leg and yanked, the knee separating painfully from the joint. I fell forward and missed his throat, but nicked his carotid artery. Blood sprayed my face and back as the wolves growled and more High Table security flooded into the room.

It took four of them biting and worrying at his arm to make him let go, and by the time they had chewed it off, his body began to shrink as he wailed pitiably.

One of the wolves, a russet-furred mass of muscle and hatred when I had first seen them, nodded in my direction and motioned to my leg. "Sit still, I'll fix it."

"Huh?" They grabbed my leg and pulled it, twisting to snap it back into place as I snarled, "Good gravy!"

The wolf just chuckled before winking at me. "You'll get used to it, boss. Good fight."

"Thanks?" My leg already felt a lot better, so I grabbed the hand they offered me and let them pull me to my feet. The knee was tender, but not unusable, so I limped over to Cassia. "How're you doing?"

"Good!" She grinned at me, then frowned at the body of

the mousy man. "Wish he had told us who his supplier was and what they were planning with that stuff."

A wet plopping sound drew our attention upward to the lip of the vat. A purple hand grasped it and pulled. The figure fell over the side toward the ground, but just as it should have hit the ground, it stopped and froze midair.

It was a woman, judging by her figure and the way she moved. "Galaxy?"

She turned her head toward me and smiled. "That's me."

"What happened?" Cassia whispered and stepped closer.

"Pure mana happened, that's what." She smiled, her beautiful features almost radiating a warmth that made me smile too.

Her skin was the same color that her fur had been, dark and purple with dots and spots like the stars in the sky. Her long, shaggy hair was golden and cascaded over her long, pointed ears.

"Elf?" Cassia whispered in wonder again. "But wait, why do you look like that? The other elves are almost human-looking except that they're too beautiful or handsome."

Galaxy looked down at herself and her skin rippled, the specks of light disappearing with each ripple until a perfectly dark-skinned elven woman stood before us completely nude.

"Is this better?" She motioned to herself and I took off my flannel to drape around her shoulders like a dress. "Thank you."

"What happened in there?" I asked her in a low voice.

"We can discuss it later when we are alone." She smiled at me and shimmered once before her feline form rubbed up against my leg, the bloody flannel having fallen onto the floor. *For now, we need to leave this place and discuss what we have learned. As well as you both leveling up.*

"Oh, that's so awesome!" Cass pumped her arm excitedly. "Ding!"

The other security staff eyed her disbelievingly until she straightened and barked, "Get your asses back to the barracks and get cleaned up. This thing surprised us; we cannot let that happen again. Any word on any kind of new drug hitting the streets—I better know within the hour, am I clear?"

"Yes ma'am!" Their roar of compliance was enough to make me flinch, but the quickness at which they complied was even more surprising.

She turned to me. "We need to destroy the evidence of this place and us being here, can you burn it down?"

I thought about it, eyeing my mana bar. I still had *30/100* to work with.

"I can do that." I took a deep breath and cast Wisp at the vat itself, the couches, and debris on the way out.

The building began to smoke and light filtered through the dirt streaked and stained windows as the flames licked at the walls from within.

It was a bit of a hike back to the car from there; the majority of the time we spent walking was spent ensuring that no one saw me covered in all this blood. Even though my flannel had covered the majority of my body, there was still a lot of blood on my face and neck.

"You fought well," Cassia observed softly as we watched a few of our people cross the street and bolt to the shadows of an alleyway across the street.

"Thank you." She nodded quietly, but stayed quiet. "I'm sorry if I offended you by trying to talk to him like that. Making you sound like a brute so he might talk to me."

"Me?" She smirked and looked around. "I am a brute, Marcus. I have accepted that role and embrace it at times when it is convenient. You saying that didn't hurt me. It was frustrating that I couldn't make him talk and I missed that needle. I had patted him down, and I have no idea where it came from."

"And he could have hurt your people," I offered and she nodded solemnly. "That's a sign of good leadership to me." She paused and frowned at me. "I like good leaders. Good leaders care about their troops and when something goes wrong, they blame themselves, even if they had no direct hand in what happened. Good leadership is hard to find sometimes."

She just made a noise with her throat and we moved on until we made it to the parking garage and her vehicle. Luckily, this was one of the garages with no cameras, and we got out of there easily.

We made it back to the parking lot at the High Table with ease and booked it into the gym area where we were met with cheers and clapping.

Cassia looked surprised but grinned before ducking out of the way so the others could rush me and lift me off the ground. "Woah! What's going on?"

"Celebrate good hunt!" Kenshi called over the din of voices chanting in a language I didn't know. I saw the massive oni standing over the others with his arms crossed over his chest while they brought me toward him. Once they put me down before him, he raised his arms and they quieted swiftly as they all took a knee.

"Tonight, we celebrate birth of bubba Marcus." His growling voice was punctuated by the growls and grunts of all the gathered security. "Bubba Marcus fought with family, protected family. Killed enemies of the High Table. This good."

Whooping and calls of agreement echoed around us as Cassia stood and joined her brother, raising her voice. "Warriors of the High Table Columbus Branch, this mage fought and bled for us—with us—to protect our High Table, to protect our people. That makes him a warrior. He has bathed in the blood of a powerful foe, and on this night, can be reborn. What say you, brothers and sisters? Is this enough to stand with him? Is he not worthy?"

A large man stood, his shorts in shreds as he raised both hands. "With these hands, I set his displaced bones, so that he might continue to serve and defend. With these hands, I would lift him up and carry him to safety, as with his hands, he saved me."

"Well said, bubba Fenrir." Kenshi put his right fist over his heart and bowed his head before looking up.

A woman stood and the crowd lifted their chins. "With these teeth, I bit his foe, so that he might be able to strike the final blow. With these teeth, I would bite him should he lose his way—so that he knows where the truth is. He does not use his teeth, but his blade is sharp, and it bit his foe well. I respect this."

"Well said, sissy Ceres." Cassia mirrored Kenshi as she bowed her own head.

"He is human, he is a mage," another voice rang out from the back of the crowd. Others muttered as the speaker pushed his way through the crowd to stand beside me. It was the moose knuckle from the chow hall. "Mages have no place among true warriors."

"All who feel same as bubba Sabbath, stand," Kenshi snarled, his eyes scanning the crowd of gathered bodies. "Now."

Around twenty security members walked into the room from the hallway as if on cue, including the two goons that had been with him.

Kenshi scanned the group behind me and scowled at them all. "No more?"

Those with us stayed kneeling resolutely, throwing scornful glares and baring teeth at the others who stood, prompting Cassia to say, "It seems that we have division amongst us, and there is an even number on both sides."

"We have to settle in the old way." Kenshi nodded as if to himself. "Warrior elder and heads not take part in vote."

"I take it that the old way is a duel of sorts?" I glanced around and found that that was the case due to the nods of those closest to me. "I'm game."

"You think a mage like you can take me?" Sabbath snorted derisively and rolled his eyes. "I would kill you."

I don't like him, Galaxy spat. *I would happily see you kill him. But this could be useful. You have yet to place your points from the last time you leveled, or this time—doing so now could prove useful.*

Yeah, but I don't have any mana, right now? Why is it not regenerat-

ing? She didn't have time to answer my question before my stomach gurgled loudly.

You aren't used to using mana, and as you heal, your body uses energy to do so, like a lycan's does, she explained with more mirth in her tone than I thought the situation deserved. *While you are hungry, your body cannot recover mana well without you being stronger.*

Stronger how, like with my Mana stat? I could inwardly feel her nod an affirmative and sighed. It would be more than mana that I needed.

"Can I have some time to eat?" I asked politely, Sabbath tilting his head with his lips and face wrinkled with disgust.

"An hour to prepare is good enough." Cassia interrupted before Sabbath could press the issue any more. "Sabbath, go and cleanse yourself and prepare for your fight."

He scowled at me and left to go do whatever he would do as Kenshi approached me. "Good luck, bubba Marcus."

Cassia grabbed my arm and herded me to the chow hall where I got some food and some of the others that seemed to like me joined us. While I ate so much food, I thought I would burst, I found that as soon as I felt full, my body started to recover mana. By the time I had been eating for half an hour, I had my mana fully restored and I felt better than I had before.

I checked over my stats and thought about it before asking, *What do you think Sabbath's stats are?*

Judging based on his personality I would say all his stats were maxed in being a prissy little turd. Galaxy's vehemence made me laugh in surprise. *I've been learning more from your memories and emotions.*

So come on, what would you think they are?

She thought for a moment then replied, *Brawn and Physique will be high, almost no mana, middling Charisma and likely low Dexterity. Feel free to open your display however you like. I am strong enough to allow you the freedom to not need my aid.*

I grinned at that, having had the same thoughts myself. So I would do what I could. I had ten points to play with and some magic too. I opted to put four points into Brawn, making it twelve. Three into Dexterity for an even six, one into Physique for the same amount and the rest into Mana for twelve.

My stomach grumbled and I sighed, shoveling more food into my already complaining stomach. My clothes were beginning to get a little tight on me as it was, but Cassia grabbed my arm and asked, "Did you spend more points?"

I blinked at her and nodded. "Why?"

She motioned to my arm. It had been well-defined before, but now it was more vascular than it had ever been in my life. "Oh, instant results. May have to watch that though, too much of a change could be telling."

She nodded, feeling my bicep then feeling hers. "It's nice, isn't it?"

I winked at her and raised an eyebrow in her direction. "You want to fight later?"

Her eyes widened and she glanced around as the discussion at the table lulled, several sets of eyes turning to glance at us. She blushed and nodded as I laughed, the others just snorting.

She's just threatened to kill you six times, so you know. Galaxy's cool voice was enough to make me gulp and make Cassia laugh.

I checked my spells and saw that there wasn't really anything open, so I took the opportunity to add a point to Bolt, raising the efficiency of the spell so there wasn't as much of a lag between when I cast it and the strike. Personally, I hadn't seen much of one to begin with, but I was glad it would be faster. Of course, I had been killing people.

Still, somehow I was completely fine with that. Maybe Connell's mother had been right?

You do not believe that, and you know it. Galaxy tutted at me from within. *Do not dwell, and look, you have unlocked a new branch of spell growth.*

Glancing back at the list before me, I saw that she was right. *Of course I am.*

I rolled my eyes and read the list.

Twin Bolt – Bolt cast from both hands at twice the

mana cost of the original spell, but double the power. 20 mana.

Arcing Bolt – Each casting of Bolt has a high chance of striking nearby enemies. 15 mana.

Embodiment – Bolt can be cast normally or consumed and used for heightened speed and reflexes. 20 mana.

"Oh, all of these are so cool." I thought for a moment and pulled Cassia aside, knowing I had precious little time to waste. "Galaxy, please share my status with Cassia?"

She can see it now that she is one of my blessed, just show her. Galaxy seemed as intrigued by the spells as I was.

"Oh, those are really cool. What were you thinking of taking?" I stared at her and she smiled knowingly. "Can't decide either, huh?" I shook my head and she nodded. "I know that feeling. If you were planning on doing anything for this fight, I would say Twin Bolt, just because it sends two spells out with twice the oomph. But Embodiment looks like it could be supremely useful in that it could raise your speed."

She took a look at my other spells and pointed to Physical Buff. "Can you make this give you a specific buff, or is everything?"

"Last time I used it, it made me faster."

She nodded to herself and thought for a moment longer. "Okay, I would go Embodiment, and put a point into it too so it gives you some kind of bonus." I selected the spell and paused, seeing that this one could be leveled up eight times. "So stronger spells can be leveled up more? That's great to know."

"Sissy Cass," Kenshi called, tapping his wrist. "It time."

She turned to me and smacked my arm. "You can help me level up after your fight."

"Not going to wish me luck?" I tried to pout at her playfully, but her deadpan look in return made me wince.

"Warriors have skill, and even skillful warriors need a bit of luck from time to time, Marcus." She kissed my cheek. "But a true warrior makes his own luck. You should know this. Now go kick his ass and we can fight after we look at my stats."

After that, she grabbed me by my bloody shirt and pulled me forward to kiss me fully on the mouth until I was breathless. "And what a fight it will be."

I took a deep look into her wild eyes and set my jaw.

Time to go make some luck, Marcus.

CHAPTER TEN

I stood in front of the whole security staff wearing nothing but a pair of clean workout shorts, having had enough time to wash the blood off and change into someone else's shorts for the fight. Across from me stood the massive, Adonis-like Sabbath, wearing a similar pair of shorts as me.

They had cleared the gym floor in seconds with everyone lifting the equipment and storing it at the back of the room so there was plenty of space for us to have it out.

Sabbath's massive bulk would have normally been enough to scare a lot of people, but Cassia's pep talk had been enough to make me even more aware that this guy had to go down. It was like the times that all of the Corporals under me got it in their heads that I needed to relax and step down, so they opted to try to handle things the way they had in the old Corps— hand to hand training.

This was just another step into the tree line for me, and he was going to fall in line one way or another.

"Fight hard, use natural weapons only." Kenshi raised his hands and the guards lining the wall each took a deep breath and began to chant and clap. Some even brought out drums and tapped a rhythm that made my heart beat faster in time with their beats.

Sabbath spread his feet and lifted his arms, his muscles bulging and warping as his body shifted and grew steadily larger. Finally, when he was about ten feet tall, fur erupted from his body, his fingers growing long claws as they flexed. "You ready to die, Normie?"

"Your mother," I spat and he trundled toward me on all fours for some reason.

Once he was close enough, I whipped my foot around and caught him in the face, but he did nothing more than take this hit and keep coming. I sighed as he swiped at me, almost too slowly, and missed as I ducked the blow and caught his arm on the follow through.

I latched on and whipped my weight over it and my feet down so that I had his arm in both of mine and leveraged it toward the floor.

He snarled, "You little runt, you think you can break my arm?"

"I think you can't stop me if I did want to." I grinned as his weight shifted and he reared up onto his back legs. I didn't try to keep his arm, instead dancing away and smiling. "Tell me, Sabbath, what's it like knowing that Cassia is with me and not you?"

He roared and charged me, faster than he had been. I laughed openly and cast Physical Buff, my muscles tightening and bulging. I didn't do anything other than mirror him. As he was about to spear his arm forward, I jumped as hard and high as I could and kneed him in the chest, punching him right in the forehead as I cast Bolt.

The spell zapped him and made him grunt and list to the left. "Magic!" he snarled, his muzzle twisting in disgust. "He's using magic."

Kenshi watched impassively. "Magic natural weapon. Fight, Sabbath."

I belly laughed, before sarcastically lowering my voice to

sound like him. "The big bad Normie's using magic to whip my ass, he's cheating." I held my fists up to my face and mimed crying. "Woe is me, I'm Sabbath and I wanna whine like a little bit—oof!"

Again, his increase in speed surprised me and this time he connected. His claws raked the inside of my bicep, shredding my flesh and sending me head over heels into the wall behind me.

"Talking shit won't get you anywhere with me, Normie," Sabbath growled. "You think that you can piss me off and I'll fight stupidly? Please."

I grinned and just shrugged as I stood, the wound itching fiercely as it closed. "Nah, I just wanted to tease you because that's what you sound like. I don't give a flying fuck how you fight."

He watched me quietly, then must have decided I wasn't worth the limited braincells he had rubbing together because he just roared and charged forward again.

I waited until he was committed to the charge and cast Embodiment. The muscles in my body shook once, but I felt alive. Almost jittery with the lightning screaming through my body. As soon as his massive paw raised to cut me down and started on the swing, I moved and stood three feet to the right with my arms crossed in the blink of an eye.

To him, it had to have looked like I just teleported and wasn't there anymore as he crashed into the wall with a resounding thud BANG.

I took advantage of his daze to hop onto his shoulders and put my hands to the back of his head, spamming Bolt every second until I had only *5/120* mana left. He drooled a puddle on the ground, the whites of his eyes the only thing showing as I stood.

The crowd went ballistic and rushed me, some of the guards pulling me away from their fallen comrade as the others checked on him. The doc shoved his way through Sabbath's cronies and checked him over. I pushed at some of the hands grasping me, but they were insistent and many, so I couldn't get back to the massive man and doc.

Finally, I stood before Kenshi and Cassia as the people touching me knelt directly where they were, their closeness and proximity suddenly hotter than it had been before.

"Marcus prove he warrior like you, let those who say he fit stand with him." Everybody around me stood and roared in their own way, the energy of it making goosebumps rise along my skin, the hair on my body standing on end. "Then let us give him rebirth."

Kenshi pulled a cup from behind his back, a large golden goblet, and a blade. He passed the blade over his thumb and pressed it to the lip of the goblet so the blood ran into it. Cassia did the same and then passed the cup on to the next member of the group.

By the time it got back to me, it was half filled with crimson and green swirling in it. "What's the green?"

"Oni blood turn green if in air long time." Kenshi motioned to the surroundings and several other oni nodded. He took the cup from my hands and raised it where he stood. "Blood of our blood, bond by oath. Sissy Cassia, give oath."

Cassia stepped forward and spoke calmly, shedding her human form so that she stood before me as her fully oni self. "Do you, Marcus, swear to uphold the laws and safety of those within the High Table as a warrior?"

"I do." I nodded and she dipped her finger into the blood of the cup and ran it over my forehead.

"Do you swear to protect your brothers and sisters at arms as they protect you?" She motioned for me to hush, then a soft drumming began and people began to hum solemnly. "Do you swear to uplift them and hold them accountable as they would do for you?"

"I do, and I will." She dipped her two forefingers into the cup and made two lines down each of my cheeks.

"Will you give your life, to protect our charges, and for the High Table?"

The question hung in the air and the noise stopped.

No. Galaxy warned me. Images flashing through my mind. I knew what was needed.

"I am a warrior. I don't give my life—someone must take it." My voice was guttural, even to me. "And I will not allow them to without making them pay a heavy toll for it first."

Kenshi crossed his arms and shouted, "Who here feels the same?"

Every voice raised along with mine, "Yes!"

Cassia offered me the goblet as Kenshi bid me drink. I steeled myself and took a few gulps until it was all gone. *Nicely done, Marcus. We can use this to grow stronger.*

I fought not to get sick, but eventually just swallowed a few times and my stomach settled suddenly.

"As elder of us all, bubba Kenshi will give the blessing of the rebirth name." Cassia turned and stepped closer to her brother. "Bubba Kenshi, what do you name our new warrior brother?"

"I call him Marcus Massacre." Kenshi placed his massive hands on either side of my face and pressed his horns against my forehead. "I call him bubba."

The rest of the security guards muttered, "Bubba," before closing around us so that they could touch my shoulder or back and sniff me. Even the ones who had been against me joined in, solemn looks of resignation on their faces as they held to the ceremony.

The last one to join them was Sabbath, his jaw set and his eyes seething with rage. "You won."

I nodded once. "I did." I offered him my hand and he grabbed it, the crushing grip I had expected not coming. He lifted my hand to his mouth, I wondered if he was going to kiss it until finally he took my scent from the inside of my wrist.

"Don't think I'll settle for second fiddle," he growled, looming over me. "I prize strength. Doesn't matter the gender."

I blinked as he walked away, looking over at Cassia. "Was he just hitting on me?"

She grinned. "Yeah, his sexuality was never really something I paid attention to, he just kept trying to get with me. Never really paid it any mind until now."

"Huh." I shrugged. Wasn't be the first time I'd been hit on by a dude, not my preference, but still flattering. "What happens now?"

My stomach gurgled annoyingly and I rolled my eyes. "This whole eating thing has to stop, Galaxy. My stomach is going to burst."

No it won't, stop being such a baby, she hissed back at me.

"Hey!" someone called from inside the gym door. "Luci is here for Karaoke Night, who's coming to watch him perform?"

Cassia looked at me with a huge grin and I just snorted. "Can we get the chow hall food to go?"

"Have you not seen him sing before?" Fenrir asked me excitedly and I shook my head no. "Cass, get his ass over there, I'll go get him food."

She laughed and pulled me along after her, bypassing the line of guests and angry college kids who weren't allowed in due to being human kids. The dance area had been converted to a stage—likely by a spell of some kind—and there was a song machine and small television in front of the microphone where Luci was finishing up a song.

Someone screamed, "Encore!" And all he did was chuckle and shake his head humbly as he tried to pass the next person the mic.

It was Arden. All she did was take it and hand it right back, pointing to the stage with a huge smile on her face. Lucifer sighed and rolled his eyes. "You guys just can't let a guy sing once, can you?"

"Hell no!" I hollered and he eyed me with a smile. "Had to come see you sing after Arden talked you up so much."

"Well, since I have a new fan here tonight, I'll take requests." He held up a hand and tiredly hung his head. "And for the love of Dad, nothing with me in it? I don't particularly care to go to Georgia unless it's for DragonCon, and even then, just to see some friends as they peddle their wares."

The crowd laughed and he smiled as he waited and listened. Someone suggested, "Take Me to Church!"

Luci laughed. "Oh, dear. How delightfully ironic that is. Allow me to make a few alterations to the words so that it makes it just a little more personal to us, will you? That's the little number that goes something like this, right?" Low key music started to play over the speakers that wasn't what I recognized the song to be, but I guessed it must have been loading the actual song.

Luci cleared his throat then began to sing, his voice as rich and melodic as the original singer's, but there was something just extra about it. Fuller. A thrill rang down my spine as his voice filled the room, the scent of food that had been set on the table near me all but forgotten at the devil's honeyed words and sweet tempo.

Finally, his eyes scanned the crowd as he sang, "I was born slick, but I love it, command me into hell, hey—Everybody go ahead and join me and say Take me to the Table in three! Two... One!"

"Take me to the Table!" we all cheered as he continued the song, the soulful melody almost cupping me and forcing my tired heart to just rest and be in this moment until the last words rang out and the only thing I could do was clap to fight the solemnity away as the solace and peace faded.

"Thank you, all of you." Luci bowed slightly and graciously handed the mic away to the young woman behind Arden who just scoffed and mouthed something about not being able to follow him and he just winked at her. "Honey, you can do better than anybody in this room as long as you're having a good time. That's all that matters."

He came over to stand near Cassia, Arden, and me and shook his head with a slight smirk on his face. "Had to get him in here on karaoke night, huh?"

"Had to." Cassia pulled Luci into a hug that he happily returned and Arden joined them. "How're you doing, dear?"

"I'm good, still reeling a little but, it's just how life goes, isn't it?"

His chagrin wasn't lost on me and I had to speak up. "What happened, Luce?"

He cocked his head and the lopsided smirk grew to a grin. "Is that a nickname of a nickname? Loose?" His initial shock was gone and replaced by a warm smile. "I love it; thank you, Marcus. The ladies are a bit concerned over one of my most recent romantic debacles, and how I am taking it."

"We know you cared about him, Luci. You brought him here to see us." Arden crossed her arms as the man just eyed her with a knowing look. "That's important. This place is a haven for you and to bring anyone here is a huge sign."

Cassia nodded her head and I was a bit confused, because it seemed that she knew at least a little bit about relationships based on how upset she seemed on his behalf.

"He was just having an asshole streak. I'm over him." Luci assured them, his placating smile almost familiar. I noticed he wasn't wearing the same kind of clothes that he had been the other night. Gone were the dark tank top and fashionable shorts, replaced by a long sleeve t-shirt and jeans.

I played a hunch based on the way he was holding himself and touched his forearm. He winced and I knew, motioning him aside. The girls paused but didn't say anything as he joined me, the slow song that the woman on stage sang the perfect excuse to get close to someone.

I stood closer than would normally make two almost-strangers comfortable, and began to sway with him as if dancing, before I spoke softly enough that I hoped Arden and Cassia wouldn't be able to hear. "Why are you hiding the marks?"

To his credit, he didn't stop moving as he responded, "You know I hate lying. Them asking indirect questions makes it easier to omit the truth, but I despise it and hate myself for it all the same."

"Artfully avoiding answering the question too." I offered a contrite smile as he glared at me, then snickered and put his head down onto my shoulder. "What really happened, Luce? I know you don't know me, but you're important to two of my new friends and I would absolutely love to consider you a friend, so talk to me."

"I'm hiding them because while I don't like my whole reputation, I still need to maintain my level of power." He sighed and raised his head so that he could look at me. "The other part is because he's a Warden. And he should not have been able to hurt me like this."

"Like what?" I asked and his grip tightened on my waist.

"If I show you, the two of them will know something is wrong and try to go find him themselves." He whispered vehemently, "I cannot risk him doing this to them as well."

"Tell me what happened, Luce," I whispered again.

The song changed and he mouthed *later*.

The ladies joined us and he frowned apologetically. "I need to get back home and check on the doggies. I know, I know, I have demons who can handle that, but you know how Zenith can be if she doesn't have Daddy there to cuddle her before bed. She can be a real bitch."

He disappeared on his own and suddenly I was left alone, coughing on a cloud of sulfurous smoke, with two suspicious women.

Cassia is probing me for what was said. She is very adept at asking the right sort of questions. I would suggest telling her the truth.

"Let's go up to my room and I'll say what I can." I worked my way through the crowd at the bottom of the stairs and then up them and into my room. Arden and Cassia joined me and crossed their arms as they watched me. "What was his name?"

"Luci?" Arden asked and Cassia shook her head, grabbing her forearm. "Oh, his lover? His name is Varlin."

"And he's a Warden?" They both seemed surprised, then suspicious. I sighed and glanced at Cassia. "We need to fill her in, and then we need to take care of this asshole."

We spent a few minutes catching Arden up on what we had

found out earlier and she got stuck on the fact that my cat was something more now.

"Galaxy, could you join us?" Cassia asked finally, tired of Arden's confusion.

Fine. Galaxy stepped out of the ether and onto my shoulder, then hopped onto the bed and became the same voluptuous woman that she had been in the factory. "I think I will need to acquire clothing."

"Yes, you will," Arden whispered before looking at us in shock. "What the fuck is going on here?"

"We told you, they're making some kind of drug with mana." I wrapped Galaxy in my blanket and she seemed fine with that. "And I have reason to believe that Varlin is on the cut."

"Why is that?" Cassia frowned and gasped. "He was here for work is what Luci said, that's why he brought him in!"

"Lucifer!" Arden snarled, her eyes blazing. "You get your ass up here now!"

A plume of sulfurous smoke burst from the floor and Luci stood before us, fuzzy robe akimbo with his toothbrush in his mouth and a charcoal mask on his face. He blinked and sighed before looking at me pointedly. He snapped his fingers and the robe was replaced by a suit and tie, his toothbrush was gone, but the mask remained. "This had better be good, I don't have DVR down there and Lucifer is on. I love the shit out of Tom Ellis and he does a really damned good me."

"Tell us what the fuck happened between you and Varlin, now." Arden crossed her arms over her chest as her hair began to wave behind her head and rise over her shoulders.

"What did you tell them, Marcus?" He seethed, but I held my hands up. "I won't tolerate any lies."

"Not even ones of omission?" I asked pointedly and his chest deflated. "Look, Luce, they obviously love you and I think you're an awesome dude. I'm an Ellis fan as well; the guy has serious chops and I'm happy you like him too. I want you to be able to get back to your normal, but things are fucked here up top and we need your help to prove a theory. Help us out, please?"

"Fine." He sighed and ran his hands through his hair, then frowned at Galaxy. "Who's this?"

"She's a part of me." I said and his eyebrows raised. "Interesting, I know, but clock's ticking? You can trust her."

He looked her up and down and nodded. "Very well." He took a deep breath and began, "Varlin and I were out on a date, it was taco night downtown at that little food truck place—you know the one, Cass, the one that Kenshi likes?"

"Their pico is shit, but I love the carnitas!" Cassia agreed and waved for him to continue.

"He had kind of been dragging ass all night and I worried that it was something to do with work; they had called him just as we got in line and he said he'd be right back." Luci scrunched his nose and his eyes closed as if he were having trouble recalling something. "He came back about fifteen minutes later and was completely boosted, like he had just woken up from a three-day nap and had a gallon of espresso. He was jittery and acting oddly, so when I asked him about it, he got all paranoid. More than usual. Started accusing me of not trusting him and being stupid."

"Oh no." Arden shook her head. "Not that shit again."

"Yeah, so when I told him I was done, he grabbed me and used a spell on me." He pulled his sleeves up and there was a blackened handprint on his forearm the size of a large man's hand. "He's a nephilim, and shouldn't even be able to touch me with his power, but yet here it is—the hand of judgement."

"What does that do?" I asked as I stepped closer to look at it, then noticed that it smelled charred still, slightly.

"It's what it sounds like." His eyes closed and put the sleeve back over it. "It means I have been judged and found 'unworthy' and therefore have been marked by the nephilim so that he knows where I am at all times and can come to end me."

Galaxy, I know that you ate all that mana—does your power boost mean you can get rid of it?

She turned her head up toward me, then stood and closed the distance between her and Luci, the man frowning as she spoke. "Let me see that mark?"

Lucifer eyed me and I nodded once, Cassia mirroring me as Arden stepped closer curiously. As Luci bared the mark, Galaxy's hands reached forth and touched it, the devil grimacing in pain.

She lifted the mark toward her face and kissed it, then ran her tongue over it, almost too slowly. Where her mouth touched, the charred and blackened skin grew ashen and gray, the burns falling away onto the floor and her bare chest.

He hissed in pain, then groaned as the pained look on his face faded, able to relax now.

Galaxy's eyes flared and she leaned her head back as she inhaled deeply, the mark fading completely and she turned to Arden. "Would you like a blessing, jinn? I can give you the power Cassia and Marcus have. The power to change yourself and grow with me to an extent. Decide."

Cassia leaned forward and whispered something into Arden's ear and she stiffened. "Yes!"

Galaxy smiled and stepped forward, her hands cupping the woman's cheeks as she stared into her eyes. "Welcome to the fold, Arden." She leaned forward and kissed Arden directly on the lips, the jinn's eyes widening in surprise as an ethereal light fled Galaxy's lips and mouth into Arden's and down her throat. At the base of her neck, an ebony star flashed into view and stayed there, the light flooding into it.

"Nice ink," I muttered to Arden as she gasped. Galaxy sagged slightly and stood still. "You okay?"

"I will be fine; it took more out of me to make her mine than I thought it might." She eyed all of us and nodded to herself. "I will sit and let you continue, if you don't mind."

I nodded and she slumped onto the bed tiredly. "Is she going to be okay?" Luci started forward but the sound of something crashing downstairs drew all of our attention.

"Where is he?" someone roared below, making me frown but Lucifer looked downright mortified. "Lucifer!"

"Oh, hell no." Arden growled, taking steps toward the door, but I stopped her. "He has this coming, Marcus."

"He does, but let me go." I smiled at her sickly sweet before glancing at Luci. "He needs you both here right now, not me."

Cassia nodded to me once and I winked at her before walking down the stairs and into the crowd. "Step aside folks, lemme see if I can't figure out what's going on?"

People moved out of my way as a guy in a biker outfit stood in the doorway shouting, "Get out here, Lucifer!"

"Woah there, big'un." I chuckled and spread my hands to let him know I didn't mean any harm. "What's the problem? Why're you disturbing all these nice folks trying to have a good time? Pretty sure you're ruining Free Bird right now."

"Yeah!" someone shouted and the man snarled and stepped forward like he was expecting me to back down.

"I'm Warden Varlin, and one of my marks was here—where is that stupid bitch?" He leaned down and sniffed at me. "Where are you hiding him, Normie?"

"I don't know who you're talking about, but you need to go." I nodded to the guards around me, Kenshi and the others moving forward. I motioned to my face and glared at him so that he might catch my meaning.

"You're obstructing a Warden on official business, I could kill you for that." He spread his arms out beside him and I could smell the scent of ozone gathering around him. "Tell me where he is!"

"I don't think so." I shrugged nonchalantly and put my hands on my belt. "Seeing as you said he was a mark of yours and you don't know where he's at—you must be a shitty warden."

"Fuck off!" He leaned forward and I cast Physical Buff as I stepped aside, his arm lashing out to try to strike me. I grabbed his wrist and twisted it back behind his back.

"Kenshi!" My voice rang out as the nephilim's face came around. "Clock him!"

Kenshi rushed forward and his fist smashed into Varlin's nose so hard that his head rocked back, blood flowing from his nostrils. I put my foot between his legs and tripped him as he leaned forward, my weight forcing him forward so he hit his face on the floor. Kenshi stood him up with my help, the dazed half angel groggily peering around.

"Help me take him to my room?" Kenshi raised a brow at me, but shrugged as the patrons cheered.

"Let me buy you a drink, Marcus!" someone called and I just laughed, shaking my head.

"Maybe later!" I grinned and took the congratulatory pats on the shoulder and back as we pressed through the room. We grabbed a stool that was beside the stairs, and took him to my room.

Lucifer gasped loudly when we brought him into the room and sat him on the floor with the stool behind him as support.

Arden reached out and flaming chains crackled into existence around him, binding him to the stool tightly, lightly scorching the leather but not touching the wood.

"What on earth are you doing?" Luci grasped my arm tightly and pulled me close enough to whisper. "He's a Warden, assaulting one like this is against the law!"

"He attacked me and I defended myself inside the High Table. He's very easy to goad, you know that?" I chuckled to myself and dropped down next to him, perched on the balls of my feet. "Hey, wake up."

He stared at me blearily through the tears his likely-broken nose left in his eyes. I slapped him a couple times to get his attention and snap him out of it. Alert, he snarled at me, "I'll get you!"

"Yeah, yeah, and my little dog too—shut up." I started to look him over, not finding what I was looking for up near his neck and shoulder. "Cass, you wanna get rid of these sleeves? They look a little constraining and uncomfortable."

"With pleasure." Cassia grasped the wrist of his jacket and yanked, a sickening, wet pop preceding a feral yowl of pain and rage from Varlin; the sleeve had come off a little, but not completely. "Whoops."

She did not look sorry, but thankfully took more 'care' the next couple of times she jerked the leather from his shoulders.

I checked the insides of his elbows and didn't see anything there either, which was starting to make me think I could have been wrong about his involvement. There was one last place that I wasn't sure about that I wanted to check, and it would be gross.

"Cass, his boots and socks, if you please?"

She screwed up her face, but as soon as he started to kick at us, I knew we were on to something.

Once the hard leather boots were off and thrown aside, I groaned at the stink, grateful my senses weren't heightened. I returned and inspected his feet. "Wash your fucking feet, and change your goddamn socks, you disgusting thing. My doc would have a goddamn seizure if he saw—jackpot."

I stopped my rant at the deep purple markings and track marks on the upper portion of his foot and between his toes. "He's been injecting that mana stuff. That's why he was strong enough to hurt you, Luce. He's been juicing."

Arden leaned down and grimaced into Varlin's face. "Who's take are you on?"

"You know nothing about me, you stupid jinn bitch." A fist collided with his face and knocked three teeth out. I glanced left and saw a furious Lucifer, his visage of being a normal man gone completely and left behind was the most beautiful being I had ever seen.

He stood eight feet tall, his face fuller and more chiseled than before, perfect lips and a strong nose that he looked down at Varlin with crimson eyes. He flexed his back and ivory wings that could have been chiseled from stone spread wide, taking up the majority of my room.

His voice was so pleasant that I couldn't tell what it sounded like really. It was deep and high. Male and female. Grating and musical all at once. His voice was beautiful and horrifying, and his words held only malice. "I will not tolerate you abusing my friends."

To his credit, Varlin only sneered. "And what are you going to do about it?"

The Morningstar reached down and grabbed the nephilim by the front of his jacket and lifted him with barely any kind of effort registering in his face or body at all.

The fallen lord of hell leaned forward until he was close enough to breathe in his captive's face and whispered, "Miss my favorite show." He regarded us, then disappeared with a sound of wings beating and a play of shadows.

Galaxy broke the silence. "Where did they go?"

"I assume somewhere where Luce could get the information we want?" I glanced at the others who looked like they were a little jilted by his sudden departure. "Or to at least get his pound of flesh."

"Likely the latter," Uncle Yen stated flatly, standing with his arms crossed in my doorway. "I would normally ask if this is a good time to talk, but I can see that all of you are here with whom I assume to be the cat wrapped in a blanket there. Considering that I just saw Lucifer kidnap a Warden, I'm not sure if now is a good time."

"What's up, Uncle Yen?" I asked, frowning.

"I don't know if I should say in front of everyone, but we've made a little headway on the search to find out who or what that being in you is." He pointedly eyed Arden and Cassia as well as Galaxy. "I can come back, or you can come with me?"

"This elven woman is actually Galaxy, the being, and Arden and Cassia have been given a blessing from her and are now involved." I explained and he actually stepped into the room to check and gasped. "What?"

"I can see the magic linking them to her, and you." He reached out and grasped something in front of me, then tugged.

My stomach flopped a bit as Arden's neck was jerked closer. "You felt that?"

I blinked, turning to look over at Galaxy who appeared tense. "Yes, did you?"

"Yes." She stared at my uncle. "You should not be able to interact with my bond like that. Where did you come across your power?"

"Hard training and more than a little willingness to kill." He smiled back, almost as if that were a veiled threat that wasn't meant to be subtle. "As well as being ruthless when necessary."

I can respect that, but if he pulls on our bonds like that again, I will be forced to drain him. Galaxy blinked at me and smiled sweetly as several dozen thoughts ran through my head. All of them threatening to her. "It wouldn't kill him."

Uncle Yen stared at her and I sighed. "Don't touch our bonds again, please. It scares her."

"Good." He grinned, shutting the door before making several swift motions with his hands. "The room has been soundproofed, so nothing said in this room should leave here unless by one of us."

"Where's Anubis?" My suspicion was rewarded with a tense glare from my uncle and a careful glance at them and Galaxy. "He's still freaking out about her?"

"Rightfully so." He nodded and stared at Galaxy. "Have you begun to recall anything about yourself?"

"Some tidbits here and there, but nothing outside of being wrapped in a blanket of stars for several thousand years before the beginning." Galaxy spoke honestly from what I could feel from her.

"That lines up." Uncle Yen sighed heavily and leaned up against the doorframe, his hands rubbing his exhausted face before going up through his hair. As I observed him, I saw a bit of his own aura, gray and light that was taller, broader than what he was currently.

You have the right of it—he is more than he seems and lets on,

Galaxy warned, catching my gaze before looking back at my uncle. "With what?"

He turned a baleful gaze on her and said, "Our theory that you might be a primordial god of some flavor, and that your rebirth could be much larger than what we thought."

She stared at him, thinking, then frowned. "I don't remember that far. All I can gather is a comfort in the void with the stars and their vacuum. Then I remember snippets of my first followers and how things were done with the other gods I knew… I can see their faces but they have no names to me."

"That supports it too, but I can't find anything on any ancient pantheons, or that your reawakening doesn't spell some kind of galactic doom." He scratched his chin, a little bit of stubble on it from lack of shaving it seemed, and yawned. "Blessing three of the more important people in my life is… worrying. We don't know what you're capable of or what you are, but it seems that they trust you?"

"She hasn't steered me wrong yet—says some troubling shit at times, but not too bad." Galaxy gave me a soft smile, and winked in my direction as she looked to the others. "As to Arden and Cassia, I don't think she's really had any time to fool them or to lie either."

"She has been genuinely helpful to me," Cass stated with a smile. "And I basically get to live an RPG now, so there's that."

"I want that too," Arden blurted, looking worried. "Sorry, I just love gaming so much and the thought of being able to grow and become stronger differently is just so amazing that I had to jump at the chance. She looks weird, but we all do and I'm not going to judge an amnesiac."

Galaxy snorted, raising an eyebrow in uncertainty. "Thank you?"

Arden just held up her thumbs and grinned. "Let me watch you level up, Cass!"

They huddled together as my uncle began to laugh and shake his head. "You kids and your damned video games."

"Don't you talk shit, Yenny," Cassia growled. "I've seen you gaming before. Elder Scrolls, Modern Warfare, and the like—I know you like hunting zombies."

He blanched and looked at me as I regarded him curiously. "Shut up!" Cassia just waved him away and I stepped closer to him. "What's up, kiddo? I'm pretty bushed."

"I wanted to know what you did before, how you control your magic and how you learned your spells. Like the one you used to calm everyone when those Fae came in?"

He stilled and stared at me hard. "I can't teach you that kind of magic because it comes with being the boss of a High Table. It's… a perk of the position. That's all I can say about that." He frowned and pulled me closer to him. "If you want to learn some magic, I can get you books and whatnot that you can use to study, but you have to promise me you won't use it in the bar. Can't have you casting a fireball into the patrons, can we?"

We shared a laugh over that as he pulled me into a hug, muttering, "Mind the cat, Marcus. I don't like how she can't remember much. Could make her dangerous."

"I'll be careful, Uncle Yen," I promised and he patted my cheek affectionately before wandering into the hall and toward his room.

"Marcus!" Arden bellowed and I flinched, turning to find her staring at me. "You can cast spells?"

"I can?" I raised a questioning eyebrow back at her and she clapped in giddy delight.

"Cast a spell for me!" she ordered and watched me excitedly. "Come on, please?"

"Why?" I frowned at how insistent she was being and eyed her.

"Because the very thought of your kind of magic is hysterical to her." Galaxy snickered, making Arden freeze. "Yes, I can read your thoughts and emotions."

She crossed her arms and scowled. "That seems invasive."

"We have the ability to level up and gain power unheard of in who knows how long." Cassia looked at Arden as if she were losing her marbles in front of her. "I'd sell what little soul I have for this gift. She can know what I think—I'd say as much without having to be told what I'm thinking and feeling."

"Do you want to level up?" I looked over at her and Cassia, the latter nodding wildly.

"I want to see you use magic!" Arden growled impetuously with her arms crossed.

"Fine!" I sighed and motioned for them to follow me. "Let's go to one of the rooms in the gym."

CHAPTER ELEVEN

Once we fought our way through the crowd with polite words and promises to return, we made our way into the gym, then found an empty sparring chamber.

"Let's see this magic!" Arden clapped her hands and rubbed them together as she watched me excitedly.

"I'm still only a low level, so please don't make fun of me too much?" She just grinned at me and made a motion to hurry. "Okay."

I cast Wisp, a ball of bright flame appearing in my hand. It was warm, but not too hot for me to handle.

"Oh my God, it's so cute!" Arden gushing over the small flames in my hand made me more than a little uncomfortable. "Throw it at me!"

I glanced at Cassia who shrugged. "I wasn't there for the time she met Yenny, but from what I heard, he cast spells at her until he passed out so… This is all on you guys. I'm going to look at my stats."

I shrugged and turned back to Arden, who looked ready to tackle me if I didn't throw the spell, so I lobbed it at her.

She cackled loudly as the wisp of a flame flew in her direction, catching it deftly and holding it like it was precious. "Oh, it's just a wittle baby flame! Look at it burn so cute!"

"You know that's more than a little disconcerting, right?" I glared at her as she tossed my spell around in her hands like it was a tiny bouncy ball and her the kid with a new toy.

"It's just so adorable, Marcus!" She stopped tossing it about and held it in her left hand, her right hand spreading wide, a ball of flame forming there. It looked like a t-ball by the time she stopped and flexed her fingers. "See, I'm a jinn of flame; my kind are a little more rare than other jinn are, and seeing you use fire like this is just—sorry to say it, but it's cute."

The flame in her right hand blazed and boiled over growing and growing. "The flames in this world are just so much weaker than home. Your flame is nice, warm and all. But against a creature like me, this is like being home."

"Then teach me how to make my flames hotter," I challenged her and she quirked her head. "Come on, throw it, let's see how it works."

She stared at me for a moment before looking at Cassia who wasn't paying attention to us, then shrugged. "Alright."

She pushed her arm forward and the flames rocketed toward me. *Let's hope this works, Galaxy!*

A hunger worked through me as I set my feet and instinct took over. Fire with fire.

I cast Wisp at the flames, the speed they flew at me diminishing a little but not enough to keep me on my feet. The blast caught me in the arms and chest, flinging me across the room with a grunt that sounded like a death knell to me.

"Marcus!" Arden called, worried, but the burns on my arms were already healing, though they itched like hell.

"What the fuck was that?" Cassia roared, stomping over to us, her eyes narrowed. "Arden, are you trying to fight my boyfriend?"

"Boyfriend?" Arden looked between us in confusion, then realization dawned on her. "Is that why you two had been spending so much time together?" She glanced down at me and shook her head. "You work fast, and you *survived* it?"

I snorted. "Fucking barely."

Cassia actually laughed at that and helped me to my feet.

Jinn Flame – Devoured – Path of spell growth unlocked.

You have other notifications, by the way, did you want to see them?

I shrugged, and mentally assented.

Oni Blood – A brackish green liquid that confers a small bonus to Physique. +2 Physique.

"Oh, that's cool." I grinned then looked at the next one.

Lycanthropic Curse – Bolstered – Slight allergy to silver developed.

"You gotta be shitting me—Galaxy, is this for real?" My anger caught Cassia by surprise, making her look up from her screen in confusion. "Drinking too much lycan blood gave me a 'slight' silver allergy."

There cannot only be beneficial effects every time, Galaxy advised coolly in reply. *How would that be balanced?*

"Is the point of a game to be OP as shit?" Arden raised an eyebrow. "Are you going to give us debuffs too? Can you warn us when there's too much of a good thing so we can avoid the bad things?"

I can try to, but that is more a thing for you to think on.

I waited for her to continue.

Silence stretched for a time before she sighed and stated, *Even I do not know when it will happen. There is something that binds a balance of sorts to my blessings. If good may come, is it not worth the risk to receive slight discomfort from an unlikely metal?*

"She does have a point," Cassia muttered and finally smiled winningly. "I've done it, I put three points into Mana."

"So how much do you have?" I asked and scratched my head.

"Five." She replied proudly with her chin tilting up. "You?"

"Twelve." Her mouth fell open before she crossed her arms

at me and I held my hands up and open. "Hey, sorry about that. I didn't know it was that high, is it?"

"Not at all." Arden snickered. "Mine is twenty-two."

"Woof." I rubbed my head, and grimaced. "Speaking of, can you teach me magic? Am I even capable of learning spells in a truer sense of the practice, Galaxy?"

I could burn mana routes for you and have you learn to harness it and manipulate it the way that the Touched do—the way Arden does naturally. She seemed pensive for a second and I could see her in me frowning. *Unless, of course, Arden would like to make a donation of some kind to you?*

Arden froze and looked over to us. "What kind of donation?"

A bodily one. Galaxy purred within me, her meaning not lost on me.

"You want her to donate blood to me?" I shook my head. "I can't ask for that—besides you just said it was like a lottery of sorts. Some good, some bad?"

Yes, but I'm not talking merely about her blood. She stepped out of the shadows at my feet in her elven form. "I'm talking about letting me rummage through her body for a moment."

"Rummage!" Arden gasped, her hand flying to her chest. "You act as if you would be sliding a hand inside me to root around and find treasure."

Galaxy smiled. "I would be." Arden gasped again, then Galaxy spread her hands before her in a placating gesture. "You can refuse me, as it will be painful and uncomfortable."

"What do I get if I do allow you to do this?" Arden frowned deeply, distrustfully.

"I can figure out how you grow and manipulate mana so that I can offer you different abilities and spells." Galaxy lifted a hand like she was offering something, then the other. "I could even mimic your mana manipulation in others, so that your friends could benefit more fully from it as well."

Arden glared at the elven woman who watched her evenly. "Try to make it less painful?"

Galaxy stepped forward and rested her hand on Arden's chest, smiling. "Only because I'm starting to like you." She closed her eyes. "Can you bring your mana into your chest? Just under my hand."

Galaxy's breathing matched Arden's and soon both of them began to relax more and more. As she focused, the elven woman led Arden through what to do and in a flash of light was gone. Arden grunted as a figure of a spectral cat floated along her skin, up her shoulder and down her back. Arden grabbed her stomach and looked down, grasping the cloth there and ripping it up to reveal her abs. The cat faded into her belly button and she gasped. "I *am* using my mana, but it's not acting right with you in me!"

It was another heartbeat before Arden grunted and roared, "Fine."

Cupping her hands together in front of her abdomen, a ball of flame guttered into life just above them and grew steadily as she breathed as raggedly as she could.

"Galaxy, get the hell out of her," I snarled, my eyes catching Cassia's as the oni surged forward to try to keep Arden standing up right.

I'm not done and she is surprisingly resilient. She is fine.

Sweat began to pour from Arden's forehead and neck, her face a grimace of concentration and pain.

I walked over and began to look over Arden, trying to figure out where the cat was, when the flames in her hand grew to the size of a basketball and she screamed loudly.

I grabbed her waist and started to really look for her, shouting, "Galaxy!"

Almost done! she spat back, and I could just make out an outline on Arden's forearm.

I grabbed her elbows to keep her steady and watched as the tattoo-like marking of Galaxy padded down into her wrist and then disappeared briefly before Arden screeched again, her flames burning brighter.

Cat Galaxy appeared in the middle of the sun-like ball of

flames and seemed unperturbed, opening her mouth and devouring the magic in lunging bites. I reached into the magic and grabbed her by the scruff of the neck as Arden's legs gave out, pulling her from the flames and getting burnt in the process.

I could see the muscles and sinew under my flesh by the time I had her out and away from my friend, smelling the extremely burnt and charred meat. The pain was enough that I should have passed out from it, but I didn't.

"You're learning." The smile I heard in Galaxy's tone of voice irked me and I turned to glare at her. "She will be fine in a moment. The magic I ate before you interrupted me was to give back to her—so I do wish you hadn't been so proactive and intrusive."

"Intrusive?" I roared, standing up to my full height. "You literally just took a fucking jaunt through her entire being and you call *me* intrusive?"

"I realize that you are upset and that you feel I betrayed her in some manner, but I didn't." Galaxy lifted her hand and stood from where she had been sprawled out. She walked over and laid a hand on Arden's shoulder and her hard breathing eased noticeably. "I shielded her from as much as I could, and I only worked on getting the main passageways while adding some for her."

I frowned, glaring at her because I wasn't sure if I wanted to believe her or not. She had basically abandoned us in that fight to go devour all that mana, and now this?

Could it be that as a primordial being you aren't too used to what it means to be gentle? The thought had occurred to me before, but it was still forming. *Do you not know what it means to give with nothing coming to you in return?*

Galaxy turned and stared deep into my eyes, a tear forming in hers. *I rely on you for protection. I rely on you for sustenance in a world I don't understand and have no current place in. I give you the ability to protect yourself and have things you otherwise would never have experienced.*

She stooped and touched Cassia's face, the oni woman

gasping and bursting into her natural oni form before stiffening and convulsing slightly.

Galaxy stood up and stepped toward me, one step at a time until she stood no more than a mere few inches away from me and whispered, "I know intimately what it is like to give and not get anything back. I don't even know who I am, but you can make demands about learning magic? Doing everything for you? Having seen everything you have up to now—do you not realize the depths of the gift I have given to you?"

She looked back at Cassia, Arden having sat up on her own and started to look after the other woman as she still recovered herself. "Having witnessed the power and abilities of the creatures you once thought fairytales, have you not yet learned how hopelessly out of your element you would be if not for me?" She reached up and touched my cheek, her touch soft and gentle as her palm cradled my face. "Imagine being that weak and not knowing anything about yourself.

"Imagine knowing nothing for unknown thousands of years and then seeing light and jumping at it, only to realize that you're too weak even to use your own voice." She put her wrists to her forehead, then they fell away so she could stare at me coldly. "Imagine taking all the mana from the world around you that you can and using it to fill the one person you hope can handle knowing that you exist, and them not being able to at least trust that you will give them anything just to avoid going back into the darkness."

She leaned forward and touched her forehead to mine, tears plopping onto my chest and slowly-healing arm as she whispered, "And yet still, I give."

She looked up into my eyes, hurt and concern weighing equally in her gaze as she leaned close enough to kiss my mouth. Her lips touched mine and power surged through me and slammed into my mind hard enough to give me a migraine that no Motrin would ever eat away at.

Blinking, I now knew how to create the pathways to control my mana and manipulate it. Galaxy no longer stood in front of me and instead I stood alone in the room with Cassia and Arden watching us, me.

"That was a lot." Arden's voice was somber as she sat cross-legged on the ground and stared up at me. "I could feel how much that sucked for her." She rubbed the back of her neck and gasped. "What's going on?" She looked down at her hands and a screen flickered into existence. "This is so weird."

"What? Is everything okay?" I wondered, still rooted to my spot and unable to bring myself to move.

Arden's right hand came to her mouth as a tear slid down her cheek, Cassia grasping her shoulder tiredly to ask, "What's wrong?"

"Nothing's wrong!" Arden cried, her shoulders shaking as tears continued to fall. "I was always treated differently by the other jinn for being a fire jinn and now I can grow and use other elements. The gift she gave me is beautiful."

"What did she give you, Cass?" My voice was a little more timid than I had wanted it to be. Maybe I was the asshole?

"She gave me the pathways that Arden has so that I can draw in mana and use it like a mage." She smiled and touched her horn and grinned. "I can use magic now, and I still have my horn."

"What does that mean?" I raised an eyebrow at her and finally my legs could move.

"Oni mages are rare, and those who pursue magic have to give up their horn to do so." Arden sniffled and wiped her face with her arm. "The fact that she gets to keep it means that other oni will still recognize her as a warrior and as a mage. It means she can stay with her family."

"What if you had to give up your horn?" I trudged toward them and she shrugged. "You don't know?"

"I hoped that I wouldn't if I could grow the way you could." She smiled and sighed in relief. "I could tell that she was hurt too. For being a warrior, you don't really read a room very well at times, Marcus."

I laughed despite how shitty I felt. "I can imagine that I don't. Can you forgive me?"

Arden just rolled her eyes and shook her head. "Dumbass."

Cassia grabbed my shoulder. "It's not our forgiveness you need, Marcus. Go talk to her and apologize, properly."

"I'm going to be completely honest here—I don't know how." They both stared at me with open confusion. "She can feel and know everything I'm thinking. And I have no clue about her."

"She literally just said everything, Marcus." Arden smacked me on the shoulder, my still healing arm stinging from the sudden motion. "Figure it the hell out."

Cassia pulled my head forward and touched her horn to my forehead. "You are handsome, Marcus Massacre, but you are also a little thick in the head. For someone with no horn? This is impressive."

Arden snorted and Cassia shoved me toward the door. "Call me later, if you can. There are things I need to do tonight so we will have to fight another time, but I would love to spend some time with you tomorrow."

"It's a date." I kissed her shoulder on my way by and made my way toward the door.

I heard a heavy smacking sound and turned to see Arden smacking the hell out of the larger woman's shoulder. "I cannot believe you didn't tell me you two were dating! Give me the details, woman!"

Cassia lifted Arden up over her head like a barrel and grunted as she threw her bodily away, before acquiescing with an, "Okay!"

I shook my head and made my way out of the gym, then through the High Table and up to my room. It only took me about twenty minutes and several promises to drink with people I vaguely recalled from my two shifts, but I made it.

I found Galaxy in her cat form staring at a paused game screen, just sitting there on the floor. I closed the door and sat on the bed. "I'm sorry."

She stayed quiet and just listened, so I continued. "It's difficult to say anything about it that won't sound like I'm trying to offer an excuse for what I said and my rampant thoughts, so I won't. I do know that without you, I wouldn't be able to do any of what I did. I would be at the mercy of creatures untold, and the thought of that makes my skin crawl."

She finally turned her head to glance my way, not fully looking at me, but just enough that I could see one of her eyes in the dim light.

"It's like you said, you don't know anything and neither do I." I sighed, more to myself and at how hopelessly ignorant I was in all of this. I truly had no idea what I was doing. "So, if you can still stand it, I would like to be your partner. You and me, me and you. Galaxy and Marcus—team. What do you say?"

She turned and stared at me for what could have been an eternity, before finally speaking, *I can tell you mean that.*

"Of course I do." I smiled at her. "Look, you're a primordial god—might be one, at least—and I am irresponsibly out of my element here. If anyone needed a friend more than you right now, it'd be me. And you just gave Cassia and Arden the very things they wanted most and have taken… what? A little energy? I don't know about any of this, but my ignorance isn't your fault. It's mine."

She watched me some more and finally I said, "If you can forgive me for being an ignorant dick, we can see if Cassia will let you borrow some clothes and we will go shopping for you tomorrow."

She shifted into her elven form and actually smiled at me, laughing a little bit as she stood up and closed the distance between us to sit down and offer her hand to me as the bed moved. "Partners. Marcus and Galaxy. No more distrust, no more hiding anything if we can help it."

I grasped her hand and shook it. "Open communication."

"Yes." She nodded slowly, taking a deep breath. "I've been thinking."

"I can imagine you have been. What about?"

"You and I have been together for months, and I wanted to try something." I froze, and she instantly took my hand. "Not that."

I sighed in relief and she squeezed my hand. "I want to sleep with you."

I pulled my hand out of hers and growled. "You literally just said that wasn't what you wanted!"

She eyed me flatly and retorted, "I've been inside you, Marcus."

"If Arden or Cassia—or any of my Marines—heard that, I'd be wading up to my waist in asses from all the ones I'd have to kick for the misunderstandings about what you just said." I sighed and rubbed my head exasperatedly.

"Would you just relax?" She snorted and giggled as she stared into my eyes. "Sleeping inside you is a level of close, but it's like being where I was before you found me."

"So you want to… What? Sleep with me in the bed?" She nodded and I scratched my head.

"I do not think it would be a problem with Cassia, but we can call her if you would like?" She seemed really hopeful.

"Uh, sure?" I raised an eyebrow at her and pulled my cell out to call my girlfriend.

She answered after the fourth ring, breathing heavily. "Yes. Marcus?"

"Hey, Cass, Galaxy and I made up but she had a request." I watched as the woman held her hand out for the phone but I motioned that she wait. "I think she wants to ask you herself?"

"Oh, that's good, I'm glad. I'm still with Arden working something out and filling her in but yeah, put her on."

I blinked and shrugged before giving the phone to Galaxy; she stared at the device for a second, then put it to her face the way I had and spoke into it as if she was uncertain. "Cassia?" I heard the oni respond on the other end and Galaxy relaxed a tad and continued speaking, "I wanted to request permission to sleep with Marcus."

There was a pause, then she nodded—remembered she couldn't be seen and stated, "Yes, I understand." She grunted and nodded again before saying, "We also made a deal that if I would forgive him, he would request that you join us to go shopping for clothes for me tomorrow?"

There was a pause and the phone fell silent, I heard a shout on the other end and then Galaxy looked at me in surprise. "I do believe she's hung up." She handed me the phone and pointed at it. "Summon her again."

"You do know that's not what happens with this, right?" I raised an eyebrow at her and fought a snort. Someone knocked loudly on the door and I got up off the bed. "Who could that be?"

I opened the door to find a bloodied Arden standing in the doorway, breathing heavily. A gash on her forehead made my eyes widen. "Arden, what the fuck is going on?"

"I attacked her while she was distracted—we'll come shopping tomorrow." She grimaced and grabbed her shirt and held it up. "I hate it when she starts fights to make sure that I'm okay!"

Just as quickly as she had appeared in front of my door, she was gone and I was staring at an empty hall. "Huh." I turned back to Galaxy and narrowed my eyes. "What did Cassia say to you?"

"She said that sleeping was fine, and that group sleeping was a thing that the oni liked, so she understood." She smiled at me slyly and added, "She also asked that I refrain from fighting with you."

"Oh my God, that woman," I cried exasperatedly and closed my door, locked it, and went to my dresser. I dug out a pair of shorts and a t-shirt that I wore to workout in and tossed them to her.

"What are these for?" She looked at them as if betrayed.

"To sleep in." I grabbed my clothes and went to the bathroom to change.

I came out and she was wearing them, but seemed disgruntled. "What?"

"You sleep nude all the time, why change now?" She looked kind of adorable in the outfit, the shirt down to her thighs and the shorts peeking out. They were silkies, they did that.

"Because I don't want to fight you?" I laughed and she just rolled her eyes at me. "Now, how do you prefer to sleep?"

She bid me lay down and I did so. She turned off the light and her eyes glowed in the darkness as she watched me.

"What's with that?"

"Benefits of power." Her voice was low as she leaned over me. She climbed into the bed closest to the wall and cuddled up against me, her head in the crook of my arm, her arm resting on my stomach and her hand on my chest. "So this is what it feels like?"

Basking in the warmth that radiated from her was… different. She was comforting like a blanket, and as I raised the blanket on the bed over the two of us, she cuddled closer.

I wrapped my arm around her protectively and felt called to whisper, "You'll not be alone again if I can help it."

"Thank you," she whispered softly against my shirt and soon she was snoring softly. The night air in the room was cool enough that I fell asleep shortly after.

CHAPTER TWELVE

I woke up to the blankets over us being pulled away, and someone scooping me into their arms. "Woah!"

I looked up to find Cassia smiling down at me. "Good morning, Marcus."

"Good morning!" I greeted her, adrenaline still pumping through my body. "What's going on?"

"We came to get you when you didn't answer your phone." Arden grinned at me, then searched the bed. "Where is Galaxy?"

"I'm in here." She came out holding my toothbrush and glared at it. "I tried brushing my teeth with this, but the chemical paste was… gross."

"Toothpaste is generally disgusting, but why did you use my toothbrush?" Cassia put me down and I collected my toothbrush from her. "Well, your toothbrush now."

"We inhabit the same body, brushing our fangs is not something that we should skip." She put the toothbrush in her mouth and smiled at me, her incisors sharp like a cat's would be.

"This inhabiting the same body is cool and all, but we're still two very different beings," I replied and threw my hands up. Cassia grabbed my waist and pulled me toward her, leaning down to press her head against the back of mine. "Hello again. Feeling affectionate this morning?"

"Yes, Arden is capable of defending herself adequately and I want to fight you." I blushed at that and turned toward her. "What's wrong?"

"We really need to figure out a code word for that. I never know what kind of fight you mean."

She frowned and looked pensive before leaning down close enough that I caught a full whiff of her shampoo and whispered, "I really can't wait until it's just the two of us so we can fight." I was about to protest her using that same word, but her grabbing a handful of my rump was enough to give me a better idea. "Better?"

I nodded wildly. "Yup!"

"He's excited," Galaxy called from the bathroom, and Arden turned to catch both of us in the act.

"Can you not wait until I leave the damned room? You just started dating, and it's to this level already?" She rolled her eyes and huffed. "Maybe I should skip this and go see Masonai?"

Cassia growled and pulled me closer to her, her arms folding over my chest. "Maybe you should." She leaned down and kissed my neck, and I could see that her eyes were locked on the jinn. "Maybe then you would be less stuck up about affection."

"It's public displays of it that bother me, and only when I know the people, and work with both," Arden shot back as the bathroom door opened a bit.

"It's not public in this room, it's private." Galaxy smiled and crossed the room to stand between Arden and us. "I can feel everything he does, and I can tell you he wishes things were even more private than they are."

I sighed and rolled my eyes. "Tell them how I really feel, why don't you?"

She turned and looked at me with a mischievous glimmer in her eyes, "You sure?" I went to say for her not to but she turned back to Arden. "He would happily do many things to all the women in this room. I write that off as him being a healthy and virile man who acts his age, but he denies himself those advances because he's in a relationship. He finds both of you wildly attractive, and isn't sure how to feel about me. Am I a separate entity? Am I a part of him? Am I both? Now he's embarrassed and wants to strangle me but won't because he feels bad for hurting me last night."

My mouth opened and fell and stayed there while she looked back at Arden. "Do these look okay on me?"

She wore a simple crop top of white and green, the short-shorts she wore hugging her waist and hips tightly, but not obscenely.

"Yeah," Arden answered and blinked at her. "Did you mean all that?"

Galaxy nodded and looked at me. "He wishes he could melt into the floor for thinking my butt looks great in these."

"Why are you so frivolous with the inner workings of my mind, Galaxy!" I roared, concerned that I was about to get my ass kicked.

Cassia's grip tightened and she kissed my cheek. "It's okay to think these things, I won't be upset." I frowned and she let go of me, putting a hand on my shoulder. "I think many men and women are attractive, Arden among them. Don't feel bad. Even Galaxy too. If she wasn't so weak right now, I would want to fight her too."

Galaxy grinned widely. "Thank you."

Cassia nodded and looked over my shoulder at Arden. "Does this information bother you? You told me just last night that the first time you saw him, he hit his toe on a stool because he couldn't look away from you."

Arden blushed a bit and looked away. "It's one thing to think it because he's watching like a normal man. But hearing it from someone who lives inside him is wholly different."

GALAXY

"She's not against the idea and is rather flattered," Galaxy interjected quickly, making me and Cass laugh as Arden stammered. "Can we go now? I would like to be able to research today."

We laughed our way out of my room, leaving our clothes on the floor for Seamus to take care of. This time, I would remember the sweets for him.

On our way out, I found a note from Uncle Yen.

Marcus,

Last night, more than a few of our patrons liked the show so much that they wanted to leave you a little present for taking care of a rather nasty "asshole" as they put it. This is for you.

Be careful, boy.

Uncle Yen.

Under the note I found an envelope with a stack of cash in it thicker than any I had ever seen in my life, and several notes of gratitude that requested drinks with me later on tonight. Arden and Cassia both laughed at that and agreed we would have a night to drink and celebrate.

As we were about to head out the front door, we stopped and I turned to Galaxy. "Can you take a more human form?"

She looked down at herself and frowned. "I suppose I do have to make an effort to hide myself, don't I?"

She closed her eyes, and the stars and galaxies across her skin faded and her skin turned less purple, becoming a more common darker shade. She kept focusing until she looked like a dark-skinned woman in her late twenties. Honestly, the only difference to her face was that she looked like she had small and normal-looking ears. Even in her human form, she was beautiful and alluring.

"Is this okay?" We all nodded and she smiled. "Let's go!"

We all piled into Cassia's SUV and she took us to the mall, where we found our way into one of the larger department stores and shopped about a bit. I found some cute pajamas that I thought would look good for her and put them into the cart we shared for the haul and went back out to search.

It took a little bit for all of us to decide on things for her to wear, things that would look good with her human skin tone and her normal skin tone. Once we had found enough for her, we found some more clothes for me and got her some shoes before opting to go get something to eat at the food court. This time, I made sure to get Seamus some buckeyes, little balls of chocolate and peanut butter, as well as some actual brownies. Arden approved.

We all got some Chinese food, Cassia complaining vividly about how the original food was so much better and she missed hand-made ramen from Osaka. "Wait, are you originally from Japan?"

She frowned at me. "Of course I am." She laughed and waved a hand in front of me. "Wait, is that question because I look like your average American woman? Like Caucasian and the like?"

I nodded and she just snickered at me. "Being Japanese in a city like this about a century back would have drawn a target on my back, and my family's as being outsiders. So we chose to look like this instead. I can change my human form without an issue, though. Would you like to see what Japanese Cassia looks like?"

I laughed and shook my head. "I was just curious. Though that does beg the question—do you ever get homesick?"

She nodded excitedly. "Arden and I were actually planning a trip to Akihabara in Tokyo later this year to go shopping and visit some of my family who stayed behind."

Arden clapped her hands and smiled dreamily. "Ah, the promised land of we weebs and nerds. What I wouldn't give to just be able to go now. I'm going to have a massive library when I come back. All the manga and anime I need to collect. Ugh."

I couldn't help laughing at that, Galaxy joining me because she thought it was funny too. Though, through the bond we had developing, I could tell she wanted to go too, for much the same reasons.

Maybe we can sit down tonight and watch some anime on TV so you can become accustomed?

She turned to me and her smile brightened before she nodded.

We continued our meal in amicable conversation for another ten minutes before someone shouting about something caught our attention.

I turned to see a younger man, probably just having turned twenty-one or so, trying to talk to a young woman at one of the tables across the large dining area from us.

Thinking little of it, I took it as he was trying to get her to talk to him and she was pissed off about it, no big deal. The way she was laying into him led me to believe she could handle her own and no knight need come charging in to rescue her.

But as I stared, a massive aura reared up around her, easily twenty-feet tall, while she started to stand and glare at him. "Oh shit, this isn't good."

"What? She's got it." Cassia shrugged, then turned back to her meal.

"What's wrong, Marcus?" Arden looked over just in time to watch her pick up the heavy stone table she had been sitting at and throw it at the young man. "Oh no!"

People panicked and began to scream, some pulling out phones to record as they left.

"Arden, try to get the Normies out!" Cassia grunted and shoved me aside so she had a clear shot at the woman who had begun to grow where she was. "Marcus, let's go see if we can't get her calmed down."

"Yup!" I took a swig of my sweet tea and shot forward as fast as my legs and maneuver under fire skills would let me. Dodging chairs and benches that were tossed aside as the massive beast of a woman, or giant… whatever the hell it was decided to wade through the area toward the new threats like a predator.

I grimaced and grabbed Cassia's wrist, her attention diverting to me. "What?"

"Throw me at her," I stated and held my hand out.

"What the hell are you talking about?" We were about thirty feet away and the massive creature had just picked up a stone bench to throw.

"Fucking throw me at her head!" I ordered and the oni grasped my arm and whipped me toward the giant just as the chair sailed out of her fingertips.

Cassia shouted something, but all I heard were bells in my head as the giant's hand whacked my upper body. I cast Embodiment and avoided the majority of the damage by bouncing off her palm and landing painfully on a knee twelve feet from her.

I cast Bolt at her knee and that just made her angrier as she switched gears and lurched toward me.

Flames burst against her head. The one eye that I could see under the thickly matted red hair scanning the room until she found whatever it was that had pissed her off. She roared as she started toward it.

I glanced over my shoulder to find the same man that she had thrown the table at, bleeding and holding his ribs as he muttered and motioned with her bearing down on him.

A red streak pushed by me and Arden stood there, flames geysering from her hands like she was some kind of magnificent war caster. The flames got the giant's attention long enough for the guy to finish what he was doing, his hands flickering blue, then a cage of sorts exploded from his palms and shot toward the giant while she tried to fend off the flames shooting at her head.

The cage wrapped around the massive creature and she froze and shrank more and more as my heart pounded and I closed in on her and the man.

He limped toward us. "Your interference wasn't warranted, but is appreciated, thank you." His mouth and head were bleeding but as I watched people beginning to gather round and take out phones, he reached into his pocket and pulled out a single blue bead. "One moment."

He stepped forward and threw the bead into the air where it detonated and sprinkles of magic flew across the air toward everyone. "What you all have witnessed just now is a terrorist attack by someone who wished the news media would be fooled, and the American public made a mockery of. Sharing anything like this will make you look simple, and you're better than that. We got him, and he's going away for a very long time."

After he stopped speaking, people began to clap loudly, whistling. Someone even broke into a chant of, "U S A, U S A!"

I glanced over at Arden and Cassia who shrugged as the guy grabbed the cage and pulled it behind him. I stepped closer. "Hey, buddy, what're you going to do with her?"

He didn't so much as pause before replying, "I'm going to take her in for questioning in my partner's disappearance. Again, thanks for the assistance, but I have it from here."

Arden stepped forward and whispered, "She had the same kind of purple marks on her that Varlin did."

"Stop, kid," I ordered and he just kept moving, so I stepped forward and grabbed his arm. "I said stop."

He turned and touched a hand to my hip and electricity jolted through my body similar to what I could imagine my Bolt spell must have felt like.

It brought me to a knee, stiffening my muscles and making me seethe, but he just turned and spoke in a low tone, "Listen, you may feel entitled to some kind of compensation or more gratitude than you think you're owed—I don't care. This is official Warden business and continued interference with that business will get you hurt."

"We know what happened to your partner," Cassia stated and the kid paused to look at her distrustfully. He pressed something on the cage and it shrank down completely, his hand and the object going into his pocket before he took it back out. "We can tell you more once we get out of here. You have a ride?"

"Where are you planning to go?" He crossed his arms and eyed us all once more. "An oni, a jinn, and a rogue Touched? Has to be that bloody hole in the wall."

"The High Table is a classy joint, fuckhead." Arden sneered openly and crossed her arms. "And you'd better recognize that."

"If it wasn't for the fact that I was looking for my partner, freaks like you would be locked away in an instant for obstruction—you sure this is a road you want to go down with me?" He leered at her and decided that she must have wised up before looking at Cass. "Where is my partner? I'm not going to that monster-mash hellhole you call a bar without backup."

"Fuck this kid." I grunted, finally able to stand on my own. "He's obviously got a handle on it, right?"

Everyone seemed surprised but I just shrugged. "Yeah, he's a boot who thinks he's got it all under control and shit's flying off the rails all around him." They continued to stare when it dawned on me that I was the only one who seemed to get it. "He's not even really a Warden, is he?"

"What?" Cassia spat and glared at him.

"It all makes sense." I continued and motioned to him. "Sure, he has the look and can talk the talk, but if you know what to look for, you can spot glaring holes in his authority. 'Warden business'? Please. It might be, but you aren't a Warden, are you, kid?"

He just glared at me hatefully and I leaned forward. "Come on, say it. Tell us what you really are, boot."

He grumbled something that I couldn't hear as he looked away and I leaned closer. "What was that? I didn't quite catch it."

He turned and started to shout, "I said!" He realized that people were still close by and lowered his tone to a growl. "I said I'm a trainee."

"Ah, there it is." I motioned that we should all start walking because people had begun to gravitate toward us. "So, I can imagine, being the naïve little boot you are, you probably didn't tell anyone that your trainer was missing and decided to investigate on your own?" When the kid did nothing more than scowl at me, I snickered. "No matter where you go—all boots are the same."

"You keep calling me boot, and we're going to have a fucking problem." He stopped walking and clenched his fists next to his hips. I stepped closer to him and he unclenched and settled himself into a fighting stance. "I'm warning you, I was top of my trainee class in magical practices and application."

I reached out and wrapped my fingers around the back of his neck faster than he could react and yanked him toward the door, uttering a simple statement, "You going rogue means that no one is watching you but the monsters you seem to hate, boot." He tried to strike me but I just leaned back and cast Embodiment, stepping around him like a blur. I grabbed the back of his neck again and hauled him outside where we were away from prying eyes for a moment. *Galaxy, drain him.*

On it. She returned and put her hand on his forehead like she was trying to check his wounds. "You're so injured, little boy, why don't you rest now?"

He started to raise his hand at her before his weight sagged against me and I picked him up as folks in the vicinity turned our way. I offered an apologetic smile and called, "He's beat to hell from being a hero and stopping a terrorist attack. We're taking him to a hospital nearby to get some help."

They cleared out of the way, some people even offering to give us a courtesy transport or something like that, but we just booked it to Cassia's SUV. Once we were in, she had me sit in the back with the kid and Galaxy sitting on his other side, Arden up in the front just in case.

"Shit, Galaxy, what about all the stuff we just bought you?" Arden shouted and made to get out of the car.

"Don't worry about it, Arden, I have it all with me." Galaxy looked back to find all three of us staring at her. "Don't we have someone captive?"

Arden pointed at her and narrowed her eyes. "We will be talking about this."

Galaxy rolled her eyes and smiled as Cass whipped us out of the space and into drive. "Speaking of talking about things—Marcus—throw you?"

"I was just trying to get her attention off of you all," I grumbled, knowing it had been stupid.

"I can take a beating, Marcus. If she had been any faster, you would be a pancake." She glared at me in the rear-view mirror for a second before stating, "You're going to come train with security in the mornings from now on."

"I'm not going to complain about that." I scratched my head and she growled in anger. "What?"

"Do you want to make it twice a day?" Her anger was a little out of place and Arden touched her elbow. "What?"

"Honey, he said he was fine with that." Arden looked concerned, then snorted. "Are you blushing?"

"I was more prepared for him to whine about it and already had the anger there and didn't know what to say," Cassia grumbled, making us laugh hard enough that the kid started to rouse.

Galaxy put a hand on his neck and he fell again, prompting me to look at her and say, "This is okay, right?"

"I'm only taking a little at a time, but he recovers faster than you naturally." She closed her eyes and frowned. "Something about the way he was trained to do magic allows him to recover his mana at an almost alarming rate. If he wasn't lying about his accomplishments in schooling, I would venture a guess that this could be why."

"Good for him—doesn't excuse him being a dickhead," I grumped, then turned to the others. "What's the deal with these Wardens? You would think they would admire the High Table for the service it provides."

"I don't understand it really, but the Order of the Staff—the people who started the Warden service—really don't care for the peace we offer," Arden explained and pointed out a car about to merge in about twenty feet from us so Cass could dodge around it. "To them, wars between the varying supernatural creatures would benefit them in keeping our numbers low so we're easier to manipulate and control. Easier to hide."

"Easier to kill," Cassia corrected darkly. Her eyes flicked up to the mirror and at the kid. "The majority of the Wardens are human Touched who have a strong sense of hatred toward monsters for some reason or another, and that is extremely telling. They usually delight in locking us away if they can, and killing us if they can't."

"I thought that us hunting helped them; if that was the case, why risk it?"

"Because policing our own helps keep their numbers small and their attention elsewhere." Cassia grunted and flipped off someone who honked at her violently. "I don't do it as a favor to them, it's a favor to us and our kind. Our patrons."

"Why don't you all rise up and annihilate them then?" Galaxy questioned as she looked over the boy. "He's so small. Fragile even. I could kill him for you right now and feel nothing more than delight knowing that there is one less threat to you in the world."

"We appreciate the thought, but their magic is what keeps them strong and in power." Arden shrugged and scratched her head. "There are factions of creatures out there, heavily Fae, who actively hunt down and kill Wardens if they step out of line or stray too far from the rest of their ilk."

"Wait, so if they hate supernatural creatures and all that, how is a nephilim one?" I found the entire premise weird and that was saying something.

"Nephilim are born of a human and an angel, but belong more to their humanity—plus, they're natural-born monster killers. All the benefits and none of the weaknesses." Arden's explanation made me snort, her eyes shifting back toward me. "Comments?"

"Yeah, I thought getting addicted to drugs was a human thing?" I rolled my eyes as I thought about him. "Now I know that a junkie nephilim is just as bad as humans are."

Cassia laughed loudly and almost hit someone sprinting across a crosswalk in front of her. She swerved and sirens went off behind us.

"Shit!" I spat and turned in time to see a cruiser pull out behind us from a speed trap.

"Arden, I need interference in three seconds." Cassia settled in and looked like she was getting ready to gun it.

"On it!" Arden got up and turned in her seat with her hands flexing as she knelt. "Give me the word?"

"Fucking now!" Cassia roared and hit the brakes as she whipped into a parking spot.

My heart could have kicked its way out of my chest that very second, but the cop car sped past us without a glance our way.

"Good job." Cassia sighed and let her shoulders sag before she used her blinker and got out of the spot.

"What the hell happened?" I blurted as I saw the cop car no more than three cars ahead of us, having moved on.

"Heat rises and creates illusions." Arden pointed to the road ahead of us and sure enough, I could see the waves of heat on the cement. "I can use those waves to make images that will befuddle those around me. I made him see the car going on as we turned." She glanced forward. "Take this street here and we can get to the bar faster without cops on the main roads."

My phone buzzed and I rolled my eyes. What a time for someone to be trying to get a hold of me.

It took a little longer to get to the bar than it could have, but we made it there without any run-ins with the law. On our way to the gym with our guest, Cassia stopped to talk to the attendant at the front of the lot. "Plates and a clean vin for my baby, had a run in with the fuzz a bit ago. Also, blood on the seats could be a little good for you, if you wanted it."

The attendant grinned and tipped his hat to her before standing up. His aura was more along his mouth and reminded me of a leech of sorts more than any other kind of monster or being I had seen before.

"Is he a vampire?" I muttered to Cassia as we stepped away.

"No," she answered simply then frowned. "I suppose he wouldn't mind you knowing; he's a hybrid of sorts. Demon and a leech? Not even sure what to call himself, but he loves blood and it sustains him. We try not to judge him for it."

"I can respect that." We made our way into the gym and into one of the lower sections of the gym that looked suspiciously like an interrogation room that we would use at the FOB. An unstable and horrifically-stained desk, wobbly chairs, and an overall stench of despair really pulled the room together.

"What're we going to do in here, you guys?" My voice was cautious, because I thought I knew but my instincts had been subverted before and I didn't want to make an assumption based on what was presented like I usually did.

"Oh, we're going to torture him to figure out what he knows." Cassia nodded and smiled enthusiastically.

So much for that, I muttered mentally before turning to Arden, hoping to find some kind of wiggle room or doubt in her, but she was just as excited for it as Cass seemed. *Shit.*

"For once, I don't think torture is the right thing to do." I sighed heavily and both Cassia and Arden glared at me. "I know, considering that I was pretty much game for it when we had hold of Varlin, I don't think it's cool now. Let's find out what the kid knows, then see what we can do with him, okay?"

"So you really do know what's going on with my trainer." The kid sat up where they had laid him on the table and licked his hand before rubbing some of the blood away from his eye. Seeing it, he sighed and muttered something under his breath, the blood flaking away along with any dirt and debris on him, leaving him completely clean. "Better. Now, tell me everything."

"Listen, boot, I'm not entirely sure that you grasp the situation you're in." I rounded on him, suddenly angry that I had been trying to protect the little shit.

"I understand perfectly." He pointed to Cass and Arden with his index and pinky fingers, "These two want to torture me and see what I know, and you're against it." He jerked a finger over toward where Galaxy leaned against the wall in the shadows. "And whatever that thing is eats mana and has the ability to incapacitate me."

I nodded, playing along for now. "Right, so listen—"

"No, you listen, Marcus, Cass, and Arden." He spat each of our names as if they were vile and glared at us. "If anyone in this room so much as looks at me in the wrong tone of voice again, or threatens me in any way, I nuke this whole fucking place and go to my superiors."

I can sense him reaching for his mana, and he has so much more than I could find in him. Galaxy warned as she stepped closer to him.

"If you fucking touch me, I will melt you to the floor," the kid snarled over his shoulder at her and I took my chance, casting Embodiment the same time she turned into a shadow to meld with me.

I touched his shoulder and pulled his chin up so that I could look him in the eyes as Galaxy in her cat form stalked out of my forearm, her hackles raised. "You better back it down, or I'm going to save us all a headache and just let her devour you."

A small cracking sound drew my attention as Galaxy's jaw unhinged and opened wider and wider as she hissed weirdly.

The look of horror must have looked weird to the others, both from the kid and me, as she closed her mouth when he muttered, "Okay."

She hopped off my shoulder and took her human form wearing the clothes that she had been in, never taking her eyes off the kid.

"I think we got off on the wrong foot here. Let's start over." I offered him a soft smile, motioning to myself. "As you know, I'm Marcus. That's Cassia, and Arden, and the being that can eat you is Galaxy."

The kid nodded and finally managed, "I'm Merlin."

"You have got to be shitting me." Arden snorted, chortling so hard that she doubled over where she stood. "Who the hell named you that?"

"I did." He replied with a sullen glare that made him look a lot younger. "The orphanage I grew up in let us pick our own names when we were old enough to become adults, and I chose this name."

"Wait, you're an orphan?" He nodded and Cassia frowned. "So then how did you get into the Warden service?"

"All of the orphans at St. Oliver's go into the service, it's what we're taught from a young age—the best use of our various talents." He must have decided that was enough talk of that because he switched gears. "I just want to know what happened to Varlin so I can complete my training and get back to protecting the innocents."

"Before we can tell you that, we need a little bit from you, Merlin." *God, it feels so fucking weird to say that name to a magical kid.* I shook myself out of it and focused on him. "What were you both doing here in Columbus?"

"We got word that something big was going down and that small fry supes and druggies were either going missing, or getting killed in big ways." He scratched his head and frowned. "Varlin was by the books before we got here, then he met up with an informant and disappeared for a few hours and when he came back, he was different. Boastful and prideful. Stronger than before but he seemed like he could swing to depressed all at the same time?"

"He tell you about what was going on at all?" Cassia crossed her arms and stepped a little closer.

Merlin shook his head, staring at her a little harder. "No. He said that he had it handled and that we would do some patrols, but any time we went out after that, he would disappear for a bit and come back as super Warden. He'd fly off on his own and 'investigate,' then come back and tell me it was a dead end but he was as chipper as before."

I glanced over at the ladies and scowled. *Galaxy, can you ask them if they think he can be trusted to know what's going on?*

She nodded once and glanced over to the ladies.

Finally Arden asked, "Do you know who his informant is? He ever give you a name?"

"All I know is that he's a Fae who lives in a place called

Bexley?" He scratched his head and frowned at us. "I've been more than forthcoming with you and told you what I know, now can you please tell me what happened to Varlin?"

I glanced at the others, then sighed. "He may or may not have pissed off Lucifer."

"Okay, seriously?" Merlin rolled his eyes and crossed his arms. "Now I know you think I'm just a kid, but come on. You expect me to believe that *the* Satan has my trainer?"

Arden chuckled and pulled out her phone, tapped the screen a couple times and held the device up to her ear. "Hey, you busy?" She listened for a second then scoffed. "You know damned well why I called, Luci. After that verbal dressing down you gave me after I ordered you upstairs, I'm not doing it without checking in first."

Merlin narrowed his eyes at her as she finished up the call.

"Yup, give us the ol' mustard, buddy. 'Kay, see you in a sec."

"You cannot honestly expect me to believe that." Merlin shook his head until a wave of sulfurous heat washed over the room so quickly it singed the hairs on my arms.

We all turned to see Luci standing as he had the night previously, in all his angelic beauty and splendor, two demonic figures kneeling before him at his side as he stepped from a corridor of darkness.

Merlin sputtered, "Y—you're just an illusion!"

Lucifer leaned down and glanced into the boy's eyes from a foot away. "And you're adorable. Hello, Merlin, Varlin spoke much of you. Have you been eating well in his absence?"

Merlin's mouth worked but no sound came out until finally he managed to eke out, "Where?"

Lucifer leaned back and snapped his fingers, the two demons dipping in unison and pulling the heavily beaten and chained Warden from the floor.

"Varlin!" Merlin forgot who was in front of him and made to pass by him, but the king of Hell itself grasped his shoulder. "Let me go!"

"As you wish." Lucifer whispered and let the boy go. He

stumbled closer to the demons, who eyed him hungrily, but a sideways glare from their ruler made them slink back.

As he came to the nephilim's side, he began casting spell after spell and some of the magic seeped into Varlin from what I could make out, but it looked like it just kept fading away.

Varlin stirred and reached out, grabbing Merlin's upper arm painfully. "Ow, Varlin. It's me, Merlin. Hey, snap out of it!" He grunted and the nephilim's hand glowed blue. "Varlin, stop it, that hurts!"

With the sound of a thousand wings preceding him, Lucifer suddenly stooped over his captive and grabbed his wrist so tightly that something snapped and the half-angel cried out before letting the boy go.

Merlin scrambled back from them both and stared mistrustingly at Lucifer. "What happened to him?"

Lucifer looked almost sad. "I don't know." He glanced up at us. "I think he's dying because of the drug."

Galaxy stepped forward and put her hand toward him only for it to recoil. "It's burnt through his mana reserves and created a funnel of sorts. Mana is the only thing keeping him alive but he can't regenerate it fast enough."

"What drug are you talking about?" Merlin demanded, suddenly furious. "Where is it coming from?"

"We don't know," I answered and looked over at Lucifer. "Can you have them take him away?"

"What are you talking about?" Merlin roared, his fists clenching. "We have to get him to the Order of the Staff; they can help him!"

"They might be able to, Merlin." Arden stepped closer to him, slowly so that he might not take it as a threat. "But all of us are heavily implicated in his fall. If we turn him in with no answers, the only people who know about this drug could end up disappearing."

"I'll talk to them, make them understand that it wasn't you all." Him begging for his junky master was a lot to take. Especially at the mention of people disappearing after what I had gone through in that temple. "Maybe they can help us?"

"They'll come in here and interrogate you, and us, and find something to stick us with so that we take the fall, and they can start killing our kind indiscriminately," Cassia finally said, her arms crossed and her shoulders set. "I will not risk my family here—especially not for an abusive junky nephilim."

"Luce, can you keep him alive?" The question was out before I completely knew where I was going with this.

"I think I can if I were to allow him to devour some of the demons I have. That or a few souls." He pondered for a little bit. "Without, he would probably make it a little while based on what he just siphoned from young Merlin here."

"Six hours," Galaxy stated, drawing all of our attention. "Provided that he doesn't try to work any magic of his own, he can last six hours before he starts to spiral out of control."

"Okay, cool." I started piecing things together in my head and found a solution, or at least a band aid for a hemorrhage. "Luci can look after him while we go look for his informant over near Bexley. We can try to get a lead on where this stuff is coming from, and then after that track it down and stop it from hitting the streets."

"Why do you want to stop it?" Merlin frowned heavily, motioning at me and the others with his chin. "What do any of you have in it that makes it so important? You should leave it to the Wardens."

"What, you think we want this crap to draw attention from the Normies?" Cassia scoffed. "Even better, *your* kind? No thanks. We can't trust the Wardens to have our best interests at heart."

"And some of us genuinely care about the humans and 'supes' here, as you call them," Arden interjected before Merlin could retort to Cassia's obvious anger. "We want to maintain what little semblance of peace we have. Our interest in getting this stuff off the streets is as pure as yours, Merlin."

He thought on it for a moment, then grimaced and spat,

"Fine. But we are not letting her drive again—that was terrifying."

Cassia stomped forward once and I turned to glare at her, stopping her in her place for now. Though I did glance from her to Merlin. "This taking potshots at each other shit stops. Now. On both sides. Because, like it or not, we need to work together to keep all sides from going at the other."

"I fail to see how the Warden service stands to lose anything in this." Merlin crossed his arms and lifted his chin as if he were untouchable.

"The Wardens had a member of their order fall to drugs, abuse one of the most influential beings in existence and royally piss him off. Which proved that his kind aren't quite so intrinsically trustworthy as they claimed to be." I crossed my own arms and stared at him in return. "I don't know about your order, but in the Marine Corps, I've seen people who caused trouble and those who knew about it sent to all sorts of shitty places. Twenty-Nine Palms… ships… Oki… the brig, to say the least shitty. What would your order do to you knowing that you knew and did nothing and tried to make yourself look good over them?"

His face paled, eyes widening as he gulped.

"That's what I thought." I glanced over at the others. "We need to cooperate and keep our cool. I'm not saying we have to like everyone and be all buddy-buddy afterward. But we will work as a unit and we will maintain professional courtesies."

Everyone muttered something, especially Cassia and Merlin.

"Open your freaking mouths!"

"Yes sir!" Merlin snapped to attention and Cassia tilted her head at the same time Arden threw a fireball at me.

"What the fuck, Arden?" I patted the flames out on my shirt and frowned at her as she glared back.

"I don't like being yelled at, and I am not a slave to be ordered about." She lifted herself to stand more erect and aloft that she had before. "I will continue to help, but it will be on my terms. Am I clear, Marcus?"

"Yeah, sure." I chuckled a bit. "Sorry, that was just something I would do to my Marines to get their attention and compliance. I didn't mean to startle you, or to make you feel bad."

"I understand." She patted my arm and we all looked over to Lucifer who stood watching us passively. "How are you, my love?"

"As well as someone whose former lover is dying in their care can be?" He looked a little piqued from it, but otherwise was a little more removed than I had seen before. "I want to help all of you, I do, but even if she says he has six hours—I cannot have him die in my care."

"Can you watch him for a few hours at least?" I broached and he turned toward me. "Listen, I know that this is a harrowing thing to ask you, and if you can't, we'll find another way, but even two hours is better than nothing. Having him off the property frees us all up for a lot more than it doesn't. Besides, what if we stumble on a way to fix him?"

He seemed reticent to acquiesce so I opted to sweeten the deal. "Can you and I step out for a moment?"

"What do you mean?" Arden stood stock still with a look of sudden knowing on her face.

"Yes, we can, please follow me." Luci motioned for me to step closer and enter a vortex of red and black just behind him.

"Marcus, no!" Arden snarled as I stepped through.

I was weightless, then heavy all at once, heat washed over me, then a cool chill, and finally I stood in what had to be the most technologically advanced kitchen I had ever seen in my entire existence.

"Welcome to my humble abode." He motioned to the kitchen and a pitcher of liquid appeared. "Water?"

"Thank you." He poured the water into a cup that appeared in his hand and I eyed him. "You know, as awesome as this place is, I really doubt you don't have DVR. I mean, your fridge could probably play a full-length movie and it would be better than a theater."

He laughed and handed me the cup. "This is the most well-to-do place in my home, because I love cooking and the modern amenities afford me the best means to work with the best ingredients. Everywhere else has taken a back seat of sorts, and I don't believe in streaming services, so there's that argument nulled. Now, what was it you wanted to speak about?"

"I want to make a deal with you." I swallowed the water, crystalline and icy, as he spit his out.

"You let me bring you to my home—the first person other than a lover in years, mind you—to strike up a deal?" He blinked at me and I nodded, then he held up a finger. "You remembered the rules from when Ardent Flame rebuffed me! Oh, how delightful. Spill it, Marcus, what is it that you desire?"

"Oh my God, do you do that because of the show or did they get that right?" I couldn't help laughing and he joined me as he leaned forward on the counter. "It was the show, wasn't it?"

He gave me a coy smile and nodded once. "It was totally the show. I cannot believe I never thought to ask someone like that, though. I am so upset over that."

I laughed again. "I can only imagine. But no, I wanted to offer myself in exchange for you holding onto Varlin for a few hours so we can go meet his contact."

He stilled and his eyes narrowed. "Offer yourself how?"

"If you will watch him for a few hours, I will let you pick one song for me to sing at the next karaoke night."

His eyes widened, and he leaned closer. "That is a delicious deal, my dear, but I'm afraid I truly must decline."

"A song per hour." His smile widened again at my offer and he shook his head, so I brought out the big guns. "It can be the sappiest song you think of, your choice as long as I can sing it, and I will personally make you a few drinks the next time I work."

"Darling, I can have the latter any time I please." He almost rolled his eyes.

"True." I sighed, then shook my head. "But I planned on

really upping the ante with some more awesome drinks and variations on my Bloody Mary. I was going to get so dirty with it."

His mouth actually fell open and he looked visibly upset. "You wouldn't dare deny me these new takes, Marcus."

I put my hand on his and looked him in the eye. "Maple bacon and apple cider, sweetheart. Oh, the sweet things, the tangy things—the sizzling heat I could bring with the right kind of preparations. But if I can't tempt you with this deal, I just have to put them on hold."

His massive wings flared and he looked wounded. "I am the devil, Marcus, me!" he howled. "I am the one who is supposed to do the damnable tempting here!"

I grinned at him. "So a song per hour and three new cocktails for you to try?"

He eyed me distrustfully before holding out his hand, "One song per hour held, maximum three hours and I want five variations on the drinks. Three of which will be new takes on the Bloody Mary."

"Deal." I reached out and clasped his hand as he laughed.

I didn't feel any different and he laughed again. "Were you expecting something much more grandiose? Lights flickering, me tearing out a portion of your soul to hold as collateral?"

Deflated, I scratched my head and chuckled. "Kinda?"

He snorted and patted my shoulder. "Sweet child, a deal between friends is always honored. If I didn't like you, I'd force you to sign a lengthy contract and make you use up your time doing so. I know that you will hold up your end of the deal, just as much as you know I will hold up mine."

I grabbed his hand and held it. "I appreciate your trust, Luce. I'll do my best to make sure it's well placed. I'll have someone grab me the ingredients and I'll blow your mind with those drinks."

"I cannot wait, my friend." He waved his hand and the vortex opened again. "Let's get you back to the ass kicking that likely awaits you."

"What?"

He shoved me through the vortex to where all three women and a very disgruntled looking Warden-in-training waited for me.

"Shit."

CHAPTER THIRTEEN

"Seriously, guys, it's not like I sold my soul to him or anything," I grumped for the umpteenth time in the back of the High Table security forces' minivan. We'd had to take it since they hadn't gotten the new tags for Cassia's SUV yet.

Arden growled low as she drove the hulking thing down the highway, keeping her eyes on the road. Merlin sat in front to guide her with what he remembered, and Cassia sat with me. She had been a little more forgiving, but still sulked.

"You don't understand, Marcus." She explained quietly, "Luci hasn't taken any of us to his place before and you get to just waltz in? We're hurt. And you made a deal with him? That's not High Table procedure."

"It was what was needed to protect the High Table," I countered and she frowned. "Look, if you want to tell Uncle Yen what I did because you have to, I understand. I respect your position as head of security, I truly do. But if we're going to get this shit taken care of, we need the High Table in the clear."

She looked out the window, then back at me. "I'm more upset that you saw his place than anything to do with the High Table. I've only been the head of security for a year or so now, and you making calls like this the way you have been shows that you have almost as good a head for it as I do. I like that about you, Marcus. I do."

She smiled at me softly and touched my thigh. "We can fight over a lot of things, and protecting the things we hold dear will always be one of them."

I was touched until I realized what she had said and how she said it. "Did you mean to say that we would always fight over things like that?"

"Yes." She nodded happily, her hand gripping my leg tightly. "So long as you are strong enough to protect what you care about, like the High Table and our patrons and family there, we will continue to fight with each other. And such fights they will be."

You really do have to come up with some sort of code word for that, Marcus. I'm inside her head and even I don't quite know what she means.

I laughed at Galaxy's statement and Cassia joined me, having heard the remark from her benefactor.

I pulled my phone out and saw that I had a text from Uncle Yen telling me he hadn't had anything turn up in his hunt for information about Galaxy, but he was going to keep searching. After that, I saw I had an email from Connell's mom.

Hey Marcus,

I know it's been a while since I was able to send any photos or anything of Connell, things have been crazy and he's been going through some things at school, but he's been playing soccer lately and he's really good at it!

I attached a video so you could see him kick some ass.

As always, thanks for caring.

Kind regards,

Aeslyn.

I opened the video and watched as a scruffy-headed boy with golden skin kicked a ball so hard past the shoulder of the goalie that the kid had no chance to even get in position to stop it.

I was so proud, and at the same time, hurt.

Something on my shoulder shifted and Galaxy sat in the van with us, between the two seats that Cassia and I occupied.

"You truly miss him, don't you?" I nodded at her question as I sent a reply to Aeslyn.

Thanks for that, he's so good!

I know you don't want me to try to come find you, and I'm not. I just wanted you to know that I'm in Columbus with my uncle. You know, if we run into each other I want there to be transparency. I'm working at a place called the High Table now too, so if you want to know where I am, that's it.

I miss Connell, and I hope he's having fun, and that things at school slow down for him. I'm sure he's going to do great things. I hope someday he gets to know who I am, and how I feel.

I frowned. That last bit seemed accusatory, didn't it? I mean, I felt that way, but at the same time I didn't want to make her feel like I was guilt tripping her.

I deleted the last paragraph, like I almost always did, and wrote:

I'm glad that he's doing so good. I hope everything at home is going well, and if you need me—I'm here.

My love and thoughts to Connell.

Kindest thoughts,

Marcus.

I pressed send and closed my phone as we pulled down a side street off of Fifth.

"We're almost there," Merlin warned.

Cassia grasped my wrist. "What was that video you were watching? It looked fun." I pulled my phone out and let her watch it. "Oh that's so cool! What a great shot!"

I laughed. "Yeah, he's eight now. He's pretty strong too. Maybe he could go pro for soccer."

"Football," Arden snarled. "It's football, you philistine!"

I snorted. "So sorry. We were watching a video of my son, I'll show you later."

Cassia's grip tightened as she stared at me. "That was Connell?"

I nodded and she leaned forward and pressed play. "He's beautiful." She looked up at me, my face as much a mask as I could make it. Her shoulders sagged a bit. "I'm sorry, Marcus."

"Don't be." I tried to smile at her. "It's not your fault. You sure you want all this?"

"What do you mean?" She frowned at me.

"Dating me is going to come with this kind of emotional baggage." I motioned to my phone. "I get one of these kinds of messages about once a week to once a month sometimes. I can function pretty well without them, but I get a little morose thinking about Connell and his mom keeping him from me. I know it isn't your fault, and you do too, but that doesn't mean I won't feel this way from time to time."

"Okay, and?" She cocked her head to the side and frowned deeper.

"And that's a lot for someone to deal with. Having a significant other with a child or a past the way I have one stops a lot of people from wanting to be with me, because the love comes with a lot of work that has to happen."

She touched my wrist. "Marcus, I do not love you."

The suddenness of the statement took the air out of my lungs in a whoosh and I floundered for something, anything to say, but she just smiled at me and Arden laughed.

"I didn't come into this relationship for love, or without knowing we were vastly different people." She touched my face. "I found you attractive, and your actions endearing. You fight well, and I desire you. I do not love you. But I also do not hold your past against you. Or in front of you. Your past made you into the man I enjoy sitting in front of me right now. I cannot begrudge you that, or anyone else."

"I'm a little confused by this," I stated openly and honestly.

"She's not saying that she *couldn't* love you, Marcus," Arden explained after Cassia looked pointedly her way with a pleading expression. "Just that she's not someone who expects it as of right now. Or that she's thinking about it actively in that way.

She likes you for who you are and what you offer. Who knows what the future holds?"

"Yes, that." Cassia nodded and stared at me for a moment. "Is that okay? Did I hurt your feelings? I know humans are a little more emotionally different compared to oni."

"No?" I shrugged and just shook my head as I laughed a little bit. "I think you just surprised me more than anything." She grinned at me and I asked, "So you have no problem with Connell or my past?"

She shook her head. "Nope! I couldn't care less about your past, though he is a handsome boy, and strong. Many suitors will come to him."

I laughed and nodded. "I'm sure if he's anything like his mom, they'll flock to him sooner than he wants."

"Was she beautiful?" Cassia asked, watching me curiously.

I nodded again. "Very."

"We're here. Let's go before I puke." Merlin groaned and stepped out of the car.

The first thing I noticed was a fifteen-foot-tall fir tree in the front yard, with a different large plant growing out of the side of it facing toward the house next to it. The house we were at was an older-looking, two-story home with a red door and large cement porch.

The front yard had been mowed recently, the grass lower than the neighboring houses. Merlin pulled out a string and let a necklace fall, the object on the end swinging like a pendulum as it settled, then lifted slightly toward the back yard.

The sidewalk up to the home had a bit of grass on it, and led to the porch, then broke off to the right of the house where we walked now. A small set of steps led to a side door for the home and past that was a medium-sized yard with a rotten white picket fence breaking apart on the right hand side.

A massive white furred dog barked and barreled toward us; Galaxy was luckily in her human form next to me as opposed to her cat form.

The necklace shook violently toward the dog and it stopped

ten feet away, as the lead it was on stopped it from coming too much closer.

"Can we ask you a few questions?" Merlin called over the din the dog was making. He looked like a Great Pyrenees, but was a little more scruffy looking. "It's about Varlin."

At the mention of the name, the dog stopped his barking and stilled, an immense aura of shadow and darkness flaring around him before a being stepped out from behind the dog. The white furred animal looked up at the man uncertainly, but when waved away wandered off and laid in the shade of the trees along the wooden fence to the left of the house.

The shadowy figure turned toward us, his pure black skin eating the sunlight around him, his piercing crimson eyes watching. Waiting. Finally he deemed to speak, his voice deeper and more menacing than a lithely built figure should have had. "You must be his apprentice."

"And you must be his informant," Merlin returned, putting the necklace away. "What are you?"

"I am many things, but servant and protector of the denizens of this home is all you need know. So long as you mean no harm to them, I will be peaceable." The figure stood waiting still. "What do you want? And make it fast, he returns soon."

"Who is he?" I asked, but the figure just eyed me and kept quiet.

"We want to know what Varlin had asked about last time he came here, something about a drug that is being put out onto the streets?" Merlin asked and the figure relaxed a little. "You know something."

"I know much, and yet not enough." Servant spread his hands and the air around us chilled a bit. "I heard tales of this world from him, my former master, and believed it bereft of magic. Imagine my surprise when I find that he was wrong, and that there were others of my kind from our world here. And that some of those others mean to poison the creatures of this world in a way that makes them dependent on their poison."

"Who?" I asked and the figure once again eyed me, but this time he stepped closer, his red eyes searching me. "See something you like?"

"No," he stated simply, then turned to Galaxy. "Though you feel familiar somehow and yet you are not Fae. At least, not in the way that I am used to."

He stilled, listening for something, then he scowled. "She must have dragged him the entire block to get back so fast. You have to leave—now."

"What about who is doing this?" Merlin asked as the figure retreated toward the dog. "Can you at least tell us who he got it from?"

"I have said much already." Servant fled into the dog's shadow and trotted over to the set of chairs that sat in the middle of the yard as a bald, stocky man walked around the corner and into the yard near a red car that sat on cement near the road.

The dog that pulled him barked maddeningly and pulled even more, but the man had no issues holding her to him, though I could tell it was a strain. "Can I help you?"

"We were a bit lost," I stated and smiled, stepping around the others to close the distance between us as he put the smaller, tan dog on the lead closest to him. "You have some really nice dogs."

"Thank you," he replied warily, left hand in his beard as he looked to be counting the five of us and eyeing us all in a familiar kind of way. "They can be a bit rowdy at times, but I've been bitten by worse."

I laughed, then noticed a sticker on the car behind him and pointed to it. "That Marine Corps sticker on your bumper—you serve?"

He blinked and nodded, then pointed to his head. "I notice you have the same shitty haircut a lot of Marines have. How long ago you get out, or are you still in?"

"Medically retired, brother." I smiled, genuinely happy to

meet another Marine and stepped toward him to shake his hand.

Servant, inside the large white dog, growled deeply and put himself between me and the man, getting a smack on the rump from him. "Spirit!" The dog backed down a little bit but still watched us with a glare. "Sorry, he's never reacted that way to anyone."

"It's okay—it's his yard and he just wants to protect you." I stepped back and motioned to the others. "Sorry, we were on our way to try to find a place to get some pizza and we thought that our friend lived on this street. Could you tell us how to get to this location?"

I pulled up a random address nearby and he pointed us in the right direction as best as he could. I thanked him and shook his hand, the dog still watching us evilly as we spoke.

He shook my hand and wished us well as he walked back to the dog.

We piled back into the car and Merlin swore. "Now we have nothing."

"No, he gave us a clue," Arden assured him, thinking. "He said others of 'my kind.' Then he said that Galaxy felt familiar and that she wasn't like the Fae he was used to."

"That could mean that he's Fae!" Galaxy smiled, looking at me in wonder. "That means that I could be related to the Fae in some way, right?"

"It sounds like it." I frowned. "But why would the Fae want to make the rest of the supernatural beings dependent on them and their drug?"

"Not all of the Fae," Merlin amended for me. "Some of them, he said some of them. That could leave the Summer Court. Have you had any run-ins with the Seelie Fae recently?"

Arden, Cassia and I all glanced at each other before I growled, "That motherfucker."

Merlin sat back and crossed his arms triumphantly. "That answers that question. And it's only been an hour."

"Do we know where they frequent?" Everyone shook their

heads at me and I socked the passenger seat, making Merlin jump a bit. "Sorry. We need to put feelers out there. Arden, let's get back to the High Table and get Varlin from Lucifer. Let's see if we can't get the information from him before he passes."

"We have to get him help, Marcus." Merlin spoke softly as we pulled away from the home. "If he dies, my career goes up in smoke."

"If he lives, you could die," Arden pointed out softly.

"What do you all care?" He frowned and glared at her, then the rest of us. "To you, I'm a member of an oppressive regime designed to keep you from killing humans."

"You're an antiquated regime bent on oppressing our kind, sure," Cassia pointed out and stopped there. I stared at her and she looked concerned. "Wait, I had to say more?"

Merlin rolled his eyes and actually laughed at that.

Cassia lifted an eyebrow and smiled at him. "Look, you're a child. You don't know a whole lot and you can make the world a better place. If I had to choose to allow Varlin to get better and risk you, or teach you that we aren't the monsters you think we are so you can teach others, I'd prefer the latter."

He blinked at her in surprise and before he said anything Cassia held up a hand. "You say something smart to me, Merlin, and I'm not going to be able to let anyone in this car stop me from crushing your little skull."

He frowned appreciatively and just said, "Then I'll shut up."

He turned around and sat in his seat quietly before Cassia snorted. "There's hope for you, boy."

It didn't take long before we got to the bar and then I went to my room. I deposited Seamus' treat before going back into the gym where I met with Cassia and Galaxy in the interrogation room. Merlin and Arden had gone to the cafeteria to get the boy something to eat while we were thinking of a way to dispose of a certain… fuckboy half angel.

Galaxy sat on the table and watched us for a moment as we thought and finally she sighed. "Kill him."

"What?" Cassia frowned and stared at her.

"We kill him." I said, her gaze flipping to me. "We kill him and gain some experience for his death, then Galaxy devours the body."

"You really are starting to get me." She grinned at me and I just shook my head.

"You want to kill him?" Cassia frowned at me. "You know killing a nephilim is a crime against the Christian god, right?"

"Not my god." I shrugged and grinned a little wider. "Lucifer, I think we're ready."

I wasn't expecting anything to happen, but the sound of wings flapping wildly preceded him once more and he stood in front of us. "Only an hour and thirty minutes, whatever is a devil to do?"

"Take two songs and all the drinks offered?" I raised an eyebrow at him and he grinned, reaching out a hand that I took. "Deal is sealed. Let us have him and you can leave. We will take care of him."

"Take care of him?" Lucifer glanced between the two of us and frowned. "Do I want to know?"

Cassia stood and walked over to him, putting her hands on his face. "No. But you can trust that we will take care of this for you. Because we care about and value you."

Lucifer leaned forward and kissed her forehead. "Thank you, sweetheart. Boys?" Two demons plodded out of the darkness and dropped the dying nephilim on the ground. "Thank you."

He nodded to me before moving toward the wall and disappearing as his demons filtered away.

Varlin, his eyes open but barely comprehending, gasped and reached toward Galaxy.

"Let's make this as quick and painless as possible." I cast Blade and the weapon materialized in my hand as Cassia brought out a small Japanese-style blade. "Is that yours?"

"Bubba Kenshi dabbles in making swords, he has for centuries." She stepped over his body and held the blade aloft over his heart. "It pains me to take a life from someone who cannot defend themselves. May you be reborn and know what it's like to be a good person in your next life."

"May you know peace," I said simply, not wishing to give him the satisfaction of knowing I was slightly uncomfortable taking his life like this, and instead offering the solace of a quick death.

He wheezed something as the blades pierced his heart and slid into his temple, his body bucking once then falling still as Galaxy, human form cast aside, strode over to claim her prize.

She reached down, her shadow passing over his body as he bled onto the floor and then as soon as her shadow touched his flesh it faded away and melded with her.

After a moment, she was done, leaning up and looking more vibrant than before. "That really did it."

Not for the first time, I wondered if she'd had a part in my platoon's fall. She turned and gazed at me, our bond letting me feel how the slight bend in my trust hurt her, but she knew the thought wasn't malicious. She also knew that she couldn't have since she was interred in that damnable necklace.

She shook herself out and her hair grew longer from where it had been, her curves growing and skin color deepening momentarily. "I can give someone something extra. Who should I give it to?"

"What kind of extra?" Cassia asked and Galaxy shrugged. "Is it something holy?"

"I think so?" Galaxy answered after pondering a moment. "Yes. It feels that way."

"Cassia should have it," I answered before she could say anything else.

She looked at me. "Are you sure? We don't know what it could be."

"That's exactly why." I grasped her shoulder and nudged her toward Galaxy. "You take it, and I'll get the next one. Or Arden, you know, whatever."

Galaxy leaned forward and placed her hands against

Cassia's head and closed her eyes before a muted golden light flooded her body.

Cassia went rigid for a moment before her body relaxed and she smiled. "Oh, it's a healing spell!"

"That's too cool!" I grinned at her and her smile widened. "How does it work?"

"I hit whatever I want to heal!" I blinked at her as the realization struck.

"Wait, you hit them?" She nodded and I just rolled my eyes. "Oni and their attacking and fighting!"

She laughed uproariously before we went to go find Arden and Merlin in the cafeteria. They had food waiting for us and, as we ate, I could tell that something was eating at the boy.

"He's gone, Merlin," I stated softly. "The drug ate him to the point that he couldn't function on his own."

Merlin picked at his food for a time more, then finally asked, "What should I tell the order?"

Arden, Galaxy, Cassia and I glanced at each other, stuck on what we could say, before Galaxy offered, "You could tell them the truth."

He looked up, alarmed but kept his voice low. "But if I do, they'll know about all of you."

"Tell them a version of the truth," she persisted, putting a hand on his shoulder. "You knew that he had taken a drug that somehow poisoned him, then killed him. The means to that death or the in between are irrelevant."

"What if they dig further than that?" he wondered out loud as he hefted a sandwich to his mouth and bit.

"Then you give them a little more," Arden added quietly. "Tell them that a group of supes found you and kept you safe until you were well enough to get back to them."

"They'll know that was a lie."

I turned to him and asked, "Is it?" He paused and looked at me. "We took you in, fed you, helped you find him, and didn't kill you. Hell, we even helped keep you safe when that hulking monster would have given you the works. So tell me, Merlin, is it a lie?"

"Huh." He chuckled to himself and muttered, "Guess not."

"When do you plan on going back to them?" Cassia asked and he shrugged. "Okay, when do you have to check in?"

"Varlin has been having me check in with them, but usually only once every three to four days." He pulled out a quill and piece of paper that looked like a log sheet of sorts. He checked his phone and wrote the time and date, then in the narrative portion wrote:

Warden Varlin and apprentice Warden Merlin okay, making the rounds and investigation ongoing. No further.

"And voila!" The message sank into the paper and faded slightly before a reply came.

Very well. Proceed as ordered.

"That's an interesting piece of hardware you have there," I mused, then shrugged. "So now we have a few more days?"

"At the most. The Wardens have a way of discerning when one is hurt or dead." He scratched his head and finally just started eating until he could think of what to say next. Which was, "I don't know what it is or how it happens, but they could know as soon as tomorrow. I can't be precisely sure."

"Okay, so we just need to try to figure out what we can." I grimaced and tapped the table in front of Cassia. "Cass, can you see if we can't figure out where the Summer Court frequents? Do they have haunts or own property in the area or surrounding areas?"

"I'll do what I can." She pulled out her phone and began tapping away.

"I think I have some friends in the Winter Court who would be delighted to help us stop something like this." Arden stood and was off before I could so much as blink.

"Are they always like this?" Merlin asked me in a low tone that made me laugh. "What's so funny?"

"Oh, nothing." I waited until the worst of the laughing

subsided and answered, "I wouldn't know, I've only known them about four days now?"

"And you all work like this already?" He whistled low.

"I don't think we're as cohesive a unit as I was used to in what I did before, but it is nice that we can work this well together after such a short time." I mused to myself more than him on this, "Though I do wonder at times who's in charge."

Galaxy cleared her throat pointedly and motioned to herself. "I would be, of course."

I laughed and Merlin joined me before he paused and asked, "What are you, Galaxy? Servant called you Fae, but you don't remind me or him of any ever seen before." He stood up and reached toward her, the woman stilling as his fingers brushed her ears. "You're beautiful, and pleasing to be around like the Fae of old are supposed to have been before their fall. Even now, they're beautiful and enticing, but their glamours are nowhere near what they once were."

"And what does this have to do with me, small Merlin?" Galaxy tilted her head and stared at him, openly curious.

"You don't use a glamour." He actually tugged on her ear and she flinched. "You feel the same way you look. You're different."

"I am aware of this, thank you."

"You're much more different than even you know, and I don't know how to say it." Merlin frowned and finally smiled. "You offer them power, am I right?"

She stilled and watched him, prompting him to speak again. "There are two other orders within the Warden service." He glanced at me. "If you were to join us, you would likely be placed within the Order of the Sword with how physical your magic and abilities are. The other is the Order of the Heart, who oversees the memories of our orders, the records of everything we do, as well as the logistics and oversight of our missions."

"This is all interesting, but what does that have to do with Galaxy?" I whispered cautiously.

He glanced from her to me, his hand falling to his side. "If I have the strength to join one of the other orders, I can access the databases from the Heart and try to figure out what she is—who she is."

"What's in it for you?" Cassia questioned with her arms crossed. Her gaze was fierce and he gulped before closing his eyes to collect his answer.

"If they don't believe me, and my inaction is found to be the reason for his death, they'll likely kill or retrain me." He frowned deeply as if the thought of either was the absolute last thing that could happen if he could help it. "I can't stand up to them on my own; they'd do whatever they wanted. But if I had a backer and the strength to separate myself a little more…"

He left the statement as open for interpretation as he could and I added, "And then the Order of the Staff won't be able to get to you with impunity." He looked dismayed, but he nodded. "So you want to have Galaxy give you power to protect yourself."

"I'm not asking so that I can give nothing back." He waved in front of himself like he was warding the very thought away. "I'm willing to earn it if I have to."

"I don't know if my blessing will kill you or not," Galaxy stated matter of fact. "If I were stronger, I could say with more certainty."

"What if we were to find you another vat of mana?" I asked and both she and Merlin looked at me as if I were daft. "They couldn't have had only one place where they were making this stuff. That wouldn't make sense, would it?"

"No, the Fae are fickle creatures, even now." Merlin scratched his head and sighed. "They would have backup after backup, and a supply close to them so that they could maintain it and ensure things were best."

"That and they would try to perfect the strain that they wanted," Cassia stated, startling me, as I had forgotten she was there. "Their guy back at the factory had used it with no fear of the consequences; maybe they have a non-addictive or non-dangerous strain of whatever they're making?"

"The problem becomes tracking it." Galaxy sighed, drawing our attention. "If I had some, I might be able to find something nearby."

"What about the giant you have secured?" Cassia wondered and pointed to the kid's pocket.

"What about her?" He seemed confused.

"She had signs of using as well. She could have some on her and Galaxy could track it, right?" I was excited now that my stomach wasn't empty and we had a lead. "Let's go to the gym and see what we can see."

"I can take everything from her person right here." Merlin waved a hand over the table and a large sack bounced onto the surface with a thunk. He glanced at me and a sheepish Cassia. "What, were you planning to fight her and rob her or something?"

My eyebrows raised and I looked away with my mouth stretching out a little as he scoffed. "That's so Order of the Sword for you."

"Order of the Whatever-the-Hell, I don't care. What's in the bag?" I snarled, more than a little embarrassed.

He smirked and unzipped it, whistling low. "More than I thought."

He pulled out three large plastic containers of the liquified mana, several iffy-looking needles and huge wads of cash.

"Was she dealing?" Cass asked in a low growl. "We need to pull her ass out and question her."

"She's in the same state that she was in when she was free, all of it." Merlin explained, pulling out a small object that looked like a coin with a one-eyed giant on it.

"So let's go pull her out and get the information we need, come on!" Cassia's almost manic grin made her punching her open palm a little less funny and more concerning.

"If I take her to the Order as she is right now, we might be able to make some kind of magical antidote for this stuff."

Merlin held onto the coin while Cassia reached for it like a stubborn child. "I could use her as a bargaining chip, maybe. In case any other Wardens have been tempted or duped."

"Like a magical Narcan?" He looked at me in confusion until I added, "What they use to quickly detox people who are overdosing on narcotics."

He clapped, the coin in his hands vanishing so fast that Cassia bodily lifted him up to check for it under him, his voice cracking slightly as he yelped, "Yes, that! Put me down, you gorilla of a woman!"

"Aww!" She dropped him and he landed in a heap on the floor with a grunt and a soft curse. "I think he's starting to like me."

"That can change swiftly, demon," Merlin hissed as he rubbed his butt and glared at her.

Someone cleared their throat noisily near where the food was and I saw Gunny separate himself from the shadows, arms crossed and glaring pointedly at all of us.

I gave him a respectful nod. "Afternoon, Gunny."

He grunted and stepped back into the shadows as he was wont to do and we knew he was watching. No one would disrespect his food again. And I sure as shit wouldn't either.

Merlin stared at the exchange in shock, then wonder. "You're a boot too?"

"Everyone is a boot to someone else, kid. Get used to it." I smiled at him and winked.

"We had better do this somewhere less… visible." Galaxy motioned to the objects on the table and Merlin shoved it all back into the bag and followed Galaxy, Cassia, and me out of the room and toward one of the matted rooms.

Galaxy reached into the bag and grabbed all three containers. The first two she emptied into her mouth excitedly and grinned as she closed her eyes, a look of euphoria falling over her.

"Uhm, is she okay?" Merlin whispered quietly to me as I shrugged. She felt fine to me.

She opened her eyes and focused on the final container for a long few minutes, the rest of us watching as she worked. Finally, she scowled and made a motion with her hand and the minimap in the corner of my vision cut out, then came back.

"What was that?" I asked and noticed Cassia seemed concerned as well.

"Your map wasn't large enough so I had to up it a little bit." She sighed, shaking her head. "I found one a little outside the city, to the east. The other ones are further up north, but this one east of us seems to be the largest concentration."

"So we go tonight then!" Cassia grinned and looked excited.

"Not tonight, no." Arden's voice greeted us from the doorway, Cass throwing her hands up in despair. "Relax, I just finished talking to a friend in the Winter Court, he's going to put some feelers out and see what he can figure out for us. He did, however, let us know that the Summer Fae are looking for whoever raided one of their dens here in Columbus, and that they're on high alert."

"So it would be dangerous for us to go and do anything about it tonight." I completed her thought and she nodded. I sighed and shrugged. "Well, there's that then. I guess we have the next few days to come up with some kind of strategy and train."

Cassia perked up and turned to me. "Training?" I nodded and she whooped. "Yes! That means we can lift weights and eat lots of food and fight!"

I laughed at her excitement, Arden shaking her head, but Merlin pointed to himself. "What am I supposed to do for a few days?"

We all froze, but it was Arden who turned to him and asked, "Do you like video games?"

He frowned and looked at her as if she wasn't making a lick of sense. "What are those?"

Cassia and Arden both shared a wicked glance with each other before slowly turning their heads toward him in an eerie unison that made the hair on my body stand on end. "Run, kid!"

They were on him before he even stood a chance and dragged him hollering out of the room with promises of introducing him to the concept as quickly as possible. Then they started to argue about what he should play, loudly, much to the chagrin of all the people in the gym lifting and working out.

"I truly think they will murder him if he doesn't like gaming the way we do," Galaxy muttered as she joined me. "So, looks like it's you and I for now. What do you plan on doing?"

"Well, it's not karaoke night yet, so I don't owe anyone songs." I chuckled to myself. "I suppose if we're going to do anything, it may as well be some research?"

She wrapped her arm through mine and smiled at me. "I like the way you think, Marcus."

I watched as she brought the last container of liquid mana up to her lips like it was a Solo cup and she was nursing it. "You okay with that?"

She raised her eyebrows at me a second before she realized. "Oh, this?" She lifted it toward me. "I can neutralize the additives they put into it and devour the mana as it should have been, like that of any magical effect that is turned against you. Look at me like a giant filter where it concerns this nasty stuff. That said—would you like some?"

"Nah." I smiled at her, the closeness of her comforting. "You know, I never got the chance to ask. Are you okay with me being your vessel?"

"What makes you ask that? I chose you, didn't I?" She laughed a bit at my consternation as we walked through the gym.

"Mainly that, even with my potential, I'm still human." I pointed to some of the oni and lycans around us. "You would be better off with one of them, wouldn't you?"

"Nope." She smiled at me and leaned her head on my shoulder. "Their growth would be stunted at best. Even Cassia and Arden, as powerful as they are naturally, won't have the same kind of variable growth as you. Besides, strength is only one aspect of my decision. I like your mind too."

I nodded. "Thanks."

"Thank you for being a good host, when you aren't being suspicious or mean." Her playful ribbing was fine and I just laughed it off.

We were outside and I saw that there was a line to get into the bar, but the bouncer on duty waved us up. Some of the college kids in line scoffed and complained, but unless they were more than they appeared, they wouldn't be getting in anyway.

We continued through the area, some of the guests calling out and telling me they owed me a drink. Which I had to oblige, according to Galaxy, so I ended up drinking much more than I thought I would.

Once I found an opening to get out of the bar, I took it and managed my way up the stairs finally to find Galaxy on the console playing some more.

"Did you really just sacrifice me to all those people down there so you could get some gaming in?" I peered at her blearily and tried to sound offended but I couldn't blame her.

"Research, Marcus, and with that little bit of power from the giant and your canoodling downstairs, I have options to lay out before you." She grinned at me as she paused her game and patted the bed next to her.

"Canoodling?" She nodded at my stressing the word and I frowned. "What are you talking about?"

"I'm strong enough to glean mana that monsters exude when inebriated around you." I blinked at her and she rolled her eyes as she touched my head. The sensation of the buzz that I had was just gone and I could think more clearly now.

"Oh, that would kick ass in a drinking competition!" I grinned and she rolled her eyes before I tried again. "So you can steal mana from people through me now?"

"Yes and no." She frowned, clearly trying to find a way to put it. "Imagine that a perfectly sober monster has a basket of balls that represent their mana. When they're aware of it, they keep their mana with them and secure. Emotions change that slightly, but when they're drinking, the mana escapes from them because their guard is down, and the mana leaves their body a little more readily. That's what I take from them."

"I see, so what are the options you had for me?"

She lifted her hand and a small item appeared. "This is something I've been working on, but I wanted to know if it is suitable." Looking at it, I saw a ring in her hand, green and simple. "Put it on."

I put it on my right index finger where she had pointed for me to and as soon as I did a screen popped up for me.

Mobile Inventory (Limited) – Allows for up to ten items to be stored within.

"Well, that's pretty cool, but what did you mean about having choices?"

She motioned to the ring. "You can keep things in the ring, and I can make it hold more. You can take less in the ring and I can make an internal inventory for you that will allow you to keep things within you. Or I can make the internal inventory larger and be your only inventory."

It took me little time to realize the perks of both. "I'll take the lesser size for the ring and an internal inventory."

She smiled, reaching out to tap the ring and then my stomach.

Mobile Inventory (Minimum) – Allows for up to five items to be stored within.

"Sweet." I smiled and frowned as she stared at me expectantly. "What's up?"

"To access your inventory, you need to be able to channel mana." She frowned. "You haven't gone through and made the mana pathways for yourself since I gave you the ability, have you?"

I shook my head. "Things have been hectic, for sure."

"I've been with you the whole time, I know." She smiled at me and touched my cheek softly. "I know that look. I asked because I figured it better than nagging at you to do it."

GALAXY

"Let me get on that then." I got into one of my drawers and pulled out my pistols that still needed cleaning, then pulled out my weapons cleaning kit.

"What are you doing?" Galaxy stared at me as if I had come unhinged. "You're supposed to be trying for a meditative state."

"This is as close to empty-headed as I get." I unrolled the kit, brushes of various sizes and form tightly secured in their pouches and trappings, just waiting to cleanse my filthy weapons.

So strange, Galaxy growled inside my mind, but quieted when she saw the Zen-like state that cleaning my weapons put me into.

Ejecting the magazines, I placed them aside on my desk, disassembling the upper receiver from the lower after making sure the weapon was clear. I started with the Fae Frame, the cool metal familiar to my touch but only in the manner that pistols were by now.

The inside was every bit as familiar to me as my other weapons had been, the upper housing where the recoil spring and pin were held. I pulled the barrel out and punched the bore of it. Likely not really needing to as it was the first time I had fired it, but I wanted to really enjoy this, so I did. I cleaned the spring with a firm-bristled brush and some gun oil, no specific brand but it worked almost as well as what the armorers had used at Pendleton and that was important to me.

While I cleaned, I fell into my body and found myself floating inside the sea of mana that I had. My hands still moved outwardly, but internally I struggled to try to figure out how to make the channels flow from this watery place into my body.

While I puzzled and reasoned based on the knowledge that Galaxy had imparted into me from Arden, glowing sections of mana shimmered underneath.

Something within me pulled me to the nearest one and told me to dive into the mana and allow it to push me along. I did as beckoned and found myself swimming through the liquid and pressed up against a hard wall. I beat against it and finally as I thought I might drown, I kicked for all I was worth and the wall caved inward.

The mana and I flowed through the space and Galaxy reminded me, *You must control it, or the mana will disperse into your body and can poison you.*

I gulped and focused again, wrangling the sensation of the liquid and pulling it in tight. Where it touched, I made it build a tube-like tunnel of liquid and as soon as it was set, it settled and became as solid as metal. I pulled and tugged and corralled it all throughout the area that I saw was lit up, for what felt like hours.

By the time I was finished, the mana that had flowed around me like a torrential river had become little more than a trickle. Coming back to the task at hand, I had finished cleaning the Silvaero and was wiping all the excess oil off the sides and grip, my mana bar flashing at zero and my stomach grumbling wildly.

"The bill for food is going to be absolutely wild," I grumbled to myself and found Galaxy sitting next to me holding my phone. "What're you up to?"

"I've ordered a few pizzas for you, as well as some salad and something called 'crazy bread'?" She seemed confused and I laughed. "That's what it's called, right?"

"Yeah, and thank you—I'll need it." I smiled at her and pointed to the screen as a text came in. "What's that?"

"Cassia asking if you would like to hang out tonight?" I nodded and her slender fingers wrapped around the device as she tapped back an affirmative. "Are you planning to drink some more?"

I checked the clock; it was only about twenty-one-hundred. It had taken that long to be able to make only one pathway? Shit.

Galaxy handed me my phone and smiled at me. "It is hard, but you can do it. And I will help you out with it as well." I eyed her and she frowned. "What?"

"Does this mean more canoodling?" She laughed at me and nodded. "I never thought someone getting me all boozed up would make me feel so dirty."

She rolled her eyes and said, "Be a good boy and let the magical creatures and myths adore you while I siphon away some of their loose mana. If you do, I'll give you better mana control." She dragged that last bit out like a mother dangling a treat in front of their child.

"You're terrible, you know that?" She nodded at me as someone knocked at my door. "Come on in!"

Cassia opened my door and scowled. "I know I threatened to kill him and bury the body in a corn field, but she could have at least let me teach him how to play that game."

Both Galaxy and I burst into fits of uncontrollable laughter as she continued to whine about the unfairness of it all for another few minutes.

Man, this was great.

CHAPTER FOURTEEN

"Oh, this is horrible." I groaned as I woke up with the worst hangover I had ever had in my life to date.

I moved a little bit and the soft snoring next to me stopped and a large, red arm draped over my stomach and pulled me in tight.

I smirked and opened my eyes a little wider to see Galaxy laying in front of me with her head propped up on my bicep. I blinked at her and looked up at a room that was decidedly not mine.

The room reminded me of a very traditional Japanese bedroom, with tatami mats, and easily the most anime memorabilia I had ever seen. It covered the walls on some of the thinnest shelves I had ever thought possible, but the more I looked I realized they were made of bamboo.

"Admiring my handiwork?" Cassia grumbled groggily into my shoulder from behind, her horn pressing into the back of my neck as her lips caressed my skin.

"You did that?" I looked at it again and it was damned-near perfectly crafted. To my untrained eye, the only way it could have been more perfect was if it held more.

"Yeah, oni are pretty crafty in many ways." I could hear the smile in her tone as she craned her neck to look at it. "Don't let us fool you, we're pretty good with our hands."

I laughed as I felt her rough, calloused hands on my leg squeezing lightly. "Oh, don't I know it."

"I know you do." Galaxy jumped a bit and I looked down only to realize that all three of us were nude. "Stop worrying, I only wanted to cuddle."

"You're killing me, and how did we end up here?" My voice no longer sounded tired and I realized I was famished. "Did we ever get that pizza?"

"It's on the table on my side of the futon." Cassia moved and grabbed the box before lifting it over to our side. "Help yourself, this thing is going to need washing anyway."

She flipped open the box on Galaxy's stomach and pulled a slice of meat lover's pizza out with a growl of delight. "Yes. The best kind."

I chuckled as she sat up and eyed me as she ate in her true oni form. I had to ask, "When did you shift?"

"Well before we started to party in here." She winked at me and I frowned. "You said you liked fighting me in my oni form, and that you liked the real me. So I offered to fight you in this form again and you agreed. Then we started drinking and one thing led to another."

"God, we really need to come up with another way to refer to that," I grumbled and bit into a warm slice of pizza. "How about we refer to sex as a 'scrap'? That way we know if we're referring to actual fighting or sex?"

Galaxy snorted at that and Cassia raised an eyebrow. "It will take me time to get used to that, but I can try if it makes you more comfortable."

I smiled at her. "Thank you, Cass. I appreciate that."

"I appreciate you too." She leaned down and kissed me on the mouth. "You bloodied me last night."

I blinked at her. "What?"

"Bloodied me." She smiled and her eyes rolled back. "I asked you to hit me and you split my lip. It was so nice."

"Oh my God." I froze, then paused. "Wait, you like that?"

She looked at me in confusion. "Oni prefer things rough." She grinned. "The rougher the better. Honestly, it's why we call sex fighting. Because it almost always involves a good deal of violence."

"Oh, that makes so much more sense now," Galaxy muttered as she nibbled on a slice of crazy bread, the look on her face as she did so curious and open as she stared at us. "You were both very enthusiastic."

I blinked at her and several thoughts ran through my head as a slow smile spread across her face. She nodded a couple times and my face reached almost supernova levels of heat before she snickered and Cassia laughed with her.

"For a decent warrior, you're very shy." Cassia put the slice of pizza in her mouth, before she reached out and bodily lifted me so that she could pull me closer to her, my back to her chest and her legs on either side of mine. The way she set me made me feel almost like a little kid sitting in a babysitter's lap. She wrapped her arm around my waist and held me tightly. "You don't have to worry about things like that. Galaxy is a part of you, and she has a bond with me. It's fine. It's a little odd, but it's okay. And besides, it's the truth."

She leaned down and pulled another slice of pizza from the box, pressing it into my hand. "Here, eat. I can feel your stomach growling through mine."

I rolled my eyes and decided to just relax. If Cassia was okay with Galaxy being so close to us and a naked cuddle, I supposed I could deal with that.

"You act as though a healthy male such as yourself would refuse me," Galaxy quipped, taking a larger bite of the bread in her hand before she glanced at Cassia with a glint in her eyes. I could tell she was talking to her through their bond, and Cass laughing enough to shake me confirmed my suspicion.

"She's a part of you—separate, sure—but she knows you

better than I do." Cassia rubbed my chest absently. "I'm not sure how I feel about it, but I do know that where I would have killed any other woman for touching you as she has, I don't feel that protective for her having touched you. It seems natural."

"That's weird?" I blinked and looked over at Galaxy. *Is that your doing?*

Not fully. I frowned openly and she added, *I want her to like me, and have worked to endear myself to her, but the bit about us is just from what she has gleaned from our relationship. I had nothing to do with that other than telling her things that you already know. Also, I was able to get another of your mana channels made for you last night while you slept. It is your left arm, much like you had done with your right.*

Huh. "Okay, thank you. I'm a little weirded out by this but as long as everyone is cool with it, I'll go along with it. I'm pretty sure you don't have any interest in me like that, so if you want to cuddle, I'm game."

She leaned forward and kissed my cheek. "Thank you." She looked up at Cassia and smiled. "And thank you as well."

Cassia reached her massive hand out and grabbed Galaxy's chin with her thumb and index finger. "Not a problem. Will you be joining us in the gym?"

Galaxy laughed openly. "I will not be, I need to research things—but you two have fun."

She rolled back and stepped into the shadows before disappearing. I felt Cassia's weight shift a little as she leaned down. "Now that she's gone, how about one of those scraps you had mentioned?"

I laughed as her arm tightened and pulled me closer.

An hour later, we were in the gym lifting, which was a new experience to me in the way Cassia had me doing it. Not by much—I lifted when I was in the Marine Corps—though it was a lot more high intensity interval training than anything else. Turned out that a lot of the security staff here lifted traditionally and I found that a little less interesting and attention grabbing than I had before.

Not only that, but when I went to bench the hundred and eighty-five pounds that I knew would be my max—it was way too light.

I blinked at Cassia and blurted, "What the hell is this?" She frowned and came over to confirm the weight. "Are you sure?"

"I could curl that easily as a warm up Marcus, yes." She actually had two hundred that she was curling easily at the moment. "What is your Brawn stat at?"

I glanced at my stats and said, "Twelve?"

"So then you should be able to lift way more than that." She smiled and came over to start taking weights off. "The only way to test it is to push yourself!"

She went to where the weight plates were and grabbed two hundred-pound plates. I lifted it with barely a thought and she added another two on. Same thing. We got up to six hundred pounds before I started to notice that I was feeling it a little more like I would when I would warm up. "You've got to be shitting me!"

Several other people wandered over and began to help Cassia pile on the weight. By nine hundred, it felt like I was starting to reach my limits, but Cassia wanted me to push myself further. She added another fifty pounds on, just twenty-five on each side, and told me to do a full set of three.

I put the first one up, slowly, my heart rate quickening as I strained. Our watchers began to clap and cheer boisterously, their calls to put up or shut up echoing around us as Cassia knelt near my head. "Come on, Marcus, push yourself. Push!"

I brought the weight down and grunted as it fought me on the way back up. "Almost there!" Cassia snarled, making my adrenaline spike. "Push it, one more!"

On the last rep, the cheers grew to almost storm-like levels, some of the wolves howling together in a low tone as someone chanted my name. "Marcus. Massacre. Marcus. Massacre!"

"A little more, Marcus, get it done!" Cassia roared next to my ear, my eyes closed.

I took a deep breath and pushed the weight back up—it felt so much heavier as my muscles screamed in protest, or had that been me calling out for strength from whoever might be listening in Valhalla?

I opened my eyes as I reached the apex of the rep and saw that Cassia held another fifty-pound plate on the bar between my hands, grinning. "Good job, for a mage."

I didn't even have the chance to set the weight down before one of the oni snatched it out of my hands and the crowd was on me. They lifted me from the bench and congratulated me for my efforts, and on the new personal best that had blown my last out of the water.

"Never seen a Touched this strong, 'specially not a mage," one of the lycans called out excitedly as they clapped my back. I growled at one subconsciously as they got way too close to my inner thigh and they just laughed and howled some more as I struggled to get free.

Finally, I was too embarrassed to deal with it and cast Embodiment to get away from them altogether. That just made them even more excited.

Cassia hollered, "Never a good idea to run from a lycan!"

One of them attempted to tackle me, but I managed to juke around them at the last second. "Why?"

"Hunting instincts," Jolly's voice rang out behind me just before he shoved past me and grabbed the next lycan by the shirt. "Cool it, you pack of rabid shitheads!"

The lycans all stood down immediately, the old man staring at them as if he was daring any of them to come at him, but they all backed off.

"Thanks, Jolly." I grabbed him by the shoulder and he turned to look at me, his eyes a blue so intense that I could hardly recognize them. His eyes had been another color before, hadn't they?

"They're not going to turn back to their normal brown

anymore after the stunt I pulled with that drink." He smiled at me apologetically. "I owe you a debt of gratitude and an apology, son. I'm sorry for getting you involved in my own pity party; it's not on you to serve me like that."

"It is, but I get that you have your issues and that it helps you in some way that I don't really get." I patted him on the shoulder and he smiled at me some more. "Why don't we get a drink some time to seal the friendship, huh?"

He blinked at me in surprise. "I'd like that."

"Maybe going a tad easier on the wolf's bane." I winked at him and he tucked his head almost bashfully.

"That's likely a good idea." I swallowed and he shoved me toward Cassia. "What's that for?"

"She's going to put you through your paces now that you can lift so much." He chuckled as Cassia's fingers gripped my shoulder. "You'll regret me stopping them. That was likely meant to be your cardio."

I looked up at her and she smirked before nodding.

All I did was lower my head and mutter, "Fuck me."

"Did you want to scrap again already?" She perked up and I snorted, and so did more than twenty of the guards around us.

She put me through my paces and it was nice to be able to do much more physically demanding things again. Running and sprints were all well and good but this was something I hadn't known my body was craving.

I was sore for a little bit, then as soon as I ate again, I felt perfectly fine. Which could have been the lycanthropic healing, but I wasn't entirely sure.

After eating, Cassia and I fought, then Kenshi came in and we fought. The idea was for me to learn how to fight supernatural creatures when I would likely be at a disadvantage.

I stood more of a chance against Cass; she was young, according to her, and Kenshi was much older and craftier, not to mention more brutal.

Each of his strikes and kicks felt like I was being beaten by a Mack truck on steroids. If it hadn't been for me being as squirrelly as I could be, I'd likely have been able to walk and only walk. Thanks to that though, I had more of an idea about how to fight supernatural creatures and that making an oni angry only worked on the younger ones.

Kenshi did not fall for my bullshit and he made sure I paid for any half-baked insults I threw his way.

I ate so that my healing would kick in and I could stop limping like I was on my last legs, then showered and got ready for my shift.

As I finished shaving, I leaned back and found that there was a sticky note on my desk. I finished toweling off my face and found that it was from Seamus.

Boy-o,

Them buckeyes were tastier'n I ever had. If you feel generous, more o' those would be 'preciated.

Thank ye, laddie.

Seamus.

I chuckled and answered, "You got it, Seamus."

I could've sworn I heard a snuffling laughter under my bed and finished getting dressed, adding my Silvaero to my ring as well as my oni blade. The Fae Frame I put in the holster that I had on my waist, then pulled a red flannel over the shirt to hide it a little bit. Luckily, we kept the bar on the cooler side in the summer months from what Arden said the first night I worked there.

The shift went smoothly despite Arden calling off, so I worked with another server named Aerin, a Fae man who looked like he had seen plenty of fights, but came out happier for it. He seemed nice enough and only gave me a little shit here and there, but in a friendly sort of way.

I had no issues with anyone, and my tip jar was looking pretty healthy by the end of the night as well. All in all, it had been a good day.

I walked up to my room to find it empty and plopped down to sleep before having to get up and get my ass kicked in the morning.

CHAPTER FIFTEEN

I woke up to someone holding my mouth and found Cassia bent down in front of me. I blinked at her and let her know I'd be quiet before she whispered, "There are some Fae outside, and we can't tell who they're with."

"Okay, do you need an extra body to defend the place?" I stood up and pulled my boots on, tying them the way I had when I was in the Corps, and summoned Thumper into my hand from the ring.

She gasped at me and pointed to my weapon. "How?"

I tapped my ring. "This. What's going on?"

"They want you to come and chat." Cassia frowned as I made to remark about them being able to come in, but I paused as she held up a single hand to stop me. "I know, but they wouldn't come inside."

"That's suspicious." I frowned and pointed to my weapon with my head. "Should I have this in hand when I go outside?"

"No, better to appear unarmed." She pulled me out of the bed and pushed me toward the door. "The longer we keep them waiting, the antsier they get, and pissed off Fae are dangerous."

"Okay, let's go." I willed the weapon into my ring and

straightened myself out, glad that I had fallen asleep mostly clothed.

The downstairs bar area was filled with at least ten security guards in uniform. As soon as my foot touched the bottom of the stairs, they surrounded us and moved with me as if they were an elite security detail and this was the most natural thing in the world to them.

Once we reached the door, one of them stopped me and four of them flooded out, before the fifth stepped with me out the door, the others bringing up the rear with Cassia.

"Finally!" a voice called out. A brutish bruiser-type man stepped forward and stared at me. He was clearly elven, pointed ears and fair-skinned with blond locks that swept back over his ears, braided into a tail that hung down over his chest. He wore a slim vest over his muscular torso and shorts that matched. "I take it that you're the one called 'Marcus' that the jinn spoke of."

"You know Arden?" I asked and he smiled in a way that made my blood boil. "Where is she?"

"I'm right here, don't be so dramatic." Arden called out from behind him as she stood with a woman whose skin was almost blue, it was so white. Her eyes were pale, and yellow in the irises, her hair pink and plaited from the back of her head and down to the side of her long blue dress. "This is the princess of the Winter Court—"

"Aeslyn," I breathed, the name fell from my lips and almost made me fall to my knees. She was much more pale than I remembered, and her hair was longer than it had been, but I would never forget the woman for as long as I lived. She was still as beautiful as I remembered and standing here in the pale moonlight from above, she looked like she radiated an ethereal light of her own.

"Oh, Marcus." Her pink eyebrows knit together and she stepped forward, then must have remembered her station because she stopped and lifted her head. "How did you become entangled in all this?"

"Entangled?" I laughed at the absurdity of it. "Me? I've been entangled in all of this since the day I met you, but you would have never let me know, would you?"

"Shut your mouth, mage," the bruiser growled and stepped forward, but I just ignored him.

"Is this why you decided to keep Connell from me?" I frowned, the memories of her telling me that she wanted me to stay away. "Because of what I was?" She stayed quiet as I numbly asked, "What I wasn't?"

"You were always a fighter, Marcus Bola." She frowned more, her demeanor cooling a bit. "I had hoped that you would fight on and forget that Connell existed. You were supposed to forget him. And me. But you didn't, and I was stuck holding your hand all these years because I had to worry about you coming to look for us and ruining my sacrifice."

"What sacrifice!" I roared and suddenly the brute was on top of me and the only reason he wasn't caving my head in was Cassia grabbing his fist and the other guards surging forward to push him away.

Aeslyn watched me with some kind of emotion on her face, but I couldn't comprehend it. Arden stepped closer to me and I watched her as she did. Anger flooded through me like a torrent. How could she? I knew that we hadn't been friends for long, but fuck.

"I didn't know," she started, and put her hands out toward me. "The sacrifice she's talking about is having given up her freedoms so that she could protect Connell. And honestly, that's the first time I've heard him referred to that way."

"I believe her, Marcus." Cassia grunted.

"It's true, I refer to him as Conellar around others," Aeslyn stated as she crossed her arms. "And I don't have time to talk about all of this with you right now, Marcus. We can talk later. Right now, we have bigger concerns."

"Our son takes a much larger priority, Aeslyn," I snarled, years of being lied to and treated like a pariah coming to the fore.

"Not this second!" she roared back, snapping her fingers. Guards stepped out of the shadows and pulled a bound and gagged man along with them. "This man has news that is going to affect you—honestly, it's life or death."

"She has the gist of it there," Arden stated dryly as she crossed her arms. "They mean to hunt you down and kill you."

"What? How?" I stepped around the guards and walked over to the gagged man and removed the cloth from his mouth. "How do you know about me?"

He spat in my face and I had to admit I hadn't expected that. From the immense look of surprise on his face, I didn't think he expected me to hit him quite so hard either. Or the other Fae holding him.

Even Aeslyn gasped at the gash my fist had made under the elf's right eye, but I lifted his face back toward me. "I just found out that the last eight years of my life have been bullshit, and now my life is in danger. Please—*please*—make me ask you again."

"They found your scent at the scene of the fire, and they recognized it." He moved his jaw a bit as if it hurt to speak. "They found your scent at the mall too where their seller was apprehended. They'll hunt you down and kill you." He turned and glared at Aeslyn. "No amount of sacrifice will protect you from his wrath—he comes for you and all you Winter scum hold dear. They already close on something precious to you, princess."

Aeslyn strode closer and growled, "What did you say?"

The elven man just cackled, staring straight at her. "You'll know soon enough! Once they do get it, then nothing will stand in their way as they take this city! And the next, and the next!"

His eyes took on a manic gleam and I just watched as he prepared to spit at me again, but moved aside before he could, slamming my Blade spell into his throat savagely. Arterial spray flung blood toward me and at the two on either side of him as I tore it out. The elves on either side of the corpse gasped and made to attack me as they let him go, but I turned and let the spell go, my anger still writhing within me at the threat.

My gaze caught Aeslyn's, a look of horror and realization coming over her as I spoke, blood dripping from my face. "I need to know everything. Why do they want you dead?"

"You aren't more concerned about yourself?" The bruiser asked from where he stood, his path to me blocked by the guards.

"I've had people trying to kill me in countries whose names you can probably not even think of or know how to pronounce—you get used to that." I glared at Aeslyn. "Tell me. And what was that precious thing he mentioned?"

"The Unseelie, the Winter Fae, are powerful and hold to the old beliefs that humans and Fae can coexist and interact to a larger degree than they have in centuries," Aeslyn began, eyeing her bruiser as she spoke. "The majority of us truly believe that leaving the humans alone until they are ready to accept the different kinds of beings there are is the right thing to do. The Summer… do not."

"The Summer Court believes that humans are a plague and should be either eradicated or made to be servile, like property," Brute added in. "Hard to believe you aren't afraid, mage."

I just hit him with an eye roll and turned back to Aeslyn. "What was the precious thing?"

"I don't know. It could have been a veiled threat for Connell to make me take our forces and put them on him, but there's no way they can find him." She stared at me and said, "They're going to be coming for you, Marcus. You need to hide where it's safe for you."

My voice was calm, dark even for me as I said, "I don't give a shit who comes for me as long as they stay away from my son."

"My son," Aeslyn hissed and stepped close enough to slap me across the face. "I don't know where these powers you have are coming from, but you will not put my son in any more danger than he's already in."

"What kind of danger?" I stared into her pained eyes and she grimaced, trying to look away, but I moved to stay with her. "What. Danger?"

"The Fae don't like when a Fae and human mix," she stated. "It's hard for our kind to have children with each other, but it's almost impossible to have it happen with a human. Yet it happened with you. Connell is a good boy, and I knew from the moment I conceived I would give everything to be with him. To see him raised properly and protected. And I did give everything, Marcus."

"All I see is a princess who hides her son from his father." I seethed, then shook my head, trying to let it go. "So even your own kind hate him. No father, a mother who knows only duty—it seems anyway—where is he?"

"Safe," she reiterated again. "You need to worry about yourself. No Summer Fae can find him where he is, and he is well cared for, at least until the threats are rooted out, but he can't stay there forever without someone finding him."

"So you think these guys are a threat to him?" She nodded and I took a deep breath. "Very well."

"What do you plan to do, Marcus?" Aeslyn spoke low, then raised her voice as I started to walk away. "Answer me!"

I whipped around and snarled, "I'm going to find them, and stop them."

"We can help you, Marcus." She stepped forward again, but I just glared at her. "I can send warriors to help you find them and do just that."

"Why would I want your help?" I replied coldly. "You kept him from me for years, Aeslyn, and now he's being vaguely threatened by people who not only hate your people for their ideals, but by your own people to boot. And the former of whom want to take my life because I've stumbled onto their b-list movie plot to take over the city with a highly addictive magic drug. If I do nothing else with my life and time right now, it's to protect my son—who probably has no clue I exist—from these assholes."

She stood there and watched me for a second before I turned and walked away, the guards conflicted. Did they stay with the potential threat, or did they come with me?

Cassia grunted and ordered, "Stand down; fall back to the Table."

I walked into the bar and made my way toward the stairs. Made it about halfway too, but someone decided it would be a good idea to grab me. I wheeled around on them and saw that it was Cassia, concern plain on her face. "Marcus, are you okay?"

My anger boiled over and it was so hard not to yell. To scream and lash out. I wanted someone to feel as barren and confused as I was. The last eight years of my life had all been based around a lie. Something that I wasn't supposed to know.

"Why?" I muttered once, looking into Cassia's eyes. "You had to have known that she was the princess of the Winter Court, why didn't you tell me when you learned her name?"

"Aeslyn is an odd name, to me, and I honestly hadn't expected it to be her, Marcus." Cass tried to console me and touch my shoulder, but I didn't much feel like being touched.

Arden walked into the bar and eyed me with concern, like she had something to say to me.

"What is it?"

"They wanted me to try to talk you into allowing them to help find the Summer Court, specifically who is doing this." I started to tell her where they could shove it, but she stopped me. "I'm not going to. This is bigger than they know and they're choosing to disregard certain elements of it, like the fact that they're making a magical drug."

"And you didn't know anything about any of this with me and Aeslyn?"

I was prepared for her to lie, to say something that I wasn't expecting. Anything other than, "I suspected, but when I went to her place to talk to her, she had photos of you in places she thought were hidden, namely an album in her closet high enough that it was hard to reach." My brows knit together and she continued. "I wasn't supposed to see them, I don't think, but I kind of appeared in her room as she was getting things out of her closet and saw it."

"And what about my son?" My tone was questioning, but I tried to keep the accusation out of it.

She sort of shook her head from side to side. "The album was when I knew that she knew you somehow. I did not know that Conellar was Connell."

I nodded, still a bit too raw to trust myself to speak, but there was something missing. "Galaxy?"

Nothing came, no sound, no stirring within me. Nothing.

"Galaxy!" I bellowed and sprinted up to my room to make sure she wasn't there. I threw open the door to find my room as I had left it. I reached out and tried to find her somewhere, anywhere within me. I found a small thread and tugged it, like a bell cord.

Something smacked into the window and fluttered around persistently before disappearing. Galaxy stepped from the shadows to my far right with a deep scowl on her face. "What? I was out doing reconnaissance for you and I only checked one place!"

"What place?"

She smiled and I frowned as another update to my mini-map brought a red arrow to me.

"About six miles down the road in another factory. There are six vats this time." She grinned and grabbed my shoulders. "With that much mana, we can do a lot of stuff, Marcus. And there are a lot of people there. More than last time by sixty. They're not as cautious, but they're better armed and the lookouts are elves."

I turned to find Cassia and Arden standing in the doorway, Cassia grinning. "We going to fuck this place up, or not?"

"Let's go kick some ass and let them know they picked the wrong guy to hunt." Arden punched Cassia, her expression serious but excited.

"Oh!" Cassia clapped. "I'll go get the others and we can do a raid!"

"The High Table staff are not going to perform a raid on the Summer Court in this city!" Uncle Yen announced, punctuated by a tired yawn. "I had wondered what you kids were up to."

"But Yenny, this place is a threat to the supernatural creatures in the area, even to the High Table," Cassia protested, crossing her arms. "As the head of security, I can't allow that."

"And I can't allow our neutral status to be blown due to a hot-headed oni, a homicidal jinn and my wanted nephew." Uncle Yen rolled his eyes. "As of right this moment, Cassia, you are no longer head of security."

"What?" I stepped forward and got his attention. "Uncle Yen, they're just trying to help. Please, don't take that away from Cass."

"I know what I'm doing, boy." He snarled and pointed a finger at me. "You and Arden aren't held to the same standards that she would be as head of security, and are free to do what you want. But I can't have someone so attached to the High Table out there killing people and stopping a conspiracy to take over the city."

"Wait…" Cassia frowned and pointed from Yen to Galaxy. "You heard all of that? What we were just talking about?"

Uncle Yen snickered. "Course I did." He reached up and patted her bicep. "Go have fun saving the city, dear. You can have your position back tomorrow."

Cassia pulled the older man into a hug so tight that he cried out and several sharp pops echoed around the room from his back. She put him down and looked over him. "Yenny, I'm so sorry, are you okay?"

He touched his back and took a deep breath before wheezing, "Never. Better." He limped back to his room and opened the door. He turned around and cracked his back once, sighing in relief, then said, "You lot be safe. Come back safe. And give 'em hell."

"Oh, we will," I growled, Cassia and Arden smiling. "Arden, you want to see if Merlin wants to come and earn his place?"

"He's already on his way here." Her face was serious. "I thought some shit might go down, so I let him borrow my bike to come here without me. Where do we go first?"

"The armory." My expression may have been grim but I was excited. "Let's get going, dark's burning."

CHAPTER SIXTEEN

I don't think I had ever seen this much ammunition even while I was deployed in the Marine Corps, but—God have mercy—we would be putting some of it to good use.

"What are these rounds right here?" I pointed to a box of gray lumps in copper-colored jackets.

"Specially treated iron rounds, hundred and forty-five grain with a lead core," Cassia explained, taking another box and placing it in front of me with empty magazines for a rifle. "These should fit your rifle, but let me know if they don't."

"What do the rounds do?"

She snickered and grinned. "Really tickle the Fae. They're highly allergic to cold iron, so the heat from being shot is a little less deadly, but still really fucking annoying."

"Fair enough." I loaded up six magazines, thirty rounds each with iron rounds and another three with traditional ammo that I marked by wrapping with dark red tape. "Shit, Galaxy, can I stack these in my inventory?"

"The same items will stack in your ring, yes, but you can only hold ten of each before it goes to the next slot," she warned me, and I grimaced.

It was good that there was a stacking mechanism, but the ring was so small and I needed to finish opening my mana pathways before I could use my internal inventory.

That left me having to prime Thumper with a magazine loaded, then inventory it. I put my Silvaero into the inventory with more iron rounds designed for pistols loaded into it. Two slots there, and another two for the magazines that held normal and iron rounds. And finally I had another four magazines for my Fae Frame that I put into it. I was full up in the ring just like that.

I loaded the Fae Frame with normal bullets for the first magazine, just to be safe. Making sure my oni blade was tucked safely where it should be, I then went to my room to change into something a little more tactical. Or I would have, if Arden hadn't been a step ahead and brought me a black turtleneck and a pair of my black cargo pants.

I nodded my thanks to her and changed where I was, not giving a shit that people could see my boxers.

Kenshi walked in. "Bubba Marcus, kid Merlin here."

"Thanks Kenshi, you can let him in," Cassia called as she tucked her shirt in.

Merlin walked into the room, his brow sweating heavily, the clothes on his body drenched. He looked miserable.

"You okay, Merlin?" I raised an eyebrow at him.

He wore a black cloak and thickly knitted pants with a dark red shirt underneath. He looked like he was in tryouts to play Dracula, honestly, but he muttered a few words and his clothes lifted and changed into a more fitting pair of black slacks, a darker cloak and black shirt that were now free of sweat stains.

"Yeah, though I wish I was a little more used to such activity." He frowned as Cassia stepped toward him with a smile I had become familiar with earlier in the day. "What do you want?"

"To invite you to the gym." She smiled almost innocently. "You can come and train with me and Marcus."

My eyes widened as he looked my way and he blanched. "I

think I'll stick to riding a bike."

"Nah, you're mine now, wizard-boy." Cassia planted a massive mitt on him and he flinched, squeaking audibly. "You have a weapon on you?"

"My staff." He produced it from under his cloak and grinned. "I can club people with it and cast spells."

"Okay, and how about one that can stab someone who is trying to kill you?" She pressed and leaned down to stare him in the eyes. "Because not everyone is going to wait for you to cast a spell, and no one is going to allow you to keep that staff once they realize what you are and what it can do."

He looked to me for help, but I shook my head. "She has a point, Merlin. They'll all be physically stronger than us, so having an ace in the hole could save your life."

Cassia grinned and turned away as the boy stammered at her back, "But I don't know how to use a knife to do anything but eat."

I blinked at him, Arden slapped her forehead with her palm, and Cassia roared with delight before shouting, "Bubba Kenshi! I'm gonna borrow a blade from your stock."

Kenshi poked his head in a moment later to glance around the room before simply asking, "Who?"

We all pointed to a now-embarrassed Merlin, who raised his hand. Kenshi's lip lifted, his horns poking the sky as he assented. "'Kay."

Cassia threw open a large cabinet, stomped over to Merlin, lifted him up, and carried him over, ordering him, "Hold out your hand."

He obeyed and she started measuring blades against it before she finally settled on a small, thick-bladed kunai that reminded me of a leaf. She found a special sheath for it and started to tie it to his belt, then around his thigh. "Tell me if it's too loose. You don't want to not be able to draw it quickly."

A few minor adjustments later and he was strapped with a blade that he looked clearly uncomfortable with having. "Hey, stop glancing at it like it's going to bite you."

"I've never used one before, it might cut me." He seemed genuinely upset.

"Isn't this something you'll need to get used to if you want to join another Order?" I motioned to my oni blade, now in my hand. "Weapons? Especially the Order of the Sword. Take the sharp end and stab anyone who gets too close to you."

He reached for it and fumbled for where it was, making me stop him.

"Watch." I replaced my blade in the sheath, then let my hand come to a rest, then slowly reached for it to pull it. I pulled it and prepared to strike, but stopped. "As we move, I want you to constantly reach for it and visualize striking with it, okay? You need to be as familiar with where your weapon is on your body as you are with your own appendages—more so—because this one could save your life."

He tried to whip his hand down to it and screwed up, Cassia grabbing his wrist. "Slowly at first. Build the muscle memory. Slow and smooth. Smooth is fast."

I smiled and finished, "Perfect practice makes perfect."

He nodded slowly and took his time reaching for the weapon as the rest of us went about preparing.

"So what's the goal of this little foray?" Merlin muttered as he moved his hands to the weapon on his hip.

"Stop them producing what they're producing?" Arden shrugged, then frowned. "Get experience and level up?"

"All of the above, but mainly to make producing it a fucking nightmare and encourage them to stop," I growled, shoving my Fae Frame back into the holster once more at my waist. I'd added another round to the mag after chambering one. It had been there for the meeting with the Winter Court and now it would serve the purpose it was supposed to. "Make it so inconvenient and costly to keep trying for this that they stop and know that we aren't to be fucked with."

"What if it doesn't work?" Arden asked uncertainly.

I smiled at her softly. "Rinse and repeat until desired results."

Cassia sighed dreamily. "We are so going to scrap later."

I laughed and Merlin frowned. "What's that supposed to mean?"

"Don't worry about it, kiddo." Arden grabbed him by the shoulders and led him out into the parking lot into Cassia's SUV.

We were moving and I tapped Merlin on the arm. "Keep practicing."

He flinched before his hand drifted to the blade and back. I nodded my head once and focused on what we needed to do. "Galaxy, how far are we from where the watchers are?"

"I will warn you when you get close." Cassia followed the route on her mini-map and before long Galaxy nearly shouted, "Stop!"

I slid forward, my face bouncing off the back of the front seat painfully as the car screeched to a halt. "What the hell was that?"

"There's a sentry nearby that drifted from his spot," Galaxy explained as a figure moved down the alleyway toward us.

"Arden, Merlin, Galaxy, get down!" I hissed and pulled Arden out of the front seat so that I could get up into the front with Cassia. They did as I ordered and I grabbed Cassia's face, pulling her close so I could kiss her passionately.

"Mmf!" She groaned, but returned the embrace enthusiastically as the sentry approached.

A knock on the window a second later prompted me to break off the kiss as Cassia rolled the window down. "Hey, move it along you can—"

I whipped around and punched my oni blade into his throat and tore it out the side viciously.

"Oh my God!" Merlin cried, then Arden clamped a hand over his mouth, trying to hush him, but he managed to duck back enough to say, "What the hell was that?"

"Getting rid of an enemy, Merlin." I sighed and looked back at him, flicking some of the blood off my blade out the window. "These guys wouldn't hesitate to kill us if they knew who we were, and they have a hit out on me too, so they really want me dead."

"But you didn't even offer him a chance to fight back." He motioned to the body as we started to get out of the SUV.

"Would a supernatural creature give you a chance if they knew you were going to arrest them?" Cassia challenged him quietly. "That giantess almost killed you; would have if we hadn't been there. There are almost never any fair fights out here, Merlin. You need to be as savage as a situation demands, or you could die."

She reached down and put a hand on his shoulder before she muttered, "I want to be able to play video games with you, kid. So, please, don't let some misguided sense of fairness or honor take that from me."

Arden opened her mouth and closed it, pointing from Cassia to Merlin, then back as the boy watched her walk toward the end of the alleyway. Finally she managed to tap him on the shoulder and say, "She just admitted she liked you. Don't fuck that up. It took her two years to say something like that to me."

I snorted and she shot me a dirty look that said she was serious and I suddenly felt very special.

We continued down the alley in silence, all three of us protecting Merlin as we walked. Once we reached the end, Arden tapped Cass and me on the shoulder and whispered, "I'll go scout a bit and kill any of the lone ones I can find. You guys going to be okay without me for a minute?"

"I will scout from above," Galaxy said and shifted into a form that looked like a raven. *I will mark the ones that I find on your mini-map in orange.*

We nodded and she took off, Arden moving from view in a warm gust of air.

"God, she's so fast." I looked back at Merlin and he shrugged. "It's true."

"Let's go." I grunted as orange blips populated on my map. A few stragglers on our right looked spread out enough that we could move toward them easily.

"Any chance you could let us know where they're looking?" Cassia asked no one in particular.

Be happy you get this for now. Galaxy harrumphed and flew on.

I shook my head and kept myself as low as I could so that we could cross the open roadway toward the building. Galaxy had been right; this place was crawling with goons, and the ones on the outside were elven alright. Their auras were a mixture of green and orange and I could see their ears in the colors.

Several of them dotted the grounds between us. A dilapidated, rusted metal fence with holes a car's width wide was all that stood between us and the lot that looked like it had several shitty beaters in it. There were construction trailers, port-a-shitters and storage containers all over the place that made the area look more like a maze than a factory of any manner.

There were walkways between the factory in front of us and another sister building along the second and third stories that had bodies on them at somewhat regular intervals.

"Whoever sent these guys here has a tactical mind. This place is going to be hard to get into," I grumbled and Cassia bounced excitedly from where she knelt.

We managed to sneak up on one, his death nothing to be excited by, but the one after that came around the corner of a construction trailer too fast and managed to make noise before Cassia grabbed him and broke his neck.

"What was that!" someone shouted in the distance.

Fuck.

"Fan out and find it!" Someone was calling the shots from up above and they were good at it.

Galaxy, pass this on for me. She gave me a mental go ahead and I continued. *I'm going to pull out Thumper and start drawing their attention. Cassia, I want you to tank for me if you can, just kill anyone in your way. Arden, I need you as my deeps. Do the damage and kill the ones coming as swiftly as you can, okay?*

Got it, Arden responded via Galaxy. Cassia nodded and pointed a thumb at Merlin as she turned toward the sound of the voices.

"Merlin, I need you to get to that car over there behind us and start laying waste to the people who come at us however you can." He looked at me in fear and I grabbed him by the cloak. "Listen, it's okay to be afraid, but you gotta pony up and do your job. You Warden enough for this?"

He gasped and pushed me, a set of hands reaching over my arms as I stumbled. Merlin tapped them and the elven figure grunted and shook before falling down. "Yeah, I am." Merlin kicked him in the head and ran toward the car.

I rolled my eyes as my oni blade claimed another life, then turned and put it away to summon Thumper into my hands. "God damn, this feels like freedom!"

"Cass, I got your six!" I pressed the butt stock into my shoulder and began to fire at the ones who got too close to the oni.

The loud report of the rifle in my hands made a thrill run down my body as I caught one of the elves in the shoulder, then neck as Cassia came forward and slammed her fist into his throat.

"You need my blade?" I called over my firing but she just started laughing and pulled out a massive club. "Never mind."

She whipped the massive weapon into someone's skull and the metallic clang made me shiver almost sympathetically, but there was no time to be distracted. One of my rounds caught an elf in the eye, his hand flying up as a massive ball of flames crashed into him and charred him on the spot.

I worked it up to three-round bursts of fire, stalling them long enough to allow Cassia to whack them, but they started to learn from it.

"Incoming!" someone yelled from above, drawing my attention as I reloaded. Tossing the empty mag into a cargo pocket, I glanced up in time to see a mostly scrapped car careening toward me from the air.

"Oh fuck." I grunted and cast Embodiment, stepping four feet forward and into melee range of one of the excitable elves. I blocked his punch with the ejection port side of Thumper, then called the rifle into my inventory and switched it with the Silvaero. I brought the pistol up to his chest, safety switching off on instinct, then fired two rounds into his midsection. He bent over as I cast Blade and stabbed him in the chest.

I kept the sword spell at the ready and waded into the fray with Cassia. I stabbed around her and worked as swiftly as I was able. It was a different sort of mentality to fire at those who were close, but stab at those who were closer to us.

My breathing grew steadily more ragged as we fought on, and I happened to catch a glimpse of elves surrounding Merlin as he furiously wove spells to send flying at them.

"Get to him, Marcus." Cassia panted and snarled as she turned and shoved her foot into one of the people surrounding us.

Galaxy, get Arden here for us. I flicked my wrist and the magazine flung from the magazine well, then summoned another full magazine and racked it. It was hard to do with Blade in my left hand, but I did it.

I ducked under a blow meant for my head and shot the elf in the junk before stabbing him in the knee. The Blade bit deep and he cried out before Arden shoved her hand toward his mouth and fire burst forth and down his throat.

"Get to cover!" she ordered and then whispered, "And close your eyes when I tell you to."

I nodded and sprinted to where Merlin was using his kunai to swat at elves as they pressed in on him. His other hand flickered with electrical energy and he managed to zap a couple of them before I got to him. "Thank God."

An elf snarled and turned in time for me to stab him in the ear and grunt, "Get down!"

"Now!" Arden howled and I slammed my eyes closed. A bright flash burst before my eyelids, several voices crying out in pain and confusion before it went dark again.

I opened my eyes, the elves around me disabled, their hands rubbing their eyes as they doubled over in agony. I put my gun away, then pulled my oni blade and got to work. I stabbed temples, slit throats and slammed my weapons into spines, killing anyone still able to move.

Retching behind me drew my attention and I turned to see Merlin tossing his guts over the side of the car he had been on. Arden jogged toward me, then around me as I joined Cassia in killing the rest.

She looked up and scowled at the walkways. "There are more and they might be blinded for now, but we have to get moving if we want to keep them from spotting us again." She turned, nodded to me, and jutted her chin toward the factory. "Go ahead, I'll work on getting those two behind you and bring up the rear. Be safe."

Sheathing the oni blade, I let my sword fade and brought Thumper back out, checking the magazine to see if it was still good, then decided against it and just ejected it and put a full one in. Better safe.

I lowered my center of gravity and walked with the muzzle down but ready as my eyes scanned the area before and above me on the walkways. There was a concentration of orange dots inside this building, but none by the door I stood beside.

Galaxy, you still with us? Her attention turned to me and I knew she was just inside in the rafters before I could ask.

You have leveled up twice, Marcus. There are many enemies in here, human and otherwise. She was quiet for a time, then spoke again, *There is no telling what will happen when you come in.*

I nodded and opened my status sheet, ten points to spend, wahoo! I rolled my eyes and grimaced. I added two points to my Physique first, then the same number to Dexterity. I put one more into Brawn, and the other five I dumped into Mana.

I rolled my neck; several muted pops and I felt so much better. Some of the bruising from the fighting and several glancing blows felt better immediately, though I was beginning to get a little hungry.

More points to spend on spells and whatnot, Marcus, I reminded myself, then opened the tab to look things over.

I had spells that were available to me above Wisp thanks to

Arden, her casting fire spells at me having opened them up as Galaxy gobbled up her magic.

I had six points to work with and decided to put a point into Embodiment, allowing me to move up to twenty-five feet almost instantly, which was amazing.

Let's see these fire spells, I thought to myself and scrolled through them.

A couple of them were lame; Flaming Hands and Flame Breath. All cool in their own rights, but fuck if they couldn't turn extremely bad in a lot of ways if not wielded properly.

An attack-on-everybody-kind of spell would be cool, but I could only use it when there was a large crowd…

Fireblast – Choose a point within sixty feet to create a detonation point for a thirty-foot blast of flames. 75 Mana.

That was an expensive spell, to say the least, but if I could get the drop on some people, I could light them up.

I checked to see if there were any other spells that I wanted at the moment, but this one held my interest the most. I spent the point to get it, then four more points to level it up to five of eight.

The perks for doing so were nice. The cost was down to sixty mana, and the range was doubled with the flames hotter and a chance to cause burning damage.

"Nice." After I put a fresh iron mag in the Silvaero, I glanced back to see that Cassia and Arden all but dragged Merlin with them, his face pallid and eyes half-lidded. "He going to be okay?"

"Witnessing so much blatant murder doesn't sit well with me," he grumbled and I rolled my eyes. "You don't believe me?"

"No, I do," I snapped back quietly. "I felt the same way the first few times I cleared a house in country, but you either get used to it or you have to watch as more of your friends die and pay for your inaction."

His face fell a little further, but we needed to get in there and put a stop to the production at this place, so his compunctions against all this would have to wait.

"We go in, see who's in that massive group and then nuke them." Arden frowned at me and I showed her my status screen. "You heard me right."

She raised her eyebrows and grinned. "This is so much fun."

I nodded and we made a slow entry. What we hadn't counted on was that there would be someone that hadn't been on our maps staring down at us in surprise, a figure with a massive, hulking aura in the shape of a gorilla-like monster with a red cap on. He opened his mouth to start saying something, but a small fizzle of electricity leaped between me and Cassia and stunned him.

He fell forward with a gasp, but what startled me most was that Merlin burst through us and stabbed his blade into the man's neck two, three times before he finally looked up. Tears were in his eyes as he stared at me. "I don't want my friends to die."

I stared at him. Really took him in and saw that his knuckles were pale from holding the weapon in his hands. He didn't have his staff. His clothes were torn and bloodied. His eyes were bloodshot and he shook all over like he was expecting someone to kill him at any moment.

We moved the body from the doorway and made our way to the corner of the entry hall we had come into and looked up. Catwalks stretched over the distances of the floors, concrete walkways and sections above us held up by steel that looked to be starting to rust. Brand-new-looking machines hummed and worked electronic paddles that stirred what was in the massive, twenty-foot-tall vats while people—humans—oversaw their use.

The vats were a stark white, perfectly clean and kept in a ratty, dusty, and disgusting place.

Several of the workers had splotches of purple along their arms and necks that made me grimace.

All of them are under the affliction of their addiction and they do not look too bright at the moment, Galaxy warned softly.

I sidled closer to the floor itself and saw that a massive crowd had gathered. This time one of the black suits that we'd had the misfortune of meeting at the High Table stood maybe forty feet in front of the vats on a set of pallets so that he was slightly taller than the rest. This time his ears were pointed.

"Hey, it's that goon!" Cassia hissed, but hushed when the man's voice raised over the crowd.

"This is only the beginning of our conquest to take over, my friends." The man smiled proudly as he motioned to the vats. "Take heed and know that if you don't join us in distributing to your own localities, your will shall remain undone!"

"What if it starts to infect the true sons and daughters of the new world?" one man called out, his hand raised as if he were in school. "What if one of our kind were to partake?"

The suit laughed and some of the others joined him, but he gestured at the man as Arden whispered, "I thought you were going to nuke them? We know this already, get on with it."

"We don't know what happens to them if they take it," I corrected her and she frowned. "Let's hold off for just a second."

"My friends, when consumed by one of us, the true sons and daughters of magic and immortality, we become stronger for a time." He quelled the unrest with a wave. "This concoction that we call Divinity is not addictive to our kind, but highly so to others. To humans, it gives them a massive boost in their magical perception, complete with hallucinations that will keep them complacent and coming back for more."

He pointed up to the maintainers. "They follow simple commands after the burnout, and will do as you say until they eventually die." He motioned to some of the more muscle-bound figures skulking in the shadows. "Others of a more powerful breeding become fiends for it and are more malleable."

He motioned one forward and to the man next to him, the

hulking figure standing over him like a shadow on steroids. "And what of an antidote?"

The suit's smile faded at the edges slightly, snapping his fingers. A great big hand wrapped around the top of the speaker's head and yanked, the skin parting like a doll's arm and coming away. Some in the crowd began screaming.

That was when I cast Fireblast in the center of the group. A flash of heat preceded the wash of flames, and more than a few of the elves present burnt to cinders instantly where they stood.

Out of the roughly fifteen who had stood there, suit and his bruiser still stood with six other heavily burnt elves. Pissed off and confused—but heavily burnt.

"Get 'em!" I roared and we rushed into the room. *Galaxy, start draining the mana if you can.*

On it! I saw her bird body drop into one of the vats on our right before several large figures barreled out of the shadows.

I growled and barked, "Cassia, get them on the ropes for us!" I ducked a fist and stabbed my oni blade into an exposed rib cage. "Arden, cover us!"

A jet of flames rammed into one of the elves that had fought his way past the searing pain to stumble toward me, then a small bolt of lightning into another. I stabbed the paralyzed one and made my way toward the suit.

"I got a bone to pick with you, c'mere!"

He snarled and leveled his hand at me, vines whipping toward me.

"Shit!" I dove forward under the blast of living plant life and slashed it with my oni blade before I cast Wisp at him.

He twisted out of the way and ducked under my slash. I dropped my oni blade into my left hand as he tried to punch me, then pulled the Fae Frame and started firing at him. The bullets just bounced off his midsection and he looked irritated, but didn't slow down.

Good. I snarled and yelled, "Fuck, why won't they work!"

He smirked and pressed his advantage, 'forcing' me to holster the weapon in frustration.

I snarled and tried to slash at him, but he tripped me and I threw myself into a roll. His foot stomped the ground where my head should have been and the concrete caved in, cracks splintering from the impact.

I used the roll as a screen to pull the Silvaero with the treated rounds loaded.

He laughed. "Oh, another toy gun."

His hands spread wide as I sighted in and fired—he didn't even blink. Which was great for me.

I managed to catch him in his left eye. His spell, whatever it had been, cast wide over my shoulder and an explosive whoosh burst behind me. I lunged forward and elbowed him in the throat, riding him to the ground before I unloaded the full magazine into his mouth.

He stopped moving except for a twitch or two, giving me time to look up and see that Arden and Cassia were doing well; the fight against the larger bruisers was all but over with now. They had managed to get them to fight each other from the looks of it, two of them trying to choke each other out still.

A soft, wet gasping came from behind me that made my heart almost stop.

I turned and found Merlin sitting on the floor with blood dribbling down the right side of his mouth as he stared at me in confusion.

He pulled his hand away from the black, singed shirt on his chest, his fingers slick with blood before he looked back up at me.

"No no no!" I stood and crossed the twenty feet to get to him in long strides. "Merlin, stay with me kid, come on."

"Mar… Marcus." He wheezed, coughing up blood. "It—it hurts."

"I know it does, buddy, we're gonna need some help." I turned back to the girls. "Cass! Cassia, get over here!"

Suddenly I was back in the temple, watching as my brothers lay around me with their eyes gazing lifelessly at me, the survivor.

"Cassia, please!" I begged, as I put pressure against his wound.

Large red hands covered mine and suddenly smaller pale ones pulled me away.

I was trying to save my Marines, why were they pulling me away? I stared down at my hands, slick crimson all over them and his chest failing to rise. He needed me!

"Marcus, we will get him, it's okay!" a woman called, her voice echoing through my mind as I fought to keep my Marine safe.

"His pulse is going!" someone else roared. "Stay with me, Merlin! Damn you!"

No! This wasn't supposed to happen again! I was stronger now. I could fight toe to toe with these bastards—why was this happening again?

I remembered the necklace. Her being able to give me healing powers. "Galaxy!"

My throat hurt from screaming so loudly, but I didn't care. "Galaxy! Help him!"

I blinked and I wasn't in the temple anymore, I was standing near Merlin, watching as Cassia beat the ground next to him in frustration. "Fucking. God. Damnit!"

Arden grabbed my shoulder and pressed herself to me, her arms wrapping around me in a hug. "No."

"Galaxy!" I screamed one more time, hoping beyond hope that she could do something. Anything.

Finally, she stepped from the shadows, looking around at each of us, then to Merlin where he now laid propped up against the nearest vat.

She lifted him wordlessly and jumped higher than humanly possible, landing first on a small lift that looked to be jammed on the side of the vat she was next to, then up into it.

After that, there was nothing.

Nothing but the troubled sobs I heard from Arden, Cassia's rage, and the fact that I had lost another friend.

I had failed again.

CHAPTER SEVENTEEN

After an hour, we looked through the bodies that hadn't been burnt to hell. Wallets, ID cards, and credit cards were destroyed, though we took the surviving cash out of the wallets to donate to a worthy cause. It was something that Cassia said she liked to do with criminals.

I was… numb. Reliving the fear and uncertainty of everything that had gone on in that temple then losing Merlin was harrowing to say the least.

"Here's hoping that they stop and leave us alone now," I mumbled to myself as I sat on the floor near where I had fought with the suit.

Galaxy? I tried, but there was still no answer.

A moment later, a buzzing sound came from my left, over by where suit laid with his eyes still open and unseeing. I forced myself onto my feet and listened for the buzzing again. I reached into an inner jacket pocket, pulling out a smartphone that looked to have been clipped with a round, but it still worked.

The phone number was saved as "Young Boss" and I answered it.

"How did the tour go, Oleth?" A younger sounding voice that I recognized asked. "I got a report that someone had attempted to get in but when no one said anything else, I assumed you had taken care of it."

"So the suit's name was Oleth?" I asked in a poorly-done tone of mock surprise.

"Who the fuck are you?" the caller snarled, then paused. "Where is my guard?"

"He's dead." The guy on the other end started to lose his shit, but I roared, "You shut your fucking suck and listen to me!"

He paused and I took the opportunity to tell him, "Oleth is dead, his goons, the other goons you had watching the place, your backers, and potential whatever-the-fuck they could have been—all of them—are dead. This stops. You leave this city alone. You leave me alone and fuck off to wherever you came from, and I will be generous and leave you alone. You can hide for the rest of your days for all I give a shit, but Columbus is off the menu. Fuck off, kid. I don't care whose nutsack you crawled out of, I'll fucking kill you if you keep this shit up."

"Who the fuck do you think you are, you slimy, pathetic piece of sh—" I hit end and crushed the phone in my hand before tossing it away.

Cassia and Arden watched me with somber interest. "Who was that?"

I jerked my thumb to Oleth's body, "His boss."

They nodded, then went back to watching for Galaxy. She had popped up out of the vat and went immediately into the next by herself and was now on the last one from what I could gather from the others.

"It may not be a bad idea to get the hell out of Dodge while they're still trying to get their forces together to come here and investigate."

"We can't leave them," Arden insisted, crossing her arms. "He may be... He might be gone, but Merlin still deserves a proper sending off. We need his body for that."

I glanced over at Cassia and she nodded her agreement. "Okay, I'll go see if Galaxy is almost done and we can get out of here. Get Merlin to… rest."

I climbed up on the metal stairs next to the vats, mounting the cement walkway then peered into the first one. It sat still mostly full, so I went to the others, noting that they had been drained dry.

Galaxy, where are you? I quested with my eyes a little bit more but there was nothing. *We don't have a lot of time here; we need to leave and take Merlin's body to be cared for.*

Splashing came out of the mostly full vat and I sprinted to it, thinking something was wrong. I got to it and found Galaxy in her elven form holding the boy—who was stark naked and shivering wildly—by the back of the neck like a kitten.

She stared up at me tiredly, but triumphant. "What body?"

"Wha—How?" I roared, probably happier than I had any right to be at all.

"Explanations later, get him out of here." I reached down and grabbed the kid and hefted him out of the vat as she closed her eyes and the liquid mana began to whirl around her as it sank lower and lower.

I pulled my flannel off and wrapped it around his shoulders, huddling him close to me to get him onto the stairs as Cassia and Arden tromped up.

"We got it, we got it—you two lead the way out of here and get us back to the SUV." They nodded excitedly and turned to move ahead of us.

Arden disappeared and came back a heartbeat later with a frown.

Cassia paused and came up short. "No." Arden nodded and Cassia cried, "I was just going to get her detailed!"

Boom! An explosion burst outside, the light from the flames filtering in as Arden explained, "There are stragglers and some other folks out there with weapons who likely want to bash our skulls in."

"I want to bash their skulls in!" Cassia raged, her eyes glowing red.

"Cass, there are about twenty of them and they are all hopped up on the juice," Arden hissed as voices closed in on the door we stood near. "We can't fight that many of them right now, not and protect Merlin."

Cassia seethed, then looked at the kid who muttered, "S-sorry, C-Cass."

She scowled and grabbed him, picking him up like a princess before she growled down at him, "Stop apologizing. We are so getting you on a good diet program and lifting weights. Let's go."

I jumped out in front of her and started to jog in the opposite direction with Arden keeping pace with ease. There was a set of chained doors and a set of stairs up to the second floor.

"That door has stuff on the other side, we should go upstairs." Arden started to move toward the stairs and I moved to join her, but Cass had other ideas.

"Graargh!" The oni's massive leg lifted and slammed into the chains and doors. The hinges squealed and peeled away from the wall and the doors burst outward, the debris and whatnot behind it moving and grating against the ground as it moved.

"Cass, what the shit?" Arden hissed as the oni woman kicked again, the doors acting as a ram to clear a path large enough for us to get out through.

"There they go, get 'em!" someone yelled behind us as we moved on.

I took a quick inventory of myself and our options before I moved out of the way so Cassia could move ahead.

"What're you doing?" She huffed and I just waved her ahead as I called Thumper from the ring.

"Don't know if it will work, but I'll try to give you guys some cover fire so you can get to safety." I turned and moved back into a small off-shooting alley that I used to mount my distraction.

I fired a few bursts then yelled, "Fuck off, you junky fucks!"

Hardly the intimidating phrase, Marcus, Galaxy sighed from above me in raven form.

I don't want them to be intimidated, I want them to follow me. I growled and shot one of our pursuers in the chest, the bullet piercing the cloth there, but it didn't look like it had done shit to the skin. *Follow the others and see them to safety, I got this.*

She crowed and fluttered off into the darkness as I continued my attack in retreat down the alley.

I fired and fired until the magazine ran dry, the soft thunk of the bolt sliding back and locking in place. I flicked the rifle as I pressed the magazine release, the empty retainer flung aside as I pressed the next magazine in. I slapped the bolt catch and listened as the round slid home.

Tat tat tat! Three rounds flew the distance to the junkies and tore into them, making two of them stumble.

A soft pop, soft trigger, and minimal recoil made me growl, as I tapped the bottom of the magazine, racked the bolt and pressed the trigger once more. Another round ripped into one of the figures moving toward me.

I turned and glanced over my shoulder, realizing that this alley had a dead end thanks to a tall wooden fence. I growled and shook my head, I still had *85/170 MP* so I could cast some spells, but what?

I put Thumper back into my inventory and cast Wisp at the fence. The flames caught and began to burn the wood, thankfully.

With these fuckers being as amped up on this shit as they are, I have one chance at this.

Galaxy's mind touched mine and she gasped, *Marcus, no! I cannot bring you back if you die here! Do not do something so reckless! They're too close.*

"I didn't ask you how close they were!" I roared so my adrenaline would start pumping as I ran toward the fence. "I cast Fireblast!"

The spell burst from my hand at the wall on my left, just in front of my pursuers, and detonated as I threw myself at the burning fence.

The force of the blast propelled me harder, the pain in my shoulder and from the burns on my ass and legs. Something heavy and hard crashed into my ankle with a sickening snap.

I hacked, the smoke from the burning fence having gotten into my lungs when the blast had forced air from me and I had to breathe in. It burned fiercely, but it wasn't as bad as it could have been.

Not all of them were caught in the blast, you foolish mortal; they climb over the rubble as we speak. Galaxy nagged at me from above. *You need to go and meet with the others.*

A line of green flickered onto my map as Galaxy ordered, *Follow this.*

"Thanks." I grunted and hobbled along after the line, keeping myself close to the walls of the buildings on my right side to keep some of the pressure off my right ankle.

Sirens blared toward the area and spurred me along a little faster, the lights flashing closer and closer.

I was about to throw myself across a thin side street when the green line blinked out and readjusted like modern GPS and told me to go right toward a brick wall divider. "Uh, Gal? Little help here?"

"Help's here, stay back!" Cassia snarled from the other side as something smacked against the barrier. "You better be pretty damn far back, Marcus!"

"I a—shit!" Pieces of rubble and debris scattered against my skin painfully.

The massive woman dialed things back down to her human form, and motioned to me hurriedly. "Come on."

I limped to her and she grabbed me into her arms as Arden carried Merlin. She started to jog as some of the Divinity junkies flew around the corner and down the way at us.

I growled and looked at Cassia. "Lift me up so I can shoot over your shoulder."

"What?" She frowned at me and almost paused, but I pulled

the Fae Frame from my holster and lifted it. "Oh, fuck, my ears are going to hurt."

"Mine too." I smiled at her as she lifted me. I put both arms over her shoulder and tried to time my shots with her steps.

The first shot went wide, but I dialed it in as Arden spat, "Watch it!"

"I am, don't be there!" I retorted and she just growled and surged forward off to the side of us.

I shot again, Cass grunting with each round. After a moment, they started to slow and blink at their surroundings. One of my rounds caught the lead junky in the chest and he fell to the ground, startling the others and making them stalk the other way.

"That takes care of them." I sighed, turning to reholster my weapon.

"What?" Cassia looked at me and I had to fight not to laugh.

Police ahead, get behind this dumpster, Galaxy warned us as she watched ahead of us.

Sure enough, as soon as we hid, a search light flooded the area brightly in a beam. "I heard gunshots," someone rumbled and the light trained on something further beyond us. "Is that someone laying in the alley?"

"Shit, call a bus, I'll go in." An officer sprinted past us, looking right at us but seeing nothing as Arden's spell worked in our favor. The only reason I knew it was working was because of the heat it was giving off.

"Car forty-six, Dispatch, EMTs requested on Jaeger and East Kossuth Street." The first officer's partner walked back with his weapon drawn as he slowly walked past us. His free hand was still on the mic attached to his shoulder when he spat, "Car forty-six, Dispatch, one subject down in the roadway, unknown reasons."

"Dispatch, forty-six, ten-four. EMTs en route." The radio on his hip chirped and he nodded before resuming a two-handed grip on his pistol.

He was a good twenty feet away before Cassia and Arden moved with us in their arms, sticking close to the side of the dumpster to avoid running into the stream of light.

It wasn't easy and it took a minute, but soon enough, we were out of the alley and on our way back toward the bar and safety.

We hurried on for more than ten minutes in silence before the pain in my ankle started to numb slightly. I looked down at it and it was bruised heavily and bent at an odd angle.

"It's not healing right, I don't think."

Cassia glanced at it and muttered, "No, it isn't." She sighed and set me in the backyard of one of the houses that looked to be sleeping still, no lights on. "Arden, you need to go and get help for us if you can, a car or something. And bring food, he's going to need it to recover enough to walk on his own."

Arden looked uncertain, but finally handed Merlin to Cass and disappeared without a word.

I grunted and looked at my foot. "That's not pretty."

"No, it isn't," Cassia confirmed again. "We will have to break it again to get it to heal properly."

I grimaced. "That's going to fucking suck."

She tsked at me and I hit her with a withering look.

"You don't get to look at me like that, mister hero-man," she shot back with a baring of her teeth; they were sharper than usual. "I like that you can handle yourself, but you don't have to play the self-sacrifice card for us. We've been stronger than humans our whole lives, and I've been a warrior since before this country was even formed—I can defend myself."

"I know that." I grunted and shifted my weight to look at her better. "I wanted you guys to be able to get Merlin to safety, and if I could distract them so you could do that, I have no regrets."

"But you didn't have to blow up that building and yourself to do it," she insisted angrily. "You have a great tactical mind, but when it comes to throwing yourself into danger, you're like a... a—Fuck! Something that just dives in head first!"

I stayed silent as she watched me, deflating a little. Finally she asked, "Do you know why I challenge you to fights and push you to be better prepared?" I shook my head, genuinely wondering. "Because that's what an oni does to show they care. They make sure the people around them that they like can defend themselves. They push others to improve so that they can survive."

She reached out and cradled my face in her hands as she stared into my eyes. "I care about you. But when you throw yourself into a situation that you could have easily come out of on top, it scares me, because I know that you are capable in a fight. What you did made no sense. You have the ability to do things differently. You could have jumped that fence with your new stats. You could have plowed straight through it! But instead, you blew up something you have no business blowing up, like you don't give a shit about your life. You can defend yourself and are very adept at dealing death, Marcus. It's why you have your new name, but you can't massacre anyone if you kill yourself first!"

She threw her hands up and growled before glaring at me. "It's like caring for a baby oni all over again, except… except…"

"Except I do dumb things," I finished for her and she nodded mutely. "Thank you for caring about me enough to tell me to get my head out of my ass."

"Of course." I smiled as she sighed and her head whipped around as a vehicle approached. She stood, ready to start fighting as I drew the Fae Frame, but when the lights stopped getting closer, she breathed a sigh of relief. "Arden, 'bout time!"

"Shut up. Summer Court goons have the High Table surrounded, let's go." She flitted around the car and opened the doors. I couldn't see the make but it was a sedan of some type, very low key compared to her last car. She went to Merlin and lifted him into the back seat with me. "There's food in there too. Cassia, we need to fix that foot and ankle."

"Oh, I know." She grinned sadistically and grabbed my

ankle. "I want you to know that your decision to do dumb things hurts you more than it does me."

"Isn't it supposed to be the other way around?" I asked quickly and Arden just rolled her eyes before Cassia crushed the bones in my foot and ankle with a smugness that made me want to curse at her.

"Arden, set it really quick and I'll help heal it." They ground it to the position they thought best and set it with a makeshift splint made from a shirt that she had in her trunk and some nearby sticks from a tree. Cassia pulled the bag on the seat onto my lap and ordered, "Eat, now."

I snarled back, "I feel like I'm about to pass out and you want me to stuff my face?" She glared up at me as waves of healing radiated into my ankle and I pulled out a burger. "Yes ma'am."

I bit into the burger, bland and nearly dry, before shooting a look at Arden.

"What? They were cheap, fast and that was all that mattered!"

I rolled my eyes and ate on, my stomach cramping, then relaxing as food was introduced. As soon as I was full, my mana began to recover and I continued eating. I turned and shoved a burger at Merlin, who took it gingerly. "I know you probably don't feel like eating right now, and we're all really fucking confused about what is going on, but we need to make sure we're aces up. So eat a little and we will get you sorted out soon, okay?"

He nodded quietly and nibbled on the burger in his mitts. I grunted at him as affectionately as I could,

Galaxy dropped onto my lap and melded with my body. *Some of them are heading into the surrounding area to try to find something—I assume that something is all of you*, she growled into my head. *I would fly ahead and scout for you more, but flying is hard and takes some of my strength, more the farther I am from you. It doesn't help that I used a majority of all the mana I drained from those vats to rebuild Merlin's body.*

Rebuild? She nodded in my head and I gasped softly to myself. *How…? What did you do?*

She was quiet for a time and finally said, *I remade him the way someone rebuilds a house on the DIY channel. I gutted all the things inside him that weren't necessary and put all the things in place that needed to be there for him to be what he needed to be to serve us.*

Us? She confirmed my question and I looked back at him. He was looking at our surroundings with a blank expression. *Is he okay?*

He will be. I had to reboot his mind and it was not an easy process. He will be okay eventually, but he will be vulnerable until he is fully ready.

Okay. Thank you for saving him, Galaxy. Her smile was nice inside my head and I turned back to my food and continued to shovel it in as much as I could stand until I felt all better.

I was sore still, and that was okay, but I could walk and had full use of my body and mana pool now, so I was good.

"Okay, so how are we going to get into the High Table?" I glanced over at Cassia and Arden. Arden shrugged and turned to Cassia. "Didn't you tell me that there were secret tunnels?"

"Huh?" She grunted as she looked to have been dislodged from a thought on her mind. "Oh, yeah, there are. We can try to use one of them, but that's if we can make it past all the goons."

"We need a distraction?" I raised an eyebrow and she hit me with a solemn glare. "I was only teasing."

"We can't implicate the Table any more than we already have, but they also aren't foolish enough to try to take it either." Cassia put the heel of her palm against her forehead and thought some more. Finally, she blinked and lifted her head to stare at Arden. "Take us as close to the back alley as you can—I have an idea."

CHAPTER EIGHTEEN

"You know, when you said you had an idea, I didn't think it would be wading knee deep through shit," Arden snarled quietly as we moved through the murky sewers beneath the street. The place was cramped and dark, but thanks to Arden's nice little spell flame moving ahead of us, we could see.

The smell was much less desirable, but better than getting murdered on the streets above. I was pretty sure Seamus would just have to settle for burning these clothes. So was it really that big a trade off?

Muffled voices ahead spoke above us in some language I couldn't comprehend. It sounded like Scottish, but not. Older somehow.

"They're looking for us, wondering how long it will be before they get to end their search," Arden translated with a gag at the end. "Let's go, quietly."

"How are we supposed to be quiet when breathing is a fucking fight in and of itself?" I whispered back and had to fight another gag, glad for once I didn't have the overpowered senses of a shifter.

"I thought you said that you had been in the shit overseas?" Cassia raised an eyebrow at me teasingly.

"That was a metaphor and you godsdamned-well-know-it, woman!" I spat and it helped a little with the intense… flavor in my mouth.

Merlin snorted and gagged, making me smile and we moved on, slowly so as to not alert anyone above us with our sloshing through the muck and detritus.

Once we reached a certain cross section of the sewer, Cassia turned toward the wall and felt around a little bit before she grinned and pulled out a small key ring. She flipped a few keys, trying a couple and hissing low under her breath until at last she said, "Got it! Let's go."

We climbed up through a small entry in the stone wall that she pulled out, then followed us in. It was cramped to shit, no pun intended, and the light that was here was even more low-key than what Arden put out.

"Arden, I need you to drop that spell," Cassia stated softly and the small snippet of light burnt out. "Thank you."

"What's going on with this chamber?" I was breathing a little heavily; tight spaces weren't exactly the absolute worst to me, but I wasn't the biggest fan either.

"This is a sworn room." She grunted and pressed something. "Only those who are sworn to the High Table in some fashion can move on, but since I know the code and the spell, I can bypass it for the kid. It's meant to keep anyone who might have chased us here, in here until we can deal with them."

A small purple panel above us lit up like a black light and the picture we painted just then made bile rise in my throat anew. A few more dull taps and thud later and another, larger doorway opened on the other side that we fell into.

This room was covered in dust and cobwebs, spiders and insects crawled all over the place, but it wasn't filled with odorous crap and refuse and I was cool with that.

"This is the hold for the High Table," Cassia explained as she lifted herself, then offered a hand to Merlin, who took it.

She lifted him and patted his shoulder affectionately. "This is where people who disobey the Laws of the Table are held. Trust me when I say that you do not want to be held in here."

"It looks cozy," Arden quipped and moved to the barred door with a little more peppy sarcasm than usual. "Want to tell us how to get out of here?"

She moved aside as Cassia stomped her way over and opened the door with no more than a twist of the knob, prompting Arden to grumble, "Oh. Thank you."

Cass just snorted and laughed as she moved us up the staircase. Soon enough, we found ourselves in a room adjacent to the armory and then the showers.

Cassia told us, "There's an emergency stash of clothes that the shifters keep in the locker rooms in the last lockers on each side. Pants and all kinds of things. Shower and help yourselves real quick, but make it a fast one, we may need to defend the Table."

Merlin and I hauled ass into the showers and turned the water on before stripping to give it time to heat up. I wasted no time in getting the disgusting clothes off of me, taking the time to be sure me and the boy had towels. I glanced over to check on him and everything around me stopped.

"Jesus fucking Christ, kid," I whispered under my breath, staring openly at the massive scar on his chest. "I thought you said that you rebuilt his body?"

I did. The scar is there to serve as a reminder to him—and to others who see it—that I am capable of great mercy. But that one should never expect to come out of something unscathed.

The scar she spoke of was a massive knot of corded flesh over his heart that sunk in and slowly became a line all the way down to his opposite hip. But instead of being pink, or even red, it was the same color of Galaxy's skin in her elven form. Celestial features and all.

He noticed me staring and covered himself modestly, and I shook my head. "I'm not going to stare at you like that, Merlin. Believe me, my time in the Corps meant that I've probably seen more naked men than the majority of the women I know, and some of them probably even combined. That's a… that's a hell of a scar, man. Chicks'll… really dig that."

He smiled and walked into the steaming showers as I just stared on, then at the floor. "Galaxy, is he really going to be okay?"

His memories have fully returned to him by now, but as to why he remains silent… She trailed off until finally she gave up trying to be articulate and just said, *I don't know. Maybe he is coming to grips with his mortality. Maybe he is using this second lease on life to learn more and assume less. Time will tell. He will let us know when he is ready.*

Once more I was reminded of just how alien the being inside me truly was, how wise and knowing she could be. *Thank you, Galaxy. Do you think once he's clean you could take him to my room to rest some more? I can't condone him being in the heat again. Not right yet.*

Yes, she answered simply and her presence receded. I went into the water with a small washcloth and scrubbed my legs and hips until they were reddish pink and even then, I scrubbed some more. After that, I got another cloth and washed my face and upper body quickly and went back out in search of clothes.

I found a set neatly folded on the bench but no socks or shoes. Grateful for the clothes, I put them on and stepped outside to find the girls waiting.

"Took your sweet time." Arden shook her head at me disapprovingly and motioned to the door. "Galaxy and Merlin left five minutes ago."

"Let's go." Cassia grabbed her phone and dialed someone's number. "Status."

Whoever answered at the other end went through a series of questions and phrases that she knew and finally started to answer her. "Okay, wait there."

"What's the news?" Cassia frowned as Arden grabbed her shoulder and let go quickly.

"They're outside saying they want to talk, but they're banned and can't come in."

I snorted. "It's obviously a trap." She nodded agreement and her frown deepened. "What else is going on?"

"We all know it's a trap, there's no doubt about that." She rubbed her temples with her knuckles. "I just can't think of why they would think we would be stupid enough to fall for it. They have nothing that we don't have. And if they do anything to the High Table, they and their Court can be banned from ever going to another one."

"Let's just go to the window and see what they want," I suggested with a shrug. The adrenaline that had been coursing through my veins previously had washed out in the shower, so now I was exhausted. "Who knows, maybe seeing the people who stomped them alive and well will make them give up?"

She frowned some more, but eventually acquiesced and we made our way into the High Table through yet another secret passage. This one led from a training room into the cooler inside the kitchen, the door opening from the inside at the press of the oni's massive hand.

We made our way into the bar area and found the majority of the security staff there, including Jolly. "Hey, look what the kitty dragged in." He smiled and patted us on the shoulders. "Touch and go for a minute there, ladies and kid. Touch and go. Thought they had you at one point, but it turned out that they got confused and grabbed the wrong guy. Poor sap."

"They kill him?" I raised a brow, ready to be angry. He shook his head and I frowned. "Then what happened?"

"They took him away into a portal to their realm, I'm thinking." Cass hissed and Arden cursed, making Jolly nod. "Yeah, he's gonna wish he'd died."

"I don't even want to know," I muttered and shook my head as if to clear the cobwebs. "Let's go see what they want."

We walked over to one of the wide windows. Sure enough, there was a massive ring of men in suits that reminded me of the mafia surrounding the place. Behind the line of suits was a black SUV that reminded me of Cassia's previous one. She must have seen it too, if her angry whimper was anything to go off of. All the suits faced out, though a few of them glanced back at the building from time to time.

I leaned close to the window, fiddled with the latch a second and opened it. "Hey, dickheads. What's up?"

The goons out front turned together, creepily in sync, and a couple of them stepped over to the SUV to knock on the window.

The kid that I had spoken to over Oleth's phone stepped out with his sunglasses on and a sneer that made me think that all of this was just a waste of his time. "So you made it inside before we could have a real talk, man to man, huh?"

"Man to man?" I snorted and rolled my eyes. "I don't even know your name, son."

He laughed, the sound more of a barking, mania-induced thing than any normal laugh I had ever heard. "That's right, you're just a Normie."

He removed his sunglasses and tossed them to one of the nearest suits who caught it and fell in line as he walked closer to the window. He was careful not to step on the sidewalk; must have been due to his ban from Uncle Yen. "Normies don't give two shits about the Fae and their politicking and their schemes. No, they just spend all their time contemplating their menial lives, their mediocre dreams, and their abysmal management—no, they don't know about us."

He smiled up at me, his aura flaring brightly, a golden aura reaching out around his body that made it hard to look at him. "But I'll let you at least know who you've pissed off. My name is Ascal Qin Moira, of the Moira clan of the Seelie. See, my father's the next in line to inherit the throne after two or three uncles pass, and that means that I am in line for the throne."

I rolled my eyes. "So what?"

Ascal stood there with a look of confusion on his face before I took pity on him and finally said, "Am I supposed to care about a whelp too big for his own britches whose daddy's men just died?"

The Fae's eyes snapped golden and he stepped forward, but

an invisible barrier stopped him and burned his nose, the skin turning a deep crimson from where it touched. "Awfully big words for a Normie outside his depth."

"Says the guy who just lost a good amount of his resources, backers, sellers, and producers for other cities," I retorted and crossed my arms over my chest. "Face it, kid, you got outclassed tonight. Take your beating and know that this city isn't for the taking. Fuck off back home and wait patiently for the throne like a good little wannabe, okay?"

Ascal seethed, flecks of spittle flying from his mouth as he shouted, "How the fuck would you know what is and isn't for the taking, you inconsequential mortal? You set me back, sure, but you can't even set foot outside that stupid little bar of yours to face me like a real man."

I just laughed, Cassia and Arden laughing with me. "Believe me, kid, you wouldn't know a real man if you'd ever seen one. Clearly Daddy didn't spank you and tell you 'no' enough, so I'm going to have to do his job."

The kid raised his hand and a whistle retorted off the surroundings before a shimmering blue light erupted before me and a slim metal piece clanked onto the ground below the window.

"Sniper!" Jolly snarled and snatched me away from the window. "You got balls, kid, I'll give you that. But you just earned your whole clan a one-way trip to permanent banning."

"Who gives a shit, old man?" Ascal laughed and shook his head. "When this whole city is mine, you'll be begging me to come in and take over. All of you will."

He looked me in the eyes and grinned wider than he had before. "And before that happens, I'll show you what it means to fuck with me. You'll beg for death, and I'll only give it to you when I'm tired of kicking your broken body around, Normie."

He shrugged and blew me a kiss as he walked away with the suits escorting him to his car. Arden's hand swam into view and Jolly grabbed it, shaking his head. "I'd have to kick you out too, love. Not keen to do that."

I turned and saw Merlin standing behind us with his left arm raised, then he dropped it and the blue shimmering shield fell away. "Was it you who saved me?"

He nodded, then spoke slowly. "I... won't... let... my... friends... die."

A pride that I knew I shouldn't be feeling welled up in me, and I stepped forward to pull him into a hug. "Thanks, little brother."

He awkwardly hugged me back for a second before someone cleared their throat awkwardly. I looked up to see a shifter I wasn't familiar with raise a hand. "We going to do extra patrols or anything?"

Jolly grinned and looked at his watch before whistling. "Well, seven on the dot, quittin' time for Old Jolly here, ask your boss."

The older werewolf smirked at Cassia as she snorted before walking my way. "Word to the wise, kid?" I raised a brow at him. "Gloating makes you look like a pud. Just tell him he lost and to fuck off. That's all you gotta do. The rest just makes them feel vindictive and want to try to hurt you somehow."

"Thanks, Jolly, I'll keep that in mind."

He patted me on the shoulder and nodded before he walked out the front door, shouting at the Fae before him to get the hell out of his way before he started to crack some skulls.

Cassia dished out orders and about half an hour later, we were all in my room to relax before getting some well-earned shut eye.

"Arden, you and Merlin can have my room if you like?" Cassia offered. It looked like Arden was about to refuse it when the oni cleared her throat and stated, "Seeing as though you look too tired to drive home, and they likely have someone watching for all of us out there."

She held up her hands and just rolled her eyes before grunting, "C'mon, Merlin, let's you and me go and get some shut-eye, okay?" On their way out I heard her say, "You know, you remind me of a certain main character that never spoke on his own, but had this annoying little fairy. I think I'll show you that game next."

I chuckled as she shut the door and turned to Cassia, her gaze on me as she drank some water. "Are we about to scrap?"

She nearly spat out the water she had in her mouth, covering her face with her palm quickly as she coughed. Finally, she heaved out a choking, "Not right now!"

"Oh good, I wasn't sure how I felt about death by snu-snu after all that." The playful sigh of relief made my shoulders bounce a little as she cleared her airway a bit more. "You okay?"

"Yeah." She finally heaved a sigh of relief and looked me squarely in the face. "He's going to come after you again."

"Yeah, I gathered as much." I grunted and threw my hands up slightly. "I was genuinely hoping he was just going to give up, but I think Jolly was right on this. Rubbing his nose in it only seemed to make it worse."

"He still has places that he can make this stuff, Marcus. He can replace what was lost." She scratched her head before punching her knees. "We should have done a concerted effort to hit every spot tonight. That would have put him out of commission."

"Or made him even more desperate," I countered before adding, "You saw how he was acting out there. He's like a spoiled kid. He's got a minimal claim to the throne, so what's pushing him to move like this? Why risk the High Table, or the other supernatural creatures' ire at a chance to grasp at power? What about the Wardens?"

"I don't know." She sighed and threw up her hands. "If anything, they just might not care. They're as much a threat to the Wardens as the Wardens are to them."

"And they had one in their pocket on the shit too." I stood up and began to pace in a tight line, needing to move despite being exhausted. "I think we need to take this higher."

Cassia pulled her phone out and called someone. "Yeah, we're back. In his room. Yup. Okay. See you in a couple."

"Uncle Yen?" She nodded her head and I grunted. "Thank you."

Two minutes of pregnant silence later and Uncle Yen barged into my room. "Well? What's the news? They all dead?"

"All the people who were there are, then others showed up uninvited, so there was that." I rolled my eyes. "The thing is, that kid I socked in the bar that you banned? Yeah, he's the perpetrator."

"I see." He scratched his chin and sighed. "So, what do you need me to do?"

"Is there anyone we can get to help us on this?" I tried to make it seem like there was more that I wanted to say so that he would continue the thought on his own.

"I can call some people within the High Table." He pulled out his phone but Cassia put a hand on his wrist. "Hmm?"

"He ordered a hit from a sniper on him, Yenny." Uncle Yen's eyes widened and he began to shake. "Ascal Qin Moira."

"High Table Command: Registry-Member Rights Revocation," Uncle Yen barked and a tome atop a table appeared directly before him. "Registry, find Ascal Qin Moira."

The massive book opened and the pages flicked on their own until it got more than half way, the final page stopping as Uncle Yen's finger slapped the page. "Ascal Qin Moira is now banned from the High Table indefinitely. Registry, ban all of the Moira clan for the actions of their kin, effective immediately."

The book's pages shuffled back and forth for a few seconds, then finally it stopped and slammed shut, both covers rising into the air with a resounding finality that made me flinch.

"There is that. They'll know soon enough that they've lost their privileges for his actions." I nodded and he pointed at me. "You mind yourself and lay low for a day or two, boy. I'll make some calls and see if anyone wants to step in or has any kind of advice."

I bowed my head gratefully. "Thanks, Uncle Yen."

"I should be thanking you, Marcus," he muttered and eyed

me weirdly. "This is hardly what you expected. Sure as hell wasn't what you signed up for—yet here you are."

He patted me on the shoulder and shuffled out of my room before holding the phone to his ear as a dial tone rang through. He closed the door behind him and left me and Cass alone.

"So is he the only one who can issue commands like that to the bar?" I glanced over at her and Cassia nodded solemnly.

"Table Commands are only accessible to the person that the table is bonded to." She yawned sleepily before she blinked up at me. "Want to take a shower and help me scrub off?"

"Only if you promise to wash my back." I smiled at her and she grinned back. "Come on. You can hold my rubber ducky."

"Mister Quacks?" She raised an eyebrow and chuckled. "Count me in."

I helped her to her feet and together we stripped and got into the shower. True to my word, I let her hold Mister Quacks. He had been instrumental in me keeping some of my Marine Corps-issued immaturity alive from my barracks days. He had gone on all my deployments and to every duty station I'd had. He was family.

After a long and blessedly fruitful shower, I tossed out my wash rag and vowed to get more, and to also get Seamus something really good as a snack for the mess we were giving him. Cassia joined me on my bed and I smiled as she began to snore almost as soon as her head hit my chest.

I was glad she was with me, and I was even more glad that she was on my side.

CHAPTER NINETEEN

I woke up with less than twenty minutes to spare before my shift started, and scrambled out of bed. Cassia grunted and sat up finally, her movement freeing me so fast that I fell onto the floor with a loud thud and a curse so vehement that it made her fly out of the bed in oni form.

"What's going on?" she snarled and looked around the room enraged, her red eyes glowing and seeking what the issue could have been.

"I'm almost late for work!" I shot back and she calmed down immediately. "What?"

"I forgot you have that schedule." I looked askance at her and she added, "I'm off today and back on tomorrow."

I frowned and pointed at her. "You said two on, two off."

Her smile grew. "Head of security gets three days off for every two on. I was just talking about your schedule at the time."

I rolled my eyes at her and she just laughed. "So what will you do today?"

"Well, I was going to browse the internet for some fun stuff to read, game a little bit, and then do some light drinking later on." She shrugged, then looked at me. "We're kind of stuck around here and I don't usually leave the place for anything, so I'm good to hang about."

"You want to hang here and keep Galaxy company?" I turned and glanced at the floor next to the TV where Galaxy had been stalking us in cat form. "I saw you there, and I know you want to do a little more research."

Galaxy shifted into her elven form. "I suppose having an expert here would be helpful. Maybe she and I could compile a list of things that we could maybe create in the future?"

"I'd love to do that!" Cassia grinned wildly before she stretched. "I'll get us a bite on the way back from my room while I grab my laptop and chargers so we can really focus."

I rolled my eyes. *Focus, she says.*

I went into the bathroom and covered my chin and top lip in shaving cream as Galaxy joined me. "Yes?"

"You wanted to know more about what I did to Merlin." Her statement made me nick myself, but the cut healed almost instantly. "I can talk to you about it whenever. I just thought that it would be easiest now."

"Go ahead." I went back to slowly clearing my chin of all stubble.

"I remade him in such a way that would allow him to hold my gifts, but as I said before, it took a heavy toll on my reserves." She paused and I stared at her in the mirror as my hand worked mechanically. "I am not fully depleted, but it took more from me than I had originally thought."

"Okay, but you can recover." She nodded. "So what else? You mentioned he would serve our needs?"

"Yes," she answered simply and it took her a moment to collect her thoughts enough to elaborate. "To put it simply, we needed another set of eyes and ears in the world. So I may have... jumbled things in his head."

I stopped and stared at her hard, my eyes narrowing. "What did you do?"

"Nothing that he wouldn't likely thank me for." She lifted

her hands and spoke quickly as I turned toward her slowly. "He had been implanted with memories that were outright lies. That monsters had killed his family; shapeshifters, if I recall correctly."

"What really happened?" I frowned and shaved a bit more without looking, thank you boot camp.

"It was the Warden service that took his parents," she whispered and frowned. "He can't get out of serving them—honestly, I don't think he wants to anyway—but now at least he knows the truth. They killed his parents because he was Touched and they were rogue mages of some great strength. I was wrong, and so was he—his ability to absorb mana isn't a learned trait, it's inborn. His innate talent."

"Oh." I deflated a little more. "I'm sorry, I thought you had really mucked around in his memories."

"Oh, I did." She raised her eyebrows a little more bashfully than I thought her capable. "But it was to do nothing more than cast a slight truth-seeing pallor on all of the so-called nice things that they had done for him. There weren't many; the Order of the Staff can be pretty damned heartless. But I still had to go digging."

"So now he knows the truth and will be able to tell us what's going on with the Wardens?" She nodded. "That's useful in some situations, I guess?"

"I did save his life, you know." She crossed her arms and stared at me flatly.

"And I'm not ungrateful, I'm really not—you know it since you can see in my head." One of her shoulders twitched and I continued. "But that was a lot of work to flip one kid for a circumstance that we don't really need to worry about as much, right?"

"It is if he's to be mine," she stated tersely. "I 'flipped' him so that I knew he wouldn't betray us the second he got what he needed and went to the Orders. So that he would actually look for information about me and tell us if he found anything."

"I get that—" I began but she scoffed. "It's true, I do."

"I know you do." She tapped the side of her skull next to her ear. "In your head, remember?" She just shook her head in near disgust. "Listen, I don't know what I am, but something in me won't take the chance that he could be a threat to us. So I stacked the deck in our favor. And no, I didn't give him a choice; he can consider it a cost of being brought back from the dead."

"Okay!" I snarled and she fell silent. "Okay. I understand. You're upset, and you're weakened, and it's bothering you."

She watched me carefully as I turned around to wash my razor and begin shaving again. "I'll be working around a bunch of drunk creatures again tonight so we can work on getting you some more mana, okay?"

She scowled and finally nodded once, sullenly admitting, "I'm not the most chipper person when I'm hungry, am I?"

I burst out laughing at that and she smiled. *I'm sorry, Marcus.*

It's okay, Galaxy. I understand somewhat. I just wish we'd had the luxury of being able to converse about it before it all went down. I finished shaving and wiped my face off with the towel beside the mirror before I turned around and pulled her into a big hug. She flinched, but eventually melted into it a bit and returned it. "Thank you again for saving Merlin. I know he's useful, but I like to think that you would've saved him if he weren't too."

She narrowed her eyes at me and I almost thought she was about to correct me before she snickered and nodded. "Yeah. He's a cute kid."

I hopped in the shower again real quick to get the sweat off my body from the night before and toweled off as I exited the bathroom. Arden, Cassia, and Galaxy all stood there with clear interest. "Well." I blinked at them. "Anyone feel like handing me my clothes, or does someone want to be blinded by my nudity?"

"Seen it, like it," Cassia grunted and leaned back against my bed from where she sat on the floor.

"I've been inside you." Galaxy winked at me lasciviously and went back to mashing buttons for her research.

Arden just blinked at me. "If I see something I don't like, this shift will be really awkward for you, Marcus. So I would suggest a little restraint."

I rolled my eyes and grumbled, "For fuck's sake…" I crossed the room and began pulling clothes out until I heard a soft clap behind me. I turned in time to catch Arden and Cass recoiling from their secretive high five and just shook my head.

This was going to be a great day already.

Arden and I walked downstairs to the bar a few minutes before our shifts started and set up before people really started coming in.

"You okay?" I glanced over at Arden who watched me steadily, concerned.

"Yeah, just a lot on my mind right now." I motioned to her. "How about you and Merlin?"

"I'm perfectly fine, though I haven't taken—or helped take—so many lives since the wars in Roman times. That was harsh." She sighed and shook her head. "I gotta say, I kind of missed getting my hands dirty. And all that experience? I leveled a couple times, how about you?"

I nodded and stilled. "Fuck!"

She scowled. "What?"

I turned and wrote down a list of things and pulled out my wallet to hand her a hundred dollars. "Can you go to the store really fast and get these things? I was so busy with everything last night and meant to go today, but we overslept."

"Marcus, I'm a jinn—not a shopping assistant." She actually looked a little offended at that.

"No, no, these are for Luce!" Her eyes widened at my explanation and I continued. "I promised him five new takes on the Bloody Mary if he helped us watch over Varlin and I need to do this right."

She eyed me and finally grinned. "What do I get in return?"

"You have got to be shitting me!" I threw my hands up and she just laughed before she disappeared in a gust of wind. I sighed in relief and waited as she was gone for a little longer than I was used to.

After five minutes, she returned breathing a little heavier than normal, but otherwise fine. She laid a few bags on the table, to my delight.

"Thank you so much, Arden!" She pulled them back and I mumbled, "Drats."

"That's right, mage boy." She leaned closer, eyes sparkling mischievously. "Drats."

"What do you want?" I asked and crossed my arms.

"Two things." She held up two fingers and smiled. "We have a little bit before it gets busy in here, so I wanna hear you spill the beans about Aeslyn and your past with her."

"And what else?" I already dreaded what might come next.

"I want you to play some more games with me." She smiled sweetly, which was really weird considering she was worse than Cassia. "Cass and I are amazing together, but you make things a bit more challenging and I like that. Plus, you're alright for a scrubby human."

I coughed and held my chest. "Ah, what the hell, Arden?" She looked worried and I coughed again. "With friends like you to wound my pride, Ascal can fuck right off."

She snorted and smacked my arm. "I'm serious!"

"That's what makes it worse!" I shot back and laughed with her. I rolled my eyes and finally acquiesced. "Let me run this bacon back and see if the cook will make it up."

She nodded to me and I fled around the corner with the bacon and into the kitchen. A large knife sliced the air right next to my ear and I stilled. The cook was a massive man with six arms and a look that sent a chill down my spine.

"No one comes into my kitchen." He growled and continued to stalk toward me. "I rule here."

The door to the kitchen opened and smacked into my back, sending me stumbling forward. The man caught me with the two other knives in his hands and a very threatening spatula as I looked back and he joined me, finding Cassia standing in the doorway, confused.

"Oh, hey Cass." The man tossed me aside, his voice much peppier than it had been. "You have impeccable timing; I was just threatening the newbie here."

She laughed. "Cyrus, he's not just the newbie, he's *mine*." She emphasized that word with an unearthly growl before smiling at him. "Is my order ready?"

"Three orders of the cosmos' best damn chili cheese fries and a side order of sour cream?" He reached to the side and pulled out three white paper bags with something greasy in each. "You bet your butt, kid. Oh, I got that burger you called for too."

"That's for him, actually." She took the bags and winked down at me before admonishing Cyrus with a look of annoyance. "Play nice."

"Yes ma'am," Cyrus and I chorused together as she fled out the door.

The cook looked down at me with a quick sneer and finally snorted before offering a hand. "Sorry 'bout that. I like to scare the new 'tenders before they get complacent. I work for the customers, not you guys."

"I totally respect that, Cyrus." I grunted as he lifted me bodily off the floor. His top and lower right hands brushed the dirt off me. He glanced down at the floor, where I had deposited my bacon and grabbed it. "I was actually going to ask if you could cook that for me? I was planning on making a cocktail with it."

"Applewood smoked bacon?" He raised an eyebrow. "I like this stuff. You know, if you put some brown sugar on these and bake 'em, it's the best."

I gasped. "Can you do that to some of it?" He grinned and nodded happily. "Feel free to have some too as thanks!"

I was on my way out the door when he grabbed my shoulder and whispered, "I like Cass, she's a good eater. Take care of her, yeah?" He shoved the burger she had ordered for me into my hands and winked before I could reply and shoved me out of the kitchen.

I prepared the other ingredients how I could, and got Lucifer's number from Arden. I sent him a text that read, *Ready when you are, big guy. Just let me know when you're coming, and I'll have one waiting for you.*

I got a devil smiley face emoji back and just chuckled.

"Spill it, mister man." Arden grunted at me firmly from where she wiped down the bar.

I rolled my eyes and just sighed. "When we met, she was just this beautiful woman at the beach in California." She smiled at me and I continued. "I'd been on a working party basically all week, new to the unit and just wanted to relax a little for the weekend, so I went to the beach near base."

I served a draft beer to a large man who sat at the bar, grunting in thanks.

"Believe it or not, she came onto me." Arden gasped and I nodded, before a wry smile spread across my lips. "I'd just gotten paid and was in the process of trying to figure out what I wanted to drink at the bar that was near the sand. I ordered and when I went to pay, this calm, cute voice said, 'It's on me, Phil.'"

"She knew the guy?" Arden crowed and I just snorted at her. The guy at the bar watched her with a shake of his head and I frowned at him. He winked at me and I just shrugged; he'd be okay.

"I turned around and there she was, this small, frail-looking beauty with skin so pale that she shouldn't have been able to withstand the sun." I shook my head and ran my hand through my hair. "We hit it off immediately. She was funny, clever, attentive. It felt like every time I spoke, she heard nothing but me. When we were together, there was nothing else that mattered and it was so… freeing."

"She's always been like that." Arden's gaze softened a tad. "All the time I've known her, she was very good about remaining in the moment with you. It's a trait that I adore as well. Please, go on."

"We saw each other for a few months, and honestly, that's the happiest I can remember being. It was perfect." I stopped moving and stood rooted to the ground where I was. "Things were going fine for quite some time, but one day, she came to me and told me that she was pregnant."

A soft cough from the man made me look up at him. He wiped his beard and I got him another drink before saying, "She didn't know what to do about the baby, but I was over the moon. Sure, it wasn't what we were expecting, but I couldn't imagine it being with anyone else. I loved her. I loved her so much, and starting a family with her was all I wanted from the moment I found out."

"But she had other plans." The man at the bar grunted and I nodded. "Sorry, kid, that's rough."

"Yeah, it is." I scowled at him, looking for his aura, but there was nothing. He looked completely human. "Can I get you anything else?"

He shook his head and continued to nurse his new drink.

"What happened next?" Arden asked curiously.

"She said some stuff that I can't remember right now, nothing hurtful, just didn't make any sense at all, then disappeared. I had her email because we had exchanged streaming stuff before, so I emailed her and asked where she had gone and why." I grimaced and closed my eyes, shrugging. "When she finally responded to my email and told me what was going on, I pled my case. Told her I wanted to be a part of our child's life. She wasn't having it. Said she wasn't ready for that kind of responsibility, especially with what I did for a living at the time. I offered to not reenlist, but she just kept making it sound more and more like I was a monster of some kind for being what I was."

Arden tsked softly and grabbed my shoulder. "Marcus, I'm so sorry."

"It's okay." I grunted, a little angry at having to relive it, but did my best to let it go. "It's okay. I get to see photos and videos of my son every now and then. He's getting so big. I can't wait to see what kind of man he will become someday."

"Maybe someday, you'll get to see him." The large stranger grunted at me as he polished off his drink. "I hope, for your sake and his, that you get to."

"What's that last part supposed to mean?" I growled, suddenly protective and defensive.

The stranger stood and pushed in his stool. "Only that a child should have an opportunity to know their father, and where they come from." He looked back at me, his eerily bright green eyes the only thing I could see in the shadows against his scruffy beard. "I'm a firm believer and advocate of that in my circles. Thanks for the drinks, friend—and the story."

He left a few bills on the table and flicked a coin into my tip jar, then Arden's before nodding and heading out.

Once he was clear of the door, I turned to Arden and she asked, "Who the hell was that?"

I shook my head and a few more people came in, keeping us a little busier so that I couldn't dwell on who he was, or what I had been talking about.

Arden brought me my varying styles of bacon courtesy of Cyrus. I whipped up the three versions of recipes that I had been thinking of to modify the Bloody Mary. While I waited to start them, I nibbled on my burger.

It was about an hour or so after seven when I got the text from Lucifer that he was on his way in. I grinned and got started on the drinks.

I used a sweeter vodka to compliment the bitters and bacon, but added a V8 instead of straight-laced tomato juice. I garnished it with some cinnamon and moved on to the next.

This one, I used tomato juice and vodka, but added a little bourbon to it for some added kick, then stirred it using the candied bacon Cyrus made.

For the last one, I hollowed out a ghost pepper with some gloves on and nestled it into the bottom of the drink, then added some of the same sort of love I had before, a little pickle juice and some Worcestershire sauce for some oomph.

I was ready.

"Lo and behold, the devil hath come." Luci's voice drifted over my shoulder as I put the finishing touches on the last drink. "I swear, if those aren't for me, I'll cry."

I turned to look at him with a grin. His diminished form was what we got tonight, and though I had been getting used to the more angelic version of him, this one was nice too. "You bet they are, boss."

He grinned and clapped his hands. "Wow me, Marcus. Daddy wants to drink and dance."

I snorted and Arden joined us, raising a brow at all of the drinks I'd made. I handed him the first one.

He took a sip of it, and grimaced. "Interesting, bitter, but I like it. Then there's the sweet undertones to it that I like, though one would expect savory from a Bloody Mary."

"That was kind of the point with this one, but thank you for the review." I smiled and handed him the next one. He grinned and downed the first one I'd made for him, much to my surprise. "Woah, really thirsty, huh?"

"I am a man of my word, Mister Bola, and I want to drink and dance and be with my friends." He smiled and lifted the next drink to his lips. He took a deep drink and his eyes closed with a groan. "Oh. Oh, that's different. Is that bourbon?"

"And candied bacon."

He gasped and pulled the bacon out and bit into it with a low moan. "Delish."

As he finished that one with a shimmy, he grasped for the last one, but I hesitated.

"What's wrong with it, Marcus?"

"This, I call the Bloody Mary from Hell." He quirked his head and lifted it. By now the ghost pepper would have infused the alcohol and juice and made it damn near hotter than lava. "It has a fiery kick to it."

"We shall see." Luci chuckled darkly and lifted the glass.

"Ardent Flame and I used to eat peppers together all the time for fun."

As he put the glass to his lips, I muttered, "Don't try this at home, kids."

He upended the glass and drained it in several needy gulps before he belched. Luci laughed and chewed on something as he put the glass down. "That is horrid, Marcus. A ghost pepper, of all things?"

Arden spat the drink in her mouth out and guffawed. "He hates ghost peppers."

"I don't hate them, Arden, I just despise how they take the sweetness out of the heat." He shook his head. "There's no… subtlety to it as you enjoy it. No silver undertones of flavor. Just spiteful heat and barren nothingness."

"Sorry, I can make you another." I started to do just that and he raised a hand to stop me.

"You couldn't have known, Marcus, it's fine. And I am a devil of my word." He winked at me. "Though, I do believe I am owed two more drinks of your choice?"

I grinned and made him an Espresso Martini, which was interesting. Luckily, we had an espresso machine in the back for the 'tenders, and the lycans especially liked it. Caffeine and animal hybrids mixed well, apparently.

Two ounces vodka, half an ounce of coffee liqueur like Kahlua, and simple syrup, add your freshly brewed espresso, thanks to a very caffeinated werewolf, and garnish with some freshly powdered coffee beans and voila!

"Oh, this looks wonderful." He lifted the drink to his lips and sipped it before lowering it with a sigh. "I was right."

He grinned and he started to sway as a song came on. "I shall relent for now so that you can make the last one for me at your leisure." He winked at Arden before moving back out onto the dance floor. A few of the other patrons took long droughts of their various bottles, glasses, and cups before joining him, and the lights dimmed over the floor making it look more like a rave than a bar.

It was a good time.

After half an hour of straight dancing and conversation, Luce came back for his final drink.

It was a short cocktail, but one I loved personally. Two ounces of rum, and half an ounce of grenadine in a shaker with ice. Shake well. Pour over a small bit of cinnamon, then add a small can of pineapple juice and Sprite. Garnish with a cherry and a small wedge of orange and serve.

Cassia came down with Galaxy behind her in human form, both women smiling at Luce while he danced.

"How's the night going?" Cass called over the music and cheers as someone started to really bust a move on the dance floor.

"Pretty smoothly so far," Arden answered for me. "On the last of his owed drinks now."

Lucifer lifted the glass and looked it over before nodding appreciatively and taking a sip. His lips puckered slightly, but the intense look on his face let me know he enjoyed it.

"This is fantastic!" He guzzled it down and his eyes rolled. "Oh, I'll need another of those. And one for the ladies as well, yes?"

He looked over at Cassia and Galaxy who both shrugged, so Arden and I got busy. She knew the simple drink and made two faster than I could make one, the show off.

All three of them drank and Cassia gasped. "It's like pineapple upside-down cake!"

I laughed and so did Galaxy. Her innocence sometimes surprised us both, and it was adorable.

As Arden and I worked, the ladies relaxed and had their fun. Playing and dancing and just generally keeping Lucifer company, which, by the look of him, he really needed right now.

The rest of the shift went well, and after Lucifer went home, Cassia, Galaxy, and I went up to my room to blow off some steam, eat some pizza, and call it a night.

CHAPTER TWENTY

A knock on my door made me jump as I woke up.

"Marcus!" Uncle Yen shouted, continuing to pound on my door. I blinked at my watch and saw that it was a minute to eight. I shut off my alarm clock, scooted out from under Cassia and walked over to open the door wearing nothing but the simple silver mesh shorts I'd worn to bed.

"What's up, Uncle Yen?" I yawned.

He pushed his hand in and pulled me out into the hall gruffly, much more easily than he should have been able to considering his age.

"What's going on, Uncle Yen?"

"I just finished speaking to some of my contacts at the other branches of the Table." He sighed and shook his head. "They can't offer much, but they did tell me that the Wardens are starting to get a little concerned for having not heard from Varlin."

"Merlin handled it the other day, Uncle Yen, things should be fine." He scowled at me and I said, "Keyword being should."

"That's right. They know he's gone, boy." I frowned and he nodded slowly. "They're sending people to investigate."

"That's good though, that means that they can help us get rid of that Moira guy, right?"

"No, it means that they will move on anyone they suspect for having had any involvement in his disappearance."

The way he paused after that made me groan. "And the last place they saw him was here."

"Now, I can spin it that he came in here and attacked—true—and that you took him away for questioning, but after that, I can't vouch for you." He ran his hand through his hair with a long sigh and continued. "The Table is sending a representative of the council here to see that the High Table's interests are upheld and that our neutrality is maintained."

"Does this mean that you could get into trouble?" I raised an eyebrow at him but he just shook his head.

"Yeah, except that I don't know what happened to him, and you lot never told me." He stopped me from saying anything. "I don't want to know. He was an asshole, and I'm glad he's not around, but what I do know is that you need to be on your best behavior while the representative is here."

I nodded and headed back into the bedroom where Cass stretched herself out under the covers. "What's going on?"

"Uncle Yen says there's going to be a collaborative investigation into Varlin's disappearance by a High Table rep and the Wardens." I pulled some sweats on and a shirt. "Says we need to behave while they're here."

"No shit." Cassia rolled her eyes and grumbled back. "Ready for some training?" I grinned and she raised an eyebrow, then snorted. "No—not a scrap."

"Call me hopeful." I fake pouted and she threw my pillow at me.

"Be serious, there are Fae who are now actively trying to kill you, and now some very dangerous people will be looking into what happened to a certain asshole whose death we had a hand in." She stood up and dressed in the night clothes she brought with her. "Come on, Kenshi will be waiting for us."

We headed out of the bar area as someone was cleaning it and went into the gym. There was the normal morning crowd, but what—or rather who—caught my attention was Arden standing next to Merlin.

He rubbed his eyes as he stood there, decidedly smaller than the massive, bulky figures around him. He wore a pair of ratty, worn down sneakers, borrowed gym shorts and a shirt that looked like it could belong to Arden that read, *I'm awake and you're still alive, what more could you want?*

The shirt made me laugh, paired with how miserable he looked, but it was good to see him here. "Hey guys, what's up?"

Cassia left us together for a moment and both Arden and Merlin greeted me with less enthusiasm than they could normally muster. Not morning people.

"I was forced away from the game I was playing by a raucous banging and told to bring the boy for training?" She looked more than a little irritated and that made me wonder if she ever slept.

"Hey, Marcus." Merlin offered a soft smile. Thinking back on the things Galaxy had told me, I clapped him on the shoulder in a brotherly manner, as he'd been through a lot and it would do us both good to support each other. At the least, I could make him feel like he was valued—because he was.

"The two of you will be undergoing blade training with bubba Kenshi," Cassia explained as she rejoined us and motioned that we follow her.

"I'm going back to gaming." Arden huffed and left the two of us with the chipper oni, who led us to a much larger training room with sturdy, solid floors and no mats anywhere in sight.

The walls were a bamboo green and the floors mahogany brown, the scent of oil and metal rife in the air here. Kenshi knelt at the far side of the room, facing one of the walls with a massive demon statue before him. It reminded me of a massive oni, wielding a katana in one hand and a smaller one in the other.

"Welcome to Hall of the Blade." Kenshi's voice drifted peacefully toward us as Cassia prepared to close the door.

"Uh, I'm not entirely sure why I'm here?" Merlin raised his voice slightly. "Marcus, I understand, but I'm…"

He looked to be uncomfortably searching for the words but Cass just shoved him in and explained, "If you want to join another Order, you need to learn how to fight and get stronger. Your life depends on this, Merlin. We can talk more while you lift here in a little bit. Pay attention."

"Sissy Cass right." Kenshi growled as he still faced the wall. "Hizamazuku."

"I'm sorry?" I stammered but Merlin knelt on the ground where he stood, sitting on both of his knees and shins like Kenshi did.

"You speak mother tongue?" Kenshi asked curiously in his broken English.

"Hai," Merlin answered instantly before telling me, "It means kneel, like this."

I did as Merlin had before Kenshi's arms raised and I was forced to look back at the oni. "Big bubba Weijin, oni ancestor, taught Kenshi Way of Blade. Teach little Kenshi to forge steel and the Earth, make weapons for bubbas and sissies to use. Protect clan, High Table, our honor."

"Big bubba Weijin fell in battle, but his sword here." He stood and claimed the longer katana from the statue and turned in a fluid motion until he held the blade perfectly in front of him in a high guard. "His Spirit here."

A chill ran down my spine as Kenshi stepped forward and gently placed the sword on the floor before him, before turning to bow to the statue and muttering something in Japanese.

"He's praying to bubba Weijin that his lesson is heeded and sinks in deep," Merlin translated for me as the oni spoke.

I was so going to have to learn more about this kid.

"Come." Kenshi motioned to the floor in front of the sword and said once more, "Hizamazuku."

We moved and went to kneel before the sword as instructed.

Even in as good a shape as I was, sitting on my knees like that was hard.

"Way of Blade simple, but hard," Kenshi began, kneeling again on the other side of the blade. "Sword, knife, blade, even hand can be weapon." He showed us the flat of his palm like he was going to slice us with the side of his open hand. "All weapon cut, but Way of Blade bring soul into weapon. Make weapon and body one."

He lifted the katana and held the hilt in a closed fist as the other hand allowed the blade to rest on the open palm. "Blade is extension of soul. The body and blade one. Sword no different from arm. A knife same as fingers. All one."

He moved the blade back from us and stood with it, placing it where it belonged once more and went to a wall to press his palm to it. His fingers slid into grooves I hadn't been able to see and the wall opened to reveal even more weapons. Swords, knives of all sorts of makes and varieties, and even some hammers and maces.

He pulled out three matching knives, all of which were simply made tanto-style blades with varying styles of hilt. The dark metal in the one I could see had light, silvery etchings in it that could have been worked or folded into the metal and brought out with acid. They were cool to look at, less so when he threw them down in front of us, the blades each sinking into the floor in front of our knees.

Merlin went to touch his and Kenshi's foot appeared and launched him backward so fast I thought he would kill the kid right then. His lip was a little bloodied, but other than his wounded pride, he looked fine.

Kenshi snarled, "Never touch blade before told, boy mage."

"Yes sir," Merlin muttered and returned to his place kneeling in front of the blade.

Kenshi knelt where he had been and presented his weapon in much the same manner as he had the katana. "All blades different. All blades respected. Blade must be part of you, you a part of it. Know your blade better than your soul. Soul and blade one now. Lift your new limb."

I reached down and lifted the weapon before me in the same way that the oni showed us. The weight was minimal, and the balance was perfect. The only issue I had with the weapon was that the metal radiated a sort of warmth that I wasn't sure of at first. Like it was alive.

"Feel the call of metal." He ran his long, sharp nail over the metal of the blade, making a soft rasping sound. "Touch it with your soul."

I wasn't sure about that, but the way the blade felt in my hand was more comfortable than even the oni blade in my inventory ring.

"Stand, take fighting stance."

This I knew, and moved into easily enough though my legs had started to shake a little from the lack of blood flowing to my feet.

I squared my shoulders and spread my feet shoulder's length apart, then put my left foot and arm forward in a fighting stance, my left fist and forearm covering my face as my right hand with the blade gravitated toward my right pec.

Kenshi grunted at me and turned to Merlin, who seemed to be confused about how to hold the weapon, though he was actively trying to mimic my stance which was a start.

Kenshi corrected his stance, then showed us both how he wanted us to use the blade. Vertical, horizontal, diagonal, and finally cross slashes. Thirty each of those movements with him correcting our form and telling us to do it again.

It reminded me of all those times in the Marine Corps Martial Arts Program that I'd had to do the same thing hundreds of times over the course of weeks to build muscle memory strong enough to make it second nature. We used everything from sticks, to practice knife combat tactics, to paint knives that left marks where an opponent had slashed and stabbed to simulate wounds.

Then there were the stun knives that used electric shocks to show just how painful a cut could be, and how to react to the pain, if at all.

"Focus, bubba Marcus!" Kenshi slammed his elbow into my wrist, throwing me off my balance and onto the ground. He was on top of me, blade at the base of my throat where a single slash or stab could end me.

"Lack focus, dead." Kenshi growled deeply, then looked up at Merlin. "Lack conviction, dead. Fight consumes all thought. All self. Whole body, mind and soul needed to wield blade."

I grunted and sat up, the door opening to admit Cassia. "Are you finished with Merlin, bubba Kenshi?"

Kenshi grunted and helped me to my feet before he turned to Merlin. "Hizamazuku, Merlin."

Merlin knelt where he was and held his blade out to Kenshi as a way to present it the same way he had been shown.

Kenshi mirrored the boy, taking the blade from him and lifting it into the air. "Bubba Weijin showed bubba Kenshi the way of blooding."

The oni slid the blade across the open palm of his right hand three times in rapid, precise slashes that bled him a little, the blue hue of his blood slowly changing to a greenish one. He placed the finely honed edge of the blade into the blood and let it sit there.

"Oni blood, a sacrifice of strength to give it to our work, to our weapons." He lifted the blade once more, then brought it down into his left hand and sliced five more times.

He bathed each side of the metal in his blood, slowly sliding it until the now-green liquid coated each side. Finally, he clenched his left hand into a fist and slid it along the spine of the blade.

"With this blood, I strengthen this blade, that it may serve a new master and be a part of him."

He brought a small cloth out of his pocket and wiped the excess blood off, then put it over the wounds in his left palm.

He held the blade out, his arms and head moving like some

kind of mechanical device. As his arms shot out, his head dipped down in a bow.

Merlin held his hands out; as soon as he took the blade, he dipped his head in return, Kenshi raising his. The boy put the blade on the floor, his hands on either side of it and bowed until his forehead touched the floor.

"Dōmo arigatō gozaimasu, bubba Kenshi," Merlin whispered before lifting his head, the look of confused pride on Cassia's face making me frown.

Kenshi bowed his head. "Practice with blade daily, hone body, and spirit—you will be great hunter. Friend Merlin."

Kenshi ducked his head again and motioned to the doorway as Cassia motioned the boy toward her with a predatory grin. "Come on, Merlin. We have training to do."

Merlin grinned and moved his hands, the blade that had been on the floor in front of him gone. "Have fun!"

Kenshi raised an eyebrow and shook his head as they left. "No fun to be had here, bubba Marcus."

A thrill of adrenaline slammed through my body as his eyes glowed amber, then red. I grunted, "Oh boy," and he was on me.

His blade sliced the air by my shoulder, the hair on the back of my neck stood on end as I rolled left.

"Good!" He snarled and came at me again.

I dodged again and stabbed at his leg, his hips shifting just enough to avoid the point sinking in, a line of blood blossoming just beneath the knee of his shorts.

He hissed and grabbed my leg before jerking his arm back, my body getting flung across the room and into the wall. "Oof!"

"Fight, bubba Marcus!" Kenshi roared, stomping toward me, then throwing his blade at me as if it was the easiest thing in the world.

I cast Embodiment and moved myself behind him, standing and slashing for his legs again; hamstringing him would be my only way to get through this.

He hopped forward and lashed out with his injured fist, his

nails slashing my chest painfully. I snarled and brought the edge of my blade up to slash his forearm on the follow through before stepping back.

"Good! Again!" He held his hand out, the knife that he had thrown coming back to his grasp.

"Fuck." I grunted and steeled myself to take the asskicking I had coming to me.

Kenshi's bulk covered my vision and it was all I could do to keep his blade away from vital organs and muscles. He was overwhelmingly skilled and it took all my focus to keep him from driving that blade into my heart.

A crash came from somewhere outside and I flinched, hesitating just enough that his weapon stabbed directly into my shoulder near my collarbone. "Gah—Kenshi, fuck!"

He turned and shoved me off the blade and grunted, "You heal fast. Come."

We walked out of the room and into the hall, moving swiftly toward the weight room.

More than a dozen people stood in a tight circle around someone I couldn't see, a stack of weights floating in the air.

"I won't ask nicely again," someone droned in what sounded like boredom. "Anyone happen to know where Marcus Bola is?"

"I'm here," I called out, the soreness in my shoulder abating already as I worked my way through the crowd.

A dark-skinned woman in a tight red dress that left damn-near nothing to the imagination held a bar with around three hundred pounds of weight like it was nothing more than a tiny barbell. Her hair was cropped close to her head on the side, with braids on the top of her head that hung down to her shoulders.

Her honey-colored eyes lit up as she smiled. "Ah! I can see that Yenasi wasn't telling me everything. Hello, Marcus."

"Hello," I greeted her in return, her eyes drifted to my shoulder and she stilled. "How can I help you, miss...?"

"My name is Amelia, and I am the representative that the

council sent to investigate Warden Varlin's disappearance." She tossed the bar aside and one of the massive staff caught it with a grunt. "I have some questions for you and your friends, if you would be so kind as to join us?"

She stepped forward, motioning to Cassia who had Merlin partially hidden behind her back. "Come along, dears."

Her small hand wrapped around the inside of my arm and pulled me along beside her. "A pleasure to finally get to meet you, Marcus."

I frowned down at her, about to ask her a few questions, but she raised her hand and whispered, "Shhh."

We walked on for another couple seconds before she stopped and thought, then pushed open a door in the hallway off to our right and walked us in. She let me go and ushered both Cassia and Merlin into the room.

"Welcome all of you!" Amelia grinned at us and motioned to the interview table.

"Welcome, council member Amelia," Cassia muttered softly, which was new for her.

"You can relax, youngster." Amelia hushed her with a touch and motioned that we all sit at the table. "I'm here simply to ensure that the High Table's illustrious neutrality remains intact. Unsullied by the hot-headed nature of children still too wet behind the ears to remain so until told to by their elders."

"Children?" I raised an eyebrow at her. She couldn't have been more than twenty—tops—though I couldn't say that she wasn't beautiful. Her eyes caught mine and I blushed. "You can't be older than me."

"I can and am." She smirked and put a hand on my chest. "By more than seven hundred and seventy years or so. I've not kept so close a count."

Woah... I blinked and frowned. "So then what is that we can do for you, ma'am?"

She snickered at my sudden respectful tone and rolled her eyes. "I want to know what happened after you had seen Varlin. I'm here to investigate what happened, and I suspect that you have something to do with it as his scent is still fading in your room."

I froze and the look on Cassia's face was just as telling.

"As I thought." Amelia's voice lowered and she stared at me. "Tell me everything."

"He was a threat to the High Table, just as much as this Moira kid who's trying to put poisoned liquid mana in drug form out on the streets."

She waved as if dismissing the thought. "I don't care about that, tell me what happened to Varlin."

"You don't care about a threat to the High Table's patrons?" Cassia stilled, the trepidation on her face now replaced by suspicion and more than a little anger.

"How can a drug of any kind affect our kind?" She sighed as if we were being dense. "Now, tell me, did you have something to do with Warden Varlin's disappearance?"

"We killed him because the drug that the Seelie Fae are planning to pollute the city with was killing him." I growled at her, her eyes widening a little. "It makes supernatural creatures stronger and harder to kill, then when they're addicted, they can be more easily controlled and manipulated."

"They've tried to actively kill us on multiple occasions." Cassia added with a nod of her head. "If that stuff gets out there, our neutrality will mean nothing if all the people we serve are junkies who will attack us for nothing more than their next hit that will slowly kill them."

"Can we stay on topic?" Amelia started to speak again when Merlin slammed his hands on the table.

"You don't get it, lady—these people are coming for the High Table, and they won't stop until they're on top." She was about to forestall him speaking again when he cut her off. "No, the Wardens don't plan to do shit for you. They hate the High Table and they want the Table to fall, because if it does, there's nothing to stop them from declaring war and killing all of you with impunity. Varlin was hopped up on that shit they call 'Divinity,' and came here to start a fight that the rest of the

Wardens would love nothing more than to finish for their own ends. If they find out the High Table was involved, this shit gets out on the streets, and the Wardens will be too busy preparing for a war to get their men and women out there routing this shit out."

Amelia, Cassia, and me all stared at him in shock and awe. Here he was putting new information out there, and he seemed to give no fucks about what happened to himself.

He serves us, Galaxy reminded me and I sighed. So this was to our benefit then.

"I can taste the truth behind your words, young Warden." Amelia swore under her breath and turned to us. "You killed him; what of his body?"

"Devoured by something that will never allow it to be found," I confirmed for her, the frown on her face growing as her tongue flicked out over her lips.

"I see." She sighed and started to drum her fingertips on the table in thought. "You swear this is what happened?"

"I have proof of what it's capable of." Merlin pulled out the coin with the giantess on it.

He tossed it onto the floor and the coin grew to the point where the giantess was bent almost in two with a snarl as she fought her constraints.

The council member raised her brow, but when she saw the purple splotches on her arms and neck she paused. "Are those the identifying marks of users?"

We all nodded and she put a hand to her mouth. "Oh no."

"Oh no?" I stilled and stared at her. "What 'oh no'?"

"There have been other places with creatures going berserk and they all had to be… put down to stop their rampages." She walked over to the cage. "They had these splotches."

"Do you see how important this is now?" I stepped closer to her and she pushed me back. "What the hell, lady?"

The cage faltered, the giantess snatching Amelia up by the waist and pulling her away from us to roar at her and throw her away. Amelia grunted and shoved her hand into the giantess's hand, blood flowing from it.

Amelia held it up to her mouth and her tongue lapped it up like it was honey and the monster holding her froze. The smaller woman placed a hand on the one grasping her and ordered softly, "Put me down—gently now."

The giantess slowly lowered her to the floor and set her on the ground. "Thank you." Amelia licked her hand again and closed her eyes, softly gasping. "Oh, this is not alright."

"What's going on?" She glanced up at me, her honey-colored eyes shining like stars in the sky. "What the hell did you just do?"

"Council head Amelia is one of the strongest living dhampyr in this world or the Grestal." I frowned at Cassia's use of the word and she continued. "One of her abilities is that she can read the memories of those she drinks blood from, the other more well-known one is that she can taste lies."

"Thank you for warning him, Cassia." She sat on the table and stared up at the giantess. "She is dying, as you said, but she has a supplier. If I tell her to, she will contact them, but she does not wish to."

"Why?" Cassia asked, stepping closer to the captive.

"She knows that if she failed to distribute what she had, she will be killed for her ineptness." Amelia hopped off the table and walked over to the other, much larger woman and whispered something that made Cassia still before the giantess wheezed and fell over.

She is dead, Marcus. Galaxy sounded panicked and Cassia stared at the dark-skinned dhampyr in absolute fear. *Cassia just told me that all she did was tell the other woman to die and she did it. You need to be careful of this one.*

Amelia tilted her head and blinked. "Did you all hear that?"

My heart damn-near stopped. "Hear what?"

"It sounded like someone speaking." She looked at me, eyes narrowing. "Someone said your name, Marcus. Who was it?"

303

I blinked at her and suddenly the door shot open. "Bubba, sissy, come!" Kenshi panted, eyes wild. "Winter here."

"Say what?" I grunted, glad for the distraction, but a crashing put us all on edge. "What the fu—"

"Marcus!" a woman bellowed.

I recognized the voice.

Aeslyn.

CHAPTER TWENTY-ONE

I sped out of the room and into the hall, around the corner, and into a group of lycans and oni unsuccessfully weathering a torrential push of ice and snow shoving them back and out of the way.

"Aeslyn?" I called over the din of the weather happening indoors.

The lycanthropes stepped aside, many of them in their animal hybrid forms to keep the biting cold away from them. As they moved, I could finally see my ex, her eyes red from crying and the muscles in her neck and shoulders building as even her own retinue fought her to try to keep her in check.

"What the hell is going on out here?" I roared, finally grabbing her attention.

"You!" She lunged for me again and this time managed a few steps before her massive bodyguard was able to grab her again. "They took my son because of you!"

My heart felt like it had dropped into a meat grinder, fell into a flaming wood chipper, and was spat into acid. "They what?" Even to me my voice sounded so... hollow.

I thought it was a possibility that he was in danger, but she had said that he was safe.

He had been safe and now he wasn't.

My son was in danger.

"They took him and said if we didn't deliver you to them, or kill you ourselves, that we would watch him be turned into a kabob after they torture him." She sobbed, finally letting the sub-arctic temperatures die down a little bit.

"Galaxy," I muttered. "Find him."

Marcus... I can't just leave you like this. She paused and I couldn't help noticing her trying to tinker with my emotions.

"Find him!" I roared and pushed her out. "I'll kill whoever I have to, to make sure that you have the energy you need—fucking find my son!"

Her face went slack before she nodded and shifted into a raven and flew away.

"What on Earth is going on here?" Amelia finally managed to get our attention, motioning to the Winter Court representatives. "Why are they within the grounds? Expel them immediately."

I turned around and stared at her. "Listen, a lot of people are about to die. A lot of Seelie, Summer—whatever the fuck they want to be—are about to die. If you want to go to the council and get on the good side of this before it all goes down, I suggest you do."

"Is that a threat?" She raised an eyebrow with a soft smile beginning to form on her face.

I took a step closer and said as calmly as I didn't feel in that heartbeat, "Yes. I will kill anyone in my way. No matter how long it takes, I will end them. There are few things you don't fuck with for me. My Marines, my country, and most importantly *my fucking family.*"

I pointed to Aeslyn. "She can clue you in on what I used to do for a living." I looked over at Cassia and she nodded once. She knew. "For now, I'm going to prep for a fucking slaughter."

I turned to look at the mother of my one and only child. "I

don't know what the hell happened that whatever you thought was keeping him safe failed, but I would suggest you figure something else out for once I get him back."

She stared at me slack jawed for a second before finally saying, "You aren't prepared for this; you need our help."

I had started to turn to go to the armory in the building but stopped and gave her my undivided attention. "That's where I'm going, to prepare. Obviously, your people weren't all that good at what they needed to do either, so if you try to fuck with this rescue mission, Aeslyn, you and I are going to have a heart to heart that you won't like. If you're anywhere near this, I'll end whoever you send."

"They said that we have to bring you, or kill you to get him back," she explained again, "You need at least one of us to go. We only have twenty-four hours, Marcus. Let us help you."

I scowled and felt like I was about to blow the fuck up, but Cassia put a hand on my shoulder the same time Merlin cleared his throat. They both gave me the look. The one that said I needed to give, if only a little, but it still needed to happen.

"Then send your best—The. Fucking. Best—because if all else fails, and we can't get him, they need to be able to take me." I stopped for a second before adding softly, "Or at least get Connell to safety if I can't."

Cassia frowned, then let go of me before I had to pull my arm away. Then Aeslyn turned on her heel. "How long will you wait before leaving?"

"You have until Galaxy returns, or two hours." I closed my eyes and tried to search for her, but she was far away. "Whichever happens latest."

She nodded and said, "They will be here within the hour." Then she was walking out of the building with her entourage in tow. I could feel eyes on me, but I didn't care.

I pulled my phone out and handed it to Cassia. "Can you see if the dwarves have that belt knife ready? Also, we need ammo and a royal fuck ton of it. Will they have anything that would be powerful enough to kill Fae outright?"

She stilled and several of the men and women around us began whispering to one another. I turned around and looked at all of them, uncertain how to feel, the rage that someone I didn't know had my son and was using him against me began to rear its head, but someone beat me to it.

"Someone has his son," Sabbath called over the others, stepping forward until he loomed over me. He stared at all of them for a moment more before calm and quiet contemplation descended. "If the same were to happen to any of you, do you doubt that bubba Marcus would leave you to sort it out yourselves?"

A few of them shook their heads.

"He fought me and won the right to be treated as a bubba. He needs our strength right now, and one way or another, he will have it." Sabbath turned to me and took a knee. "I cannot abandon my post, but I will do as you ask. I can train you, I can coach you, I can lend you my own power however it has to happen. You ask it, I will give it—even if it has to be my life. This is the way of our family."

He turned and looked to the others before saying softly, "This is our pride."

"Our pride!" The whole of the group surrounding us dropped to a knee and beat their fists against their chests. Men and women of all shapes and sizes devoted to their solemn oaths to serve and protect one another.

For so long, I had felt like I was alone out here among all these civilians, like I had no place of my own and it hadn't truly been realized yet that it was wrong.

Because now I felt like I was home. I was a part of something bigger than myself again.

I belonged.

A stirring in the air behind me made me turn to see Amelia staring at me intently. "It seems there is yet much to you that surprises even me."

"I try." I shrugged back. "Well? What's your stance on all this, will the High Table stand with us to put a stop to this? Or are the patrons you claim to want to offer succor to not worth standing for?"

She grimaced and stepped closer to me. "When you put it like that, with the support of an entire facility behind you, you make it damn hard to preach neutrality." She touched my cheek, her hand cold against my flesh. "I can still taste your bloodlust. The truth you speak drenched and soaked with the blood of others. When you say you'll kill, you will. I have much to discuss with my counterparts, but you should have an answer before you go to run your errand."

She stepped around me and stopped, standing at my side so that she could look me in the eyes. "Do make us proud, won't you?"

I said nothing as she made her way out the front of the building, the glamour veil making her invisible to sight.

An umber figure passed out of my shadow, a large cat-like creature with eyes of gold holding an equally dark raven in its jaws.

"Galaxy, what the fuck?" I stepped forward, the Fae Frame in my hand and pointed at the creature.

"Shoot me, I dare you." The creature's voice was the same as Servant's from before. "I do you the favor of bringing your injured friend to you, and this is how you repay my kindness? Humans. Scum."

"What happened to her?" I asked, touching her and pulling her into my body with no resistance from her at all. True to his word, she was hurt, but not life threateningly if I could get her some mana to snack on.

I blinked at the variety of lycans and oni in the room and sighed, *Galaxy, give me just a second and I can get you some mana. Okay?*

Out loud, I asked Sabbath, "You want to make good on your word to help?"

He held out his hand and nodded stoically.

"I need to skim some of your mana away from you to help Galaxy heal. Is that okay? If I take a little from all of you, it shouldn't be too bad."

"Take as much as you need," he confirmed and his two cronies came over to join him.

Galaxy, start siphoning through my palm, I'm going to get you some mana.

She opened her eyes inwardly at me and gave a little effort, but there was nothing for a long moment.

Finally, someone touched my shoulder and an influx of mana hit my mana sea and she was more aware. At least enough to turn the Hoover on in my hands. I reached out and touched Sabbath on his head, his vitality rushing into my body, then Galaxy's gaping maw.

Sabbath's eyes half-closed as I finished, though it was hard to stop, but now that I knew what it looked like when I took too much, I could go to the others. I waded through the other lycans, some of the others like Keith grabbing my arm and forcing me to take more until finally she was replenished.

I turned back and saw Servant watching me again, weirdly interested. "What happened?"

"I was watching you, what are you talking about—oh!" His mouth opened and his shadowy teeth flashed at me. "The birdie, right. She was on her way over my charge's home when she fell. When she plummeted into my yard, the other dog tried to eat her, injured as she was already. I managed to wrest Galaxy from her and brought her to you as she requested. It is what my king would have wanted me to do if he were in his… right mind."

"The man you're guarding is your former king?" Merlin asked nonchalantly, though the shadowy Fae creature stilled and turned to stare at him. "Don't act surprised, Servant."

"Do not think to understand my duties or feelings on the matter, whelp." Servant growled and padded toward him. "You could never understand his sacrifice, or that of his queen."

"He seemed like a good dude and all, and I would love to drink a beer with him, but we got other shit going on here." I interrupted their posturing. "My son has been taken, and if I don't get shit under way, he's in even more jeopardy."

"I cannot give you any of my strength, though if my masters knew of your plight, they would assist you in your quest to retrieve him." Servant growled softly to himself before finally looking back up. "Release the one called Galaxy. I needs must speak to her privately."

Galaxy stepped out of me in her elven form and Servant shifted into his humanoid form and bowed his head. "My queen."

"I do not know you," Galaxy replied. "You said you wanted to speak to me?"

"You look just like her... how can this be?" He scented the air and grew even more discomfited. "You do not lie either, how is this possible?"

"I do not know of what you speak, but I will speak to you." She motioned the hallway behind me and Cass. "We have a deadline and my chosen has preparations to make."

She eyed me carefully and said, *Go and prepare, I have found him.*

The relief I felt was almost enough to floor me, but I had to go and get him first—then I could collapse.

Merlin joined me and Cassia in the armory while she made a couple phone calls. I sat Merlin down and stared him straight in the eyes when I told him, "You've gotta sit this one out, Merlin."

"What?" He was aghast and the look of hurt on his face after that was enough to almost make me reconsider. "But I can fight! I know I may not be as good with guns or weapons as you, but I'm better at magic! I can cast spells and kill a lot of people."

"You can." I assured him and put a hand on his shoulder in an attempt to calm him a bit. "You can magic circles around my ass, and I damned well know it."

"Then why can't I come help you guys?" He motioned to Cassia, who was whispering something into the phone, saw us talking, and quickly turned away to avoid being pulled in. "You need the magical back up."

"Right now, you're a glass cannon, kid." He looked sullen but stayed quiet as I spoke on. "You can hit hard as fuck, but until you're stronger, you'll break easy. You went down once and that fucked us all up, Merlin. I'm still not dealing with that properly, but you gotta understand that this comes from a good place for me."

He stared at me hard and I sighed. "Don't even think about trying to sneak in with us, Merlin. That's my son out there behind enemy lines. The fact that I'm sitting here right now shows the restraint I don't fucking feel, and that's all there is for me. If I have to worry about you as well…"

I trailed off because I just couldn't think of a way to put that I wouldn't hesitate to choose my son over him.

He punched me in the chest, pretty hard for how scrawny he was, and my eyes rose back up to his. He said, "Hey, I get it. That's your kid out there in trouble. That's why it's so important to me that I help you."

"I know, Merlin." I patted his shoulder and gripped it before letting go. "I need you to stay here and watch over the High Table. If anyone attacks while we're gone, you have free reign to fuck them up however you can—just don't be a hero, okay?"

"Why would I try to be something I know I am already?" He winked at me and I shook my head.

"Hey, when this is over, I'm going to take you shooting, get you trained up properly." I reached my hand out and he shook it.

"I'll hold you to that." He grinned at me and walked out of the room.

"Is it safe to come back yet?" Cassia asked on the other side of the wall to the changing area within the armory.

"Yeah, it is." I watched as she came around the corner in a loose-fitting black hoodie and sweats that did a lot to hide how curvy she was. They would probably fit her oni form as well, which was good. "Why'd you hide like that?"

"He reminds me a lot of my little sister and makes me want to protect him." She frowned at me when I snorted. "It's true.

My little sister could snap you in half. But it's not the oni way to tell someone that they can't fight. If he would have asked me…"

"You'd have fought me for him to come." She nodded and I could respect where she was coming from. "What did the dwarves say?"

"They're sending a drone now with some supplies." She looked a bit piqued and I hit her with a raised eyebrow. "We need an ingredient to make the Fae-killing bullets and it's not going to be easy to acquire."

"What could it be?" I was wary; if it was too hard to get, we would be at a serious disadvantage going into this.

"Fae blood, given willingly," she explained and I released a long gout of air.

Shit, that would be hard to get after all. "Okay, what else are they sending?"

"Some more ammo with a higher iron content than the ones we have here just to be thorough, a few of the knives that they had made with your blueprint which they said are yours." She opened her phone and scrolled up for a second, then added, "Oh, and extended Fae-blocking magazines for your Fae Frame. They were excited to get rid of them, so you got a good deal."

"It was expensive, wasn't it?" I almost dreaded the cost, but it was too late to care.

"Yeah, but I helped a bit with it so it wasn't too much." She smiled and looked excitedly at me. "Will you take me shooting too?"

I sighed tiredly. "Yeah."

"Marcus, we'll get him back." She put an arm around my shoulders and squeezed lightly. "The other calls I made were for some… reinforcements."

I frowned at her before a wash of sulfurous scent wafted my way. "Yes."

I turned around to find angelic Lucifer staring down at me with his arms crossed. "What are you doing here?"

"He's the reinforcements. Well, part of them." She looked a little bashful. "I called Arden because she belongs to Galaxy like me, and then I called Yenny to let him know what was going on."

"I hope he wasn't too put out." I sighed, then looked over at Lucifer. "I don't suppose I could get you to go and get my son for me and avoid him being in the line of fire?"

"That would be something I would sell my soul to do, but they have the place warded from angelic presences, likely thanks to our former mutual friend." He grimaced and closed his eyes. "I cannot even so much as think about the place without feeling like I'm going to vomit."

I filed his reaction and information away for later. "Okay, so how will you be backing us up?" I raised an eyebrow at him as he stepped closer. "And we aren't allowed to make deals, otherwise I get my ass kicked."

"It wasn't the deal that you made, my dear." Luce put his hands on my shoulders and looked pointedly at Cassia.

My heart rate sped up. "What did you do?"

"She gave me a part of herself freely." Lucifer spoke with a note of near admiration in his tone.

"What was it?" I pressed and she scowled. "Was it your soul?"

She shook her head and sighed. "It was my signed copy of my favorite game—the one that he absolutely loves too."

I frowned and Lucifer patted me on the shoulder before whispering emphatically, "Friends, remember?"

"But how do you know we won't take advantage?" I growled. Even worse than the growing feeling of being indebted to the devil was the thought that I was refusing valuable help in getting Connell back safe. *What the fuck is going on with me?*

You care about what happens to these people and this place. Even though you would likely kill many of them to keep your son safe, there are some you would hesitate over, Galaxy explained to me as if it were the most natural thing ever. *You care. And that emotion makes you human. But they care about you too, and that thought in them made them rise to action. They wish to help you—so take that aid.*

Yes, ma'am. I turned to Cassia and stared her in the eyes, "I'll make it up to you."

She smiled and left it at that before glancing up at Lucifer. "Can you do it?"

"I can, though there will be some who pay dearly for it." Rather than the sad tone he led with, he just grinned a little. "But what's a few dozen souls of the damned to a rescue mission for a friend who owes me a few songs at karaoke night?"

I rolled my eyes, then stilled. "Wait, what?"

He gripped my shoulder and muttered, "Frankly, some sinners who've probably suffered enough at the hands of Big Daddy whose time can be… repurposed."

I was still at a loss when Merlin and Galaxy joined us.

"I believe we will be needed for that." Galaxy smiled and motioned that Merlin sit on my other side.

"What are you talking about?" I frowned and they surrounded me.

"The experience I designate to all of you comes from the souls within those who fall to you." I frowned and she caught my thoughts, saying, "I can also glean some from pure mana to give you boosts in power. I can also glean some more from new experiences, like fighting more powerful creatures and you doing things."

"Okay, so then you are going to… what? Transfer souls to her, then she's going to power me up?" I snorted and Lucifer gave me that same soft smile he had the first night we met that made me feel… simple.

"Not just you," Galaxy corrected, the door opening to admit Arden in her own version of battle rattle. A leather jacket and dark clothes, not black but dark shades of green and brown. "All of you."

"Then why don't we power level the fuck up and go in guns blazing?" Cassia smiled. "I set up the deal; if I pay more, I can get more souls, right? Or all of us?"

"A few souls missing before they disappear forever I can explain away to the boss man." Lucifer tapped on my shoulder lightly before he came around to the side of the bench facing me. "Enough to give all of you more than a taste? That would get me shitcanned and killed, and a devil simply cannot have that before the season finale of his favorite show."

That was reasonable. If we took too much, he would be found out and would have to pay for it; and the price for our avarice would be too high.

But will it be enough to save Connell?

I glanced over at Galaxy and she nodded. "It will be, but you need to complete the mana pathways in your body. You have both your arms done, but you need to finish your legs. Merlin will act as a catalyst and battery for you to get it done, I will help you do it faster, but you must put everything into it."

I gritted my teeth and closed my eyes, withdrawing into myself as I did when I cleaned my weapons. It was a little more difficult to do sans pistol or rifle. But without a cleaning kit, it would have to do.

It's okay, Marcus. This is one of the first things they taught us in the Order of the Staff. I got your back. Merlin's teasing tone grated on me a little, but my annoyance abated swiftly when a tug pulled my mind into the center of my being where my sea of mana resided. I found Merlin standing there, grinning at me like the kid he was. *You get one leg, I got the other. I'll be funneling some of my mana into you since my supply replenishes faster. Come on!*

He took off to the left of me and I turned to orient myself toward the glowing spot on the wall where I was supposed to go. I moved to it at a run and as soon as I was about to meet the wall and crash into it, I forced my mana to swirl in front of me like a drill. I charged forward and it wasn't until my mana began to flag that I realized this one tunnel was larger than both of my previous ones had been.

Slow your roll, Marcus! Merlin chided me cheerfully. Some more mana flooded around my feet. *The less control you have of what you're doing, the sloppier your work. Precision is key.*

I closed my eyes and worked on slowing myself down and taking my time. I wasn't anywhere nearly as good at it as it felt like Merlin was, but I was making real progress. I realized that I was in the area of my knee, maybe a little above it when Merlin joined me.

I said slow down, not to a damn crawl. Damn.

I rolled my eyes and together we pressed on. I was the battering ram to his steady tunneling. I would clear the section that he then beat to the side and molded the walls of the channel to.

Once it was complete, I was mentally drained and my stomach rumbled worse than the time I had hiked nine miles with a full pack on for the crucible. Yeah, that bad.

Food waited on the bench next to me and I looked over to Galaxy. She held up two fingers and I knew—I had points to distribute.

I put three points into Mana just to even me out at *200/200*, then added two to Physique to keep me standing and enduring a bit more. Thinking about it, I was already strong enough that I could bench a thousand pounds or more, and these Fae were fast. I dumped the other five points I had into Dexterity, which put me at pretty close to even for all of my stats except Mana.

Level 7
Stats
Brawn: 13
Dexterity: 13
Physique: 12
Mana: 20
Charisma: 10
Points to spend: 0
Spells Known
Wisp 1/6
Physical Buff 1/6
Bolt 3/6
Blade 2/6

Embodiment 3/8
Fire Blast 5/8

I made note of my current abilities and checked into the other spells I could get. Nothing truly interesting had developed for me, so I decided it was time to bring at least one spell I had come to count on to the next level and upgraded Embodiment to the eight point mark.

Galaxy looked over at me and I saw little sparks in my vision like fireworks.

Congratulations on fully investing in a spell. Here is your fully upgraded and realized spell.

Embodiment of Lightning – Internalizing the spell Bolt is no longer necessary for you to call to the lightning within in order to move. Now, you are the bolt. 25 mana.

I whispered, "Woah," and clicked open the upgrades.

Upgrades*

Under the effect of this spell, you move with the speed of lightning itself, traveling anywhere almost instantaneously within a 120-foot range around you, before a bolt of electricity attacks a nearby enemy within ten feet. Additionally, the next casting of the spell Bolt will be at half cost.

"Holy shit!" My eyebrows could have shot off my head, they rocketed so high.

"What?" Cassia looked up from her status screen to stare at me.

"Spend your spell points to fully upgrade your spells," I advised them and tried to decide on what to spend my last point on. Embodiment had another section behind it that was lit up now and I could see that it was an aural spell of some kind called Bolt Aura.

Bolt Aura – Electricity pervades your being enough that it begins to leak from you. Lowers cost of lightning elemental spells for ten minutes.

At level one, that would be… decent, but with us going into

a knock-down-drag-out fight to rescue my kid, this wasn't the time to experiment with something too new. I decided to put the point into Blade, noting that it would allow me to throw the weapon now, up to so many feet away, and not have it disappear right away. Cool.

Now that your mana pathways are fully opened, I've opened your inventory for you.

I grunted a thank you to her around a mouthful of fries and peered into my inner inventory, finding that I had thirty spaces that would act the same as the ring did. Awesome.

"Do we have grenades?" I blinked at Cassia and she just snorted.

I stared at her and finally she looked up again from her status, but it was Arden who said, "Wait, you were serious?"

CHAPTER TWENTY-TWO

"Where the hell is their guy? He was supposed to be here within the hour and we're starting into the second one." I tapped my toes impatiently as I cleaned my rifle in order to keep from pacing. Again.

"If whoever it is isn't here in the next fifteen minutes, we'll leave." Arden sighed exasperatedly. She wanted to go too, but I had been getting on her nerves a bit with my constantly wanting to be off. "Where was this place again, Galaxy?"

"East of here in a more... backwater area, out of the county, in the woods." She looked contemplative too, and I wondered if it had something to do with me having yelled at her or what Servant had said.

More the latter, though heading into this distracted won't be good. She sighed and put a hand on my shoulder. *We can talk about it after. Also, don't worry too much about yelling before. While it shocked me a bit, I know more about your son than anyone else. Not to mention how you feel about him. I want him safe too.*

"Thank you." I whispered and continued to punch the bore for my barrel.

I had reassembled Thumper and was on my way through

checking my work for the rifle when a light knock echoed in the room.

Cassia blocked the majority of the door from where I was sitting but when she opened it and growled, "About damn time," I knew it was our guy. Good.

She walked in as I stood, listening for the click of the trigger releasing, then squeezed it where the hammer fell. Good. Functions check complete.

I glanced up in time to see the same scruffy man that I had the previous night. "You're with the Unseelie Fae?"

The figure sighed and took off the hat that hid some of his features. As he did, the entire scrubby outfit he wore changed completely.

Now, his lithe build was covered in brown leather, soft and supple that faded at the edges, broken up by black and dark greens that looked to move as he did. His face was handsome, high cheekbones and a broad jaw which looked weird even for an elf and his hair was a sandy brown color. But what struck me the most was that his eyes were the exact same shade of green that I remembered.

"My name is Luca." He smiled softly at me and Arden knelt in his presence. Cassia stayed standing, but it was the sudden action on Arden's part that startled me. "A pleasure to see you again, Marcus. Though I do wish it had been under better circumstances and without the need for guile. Please, Arden, you may stand."

"Don't tell me that you're the prince." I closed my eyes, dreading the answer already.

"I am." He spoke softly, but with a tone of finality. "I am the man who has been raising Conellar—Connell—as if he were my own."

I narrowed my eyes at him and he just watched me passively. "So the story I told, you already knew."

"No." He shook his head and that gave me pause. "I suspected that something was wrong and found out the truth from my wife only days ago. When I learned that you retained your memories of her and him, I thought to kill you to keep them safe, but she told me you were a warrior in your own right. I had to meet you to see what kind of man you were."

I spread my arms. "Well, here I am. We have a car ride ahead of us, so let's go. We can talk on the way."

He acquiesced and stepped out of the room, but when I went for the front door, he stopped me. "They have eyes in the streets and on the High Table. We have a plan to distract them, but I must collect something from you. Are you willing?"

"Is it going to help my son?" I watched him and he nodded once. "Fine."

He reached up and plucked a few of my hairs, then pulled a needle and stuck my left thumb before pulling a small clay figure out of a pouch on his hip.

He touched the blood and hair to the small clump of clay before muttering some words and throwing the object onto the ground. He stepped back and a perfect version of me stood in the doorway. "This is a golem of you. There are a few Unseelie out there who will take this thing 'hostage' to then kill it for show. That should allow us a little leverage and a way of getting to Conellar before they do anything they would have to have their whole Court pay for."

"They will anyway," I growled and watched as he sent the golem out of the door to be ambushed rather violently then shoved into the back of an unmarked van that sped off from the sounds of things. "That went well."

"Exceedingly." Luca seemed pleased as he turned to me. "We will need another exit."

He turned to Cassia. "Did you want to take us to the unmarked van outside in the parking lot just out of sight in another glamour, or did you want me to?"

She was absolutely shocked but he just shrugged and turned to walk down the hall into one of the occupied training rooms where ten of the guards were rolling around in a judo fight.

"Where are you taking us?" He didn't answer right away,

but I looked over at Cass and saw that she watched him with clear grudging interest.

They paused as he pressed in a small panel, then tugged something within that released a secret door that he pressed aside and disappeared into.

"What kind of ninja assassin shit is this?" Arden whispered to herself as she moved in front of me.

"I thought you knew him?" I followed behind with Cass bringing up the rear to close the door.

"I do in passing, and what I've heard from Aeslyn." She ran her hand through her hair as we moved along the straight line. "He's a good man and, from what I understand, he treats Conellar as if he were his own. Treats him with dignity and respect."

"That's... good then." I was honestly uncertain how to feel about that.

Light flooded the passage ahead and we came out under cover of a section of brick wall that didn't perfectly meet the next building, then clambered into the back of an unmarked work van. The back section pushed aside so that the driver could get into the front and that was the prince's spot. He put his hat back on and suddenly he looked like a human painter in paint-smeared coveralls.

I sat in the seat up against the back of the passenger side and waited until we were out of the lot. "So... how's Connell?"

"He's a good boy," Luca said softly. "He loves to play, and run. He's very adept at human sports, and I do believe he and his team will do much better this year with a more observant coach."

I snorted and rolled my eyes, though inside I was seething. I wanted that. I wanted to watch my boy go for the goal. I wanted to be able to cheer him on and lose my mind when he made a shot.

"I meant what I said at the High Table last night, Marcus." He made a turn and I tightened my core to keep from leaning too much and falling over. "About a boy being able to know his father."

"What about it?" I frowned and looked at him as much as I could. "What, you want to just come and let me see him and hang out with him? A total stranger?"

"Not a total stranger," he corrected me, and for the fourth time, I wondered what could be on his mind. "You've seen photos and videos of him over the years. And he's aware that I am not his real father, despite the fact that his mother would have him believe otherwise for his own sake. The fact that you would so readily risk yourself for him means that you care."

"Caring and being a father are completely different," I muttered and he whistled. "What?"

"That's true, but your resentment is deeper than I thought it would be."

"Can you blame him?" Cassia growled as she scooted closer to us. "His son was stolen from him, his opportunity to watch him grow gone. And he just found out that it's because the woman he once loved was something that had been a myth before all this. That he wasn't supposed to remember her at all, and now here he is working with the same man who has been raising his son in his stead. Marcus has every right to be resentful."

"I agree." Luca merged onto the highway and looked back at me for a cautious second. "I just hadn't been expecting it with how Aeslyn spoke of you."

"How did the two of you get to be a thing in the first place?" I asked quietly. "Arden mentioned that Aeslyn paid a price of some sort to become the princess. What's that all about?"

"She approached me knowing my... own parentage was of similar nature to Conellar's, and knew that by marrying me, my power could protect her," Luca explained, switching lanes expertly. "That power comes at a cost, however. She had to give up her own freedom and individuality in order to prepare for the throne, and at some point, she may be required to give her life if the Winter Court so desires."

"Give it how?" I pressed and he remained quiet. "Finally decided to stop talking?"

"No," he grumbled. "It is simply something that I have no right to speak of."

"So how the fuck do you know about all of our secret passages?" Cassia snarled, her eyes flashing red for a moment.

Luca chuckled. "I make it my business to know my surroundings and the layouts of interesting places." He glanced back at me. "I knew one day that I might have to take someone inside the High Table and prepared for it. Learning that they wanted Marcus dead, I did some more digging and found other ones. Don't give it too much thought, though—I have abilities that allow me to find ways around."

"Plan to use them for this operation?" I asked simply and he nodded. "Good. What's your fighting style like?"

"Up close and personal," he answered simply. He was quiet for a time before he looked back at me. "Marcus, I have a request."

"What, Luca?" I was in the middle of checking my fifth magazine for malfunctions when he asked and didn't want to look up from my work in case I missed something.

That's what you're saying to rationalize not looking at him? Galaxy snorted and I could just hear her rolling her eyes in the tone she used. I ignored her and she just huffed quietly.

"I want to teach Conellar how to fight, but I believe that one needs to learn either on their own, or from their father." That statement caught me well and truly off guard. "What do you think on the matter?"

"That's not a request, Luca." I sighed tiredly. He was making it really hard to be angry at his existence.

"Then make it a request for a father's guidance for his son's life," he corrected and I growled. "Come, please, this is important."

"Knowing how to defend yourself is something that a father,

or mother, or family member should be able to assist with." I believed it to be true. My uncles—not Yen—had helped teach me how to fight. The constant wrestling and bullying my cousins threw my way hadn't hurt either. They had all been bigger than me, and it had helped me when I was in the Corps. "Look, Luca, you know him better than I do, and while I don't know how you fight, he can only benefit from it. Right?"

"I thought so, but I needed to be sure." He sighed and rubbed his head. "It will be hard. I am not used to teaching, and I was taught in a way that left me battered and bruised on the best days. Is this an acceptable way of teaching?"

"So long as it isn't abusive, sure." I shrugged, not because I didn't care, but because even I wasn't sure of a much better way to approach it. Sure, you could go through the motions, but until someone is up in your shit and you have to actually put the motions into play, you have no idea how you'll react.

"A good point." He remained quiet for another few moments before he said, "I hope I do not have to kill you tonight."

That made me laugh. "Thanks?" He smiled and I shook my head. "Look, I don't care what happens to me, but if you see a way to get him the hell out of there safe—you better fucking take it."

"I will," he replied easily. "I think a boy should know his father; I do not believe that he should die for him."

"Neither do I." A voice that I hadn't been expecting whispered quietly from the window by the passenger seat a second before the door opened and Jolly hopped in.

"How in the fuck—Jolly?" Cassia cried and crawled closer to get a look at him.

"In the flesh, girl." He nodded to her, but his easy smile wasn't there right now. His face was a mask of grim determination. "When Yenny-boy told me that Marcus's boy was taken, I couldn't sit on my ass and do nothing, so here I am."

He looked me dead in the eyes as if daring me to say

anything about his arrival and I wanted to, but something in the way he stared at me made me pause and forget how to speak.

"I take it that you are a friend of the High Table?" Luca looked at the newcomer curiously. "How did you get here so swiftly?"

"I had a friend on a motorcycle swing me through and I hitched a ride." He grinned menacingly before he faced forward. "Ain't letting another man go through that mess. Let's get on."

The determined set to his jaw made me once again not want to question him. Here was hoping he was sober and ready for a fight.

We drove on for another twenty minutes in tense silence, my constant gear checking almost annoying me, but it was fine. It had to be fine. All my gear needed to be perfect.

I had enough magazines in my inventory with high-iron rounds to supply a small garrison, and my ring was full to the brim of goodies with which to fucking murder these fools. I took a deep breath and decided to give it to the gods in a silent prayer to Odin.

All Father, if you hear me, I pray you give me the strength to carry out justice this night. That I can strike fear into the hearts of creatures who wish me death. Should I fight and fall in glorious battle, I hope that my fall brings the rise of another who might protect my son, and the people I have come to care about.

I fear not, for I know that if I am to fall, I will take many with me.

I lifted my gaze and saw that both Arden and Cassia were openly staring at me. "Thank you both for coming with me. I know that being here is kind of a requirement for Galaxy, but it still means something to me."

"I would be here anyway." Cassia smiled at me comfortingly. "I never run from a good fight." I raised an eyebrow at her and was about to say something when she allowed, "Well, never without good reason. That was a first for me, I'll admit."

I snorted and shook my head. "I can imagine it was."

"Oh, it was," Arden confirmed and Jolly snickered. "Good to have you aboard, Jolly. Will you… be okay with all this?"

He glanced back at her and nodded a couple times solemnly, then turned around. I felt like I was missing something. Something important. I sent Arden a text asking what it could be.

She responded, *Not really in the business of telling other people's tales if I don't have to, and especially not Jolly's.*

"You kids and your technology." Jolly sighed, thumbs working like he was texting. "Back there talking to each other about me?"

He turned and I frowned at him. "You can tell?"

"I can smell the discomfort in all of you." He sighed and eyed Luca. "I can imagine you might know what happened just because you have a network of spies and information that rivals our own."

"Fair, and true." Luca stared ahead at the road while the old man growled at him, his locs shaking as he turned his head back toward us.

"The reason I'm so gung-ho for this is because something similar happened to me once." He scratched his chin and closed his eyes. "Fresh alpha, just took over the pack of local wolves for the High Table, and planned to start working for them full time with the support of the other 'thropes in the city. I didn't know that a rival pack had come down from Michigan to go in on the deal too. They wanted all of it, the benefits, the rights, everything. So instead of coming to the Table to negotiate, they wanted to settle things old school."

He reached into his pocket and grabbed something, then snarled at himself and pulled his hand out as if he had been burned. He took a couple deep breaths and continued on with a hint of a low growl under each word. "I wouldn't come to the duel—I thought it was too base for the dreams I had for my pack and where we were heading. So, in an attempt to get me to comply, they took my son."

My blood boiled and I could see that both Cassia and

Arden were angry too, but their anger was different. More primal. Personal.

"So, I went on my own and faced their leader." He snarled, his hands clenching hard enough that his knuckles popped and crackled. "I beat him. Trounced him. Dragged him through the dirt so thoroughly that not even his mate would look at him."

A dropping sensation filled my stomach. "But you didn't kill him."

He sighed heavily. "I didn't kill him." He rolled his head around on his neck and grimaced. "I should've. I should've fucking caved his skull in like my instincts told me. But I wanted to be better than our ancestors, and when they were returning my son to me, my precious boy—the disgraced bastard tore his heart out in front of me."

I flashed back to images of my Connell, smiling face with his perfect hair and giggling. I couldn't imagine that being torn away from me that way. I would go insane.

"That feeling you're going through right now, I recognize it." Jolly pointed at me and nodded slowly. "I lost my mind. I lost my beast. The wolf roared out of me and I slaughtered the whole pack on my own. For weeks, I was inconsolable and hid myself away. Then I threw myself into my work, trying to be the best damn head of security I could be, but now, in my age, I fall back to that moment and suffer."

"And that's what drives you to poison yourself like that?" I whispered, his affirmation almost driving a spike into my heart.

"A father should never be forced to outlive his children." Jolly sighed, his eyes meeting mine. "I won't let that happen to someone else. I know we just met not too long ago, son, but you let old Jolly help you out. Think of it as a return on your kindness the other day."

I nodded solemnly and after another five minutes we pulled into a gas station on the side of a four-way-stop and abandoned the vehicle in the darkness toward the rear of the building by the dumpsters.

The air was muggy in the slowly darkening dusk light, but cooling steadily. It would be a good night to travel.

Luca walked out of the shadows, lifting a hood up to obscure his face, and I did the same. We moved as quickly as we could toward the massive red blob on our mini-maps, Arden taking point because she could move so fast.

Without needing to be asked, she plotted the elves she found, Galaxy passing her thoughts to us. *These guys are expecting a fight, dressed for a battle and they all have bows and swords. Some of the ones closer to the compound have rifles and they look like they know how to use them.*

I put up my fist and halted, the prince colliding with me quietly before he muttered, "Apologies."

"You need to watch for our signals," I muttered and looked at him, Cassia, and Jolly. "There are hundreds of them here." I saw Cassia look at her map and grimace. "They're well-armed and prepared for a fight, so we need to hit them hard and quietly, or avoid them altogether and take the compound."

"Compound?" Cassia whispered sharply. "This place is that big? If there's a compound, it'll likely be a fortress, and if we have any kind of issues getting in there, they can turn on us and surround us."

"So then we must take the fight to them and kill all in our path." Luca smiled and looked over at Jolly. "Think an old werewolf can still do it?"

"I might be old, but I'm still the alpha." His eyes burned red and his body cracked and bucked as the change overtook him. His fur was graying around the chest and shoulders, but his muscles were massive and strong. His deep, guttural voice growled out of his muzzle, "See if you can keep up."

He started into the trees, walking up them with strides like that of a werewolf in the movies. Before Luca could go, I had an idea. "Luca, wait."

He turned to me, glanced back, and frowned at me. "I have a homicidal werewolf to catch up to."

"I need some of your blood, freely given." He frowned at

me and I added, "Please? It's for a few of my rounds. If we get into the shit, and I get the opportunity to use them, it could help you get Connell out."

His frown deepened, but he pulled out a small blade of a delicate-looking design and slid it towards his forearm. "Wait, I need a bowl or something!" We turned back as Cassia cleared her throat and handed me an empty Styrofoam cup.

"Humans throw trash everywhere," was all she said as she walked slightly ahead.

I dumped the contents of it out and grimaced, but it was what we had. He rolled his eyes, pulled a flask of water from his hip and washed it a little before replacing it and staring at me. "Freely given."

He sliced his forearm and the blood drizzled into the cup for a good few seconds, giving us maybe a half an inch or so, it came so fast. He held his hand over the cut and shut his eyes, whispering something in a language I didn't understand, then the gash was gone.

He nodded and said, "Hurry with your preparations."

I nodded and pulled out a magazine of rifle rounds and started emptying the contents into the cup. Once I had all thirty in, I took the lid and shook it three times, coating the bullets in blood. I fished them out and had Cassia load them while I unloaded a magazine for the Fae Frame. The rest of the blood went to those rounds and then it was gone completely. I wished I had more, but that was what we had.

I reloaded the magazine, and Cassia handed me the one she had. I loaded that mag into the Fae Frame immediately, and the rifle mag when into my inventory.

Blips on the map began to fade slowly and I smiled. "Let's go."

She took out her massive club and kept her human form, while I pulled out my oni blade and we started forward. Dead elves littered the ground near the trees, some with slashed throats that looked like multiple blades had been shoved in, twisted and slung to the side.

The ones that didn't look like werewolf horror movie victims were found with similarly slashed throats, but the gashes were only opened wide because the fall had jostled their heads around enough to tear the flesh beside it.

What I wouldn't give for a suppressor for Thumper, I growled to myself.

Arden would like to know if drawing those outside into a trap would be a good idea. Galaxy's question made me smile, but the idea wasn't necessarily a smart one. *I didn't think so either, as it could alert those inside the compound. I've passed that along.*

Thank you. I pressed on with Cassia next to me, alert and watching for any sign that someone could have seen us. A figure ahead of us moved into sight and Cassia clobbered him as he leaned over one of the dead elves on the ground. He had been reaching for something on his hip, which I grabbed, and found a radio.

"Tech savvy was not how I would have put these guys, but I'm glad you clocked him before he could radio for help." I patted Cassia on the shoulder and pulled the radio away. I turned the volume down a bit, but kept it on my belt so we could hear in case the call came out. Maybe intercept some of the traffic and stay ahead of them. "Good hit."

She winked at me and we moved again, but something caught my attention off to our right. I grimaced and kicked Cassia out of the way of an arrow as I threw my blade and dove to the side.

A gasp and curse confirmed my throw, and I was up and sprinting for it when another arrow whizzed by my head. I tackled our attacker and cracked their head on the roots of the tree behind them.

While they were dazed, I pulled my blade from their upper leg and jammed it into their temple twice before rolling to the side. The result was spectacularly gory, and I couldn't even tell if they were a guy or a girl. Just a corpse now. The bow was a compound bow, the arrows more fantasy looking than anything I had ever seen before.

I wasn't the best with a bow, or I would have taken the weapon, but rather than taking it and letting it slow me down, I put it to the side and turned to check on Cass.

She was alright, but had found another person to clock from the looks of the body at her feet. I used my victim's shirt to wipe off my weapon and cautiously skulked on.

Galaxy, are you okay to scout ahead a little bit? She stepped out of me in her cat form and padded away. *Thank you. Getting skewered is not ideal, right now. Or ever, really.*

The radio on my hip beeped and a male voice said something I couldn't comprehend before cutting off. Sounds of gunfire in the distance that were silenced swiftly made my heart race.

Arden says that someone spotted Jolly. They think he's a random werewolf out on the prowl, but there's no telling how long that will last.

"Let's go." Cassia sprinted ahead, growing as she went until her massive figure blocked some of the remaining light on our way. We headed further north into the trees until we had to be little more than a hundred yards from the facility.

And what a facility it was. There was nothing there but a large concrete wall that looked like it could have belonged to any doomsday prepper with money to blow, or a lot of know how. Or both, I wasn't going to judge.

Flashes of light and the reports of weapons firing made the hair on the back of my neck stand on end, reminding me of the firefight that had taken more of my unit from me after my life had been changed forever.

I took Thumper out and loaded a normal magazine, chambering a round and taking the weapon off safe. I could see that the guards were pretty evenly spaced and firing southward from the compound at something that was moving too fast for their rounds to hit, but they were still trying.

Galaxy, have Arden come to this side and get Cassia over there to the wall as soon as I start firing.

Her answer was Arden appearing next to me where I slowly moved into the prone position, her face close enough that I didn't have to speak too loudly for her to hear. "Every time I fire at someone, you and Cass drop 'em. First shot will catch them off guard, but I can't promise what will happen if Jolly gets hurt or you are seen. Be careful. Go."

With my order given, I sighted in on my first victim and tried to time my shot with one of theirs. His rifle barrel recoiled and stilled then moved again as Arden appeared behind him and shoved a sword through his chest.

Where the fuck did that come from? My eyes widened, but Cassia's movement made me pull myself back to the mission. I fired again at the figure in front of her, but the shot just missed and their muzzle moved toward me, flashing immediately.

A large weapon rose and fell in the blink of an eye and they were down. My trigger finger squeezed on, my shots more cautious and carefully timed than the last as they slowly lost more and more men. Once the last one on this side was down, I rose from prone and cautiously moved forward, swiveling my eyes to see if there were any others who might see me.

I pulled the magazine and reloaded with the high iron content rounds and met up with Cassia and Arden.

"Where's Luca?" Arden whispered a little loudly, her fingers digging into her ears a bit, likely from all the noise. There were still people shooting, but it was on the other side of the wall.

He has made his way over the wall and goes toward the shed at the rear of where you are currently, while Jolly rampages outside, Galaxy informed us, a bright orange glowing beacon appearing on the other side of the wall in our mini-map.

Arden was gone from sight almost instantly and Cassia just put her hands on top of the wall and heaved herself over. The wall was almost eight feet tall, so if I had been a normal human, I would have needed to find something to climb or just gone another way. Now, I figured it was a good time to see how good my vertical jump was.

I stepped back about three feet from the wall and took a couple steps before jumping as hard as I could. My body lifted five feet and counting long before I even thought to grasp for

GALAXY

the wall, and I scraped the hell out of my forearms for it. My nose crinkled at the stinging pain, but I was glad that I was good enough to get over this obstacle on my own.

The grass inside the wall was much higher than outside it, and the buildings here looked to be more tree than anything I had seen.

According to books on the Seelie, they prefer to have homes like this, but they also have an in-depth knowledge of what happens in their realms. Whoever grew those buildings likely will know if someone enters uninvited.

I mentally thanked her and crouched to take inventory of our surroundings. The grass was higher than my navel as I knelt and it moved as if in a breeze, which was weird to me. I decided to put Thumper back into my ring and pulled the Fae Frame.

I went to move forward and the grass around my legs bit into my skin a little and I couldn't stand. I tried to move and found that my legs had become trapped.

I freed my oni blade and began to saw at the grass, but when I cut one strand away, two more replaced it. Finally I grimaced and just grit my teeth, casting Wisp at my legs. The fire burned the grass and something shrieked loudly in the distance, the deep and horrid sound making the hair on my body stand on end and my teeth feel like they were on edge.

Something is coming toward us at a frightening rate of speed; you need to move. Galaxy, panicked and running just in front of me, led me toward one of the larger tree buildings.

I moved as swiftly as I dared and found Cassia and Arden just inside the door, motioning for me to run faster. Something crashed into the wall near where I had been and beat at it, the material beginning to crumble and fall inward.

"Go!" I hissed and they turned as the wall caved inward. Something sailed through the air and grabbed my leg, putting me on the ground, my face skidding on the ground where the grass should have been. I turned and cast Wisp at whatever it was that had grabbed me and it screamed again as a lithe figure crashed into it and howled madly.

Jolly had tackled it and was slashing at its violet eyes as it let me go to deal with him.

The snarling and screeching had drawn a lot of attention and it was hard for me to stand, but a pair of hands grasped me and pulled me in. Galaxy was ahead of us and moving down a set of stairs as if she was as ready to flee that thing as I was.

I can sense a large amount of liquid mana here. This is it.

I growled, the sensation of flesh regrowing on my injured leg a little distracting. *Can you find Connell?*

She was quiet a moment before I heard, "Someone shut that kid the fuck up!"

I lowered my head and put my leg down—healing would go on, and I needed to get to him. He was close, and whoever put hands on him was going to pay.

I heard a slap and a pained grunt, then crying. My mind blanked as I rounded the corner and found myself face to face with some unknown Seelie thug. Without pause, my pistol lifted as his mouth opened and I squeezed the trigger, his head rocking back in slow motion.

Get to my son! My internal order was so loud that it was mentally deafening.

Cassia snarled and threw herself into a cluster of goons on our left and Arden blasted another in the face with a fist covered in flames.

Another figure slunk from the shadows and stabbed a man who raised a semi-automatic our way, Luca separating himself from the wall. "He's ahead, come!"

Luca ran ahead, but every time he closed on someone who ran toward us, I shot them and killed them with the Fae bullets. I had one round left, and I wanted to save that, so I put it back in the holster before calling Thumper to me from the ring. A combat reload saw that there was only one high iron round in the chamber, then the rest were Fae bullets.

I shot a goon trying to come up on Luca from the side, distracting him long enough for the prince to slash his throat. Pain exploded through my left shoulder and I snarled as I realized an arrow had hit me. I kept the rifle pressed to my right shoulder as I dipped behind a metallic post of some kind that held the roof above us. While I hid, I grabbed the shaft of the arrow and yanked as hard as I could, the pain enough to make me grimace and spit, but not enough to stop me. Not now.

The wound began to heal and I threw the arrow away before ducking down and looking out around the barrier to check for my attacker. I saw them in a murder hole at the end of the passage and I rolled my eyes. The murder hole was about an inch and a half in diameter and that was it. Hitting that from this distance would be hard, hitting it with arrows coming out of it, more so.

Galaxy, anyone who goes near there will be pin cushioned. Can you go in and drain the archer?

May I? she asked back, an edge of excitement to her tone, and I nodded. My shadow lengthened around my feet and she was off. Her incorporeal form slithered across the ground in the shadows and up the wall shortly before the archer behind the wall began to scream and cry out for help.

I found Luca, his eyes wild and a look of confusion on his face. I slapped the floor a few times and the noise reached him, turning his head toward me, so I mouthed, *Go find Connell and get him out if you can.*

He nodded and was off in a flash.

Have you always been able to kill someone like that? I called to her as she returned to me.

No, I just now started being able to do it. All of you killing so many creatures has really given me a boost. Kill more.

I grinned savagely and thought, *Yes, dear.*

We moved on, Cassia having trundled forward like a massive bear and bashed another goon's head in and we were down another level. This one opened up to a series of see-through vats that had creatures inside them hooked up to several long machines that operated silently.

Some of them looked like they were just this side of being

husks, shells of their former selves, but what really made me cringe was that some of them even looked human.

"These look like Wardens." Arden whispered, then pointed to one of the ones in the back and she covered her mouth. "Oh my God."

We walked over to the portion of the area she had been looking at and she dropped to her knees, her hand on the glass as she stared inside. "Soiphra."

The woman floating in whatever soft green fluid it was had her eyes closed, looking almost serene, but she had clearly been beaten from the bruises on her arms and shoulders.

"She's Unseelie, a Winter Court noble. This has to be how they're making the liquid mana." Arden sobbed quietly before looking back at me and Cass. "We need to stop them."

"We will." I put a hand on her shoulder and looked around. I couldn't really recognize any of the symbols on the machinery, and I worried that if I screwed something up, I would only make things worse.

Since there were innocents here, that really put a damper on blowing the place sky high after we were clear.

"Someone's coming." Arden sniffed and stood up, her sword flashing in the dim light, the scimitar held low as she moved forward.

A set of guards came through the doors at the end of the room opposite where Soiphra was being held and raised swords of their own. I shot one in the head and the other moved to Arden. Their swords clashed and metallic scraping and dinging rang out three times before Arden's blade sliced cleanly through his shoulder to his left hip, the top-most portion of his body sliding off grotesquely.

We moved into the room and found a series of hallway-connected labs, high-tech machinery and instruments where workers still created inside, some human but the majority of them elves.

They wore white lab coats and didn't look to be able to see

us as we moved through. "Should we kill them?" I asked Cassia and Arden.

"They aren't combatants." Cassia grunted and shouldered her massive club.

"Some of them may even be able to craft an antidote or something for the drug, if they haven't already." Arden scowled at them all. "Much as I want to kill them all, they should be allowed to reconcile what they've done."

"Okay." I scowled around and wished I could figure out which way to go to get to Connell.

Forward, down the hall to the right and then in the back behind a panel in the wall of the room on the left. Galaxy stepped out of my shadow and started in the direction she had told me.

We opened the door and there was a rather large hallway with a mess of guards in it. All of them looked ready to brawl.

This is why we needed fucking grenades, I swore to myself.

This was going to be shitty.

CHAPTER TWENTY-THREE

Arden was the first into the hall, motioning for us to close our eyes, which we did, I even went so far as to cover my eyelids with my right arm. A vivid flash of light burst in front of us, goons screaming wildly as their eyes burned. The door had slammed shut behind her and I was wondering if it was supposed to be now that we went in.

"Get 'em!" I heard someone on the other side of the hall yell and the sound of footsteps cascading toward Arden made me set my teeth and kick the door in.

The door caught some flunky in the head and I shot his nearest friend in the neck with Thumper. Cassia waded in with a bellow and started to shove people back down the hall with her club held out like a battering ram. Arrows bounced off cold white walls, some finding homes in her shoulders painfully, others in the Fae in there with us.

I shot again, and again. Rounds killed whatever they hit and severely injured what wasn't dead already.

Waves of heat roiled along my back and I glanced back to see Arden using her fiery magic to cook the people around her as she sliced and diced.

"Marcus, go to Connell." Cassia had joined me, her previous victims rising as they could with various broken limbs. "We'll handle these assholes and meet up with you after. Go."

I trusted her and vowed to give her a proper reward later before I cast Embodiment of Lightning on myself and moved to the end of the hall, bypassing all of my would-be attackers. A bolt of electrified energy leapt from me and rammed one of the Fae in the back, putting him on the ground making weird chortle noises.

I checked the door handle and found it unlocked, then opened it inward to find a dozen Fae surrounding and pummeling Luca. He got some good swipes in here and there, but he couldn't keep twelve Fae in sight at all times.

I grit my teeth and hoped I had enough rounds left to make a difference. I took a stance and marched forward, Thumper spewing Fae-killing bullets at the fuckers before me.

I was careful not to miss, so Connell was safe, and kept firing. Some of the rounds hit stomachs and lower things like legs, but the pain was enough for the prince to capitalize on and kill some of them.

Panting, he glanced at me and pointed to the far wall. I nodded and fired another round into one of the thugs who had smartly decided that it was a good idea to attack me. I fired a round into center mass and he paused, blood coming out of the wound as he tried to get some air, but the sucking chest wound wouldn't let him take a full breath.

I kicked him in the neck and laid him low, his hands reaching to his chest as I fired another round into his head a foot away.

The other three punks managed to flee from the fight and back up to the panel before one of them pulled out two syringes and passed one to his buddy on the right.

"Fuck." I snarled and raised my rifle, the report of it firing and hitting him in the head as his friend managed to juice up. "This is going to get harder!"

The other one fell to the ground as his buddy cackled maniacally and rushed us. He was on Luca in a heartbeat and flung the prince away before I could so much as squeeze a round off.

I ducked one blow by sheer accident and the other sent a now-bent Thumper flying out of my grasp.

The still-growing figure chuckled at me. "Ain't gonna kill me now, human. Should've listened to the little master."

"I think next time I'll just kill him, how's that?" I smiled as I backed up a little bit and prepared for the fight by loosening my arms up a bit. "Speaking of, where's that little bitch hiding?"

"Nowhere you'll get to!" the other punk by the panel said. He was hesitating putting the needle into his body.

Luca groaned and sat up, his eyes a bit bleary and the massive Fae in front of me swung at me. I took the hit and cast Bolt at the same time, hoping it would do something to him, but all it did was piss him off. I pulled my oni blade and stood up, glaring at him. The blood trailing down my mouth from him hitting me dried pretty quickly with no wound to bleed from.

Healing was such a good fucking thing to have.

He shot toward me and I jumped forward and up over his grasping arms, lashing out with my blade to stab him in the shoulder; the edge bit at his flesh, but it wasn't as good a hit as I could have hoped for.

He swung his arms up and caught my leg, slamming me down onto the ground, my leg crunching slightly at the impact. It was just a dislocation of the knee, but fuck that hurt.

Woozy from my head hitting the ground, I slashed at his hand and he let me go with a hiss. Luca clambered over his shoulder and stabbed a piece of what looked like ice into his neck viciously.

The ice melted and the massive Fae screamed, his eyes bulging as the water turned to acid against his flesh, it bubbled up and sloshed down. I cast Blade and launched the weapon end over end, the ethereal blade slicing into his open mouth as he fell. The spell's hilt hit the ground and the weight drove it all the way through.

I flipped and kicked the top of the Fae's head hard enough that it split a bit and retrieved my bloodied spell sword.

Luca nodded at me once before we turned to where the panel was. It was slightly ajar and we moved toward it carefully.

Luca tossed open the panel and a small room opened up with two scared-looking children, both of them Connell. Both looked to have their wrists bound and had split lips and bruised cheeks.

The one on the left cried, "Daddy," and started to limp toward me.

The other one's eyes just widened as he yelled, "Tapioca!"

I raised my spell blade and pressed it at the on-coming child as Luca went to the other boy. With the blade pressed against his throat, the boy in front of me began to cry. "Dad, it's me, can't you tell that it's me?"

"My son doesn't know me," I replied coldly as Luca cut Connell's bonds and pulled him to safety behind me. I kept my eyes on the creature in front of me and titled my head toward them. "He okay, Luca?"

"Yes." Luca replied with a sigh. "We will be just outside. Hurry though."

I nodded once and the panel behind me closed slightly.

"What are you going to do to me?" the creature who looked like my son asked quietly.

"I'm going to ask you some questions, and based on your answers, I'll kill you." His eyes widened but I didn't give him a chance to speak again. "Where's your fucking boss?"

"He was called home by his boss for so many failings." The kid creature tried to step back but I stepped with him to keep my blade there.

"So daddy called him home?" The creature remained silent; I raised my voice. "Is there a cure? How many other facilities are there?"

"I don't know!" He motioned to the outside and I pressed the sword further into his vulnerable throat. "The scientists mess with all that stuff, I'm just hired muscle that got left behind in hopes you'd show!"

"Why'd you take my son?"

He looked at me as if I were stupid. "It got you here, didn't it?"

"Yeah, it did." I snarled and lunged forward, the spell blade piercing his throat, his gurgled panic and clawing ineffectual. "Let me say this now, so that whoever might be watching knows. Come for my son again, and I'll come for the whole goddamn Summer Court."

I slid the spell out of the wound and lashed out once more, cutting his head off completely before dismissing it.

I turned and walked outside to find Cassia and Arden standing with Luca and Connell. The latter turning to look at me with wonder in his gaze. "You're real."

I chuckled and took a knee. "Yeah, I'm real." It was so hard to work through all the emotions I felt. Joy at finally being able to meet him, relief that he was safe, if a little beaten. Finally, I asked the question that I thought safest. "Why'd you yell tapioca?"

Luca laughed and Connell just rolled his eyes up at him. "Luca taught me that phrase in case I was ever kidnapped by a shapechanger like that guy. It happens a lot, and he wanted me to be safe since Mom won't let him teach me how to fight."

Luca put his hand on the boy's shoulder and gave me a look. "See why I asked?"

I nodded and looked Connell in the eyes. "You suspect who I am, right?"

"Well, that thing called you 'Daddy' so that means that you must be Marcus, the man Luca told me about." I glanced up at the Fae prince who looked away. "He didn't tell me much because he was worried I'd say something to Mom and she'd get mad."

I snorted and reached out to touch his chest with my index finger. "Smart guy, huh?"

"Yeah, Mom can be real scary." He shivered a little and

Cassia barked with laughter, making him jump. "She can too. What are you, miss?"

"I'm an oni, and my name is Cassia." Cass knelt down next to him and looked him in the eyes. "Cute little boys like you need never fear me, Connell. I will protect you."

"Are you Marcus' girlfriend?" She nodded and he looked back at me. "Nice."

Luca sputtered and almost choked but the rest of us laughed. Finally he asked, "Can we go now? I'm sure Mom is worried, and I'm kind of hungry."

Luca looked at me and I nodded. "Yes, we can leave now. I think we need to go and meet Mom at the High Table though."

"We have really good burgers," Arden piped up at last, though she seemed a little concerned. "Luca, can I talk to you in private a moment?"

He looked down at Connell and then over at me before replying, "Yes, Arden. Conellar, I am pretty hurt and sore from all the fights we were in, but I know that Marcus would like to carry you out of here. Why do you not go with him while Arden and I speak?"

He seemed a little concerned, his eight years of life showing on him, but finally he nodded and shuffled over to me.

"You ever ride piggy-back before?" I raised an eyebrow at him and he shook his head. "Cass, Thumper is over there, you think you could grab her for me? She needs to be fixed."

The oni nodded and paced away to go grab my bent rifle while I picked Connell up and put him on my shoulders. He grunted and muttered. "Woah, I'm taller than you now!"

I laughed and said, "Yup! Sure are."

Cassia came back as we walked toward the doors. Connell looked over at her. "We are nowhere near as big as she is."

Cassia preened a little upon hearing this and made sure that the boy could see that she was teasing him. He swatted at her and she acted injured before grinning, making him laugh and giggle.

On our way out, a horde of figures confronted us in the lab

hall, and I almost had time to put Connell down before I realized that at the front of them were Merlin and Jolly.

Jolly was severely injured, missing his left arm and walking with a limp, but he had a massive grin on his face. "You got him? Oh, good then. Good."

"Jolly what the f—heck happened to you?" I was grateful that I had been able to avoid swearing in front of my son, but the injuries he'd sustained were intense.

"That grass fiend was a little older than I thought it was, and it took a lot longer to take it down than it would've in my prime." He motioned with his head toward Merlin and the others. "These'uns showed up and killed it for me and have been tending my wounds since then."

I turned to Merlin who looked concerned but had a soft look on his face as he looked at us. "Glad we will get a chance to go to the gun range now after all."

"So am I, but why aren't you at the High Table?" I asked cautiously.

Amelia stepped out from behind some of the taller figures and motioned to herself. "Because we needed a way to track you and send in back up. It was quite annoying to find you had already left, but Merlin has a way with knowing where you are, so we conscripted him."

"I guess thanks are in order, then." I shook my head and motioned to the labs. "They may know of a way to cure what happens with the drug."

"And we will oversee that," Amelia assured me, motioning to the men and women around her that soon got to work entering labs and arresting some of the members of the staff. "For now, let's focus on you. I have something I wish to speak with you about. Something highly important."

I nodded, then grunted. "It'll have to wait." She froze and I motioned to Connell who clung to my hand. "I have to get my son home and fed, or his mom is likely to kill me."

"You're most welcome to join us at the High Table for a

drink in celebration, council member Amelia," Cassia added with a bow of her head.

Amelia scowled my way a second before a smile spread across her face. "Certainly."

We continued on and made our way up and around the area, the bodies having somehow disappeared before we made our way back. Which I wasn't going to complain about, since it was already bad enough that Connell had been kidnapped, but having to see the corpses of his captors would have just been cruel.

Before we made it out of the wall, Arden and Luca caught up to us and we were on our way back to the High Table.

Mission accomplished.

CHAPTER TWENTY-FOUR

"That boy can eat." Cassia hooted after Connell had left with Luca, wanting to spare me having to weather Aeslyn's fury.

And boy had he. He had devoured a whole basket of french fries, a burger, and a large pickle. Hell, Cyrus had even come out of the back to watch his work be appreciated with a gleam of joy in his eyes before pulling a baggy of cookies out of his chef's jacket pocket to hand to the boy. "You come eat here anytime, Connell. I got you."

I laughed at that and he winked at me before heading back into the kitchens. Connell passed out soon after that and watching Luca scoop him up and take him out the door was painful, but necessary. Though he promised to return and have a talk with me, Luca still had to take my son home. Besides, Aeslyn likely would have killed me for my actions having gotten the boy involved, even though there was no proof that he hadn't been taken just because she was of a different court and valuable to her too.

"Good job tonight, Marcus," Cassia said softly. She smiled at me with a large mug in her hand and held it out to me. It was the wee hours of the morning and the bar should have been closed hours ago, yet here we were celebrating with almost the whole staff. Lucifer had been there too, watching quietly, but I could see from the look on his face that he was truly glad to have been able to help us, even if he hadn't been able to do much physically.

His contribution made sure that we could do what we did, and that was what mattered. I hugged him like a brother and everyone else there who helped got a similar show of affection.

We drank, remembering the fighting and finally Galaxy chose then to tell us that we had all leveled up again. I laughed and she joined us for a mug of booze of her own.

It was a good night of drinking and I was happy to have these people around me. This was my new family. And who knew—maybe Aeslyn would come around and let me spend time with Connell too someday soon. Holding on to that hope was what kept my drinking from turning into a pity party.

We went to bed, Galaxy, Cass, and me, smelling like a bar, and I couldn't have been happier.

Snoring and snoozing, I slept and dreamt of the sea of stars that made up the area above my mana sea. Galaxy joined me and smiled with me as we sat and watched the moving constellations until I woke up in the morning to someone once again beating on my door.

I stumbled to the door, greeted by Uncle Yen in the doorway shoving clothes into my hands, "Shit, shower, and shave, son—the council has called you to a meeting."

"Wha?" I muttered and he shoved me again. "Okay!"

I nearly tripped over Cassia's massive oni leg hanging off my bed and went to shower. I put on the suit that Uncle Yen gave me after shaving my face and was out in five minutes.

"What's this all about?" I yawned tiredly and he just ignored me. Instead of just going into his office, he opened the door, closed it, locked it using a key I hadn't seen before, and unlocked it again before swinging it wide.

The door opened to a massive round table with chunks of it missing here and there, with a council of thirteen sitting around it. All of them appeared to be humans and I had no idea what their auras looked like because the air here was so thick with magic that I couldn't tell one from the other.

"The council has called, and the call has been answered—Marcus Bola has arrived," Uncle Yen called in an almost sing-song-like tone.

"Thank you, Yenasi, you may step back." Amelia waved and my uncle grimaced as he did what was asked. "Marcus Bola, having been named Marcus Massacre by the security forces of the High Table Columbus Branch. How apt a name."

The council muttered something among themselves for a second before I made to speak, but no sound came. *Speak when spoken to.* Galaxy's warning echoed through my head and I closed my mouth.

Someone at the table clapped. "Intelligent of you."

I looked and saw a walrus of a man, his majestic mustache almost as large as his face.

Amelia rapped the table with a gavel. "Yes. Cunning and creative are some of the things we have seen of you, but mainly your propensity for great violence." She watched me for a second, then said, "Since your placement at the High Table, you have maimed and injured some, while killing dozens more. Some of this to protect yourself and others, but others still in what you would call service to the High Table and her patrons. Is this true?"

"Yes," I answered solemnly.

"And none of this was for personal gain?" another asked quietly. I couldn't see their face over the table, but the voice sounded feminine.

"I gained from every fight I had," I answered truthfully and they paused, staring at me, so I continued. "Every fight I go into and come out of alive, I learn from and gain from. I become more competent and dangerous. Soon, I'll develop a reputation of violence so thick that anyone who dares think about getting involved with something or someone I don't like could be hazardous to themselves or their business. That protects me, my family, and the places I work."

I looked at each of them, sitting here so far removed from everything. "The High Table prides itself on its neutrality and in people being able to relax in its proximity. So much that it can blatantly ignore the fact that times are changing and that we need to protect our people. Our beloved patrons."

"I know nothing of this." The man with the mustache grunted and crossed his arms. "A few magical junkies and everyone is up in arms and wants us to break eons of tradition?"

"One of those patrons was being physically, mentally, and emotionally abused by a Warden who was hopped up on the stuff you speak of, and said Warden came to the High Table branch in Columbus to investigate what happened when his victim was no longer under his thumb." The man started to harrumph and haw at me, so I bellowed, "I defended him and took care of the issue. Maybe if you took the time to interact with the patrons instead of sitting on your high horse to keep your mustache clean, you'd value them enough to want to protect them."

"Now see here!" The man slammed his hands on the table and stood, his chair clattering to the floor.

"Enough!" the mousy feminine voice shouted, higher pitched this time. "I propose we allow him to stay. All those in favor?"

Twelve hands rose, including Amelia's, her voice echoing around the chamber, "Marcus Massacre will be allowed to stay on and work at the High Table Columbus Branch. Now, to the next order of business."

Uncle Yen moved to grab me and turn me to leave when she asked, "What are you doing, Yenasi?"

"We're leaving, unless there's more?" He sounded almost hopeful that there wouldn't be.

"There is but one last issue that we need young Marcus for." She smiled softly and motioned that he step aside. "This last issue is to vote on whether or not the rebirth of the Wild Hunt is necessary."

She stood and hopped onto the table, walking until she stood on the side of the table closest to me. "As some of the older council members may remember, the Wild Hunt was a tool that used to operate at the behest of the High Table in order to protect the patrons and beings of the supernatural world. It is my firm belief that we have a strong candidate for the Huntsman in our presence now."

"The Hunt hasn't been needed for thousands of years, Amelia, and even then, that was to stop the Cull," the mustache barked, his face turning red. "You wish to give that power to a mortal who thinks he can make a mockery of this council?"

"I wish to let him earn it to prove that he truly does care." Amelia smiled, looking at the other council members with a knowing look on her face. "This man found and ended a budding drug cartel that planned to take over the continental United States in less than a month's time, and he did it before any other organization with power and reach that makes his look infantile."

"Because it is!" the mousy voice piped up and made me frown. "He's human, and wouldn't be able to handle the power. It would corrupt him."

"There are forces in this world that would love nothing more than to get their hands on a human Touched with the power of the Huntsman," someone else said in a more bass tone.

"And it is precisely because those forces exist and wish to hold such power that they need something to cause them to fear!" someone else cried.

"All I ask is that we put it to a vote." She raised her hand and voice over the bickering of the others. "Ultimately, it will be up to Marcus as to if he wants to risk the journey to get the item needed to claim the Huntsman's power. All those who wish to support?"

Several hands raised; four, five, six in total. Mustache looked smug and raised his hand as the others fell. "Those against?"

Six hands total raised, and another figure jumped onto the table. A small green woman with large, pointed ears that reminded me of Galaxy a bit sprinted toward me.

"We need you to vote, council member Serpath," Mustache whined and she shot him a look that shut him up.

She stared me deep in the eyes and asked, "Were you serious about what you said? About getting to know our patrons and protecting them?"

I nodded and she leaned back. She raised her hand and announced, "I vote for, provided that once he has the power, he goes to work immediately."

"Doing what?" I asked and she looked back at me. "Is something going on?"

"Worry about it when you have the power to do something about it," she muttered quietly. "Until then, focus on preparing for your journey."

"Journey to where?" I called out.

Amelia grinned at me. "To hunt for the mantle of the Huntsman." The others were quiet as she stepped closer to me, Uncle Yen stepped in front of me, but she just looked over his head at me. "You'll be going to Grestal to hunt it down."

Silence hung in the air for a moment as she watched me, as every eye in the room watched me, before she added, "We will see if you have what it takes to hunt down one of the most powerful artifacts in Grestallan existence—and then if you are even worthy of wielding it."

After that, no one seemed content to answer any more questions as they all focused on bickering with one another about their vote this way or that.

Uncle Yen grabbed my arm and pulled me toward the door, ignoring my questions until we were back and his door slammed shut on its own.

"Uncle Yen, what the hell just happened?"

He stared at me as if he had just aged more than twenty

years. "You just agreed to go to the monster home plane and find a mystic treasure thought lost for thousands of years since the dragons roamed the realms." He grabbed my shoulder and sighed. "You basically just signed your own death certificate because they didn't give you the chance to refuse."

"I thought I could choose to go or not?" I was uncertain with how he was acting and Galaxy remained silent within me.

"You can, but if you refuse the call, they can out you for inaction, and if you go, the creatures there will kill you." He shook his head. "It's a no-win situation my boy. And I could do nothing for you."

He walked away and collapsed in his office chair before motioning for the door to shut as his head fell into his hands.

I would have to go to Grestal? The monster plane? To get an ancient relic of power?

I could feel Galaxy drooling inside me. *What would happen if she ate that?*

We will grow stronger. She smiled at me inwardly. *And we will go, and have our party come with us, so long as they are willing.*

"I'm sure they will be." I smiled and walked back down the hall toward my room.

The future just got a whole lot more interesting.

ABOUT CHRISTOPHER JOHNS

Christopher Johns is a former photojournalist for the United States Marine Corps with published works telling hundreds of other peoples' stories through word, photo, and even video. But throughout that time, his editors and superiors had always said that his love of reading fantasy and about worlds of fantastic beauty and horrible power bled into his work. That meant he should write a book.

Well, ta-da!

Chris has been an avid devourer of fantasy and science fiction for more than twenty years and looks forward to sharing that love with his son, his loving fiancée and almost anyone he could ever hope to meet.

Connect with Chris:
Facebook.com/AxeDruidAuthor
Twitter.com/JonsyJohns

ABOUT MOUNTAINDALE PRESS

Dakota and Danielle Krout, a husband and wife team, strive to create as well as publish excellent fantasy and science fiction novels. Self-publishing *The Divine Dungeon: Dungeon Born* in 2016 transformed their careers from Dakota's military and programming background and Danielle's Ph.D. in pharmacology to President and CEO, respectively, of a small press. Their goal is to share their success with other authors and provide captivating fiction to readers with the purpose of solidifying Mountaindale Press as the place 'Where Fantasy Transforms Reality.'

Connect with Mountaindale Press:
MountaindalePress.com
Facebook.com/MountaindalePress
Twitter.com/_Mountaindale
Instagram.com/MountaindalePress

MOUNTAINDALE PRESS TITLES
GameLit and LitRPG

The Completionist Chronicles,
The Divine Dungeon, and
Full Murderhobo by Dakota Krout

King's League by Jason Anspach and J.N. Chaney

Arcana Unlocked by Gregory Blackburn

A Touch of Power by Jay Boyce

Red Mage and
Farming Livia by Xander Boyce

Space Seasons by Dawn Chapman

Ether Collapse and
Ether Flows by Ryan DeBruyn

Bloodgames by Christian J. Gilliland

Threads of Fate by Michael Head

Wolfman Warlock by James Hunter and Dakota Krout

Axe Druid,
Mephisto's Magic Online, and
High Table Hijinks by Christopher Johns

Skeleton in Space by Andries Louws

Chronicles of Ethan by John L. Monk

Pixel Dust by David Petrie
Necrotic Apocalypse by David Petrie

Henchman by Carl Stubblefield

Artorian's Archives by Dennis Vanderkerken and Dakota Krout

Printed in Great Britain
by Amazon